THOR'S DRAGON RIDER COLLECTION 1 - 3

SAFEGUARD, PURSUIT, & ENTRAPMENT

KATRINA COPE

COSY BURROW BOOKS

Hoodwinked

More to come

KATRINA COPE

SAFEGUARD

THOR'S DRAGON RIDER

BOOK 1

EDITORIAL REVIEW

Cosy Burrow Books

Thor's Dragon Rider
Book One

SAFEGUARD

"Kara's back for another adventure in Katrina Cope's latest book, *Safeguard*, with Kara's loyal dragon, Elan, and her wingless Valkyrie friends. Just when her new life seems to be drearily peaceful, a terrifying prophecy about Loki's illegitimate children threatens to destroy Asgard's hard-won tranquility." Amanda K., Line Editor, Red Adept Editing

Safeguard

Ebook first published in USA in August 2020 by Cosy Burrow
Books

Ebook first published in Great Britain in August 2020 by Cosy
Burrow Books

www.katrinacopebooks.com

Published by Cosy Burrow Books

❀ Created with Vellum

To the lovers of dragons - your next dragon friend awaits within these pages.

Chapter One

"**B**attle Maiden! Get me another mead!"

I glare at the bushy-haired redhead raising his pewter cup. Remnants from his last mead dribble down his wild auburn beard.

He smiles, showing off his straight teeth. "Please," he says smartly, as though it were an afterthought. His smile broadens. The warrior's muscles along his thick arm ripple as he pushes the cup forward, holding it high.

With my hands by my side, I flick each finger, one by one, and shake my head in disbelief. Sometimes it takes all of my effort not to clop the god of thunder over the head. If he weren't so lovable, by gods and myself alike, I probably would have pressured Odin for a different position. Scattered food and empty plates cover the table, proving hard to avoid as I lean over the mess to grab the tankard out of his hand. I prop a hand on my hip while still leaning over his mess. "Thor, you know I don't like being called that."

He smacks me on the arm as a friendly gesture, and my thin form lurches to the side from the force. "I know that. I was just making sure you didn't miss my father. I'm sure you miss Odin bossing you around and not calling you by your name." He winks.

A strand of my long dark hair falls over my face, and I hook it behind my ear. "Ah, actually. I don't miss him and the way he used to rule the Valkyries, but you know, even he calls me by my name now."

Thor grabs my cheek and shakes it. "Ah, Kara. I know the name to your pretty little face. I'm just messing with you. Now, be a dear and get me that mead."

With a numb cheek from Thor's grasp, I walk through the ruckus of the hall. Merriment surrounds me as warriors dine and celebrate. Serious battles have been rare lately. They've had ample time to fill between practices, and celebrate they do. The Valhalla warriors pack these hours with gaiety and celebration that impress the gods immensely, several of whom have joined them.

The large bowl containing mead lies outside the hall under some branches of Yggdrasil at the far end of the celebration. Of course, the world tree with the never-ending pot of mead is on the opposite end of Valhalla. I sigh and weave through the crowd, proving my hours of sparring and training were useful—at least to dodge rowdy warriors. It's a tight fit through the hall crammed with einherjar, making me glad I'm wearing my black fighting leathers instead of a dress. It wasn't a hard choice, seeing as someone has to work and keep an eye on Thor when he's celebrating.

A warrior crashes into me from behind, shoving me forward and straight into a wall of fur. I push against the coarse fibers and crane my neck to stare into the deep-brown eyes of a large hound at least a head taller than the majority of the warriors here.

A deep growl rumbles in the hound's throat. "Watch it!" The hound pulls back his lips, showing off his long canines.

I blink in disbelief. "Sorry, Fenrir." I'm used to the hound speaking our language, but usually, he's an adorable pup.

"Stop it, Fenrir. Kara is a friend. You know that." Tyr pushes his bulky form past Fenrir and stands between us, making my average height feel small against the tall god and massive hound. Tyr scratches his trimmed beard, and his brown eyes gaze at me apologetically. "I'm sorry. I don't know what's gotten into him lately."

Fenrir snorts at the back of the god of justice's head, blowing Tyr's long dark hair over his face.

I got to know this large hound over the last couple of years. Reminding myself that he is usually an adorable pup, I slowly raise a hand to Fenrir's crest. My Caucasian skin tone looks paler against his dark fur as I rub him. I add a special sweetness to my voice, trying to calm the oversized hound. "Oh, Fenrir. Are you feeling unwell?"

Fenrir growls, exposing his large canines again, and I hastily retract my hand.

"Come, Fenrir. Let's get you out of here." The muscles in Tyr's arms bulge as he coaxes the hound away from the crowd.

I watch Tyr and Fenrir retreat, the god's hand resting comfortingly on the hound's shoulders as they exit. The god of war and justice took a liking to the large hound when he was a pup and continued to raise him when the other gods were intimidated by his size.

A drunken warrior stumbles and collides with me, the pewter cup in my hand clashing with his. The noise reminds me of my task, and I continue to the large pot of mead, dipping the mug into the barrel.

A large goat's head pokes out of the leaves, startling me by the sudden appearance of horns and eyes.

I throw my hand over my heart. "Oh, Heidrun! You made me jump."

The goat bleats, and I scratch it around the ear, burying my fingertips in the brown fur before picking a few leaves from Yggdrasil and feeding them to the goat.

"Eat up, special goat. You have a lot of thirsty warriors to keep happy."

I saw goats on Midgard and was surprised to discover that they produced milk, not mead. It was then that I learned that Heidrun is one of a kind. If her food source consists only of foliage from the world tree, then she will continue to supply mead for the warriors of Valhalla.

With Thor's flask full of mead, I weave through the crowd and return to the burly redhead.

"Oh. Thank you, dear," Thor booms, grabbing the cup from me. He sees my face and chuckles. "Kara. You know I like you."

My mouth quirks to the side, unimpressed. "I know."

The leaves of Yggdrasil rustle under a sudden forceful wind followed by the ground shaking lightly.

Mead drips from Thor's beard as he lowers the

cup from his mouth. He trains his eyes on the outside. "Is that your dragon?" He stands and twists his head to the side, undoubtedly searching for a clearer view of the door. "Oh please, let it be your dragon. I'm in the mood for an eating competition."

My sight falls to the scattered mess in front of him. Empty plates and stripped carcasses are strewn through the food spread from one side of the table to the other.

"Haven't you eaten enough already?"

"What? No, of course not." He spreads his strong muscular arms out wide. "This is a feast. Nothing is better at a feast than an eating competition, and there is no better opponent than your dragon." His eyes turn hopefully to the door again. "Is it your dragon?"

I roll my eyes and speak her name, "Elan?"

Her voice sounds in my head. *Oh, I am in. I'm so in*, she repeats.

"You two are terrible. You shouldn't be encouraging him."

She sounds offended. *Hey, he's the one who asked for me.*

Anticipation fills Thor's face as he waits.

I release a deep sigh. "She says you're on." My voice lacks enthusiasm.

Thor stands, hoisting his fist. "Yes!"

I shake my head in disbelief. "I don't know why you two don't just talk to each other."

Ignoring me, the god of thunder flexes his muscles and yells, "Bring out the cows!"

The room falls silent, and he points at the door.

"An eating competition is on!"

A loud cheer erupts, and the hall empties to the outside.

Elan's golden scales shimmer in the moonlight as she eyes the exiting warriors, searching for Thor. Within moments, two cow carcasses are brought out. One raw, with the skin on, and the other cooked to perfection. Elan stands over the raw cow, her wings tucked by her sides, posture ready, and determination set on her face. Large teeth shine through her parted lips as she challenges Thor with her eyes. She tosses her head, swinging her horns menacingly in a gesture of battle. A deep hunger burns in her eyes.

Opposite her, Thor stands over his cooked carcass almost the size of his table. He rubs his hands together, eyeing the cow and rubbing his belly before grinning at Elan. The light from the hall shines behind him, highlighting his red hair and thick beard, making them appear to be on fire. A roar of support bursts through the crowd as he shuffles his feet from side to side as if readying himself for a fight. He is not the most handsome god, but his loyal heart and dedication to charge into a battle first have won him the support of his warriors. He sits his stocky form on the chair and pulls out his dagger, ready.

I face Elan. "You don't have to do this, you know. Even though he's already had some dinner, he has a solid reputation for eating a lot."

Elan scoffs. *Pfft. Don't be ridiculous. When would I ever refuse a free meal? Besides, I can beat him.*

I tilt my head to the side. "This competition has been close in the past."

You don't have to rub it in. This time, it's going to be different. I'm starving! She nudges me with her nose, pushing me toward the spectators. *Go on. Announce that I'm ready.*

I face Thor, amazed at how he could still consider starting an eating competition after everything he has already consumed.

He wipes the smug smile off his face, and a firm determination sets in. "Well? Is she ready?"

I nod. A loud cheer reverberates through the crowd. The god of thunder thumps his fists wide on the table, one holding his dagger, point up, ready to go. I raise my hands, indicating for the crowd to quiet. It takes a while for the group to fall silent.

Every warrior and serving Valkyrie circles Elan and Thor.

After waiting a moment, I begin the countdown. "Three, two, one, begin."

Elan plants a foot on the cow's leg and rips into its body with her teeth, tearing out large chunks, swallowing them after a few chews. Thor cuts away at the cooked meat with his dagger before sinking his teeth into it and ripping out large mouthfuls. The speed with which he devours the flesh is astonishing, especially considering his stocky form is much smaller than Elan's.

Within fifteen minutes, the golden dragon consumes her carcass. After only another five minutes, Thor devours the flesh on his.

Puffing out his chest, Thor stands and wipes his beard with his arm, knocking the remaining mess from his mouth. He rubs his belly and cries, "More!"

A cheer erupts from the crowd.

The young Valkyries from the academy clean Thor's table before bringing out two more carcasses, one raw for Elan and the other cooked for Thor. Other Valkyries, winged and wingless, dart through the mix of einherjar and divine warriors, refilling their cups of mead. As they bustle, I take in the faces of the young Valkyries from the academy. They are unknown to me, as I graduated from Valkyrie Academy two years ago.

Long folds of light-blue fabric sway near the entrance of Valhalla Hall, and I'm surprised to find Mistress Sigrun propped up against a wall. Her arms are crossed over her chest, her face an array of strange amusement. She looks so different. She has replaced the Valkyrie uniform with an elegant one-strap dress that hangs from her left shoulder, displaying her muscular arms. The fabric hugs her thin figure and flows down to her ankles. Her blond hair falls in a braid down her back. She is a picture of beauty. Even though she is much older than I am, she has the Valkyrie blessing of eternal youth. Only a few slight creases betray her age. Her off-duty face looks relaxed—a strange sight to see, even though it's an expression I've seen more often recently.

My focus returns to the eating competition. I stare in disbelief as they devour the second cow. Elan tears at the raw cow flesh, each bite slightly slower than the last, yet somehow, Thor continues eating, managing to keep up with her.

Mead sloshes on my foot and seeps into my leather shoes, distracting me from the competition. My toes are wet and sticky.

"Sorry." A young, nervous wingless Valkyrie eyes

me and cowers, as though waiting to be reprimanded.

Despite feeling uncomfortable and annoyed, I smile at her. "It's okay."

She dashes off, almost at a run, and I sigh. In the last couple of years, there have been rumors of my success, blowing me up into some kind of hero. I often find it makes the young ones nervous. Me a hero? That's rubbish. It all started because I didn't want to grow up as just a servant. I guess, really, I was working toward my own interests. I'm just glad it expanded to help others also.

"What's going on?" Hildr joins me. Her spiky red hair is not much different in color than Thor's, but it's much better kept. Her freckles stand out on her pale skin in the light. Her green eyes follow the commotion. A trickle of sweat runs down her neck, and she wears her leather fighting uniform. She faces me, and the sword strapped to her side clicks against a metal buckle on her belt. She looks as though she's just finished a round of combat training.

"Thor challenged Elan to another eating competition."

A giggle sounds on my other side. "Oh, Elan would love that." Eir's peaceful face fills with joy at the sight of a dragon and a god getting along.

It's been a couple of years since the dragon alliance

was revised and the dragons were released from slavery by the gods and the Valkyries. But the peacekeeper, Eir, is always happy to see this physically in motion.

The peaceful wingless Valkyrie's pale-brown hair is back in a ponytail, and she is also wearing leather —a very unusual sight for her.

"Have you been combat training with Hildr?"

Eir nods, her eyes serious.

"And me." Britta stands on the other side of Hildr.

My jaw drops. "Eir, how uncharacteristic of you."

Combat training is a usual pastime for Hildr and Britta, especially since Odin changed his attitude about wingless Valkyries. Still, Eir has always despised fighting or anything less than peaceful.

Eir sighs. "I know, but I need to practice my battle skills, too, just in case. After all, I am a Valkyrie."

I place a hand on her shoulder. "And a very good one at that."

"Who's winning?" Britta asks, wiping sweat off her forehead.

I study the contents of both the carcasses. Both contestants seem to be slowing down.

"I don't know. It seems to be a tie."

"And who's that?" Britta nods, and I follow her gaze.

In the distance, a group of warriors gathers. A blond muscular god with a kind face stands in the middle. They are all entirely under the influence of mead, and they joke and slap each other around. The blond seems to be the center of attention. He puffs out his broad chest, and in the dim light, he appears to have a soft glow about him.

I shrug. "That's the god Balder, one of Odin's sons."

Her eyebrows rise. "I've heard about him. I thought they were exaggerating. He's so handsome," she swoons.

I roll my eyes when I look at her. Her eyes are open wide, and she twiddles the end of her hair.

"Seriously?" I shake my head. Then I remember that he seems to get that reaction from all the Valkyries. "He's married."

She grins. "That can change. These gods seem to go through a lot of wives." Suddenly her smile drops. "What are they doing?"

Returning my gaze to the group, I find that they have stepped back, leaving a large opening in the middle. On one side, Balder stands with his arms open wide. On the other side, a warrior raises a bow and arrow and points it at him. The rest of the warriors stand aside, watching, grinning.

"I thought he was well-liked." Britta's voice is shrill.

"He is," I say.

"Then why is that archer pointing an arrow at him?"

The archer draws the string back with the arrow nocked. A moment later, he releases his fingers and sets the arrow free—aiming directly for Balder.

Britta screams.

Britta charges forward, aiming for the group of warriors. I clasp her arm just in time, and she moves to shake me off.

I croon to her, "Wait."

She frowns.

"Trust me."

She spins to look at the handsome god with a kind face.

The arrow's aim is true. It hits Balder directly in the heart then falls to the ground. The group laughs, Balder joining them.

Britta's mouth drops open. "What?"

I smile. "It's one of the god's favorite party tricks."

"What on Vanir? Why?" she stammers.

"Balder had a dream that he would be harmed, and when he told Odin, word got back to Frigg, his mother. She made everything promise not to hurt him. Now everything that should be able to harm or kill Balder bounces off him. These warriors have no intention of hurting him. They do this because it amuses them that these things can't harm him."

Britta crosses her arms over her chest. "What a stupid game." She huffs. "Men."

"Indeed," I agree.

Kara.

I spin around, searching for the owner of the voice in my head. It was deeper, more mature than Elan's, and I know Elan is too busy trying to out-eat Thor to talk to me. Her mind is on one track only. As I gaze in the distance, in the opposite direction of the competition, golden scales glisten in the moonlight, catching my eye.

I call over my shoulder to my three friends still engrossed in the eating competition, "I'll be back soon. Eingana wants to chat."

I weave through the crowd and approach the dragon. "Eingana, what brings you here?"

Certainly not the eating contest my daughter is competing in. She shakes her head, gazing at Elan and Thor. She shrugs. *At least it builds relationships with the gods of Asgard, but it's not the way I would have done it.*

The image of the leader of the dragons partaking in an eating competition fills my head, and my mouth quirks with amusement. "I'm certain that it's not." I have only known this dragon to be responsible.

Eingana's gaze returns to me and catches the expression on my face before I can wipe it away. *Oh. You find that amusing, do you?*

I toss my hands out to the side and shrug. "Well, you're always so serious, and at one point, you threatened to eat me."

She tilts her head and gazes down at me with one eye. *Indeed.*

"What brings you here?" I ask again.

Even though Asgard has changed the alliance with the dragons, Eingana rarely makes a social visit.

The leader of the dragons sits on her haunches, the scales between her horns puckering in the form of a dragon frown. *It's Odin. While undergoing my surveillance of Asgard, I spotted him at the entrance of the world tree that he uses to access Mimir's well.*

"What's so unusual about that? I've heard that he goes there often to consult with the wisdom of Mimir's head. Why wouldn't he? He relinquished his eye in exchange for the wisdom."

This time it's different.

"How?"

He's writhing on the ground, screaming troubling things.

I place my hands on my hips. "So why tell me? Shouldn't his sons and the gods be told first?"

She lowers her head, staring intently into my eyes. *You know how proud he is and how he needs to appear in control.* She gazes over my shoulder at the rowdy crowd. *I don't think they are the right people to tell, especially right now.*

I peer over my shoulder at the group. Adding to the eating competition, Tyr and an einherjar are starting a mead-drinking competition.

"No. They aren't. Let's go."

Eingana squats so I can climb on, and I balk. This will be the first time I have ridden on her back. In fact, I haven't seen anyone riding the dragon ruler of Asgard's wastelands.

As though sensing my hesitance, she encourages, *Come. Climb on.*

She doesn't have to ask me twice. I climb up her saddleless back and press my legs around her neck, her golden scales digging into my flesh. It's been a while since I've ridden Elan bareback, and the memories flood back to me. Leaning forward, I clasp Eingana's golden scales as she pushes into the sky. The steady motion of her wings flapping speaks to my soul.

Ever since the dragons found me and I took my first ride, I knew where I wanted to stay—right on the back of my best friend. In this case, it's her mother, and that is almost as good.

The flight is short. The entrance of the world tree to Mimir's well is located on the other side of Yggdrasil. We circle the tree, and I spot Odin's form hunched over, on his knees, his face planted on the ground. He looks so small and dejected that it takes a moment for me to realize it is the authoritative god.

Eingana lands with a soft thud, yet the god still doesn't look up. Odin was nasty to me in the past, but looking at him like this, I can't leave him. I survey the surroundings, just in case he was attacked. Although his spear, Gungnir, lies next to him on the ground, it's better to be safe than sorry.

Cautiously, I approach him and place a hand on the back of his shoulder. "Great Odin."

An unintelligible mutter rises from his form, and he rocks.

"Great Odin," I say again, slightly louder.

Suddenly, he sucks in a large breath and sits on his heels, turning panicked eyes on me. His shoulder-length gray hair sticks out from the sides of his head as he grabs my arm with a vice grip. Instantly I feel the bruise coming.

"His children. We haven't contained his children."

I frown. "Whose children?"

"Loki's. Mimir has predicted that they shall be the

beginning of Ragnarok, and they have recently found out about their father and where he is tied. They're out for blood."

My frown deepens. "But the gods changed Vali into a vicious wolf, and he killed his brother, Narfi, Loki and Sigyn's son. They used Narfi's entrails to tie Loki under the serpent. Remember?" I screw up my nose at the thought.

His grasp on my arm tightens to the point I almost scream. "No. His other children to the giantess Angrboda."

"Who are they?"

"Jormungundr."

"The Midgard Serpent?" I scrunch my chin with my hand, trying to work out how that happened.

Odin nods. "Hel."

I squash my lips together. "The weirdo goddess that rules Niflheim?"

He nods again. "And the big hound, the one they call Fenrir."

My forehead pinches into a frown. "I didn't know he was Loki's son. He snarled at me today. Tyr said he's been acting up lately."

"That's why." His piercing blue eye turns fervent. "The children must be stopped."

I contemplate, trying to process the information.

"But other than Fenrir being a little out of sorts, none of them have caused us any trouble."

Odin waves a hand dismissively. "That doesn't matter. Mimir has predicted that these three will wreak havoc on Asgard and even aspire to take over as leaders. Take me to Thor." Odin pushes up from the ground and instantly fails to stand. His face pales.

I hold him steady. "I don't think that's wise, especially considering the condition Thor is in right now. I think we need to take you to bed, and I'll tell Thor as soon as possible."

Odin protests, "But I need to tell him."

I keep my hand on his chest, holding him in his seated position. "I'll tell him as soon as I get the opportunity." I hook my arm through his and lift him off the ground. "Come on. I'm going to help you safely to your bed."

Chapter Three

When I return to the eating competition, Thor and Elan are at the end of a carcass. I move next to an einherjar. The warrior's massive form towers over mine. He crosses his arms over his chest, and his mead bounces around in his cup as he laughs.

I rise to my tippy-toes. "What number is this one?"

He gazes at me from under bushy brown eyebrows, and his mouth moves just as a loud cheer erupts through the crowd, blocking out his answer.

"How many?" I yell.

He holds up two fingers.

I nod my thanks. They're slowing down. I work my way through the crowd to stand near my friends, inching between Hildr and Eir in the front row of spectators.

Elan's eyes meet mine. She just beat Thor in that

round, yet her victory is quiet. She looks full, her eyes drowsy, a giveaway only because she's my best friend. My beautiful golden dragon companion raises her head high and stands to attention, ready to go through another round. She won't have to go hunting for a while.

Another loud cheer explodes through the group. Thor stands, pushing his belly out and rubbing it in large, exaggerated circles as he swallows his last mouthful. Pieces of meat stick to his red beard, and he wipes them away with his arm before unbuckling his belt and hanging it over the back of his chair. The crowd falls silent as the god raises his hands.

He arches a hairy orange eyebrow, leveling his gaze on Elan. "Are you ready to go again, dragon?"

Elan nods once, her golden scales catching in the light of the building.

The god stretches and glares competitively at Elan. He tilts his head. "Okay." He raises his voice. "Let's go again."

Again, the crowd shouts their enthusiasm. I blink at Thor in disbelief.

Hildr scratches her head. "I can't believe these two are still going."

The Valkyries bring out the next cows, and I survey the crowd still coaxing them on. "Two was Thor's limit before. How does this Aesir think he's going to finish three, especially after he has already eaten at the feast?"

Eir gasps. "Thor's already eaten?"

"Yep."

After several more minutes, Elan takes a lazy mouthful of her carcass, and Thor's chewing becomes much slower than before. Slowly, Elan drops to her haunches before taking another bite then gazes sluggishly at me.

Who is winning? Elan's eyes almost show defeat. *Have I eaten more than Thor?*

I reassess the two carcasses. "I don't know. It looks about even."

She rips off a leg then swallows it whole. It takes a while to get past her throat, and her eyes appear to be swimming. *How about now?*

I double-check what's remaining of Thor's cow. "It looks like you're ahead now, a whole leg ahead."

She groans. *Finally.* She pulls back from the remainder of the cow. *I'm done.*

Thor notices and calls out across the distance, "What's the matter, dragon? Are you finished?"

Elan nods.

Thor's torpid eyes assess the two cows, and he slowly takes another bite. It's evident that he's struggling, too, but his competitive side shines forth. He slowly eats another few mouthfuls. The minutes tick by until eventually he lies back in his seat. "I'm pretty close. What's the score so far?" he asks one of the warriors standing next to him.

The einherjar walks up to Elan's carcass and assesses the amount while one of the Valkyries from the academy does the same to Thor's.

Hildr rubs her palms down her leather pants. "It looks pretty close. Don't you think?"

"You're about even," the warrior says.

Thor pushes up from the backrest on his seat. "That won't do." And he eats another five mouthfuls, each one clearly more painful than the last. He barely swallows the last mouthful then points at Elan. "See, dragon. I beat you."

Elan looks mournfully down at her carcass and shakes her head. *It's not worth the pain.*

Thor stands and cries victory. Suddenly his face turns green, and he runs from the gathered warriors to empty the contents of his stomach.

Elan tilts her head. *Is that allowed? I don't think that's permitted. If it's not approved, then I've won.*

I approach Elan and rub her snout. "I know, Elan. I certainly think you won, but consider his size. He's much smaller than you."

She lowers herself down to her stomach and groans. *I guess you're right. I'm not moving for another week.*

Mead sloshes over the edges of their pewter cups as the crowd clinks in celebration of Thor's win, then they disburse and head back inside. Loud slaps reverberate off Thor's back as the einherjar congratulate the god of thunder as they pass, giving little consideration as he continues to empty his stomach onto the garden.

After the crowd clears, I wait for Thor to finish being sick before hooking my arm in his. Hildr mirrors me on his other side. "Come on, Thor. It's time to go home."

He swings his hand dismissively at me, his body still lurching over the garden. "No, no. I'm fine. Just take me back inside. I have a victory celebration to lead." His words slur, and his breath smells of mead and vomit.

I screw up my nose and breathe through my mouth. "I'm pretty sure you're done for tonight. Come. Let's go. You can celebrate again soon."

He mutters something disagreeable under his breath and starts to struggle toward the hall before stumbling. Hildr and I hold him steady.

"What would I do without you two, especially you, Kara?"

"Actually, I was wondering if you would let me go, Thor."

He lifts his head, and it wobbles from side to side

as he attempts to look at me through slushy eyes. "Whadoya mean?" His words garble.

"Well, Odin said that you needed me when he sent me to be by your side. I thought he meant that you needed me to help you defeat Asgard's enemies. The last couple of years have been… interesting, but I've basically just been your servant."

We reach the palace and make our way up the stairs, a feat that proves difficult with a sizeable drunken warrior, and I'm glad for Hildr's help.

Thor shakes his head and raises a finger as though ready to disagree. We sway slightly.

I brace myself, steeling my core, and cut him off before he starts muttering something indecipherable. "Okay. A Valkyrie companion."

He pats me on the back. "Yeah. You're my Valkyrie companion. I love having my Valkyrie coommpannnion around," he slurs.

My mouth lifts in a one-sided smile. "That's nice, and you do treat me better than Odin used to, but I was hoping for more. I want to help Asgard, not just be a companion."

"Aww." He pinches my cheek again, roughing it like an old woman does to a child. "But I love having a Vallkyyrrie friend." His words are hard to understand, but I know he means well.

We reach Thor's level, and Hildr gives me a good-luck smirk.

I smile at Thor, his blurry eyes still trained on me. "You're drunk. Let's talk about this tomorrow." I take him through his door and into his bedroom.

"I'm not drunk. I'm sober. Let's drink more mead."

I pat him on the back, and with Hildr, I help him down to his bed and remove his boots. "Sure. Let's do that. Tomorrow. Okay?"

He holds up a finger. "I'll hold you to that."

I smirk, knowing he won't remember a thing. "Tomorrow. Your father also wants me to tell you something, but it can wait until tomorrow too." I pull a blanket over him and shake my head. It always amazes me how a grown man, or god in this case, can act like a child when drunk. With a heavy heart, I walk away with Hildr.

"I thought you loved being by Thor's side." Hildr watches me as we walk back to the hall.

"I do, and he has been kindhearted and encouraging to me. Except he often uses me too much as a Valkyrie companion. There haven't been many wars in the last couple of years to put my skills to use. Since they locked Loki away, there hasn't been much disruption or mischief. I want to do more with my life, and even though Thor is an excellent warrior, I feel as though my training is being neglected."

Hildr nods, her face full of understanding. "What did you need to tell Thor from his father? Was it about where Eingana took you?"

I look directly into Hildr's eyes. "Don't tell anyone, but I found Odin in a state near the entrance to Mimir's well. Apparently, it's prophesized that Loki's children are going to avenge Loki."

"What children?"

"He has three children from a giantess. They are Fenrir, Tyr's hound, the Midgard Serpent, and Hel."

"What?" Her jaw drops.

"Yeah. I know."

"If it's true, you know that your life with Thor is about to change. In fact, I wouldn't mind joining him myself if all that is about to begin."

- Chapter Four -

Where's the big cheater? Elan flaps her wings in frustration, lifting her front feet off the ground. She hops on her hind legs before slamming them back to the ground. The early-morning sun catches in her eyes, and they ignite with color, making them seem as though they are on fire.

"Now, Elan. You know he's not a cheater." I tilt my head to the side and gaze at her under a raised eyebrow.

Yeah, yeah. I get it. He's a puny god, and I'm a big dragon. Of course I can eat more than him. Irritation laces her tone, and her words are crisp. *I'm supposed to be able to eat more than he can. Whatever. I don't care. He should be here by now.*

"What's gotten into you today, Elan? Did you sleep on the wrong side of a rock?"

Ha, ha. Very funny. The emperor dragon swings

her head from side to side, sarcasm oozing from her voice.

Three thumps sound on the ground behind me, and the ground shakes. I turn to find Naga, Drogon, and Tanda tucking their wings by their side as their riders, Hildr, Eir, and Britta, dressed in black leather fighting attire, slide off their backs.

"Hey, guys. What brings you here?" I ask.

Hildr kicks the dirt with the toe of her shoe and looks at the ground. "Um. I kind of told them about the three children."

My cheeks turn numb with shock, and I lean closer to Hildr to eliminate anyone else hearing. "You didn't mention Odin's meltdown, did you?"

She shook her head. "I only told them about the children and the havoc they could cause. We're here because we want to help."

Elan's snarky voice sounds in my head, dragging my attention away from the wingless Valkyries. *You didn't let me finish. Mother has told us about what Odin said. That's why I'm so irritable this morning.*

I plant a hand on my hip, facing her. "Oh. It's not because you've got a bellyache from eating so many cows?"

She shakes her scaly head. *Nope. Not at all. The dragons are here to help round up Fenrir, just in case he decides to run or cause any trouble. First, though, we need to get Thor out of bed. Where is he?* She stares at the palace.

Naga's seen him. Naga snuck by his room this morning and saw him sound asleep on his bed. Naga's blue eyes are wide, displaying naivete. *Naga snuck away before Thor knew Naga was there.*

I stare at Naga with wide eyes. At first, I want to write off what he said as bad language skills, but then I remember that his communication has improved immensely over the last couple of years. "Okay." I hesitate, trying to place myself in Naga's shoes before judging. "That's an interesting thing to do, Naga."

Eir chuckles, rubbing her dragon around the ears then down his snout, and Naga nudges her with his head affectionately.

"It's been Naga's favorite thing lately. I know it's a little strange." The wind blows wisps of Eir's brown hair over her eyes, and she grins, peering through the strands. "But I am okay with that. He's only watching them sleep." She cups her hands around her mouth and whispers in my ear, "Between you and me, I think he's trying to find me a nice partner, you know, one who doesn't snore." She giggles and shrugs. "Don't ask me why. I think he thinks I'm getting old."

Naga's big blue eyes blink slowly, making him

look innocent. *Eir is aging. Eir is over twenty years. She must find a man before she gets too old. That's how it works in the dragon world.*

Eir rubs his ear again and presses her side braid against his scales. "Oh, Naga. How many times do I have to tell you? Valkyries live a very long time. On top of that, they also look young for a very long time. Look at Mistress Sigrun."

Naga shivers, like something ran down his spine. *No, thank you.*

Someone nudges my back, and I turn to find Elan's golden eyes level with mine. *Come on. That's enough time wasted. Just because he's a god doesn't mean he can keep us waiting.*

"Actually, Elan, it does mean he can keep us waiting, but let's give it a try anyway. Thor can be a bit more lenient than other gods around here, and it is a matter of importance."

We trek up toward a segment of Odin's palace. The massive balcony off Thor's bedroom makes it hard to miss. Elan lands on the open part of the balcony and crouches to her stomach. I climb off her back as she ducks her head under the eaves and peers in the window.

I try the door, find it unlocked, and ease my way in. Thor's large form lies sprawled across a king-size bed framed with thick posts in each corner. Red curtains drape from the beams. His body is spread expansively, instantly explaining why he sleeps alone and not with his wife. Lack of space would be a big enough deterrent, let alone the earth-rumbling snore that bellows from the depths of his body.

Dragon scales! Would you look at that? Elan tilts her head, her mouth filling the doorway, and breathes out a plume of steam.

Instantly my skin becomes damp with sweat. "Elan, stop," I hiss. "What are you doing?"

Her golden eye looks eerie as she peers through the small window at me. *I'm waking him up. Isn't that what we're here for?*

I shake my head with disbelief. "There are nicer ways to do it."

You're right, although he looks pretty out of it. Her window-framed eye looks at Thor. *I was just trying to help.*

"Thanks, I guess, but let me try first."

Elan harrumphs. *Fine. Whatever. Good luck.*

I gaze at the snoring Thor. A slight sheen of sweat coats his skin after Elan filled his room with steam, and still, he hasn't moved an inch.

Sitting on the edge of his bed, I lightly shake his shoulder. "Thor. Wakey, wakey." He doesn't budge. "Thor, wake up," I say in a singsong voice.

Loud snores answer me, interrupted only when

he rubs his nose and flicks his arm to the side, narrowly missing me.

See. I told you, Elan chides, her snout barely fitting into the door of his room.

I glare at her eye peering through the window.

All right, all right. I get it. Quiet!

I shake the sleeping god harder, moving his torso roughly from side to side, yet he still doesn't stir. Raising my voice, I call, "Thor. Wake up!" A groan escapes my lips as I'm answered with more snores. My shoulders slump, and I spot a spare pillow on the other side of the bed. With a spring in my step, I work my way around the posts and grab it, restraining myself slightly when I hit him over the head. "Wake up."

Thor mutters something, grumbles, and turns to the other side. I let out an exasperated sigh before following him to the other side and whacking him with the pillow. Thor snorts and works his mouth loudly before progressing with his snores.

"Vanir! This man can sleep." I gaze at Elan, feeling lost.

Excitement fills Elan's eye. *Can I help now?*

I shrug. "Sure. Why not?"

A grin spreads across her mouth, framed by the doorway, giving her a conniving look. She twists her mouth to the side farther and shoves it through the door. *Okay. Ready yourself. This could be uncomfortable.*

I frown. "What do you me—"

I'm cut off by Elan's voice blasting through my head, followed by a puff of hot air. *Wake up!*

I jump. Next to me, Thor flies out of bed, grabbing his hammer from his bedside, and stands at attention. His bare chest heaves with anticipation as he surveys his surroundings, dressed in his boxer shorts. His eyes are wide, and his muscles flex as he waves Mjollnir threateningly until his eyes land on me pressing my back against the wall, trying to keep out of his hammer's reach. "Kara?"

Elan snorts through the door, and Thor spins and cries out, puffing and holding his spare hand over his heart when he spots Elan's eye through the window. "Argh! You two are going to be the death of me."

Elan smiles, exposing her extensive array of sharp teeth, managing to look more scary than friendly. *Glad I could help.*

Thor sets Mjollnir on the floor. "What is the meaning of this?" He searches for some clothes and pulls on leather pants and a tunic. He pauses, rubbing his head. "Why do I feel so terrible?"

Ah. That was me, Elan says. *I beat you in an eating competition.*

I scowl at Elan.

Thor rubs his stomach and looks thoughtful. "Really?"

Yep. Elan's eyes dance with mischief.

"Hmph! We'll just have to have another run, won't we? Not right now, though. I expect you feel just as terrible as I do."

Um—Elan looks at me, and I frown at her—*sure, but I guess all that mead you drank on top of it didn't help.*

Thor holds his head again before looking at me. "I guess not. Why are you two here, anyway?"

"Your father wants me to tell you something."

"Oh. What is it?"

"While you were partying last night and partaking in your eating competition, Eingana dropped by and took me to Odin. He was huddled next to the entrance of the world tree that he uses to access Mimir's well, overcome with a vision. He was quite distressed, and he needs us to deal with it right away."

"What do we need to deal with?" Thor asks, pulling on some strings to tighten his clothes and securing some bands over his arms.

"He had a vision that Loki's children from his giant mistress, Angrboda, are going to cause havoc."

"Do you mean Fenrir, Jormungundr, and Hel?" Thor asks.

"So, you know about them?" I ask hesitantly.

"My father sent two of them to the ends of the realm to try to keep them out of trouble. He sent Jormungundr to Midgard, and the beast circles the oceans there. He sent Hel to the realm of the shameful dead because she prefers their company. And last of all, we kept Fenrir here because, as you know, he's a puppy, and he's so adorable. What's the problem that my father saw?" Thor secures the final strap on his clothes and armor.

"He's worried because Loki's children just found out what happened to him. Somehow the information was delayed in getting to them. I think he might be right. Last night, I ran into Fenrir with Tyr. Fenrir wasn't friendly. He growled at me and was quite cranky. It's not the way I remember him. With him being so big now, it was quite disturbing. He needs to be contained."

Thor's shoulders sag. "Fine. I'll chain him, and we can monitor him from there."

Is that your answer to everything? Elan snaps. *You gods love your chains.*

Thor spins to look at her one eye peering through the window. "It's not the answer for everything, just when something is dangerous and needs to be restrained before it hurts anyone. I'm sure Tyr will look after Fenrir and let him off occasionally."

Elan huffs.

Thor shakes his head. "But first, we must see if we can chain him. It's a simple solution." He walks toward the door and opens it. "Are you coming, Kara? Or shall I meet you outside?"

"I'll meet you outside in a couple of minutes," I call over my shoulder as I follow Elan's snout onto the balcony.

- Chapter Five -

"Where's Thor?" Hildr calls to me before Elan lands.

Elan's body shudders underneath me as her feet hit the ground before my wingless Valkyrie friends and their dragons.

"He's coming," I say, climbing off her back.

Chains rattle behind me, and the faces of Naga, Drogon, and Tanda drop as their eyes widen. I follow their line of sight and spot Thor carrying massive chains draped across his arms. With every movement he makes, the chains clang together.

Thor eyes each of the dragons' expressions, and the small amount of face showing above his bushy red beard softens. "Oh. It's all right, you fantastic beasts. It's not going to be the same as when you were chained. Tyr will look after Fenrir and hope-fully tame him so we can remove these soon."

Drogon huffs steam. *Then you won't mind if the dragons supervise. Let us be the ones who decide that.*

Thor chuckles. "Be my guest. I promise you it's all above board. I've known Fenrir since he was a pup, and Tyr is my brother. He adores Fenrir. I wouldn't want to jeopardize that." Gazing at the dragons in front of him, his muscles strain as he holds up the chains. "Would one of you mind carrying these, please?" His eyes land on Drogon, and he studies the many horns on the dragon's head. "Drogon. Would you mind carrying them? They could easily rest across your horns."

Drogon looks displeased, and his eyes carry distrust as he huffs another plume of steam. *As long as you abide by your word and let us supervise. We're not going to let something happen to Fenrir like it did to us.*

Thor smiles, showing off his straight white teeth between his bushy red beard and mustache. "Of course. It's exactly as I just agreed. I have no interest in treating any animal with cruelty. However, a dangerous animal must be contained, especially if it's going to be a threat to Asgard."

Drogon lowers his head, and Thor drapes the chains over his many horns.

"In fact, I suggest we get Tyr to make it into a game for Fenrir."

As a group, we set out to find Tyr, following Thor

to the spot where the gods usually like to spar. The clashing of weapons greets us as we near. Following the sound, we find several gods deep in battle against each other.

"Ah," Britta moans. "If I'd known where you were going, I could have waited for you here."

I follow her line of sight until my eyes fall on Balder in the corner sparring with Tyr. I roll my eyes. Balder catches sight of us and waves, flashing an impressive smile that I'm sure would win many maidens' hearts. While the friendly god is distracted, Tyr's muscles ripple down his bare arms as he swings his sword at Balder. The sword swipes across the invincible god's torso, cutting the material yet leaving Balder's skin unscathed. If Balder weren't protected against all items, he would have been severely injured. The difference between this day and the party is this was not executed as a joke.

Balder pulls his gaze from us and glances down at Tyr's sword as though it were a distraction before fighting Tyr back, his friendly face relaxed and unthreatening as he practices with the god of war. The muscles in his exposed torso flex as he swings his sword.

Britta expels a loud, swooning sigh.

"Tyr!" Thor calls.

The god of war pauses of his battle and looks up, his questioning eyes squinting through sweat.

"Can we talk for a minute?" Thor's eyes travel to Fenrir, sleeping in the corner.

The hound opens one eye, watching Tyr's every move, and his ears twitch, twisting in the direction of the two gods. Moving farther away from the hound, the two gods lean their heads closer together, their mouths barely moving and their voices low.

Worry covers Tyr's face until eventually he slaps Thor on the shoulder and pulls back. "And a game it shall be." He gazes at the hound and calls, "Fenrir!"

The hound leaps to his feet and runs to Tyr, his long bushy tail wagging as though he were a pup called by his best friend.

"Yes, Tyr?" Fenrir's friendly gaze fills with distrust and curiosity as he glances at Thor, the dragons, and their riders.

Tyr pets Fenrir on his shoulder. "We want to see if you're stronger than a dragon."

Instantly the scruffy hound's eyes fill with excitement. Fenrir sits on his haunches with his back straight, and he's taller than any of the gods. The dragons still loom over his bulky, intimidating form.

"This sounds like fun." His long brown tail wags.

Thor retrieves the chains from Drogon's horns

KATRINA COPE

and carries them to Fenrir. The wolf's eyes widen with surprise, and he retreats slightly.

"Don't fear, Fenrir. These are the chains that held the dragons captive. The dragons think that they are the strongest creatures around." He challenges Fenrir with his gaze. "If you're happy to agree with that, then that's your burden to bear."

The four dragons puff out their chests, and Fenrir's furry eyebrows crowd his eyes, displaying his displeasure.

Thor nods at him. "If you want to see if you're stronger than the dragons, then let us place these on you to prove that you are indeed the strongest creature."

The dragons huff, showing their distain at the notion.

Fenrir's gaze falls on each of the dragons, taking in their displeased faces. His mouth forms into a strange smirk, exposing his big teeth, and he moves closer to Thor. "I'd love to have a go. It sounds fun."

Balder and Tyr help Thor drape the chains around Fenrir's throat and secure the chains to a boulder. Thor pulls and pushes against the chains and their anchor, testing the strength of the attachment. The connection doesn't budge.

Tyr turns to Fenrir, a challenging grin plastered

on his face. "Okay, Fenrir. You're on. Let's see what you got."

Fenrir pulls and strains, stretching out his neck and shoulders, hunkering down and pushing with his haunches. The chains clank against the stone several times, the heavy metal whooshing as it swings wildly from the test. Moments later, the chains snap, and the metal clunks to the ground and clangs against the rock boulder.

Fenrir stands tall, his face filled with victory and pride. "Look at me, dragons. I'm stronger than you. Look at the chain you couldn't escape lying broken on the ground."

Drogon's displeased eyes narrow on me. *Is this guy kidding? The dragons didn't break free because they were protecting the alliance, not because we couldn't.*

I try to look understanding while holding my finger to my lips in a shushing motion.

Elan picks up on my sentiment. *We know, Drogon. This is just a game. Relax. All of the dragons were bound by the alliance and did not flee because of that.* She nods to Fenrir, her golden-brown eyes filling with worry. *But you must admit, he's strong, and that is worrisome.*

Drogon nods.

Tyr claps his hands in approval. "Well done, Fenrir. You beat the dragons."

Tanda's grumble echoes through my head, and I glance at her and wink only to be rewarded with a fiery-red glare.

"Yes, Fenrir," Thor agrees, his voice booming. "You're very strong. This was hardly a challenge at all. We'll have to make a stronger chain and see how you do next time." He spins to greet the gods. "Why don't you work on that?"

Tyr unfastens the chain around Fenrir's neck and rubs him behind the ear. Fenrir happily tilts his head to the side, his tongue drooping from his mouth.

Grabbing the remaining chains, the other gods who had gathered to spar head in the direction of the smith, their brows furrowed in confusion.

Watching them leave so soon, my shoulders slump with disappointment. "Oh, great!" I grumble. "I didn't even get to partake in anything exciting or useful today. My friends even lined up to help me." I search for Thor and spotted him heading back to the palace. "Thor!" I yell. "Can I talk to you for a minute?"

My leader turns and calls over his shoulder, "Of course, Kara!"

He pauses, and I jog to catch up with him. When I reach his side, he slaps me on the back, sending a painful jolt through my upper back, and I grit my teeth.

52

"What is it?" he asks.

"Well," I hesitate. "I've been meaning to ask you for a while. Do you really need me to be around?"

His red bushy eyebrows push together. "What do you mean?"

"Well, Odin sent me to help you. He said it like you needed my help."

"You are helping. You let me have competitions with your dragon."

I place my hands on my hips. "We did have this conversation last night, but you were a bit out of it."

"We did?"

I nod.

"Can you remind me?" A slight amount of sympathy enters his voice.

"I'm kind of sick of being a Valkyrie companion." I hold up my hand in a stopping motion. "Don't get me wrong. I don't mind being your friend, but I'm bored. I want to do something important with my life. The way things are going, I don't feel like I'm achieving anything."

Thor slaps me on the shoulders again, and my body lurches forward with his force. He has got to start remembering that I am much finer than he is. "Kara, Kara. You are my Valkyrie friend. Surely you know I appreciate you. Threats against Asgard have been a bit quiet of late." He shrugs. "But if what my father predicts becomes true, you're about to become a very busy Valkyrie."

"I will?" With a blank face, I stare at him. "What do you mean?"

He smirks. "For starters, you can go down to Midgard and start searching for Beowulf."

"Who's that?"

"He's a human who hasn't died in battle yet but is a great warrior. He takes down all the hideous creatures in Midgard, and he also fights spectacularly in battles."

"Okay," I say hesitantly, unsure of where this is going.

"I need you to look for him. He should know where the Midgard Serpent is. When you find Beowulf, ask him if he knows the location of the serpent, and send me a message through the world tree."

"How?" I frown.

"Call Ratatoskr. He lives in Yggdrasil and loves to spread messages. He will find me and get the message to me." He turns to leave then pauses and turns back. "Oh, and take your friends and your dragons with you. You lot work well together, and a trip will be great for you."

We mount our dragons, heading to Heimdall's tower and the Bifrost portal. The large watchman stands at attention, looking out over the void, scanning for any threats. His massive body is covered in armor with a horned helmet on his head. A large sword hangs from his belt, following the length of his thigh.

After circling the gatekeeper on our dragons, we land on the large platform in front of his tower.

Elan lowers her torso to the ground, and I dismount. "Good morning, Heimdall."

Remaining in a ready stance, he pulls his gaze from the space and focuses it on me. A subtle friendliness leaks through his dark-brown irises, a change from not so long ago when he had been suspicious of my actions and my motives for wanting to go to Midgard. He remains standing at the ready, a staff propped in front of him, balanced between his large hands. Even though his gaze is friendly, his all-knowing eyes seem to peer right to the bottom of my soul.

"Good morning, Valkyries and dragons." His eyes pass over my friends. "It's been a long time since I have seen any of you come this way. Things have changed over the years." His eyes return to me.

"Yes, they definitely have changed," I agree as I weigh the differences between his greetings then and now. "And pleasant changes they are."

A slight smirk quirks his lips. "It's been a while since you have tried to sneak into Midgard. Have you lost interest now that you're allowed to go?"

I shake my head. "Thor's been keeping me busy. We're here today because he's sending us on a mission."

A small crease appears between his eyebrows. "I can't see any battles on Midgard today."

"It's not for collecting souls. He wants us to find someone on Midgard."

Heimdall lifts an eyebrow. "And who might that be?"

As I move closer, I crane my neck to look at his face. "He wants us to find Beowulf. Have you heard of him?"

He lifts his chin and lowers it slowly as though in confirmation. "Ah, yes. The great human warrior who fights against the monsters on Midgard. I will send you in his direction." In one big bound, he steps up to the portal, ready to send us through. "Kara. You and your dragon can go through first, then I will send the rest of you through individually with your dragons."

I mount Elan's back, and she stands on the portal. Heimdall pulls the lever, and the bright rainbow colors of the Bifrost flash around us before we're sucked into its portal and delivered to Midgard.

Elan lands, her feet hitting the ground with a thud that shudders through her body and rattles mine. When my vision calms from the vibration, I study my surroundings. Once again, I'm awestruck by the beauty of Midgard. This time though, the stark greenness of the land and rolling hills contrasting with the deep-blue lakes is striking. Its beauty calls to me. Filling my eyes with the greenery of the land, I ponder how strange it is to be here and not searching for the destruction of war to reap warriors' souls.

One by one, three thuds sound behind me as the rest of my small team of wingless Valkyries and dragons join us.

An insect of some sort emerges from a nearby flowering bush. Its big white wings flap slowly as it flutters past my head and lands on Eir's extended hand.

Eir squeals, her face beaming as she observes the insect. "This is what they call a butterfly. I've always wanted to see one of these. There are so many different types with many different colors." She twists her hand around to observe the white wings with a couple of black dots and the dark, almost-black body. "This one is quite bland, although it's still beautiful and fascinating. So many of their kind display vibrant colors." A dreamy expression covers her face.

The butterfly rests on her hand for a moment then lifts off, fluttering into the distance. I observe its progress until I realize there's a village snuggled not far behind the mountains.

"We should try there first." I point in the direction of the village. "It should be a perfect place to ask questions and see if they know of Beowulf."

Hildr presses her sword against her thigh as though ready for action. "Sounds like a plan."

Our dragons take flight, carrying us to the village with a few flaps of their wings, and land on a plain just outside the village.

Before we can dismount, a half-dressed man with animal leather wrapped around his waist charges us with a spear in hand. He points the spear at Elan, the closest dragon to the village, and waves it threaten-ingly. "Begone, you terrible creatures."

Elan retracts her head and stands tall. *Who does this guy think he is?* Her voice booms in my head.

Unsure if we reached the right village and in need of information, I call, "We come in peace. These dragons will not harm you. We're searching for someone."

"These are monsters! They will slaughter our village." He crosses his forearms then thumps his chest with both fists before flexing his arms to the side, showing off his muscles. He does all of this while still managing to hold the spear in one hand.

Would you look at that? This guy has more brawn than the gods, Elan comments snidely.

The man before us puffs out his chest. "I am Beowulf. I kill these monsters for a living. None will survive me."

Elan shoots a plume of steam out of her nostrils. *Yeah, right. There's four of us and one of him.*

A strange sound reaches me from behind. Curious, I turn to see Drogon's head nodding and his lips working hard to cover his teeth. I admire him for his effort, even though he isn't very successful. Hildr must have told him how vicious a dragon looks while exposing its teeth.

"Are you laughing, Drogon?" I call over my shoulder quietly to refrain from letting Beowulf hear.

Naga looks at Drogon then at me, amusement

shining in his big blue eyes. *Yes. Drogon laughs at this man. Naga thinks he's funny too.*

I agree with them. His display was interesting, to say the least. However, I don't think laughing at him is the best idea right now. I motion with my hand, my palm facing the ground in a calming motion. "All right. Settle. This isn't helping." My voice remains slightly louder than a whisper, and I hope Beowulf doesn't hear me.

I turn to face him only to be confronted by Beowulf as he hunkers down with his spear pulled over his head, ready to throw it at the dragons.

"Beowulf!" I yell. "Thor sent us to find you. He needs your help."

Beowulf halts just before throwing, his spear poised in his hand as though he's a warrior statue. "What?" His face screws up as though he's half deaf, then his expression flattens. "But these are monsters, enemies of Beowulf. Why would Thor send monsters?"

Elan lowers her body, and I dismount to approach him.

"Thor sent his most trusted warrior maidens and the mounts they ride. These are not monsters." I indicate the dragons. "These dragons are our friends and fierce protectors to have by our sides. We have an agreement with them, and they help us protect Asgard."

Beowulf lowers his spear, his fierce face distorted with confusion.

I repeat, "I am here because Thor needs your help."

"What with?"

"We've received some news that Jormungundr might be about to wreak havoc. Thor asked me to come and see if you have noticed the Midgard Serpent acting strange and causing any trouble. Also, he wants to know if you've seen where it likes to spend most of its time."

Beowulf's face straightens, and his eyes look distant as he gazes far away. I follow his line of sight to the large body of water several miles away from his village.

"The sea is restless. We didn't know why, but this would make sense. The serpent's head has emerged every so often, and it seems to be circling Midgard. Many fishermen are missing. The fish numbers are diminishing, and the serpent appears to be growing."

"Do you think you could assist Thor in containing the serpent?" I ask, scanning his body for any sign of fear.

Beowulf puffs out his bare chest. "Beowulf doesn't back down from any challenge of defeating a monster." His chest caves slightly, yet pride remains on his face. "Although sometimes I need the help of others to do this. Thor is a worthy accomplice, and I'll be proud to help him with this."

"Wonderful," I say, my attention caught by a movement in the distance.

A massive wave careens toward the shore, evolving in size, and washes over several trees.

Eir gasps as a giant serpent's head covered with murky-brown scales emerges briefly out of the water. "This would be the perfect spot for Thor to come."

Beowulf's face looks troubled as he watches the serpent. "This is what the serpent has been doing. It must be stopped. Thor must come soon, as Jormungundr only travels this way once a moon cycle. You can see it is already here, and it will leave soon. Once gone from here, I don't know where it goes."

I mount Elan and turn to leave, calling over my shoulder, "I'll get the message to Thor!"

Beowulf nods. "Come and get me when you're ready, or perhaps your colleagues and their dragons can defeat the monster."

"Now, there's an idea." Hildr shines with enthusiasm and points at Beowulf. "I like that one."

- Chapter Seven -

The water in the ocean continues to swirl higher, the swell of the waves rising with the squirming serpent's body. The waves lap at the edges of several houses that line the coast, and I fear for their fate, my heart racing with apprehension over the peoples' safety.

"Come on, Elan. We need to get to Yggdrasil and find that squirrel."

Elan pushes into the air, and within moments, we're at the base of the world tree.

I stick my head inside one of the holes and call, "Ratatoskr!"

It feels stupid calling to an overgrown rodent that I've never met. I have no idea what to expect from the squirrel. Although, when I think about it, I have done far crazier things for the sake of Asgard. I trust Thor's information is correct, and I've heard rumors before about this little creature that runs up and down the world tree, delivering messages.

A loud splash sounds behind me, and I turn to see a massive wave crashing onto the shore. The slippery scales of a serpent rise then fall beneath the surface of the water. Thor needs to come down now. It's crucial that I get this message to him as soon as possible.

"Ratatoskr!" I don't know how long it could take the squirrel to get to me. Usually, squirrels are fast movers, but maybe this one is different or only comes when it suits it. I'm desperate to get this message to Thor.

I hear a loud *yahoo* behind me. Following the sound, I spot Beowulf riding on Drogon's back, his hands clasped around Hildr's waist. Their forms rise and fall with the flapping of Drogon's wings. Britta follows on Tanda's back with Naga and Eir not far behind them. They must be heading toward the Midgard Serpent. Fear twists in the depths of my stomach. The monster needs intervention, but I'm worried about them. Despite his boasting and strength, Beowulf isn't Thor. He doesn't have a magical hammer and the bonus strength of a god, especially one with Megingjord, the belt of might that doubles power.

I worry my bottom lip. Thor needs to come straightaway, and I need to get this message to him so I can join them. I can't stand the thought of my friends approaching danger without me, even if they are adept fighters with three dragons.

I call up Yggdrasil again, "Ratatoskr! Ratatoskr!"

Spinning around to check on my friends, I catch sight of Jormungundr's head rising out of the water. My jaw drops, and my cheeks turn clammy. It's huge.

A strange rustling sounds behind me, and I jump. Turning, I stare straight into the beady eyes of a little red squirrel. It's almost double the size of the typical squirrel I've seen on Midgard, and its red fur stands on end. The squirrel sits on an outside branch of the world tree. Its whiskers twitch as its nostrils sniff curiously at me. It rises to its hind legs, and its fluffy tail twitches in an agitated motion.

My forehead pinches together. "Ratatoskr?"

With crossed arms, the squirrel leans against the tree and hooks one leg in front of the other. He tilts his head to the side, wearing a curious expression. "And who asks?"

I hold a hand over my chest. "I'm Kara. I'm a Valkyrie serving under Thor."

"So, I guess you think that gives you special privileges." He flicks a hand at me while shaking his head with attitude. "You know, because you serve under Thor." His words are exaggerated and slow. He gazes over my shoulder. "Valkyries are supposed to have wings. Where are yours? Or are you just lying to me?"

I raise an eyebrow. "Where have you been? Some Valkyries have wings, and some don't. Have you been hiding under a log?" I fill my words with the same attitude that the squirrel gave me.

Ratatoskr holds out a forepaw, indicating the world tree. "Actually, I've been living under the leaves of Yggdrasil. That's kind of a log. Why are you calling me?"

"I need you to run up and tell Thor something."

"What am I, your messenger?" He places a fisted forepaw on his hip.

I arch an eyebrow. "I've heard you're a messenger, especially along the world tree."

His eyes narrow. "Yeah, I'm a messenger, but not for stupid messages like that."

I pull back my shoulders. "Thor told me to use you as our messenger."

Ratatoskr grunts. "I only carry messages with insults, not serious information."

My jaw drops. "What's the point of carrying insulting messages?"

He gazes casually at his claws. "They get the reactions I want. You should see what happens when I send a message from the eagle down to Nidhogg, the dragon, or the dragon up to the eagle. It creates all sorts of mischief." The squirrel shrugs. "I guess you could say that's my payment." He lifts his head. "I don't do these things for free."

I bunch my lips to the side. "No, I guess you don't."

A war cry erupts behind me, and I turn to see Drogon diving toward Jormungundr with Beowulf and Hildr on his back. Hildr remains in the prime seat with her sword held high, and Beowulf holds a spear poised in his hand.

I growl. They should have waited. I need to get Thor here quickly. My mind whirls, trying to think of an insult to send Thor, hoping he can read between the lines to understand the meaning behind my message. "Okay. Then, tell Thor to get his ugly butt down here. If he doesn't, then I will personally make sure every part of his body is shaven. Then we will see how tough he is when he looks like a boy."

Ratatoskr's eyebrow rises. "He's pretty hairy, isn't he?"

I nod.

He huffs and looks thoughtful. "Okay. I guess I can give you that one." The squirrel scurries up the tree, and I watch the red-furred creature jump from branch to branch, weaving in and out of the world tree leaves until he's out of sight.

Breathing a sigh of relief that a message is finally getting to Thor, I turn around and jump onto my dragon's back. "Come on, Elan. Hopefully Thor will understand the real meaning of the message. If not, then he's going to take it as an insult."

Why would he be insulted? Elan asks. *You just stated the truth.*

"Yeah, but he is a god. I'm supposed to respect him and all that."

Even so, they have to earn respect.

"He has, Elan." I laugh. "Just don't tell him that."

She takes to the sky, unfurling her gorgeous golden wings. It only takes a few minutes before we arrive at the spot where our friends hover around the Midgard Serpent. It churns under the water, its head submerged in the ocean. Elan circles the area. The serpent's eyes follow the dragons' every move.

I call to Hildr and Beowulf, "Was that really a smart idea?"

Beowulf bellows, "We had to do something before it disappeared to another section of the ocean! It would be hard to find the head again." His spear remains poised in his hand, ready to strike, as he glares at the serpent below. "As you can see, it has us in its sights now and is not about to leave."

"Yeah. It looks like it's eyeing us as prey. Great job!" Britta calls, a hint of sarcasm in her tone.

"Can't we just speak to it or sing it a song or something to calm it down?" Eir asks.

Hildr huffs. "I'm open to ideas, Eir. If you can sing it to sleep, you go right ahead."

Eir's eyes open wide. "I'm not a siren."

"Did you get the message to Thor?" Hildr calls to me.

"I hope so. It's a rather interesting squirrel."

Hildr frowns. "What do you mean?"

"He would only take the message if I sent an insult. So I'm hoping Thor gets the meaning. Has anyone gotten close to the Midgard Serpent?"

We have. Elan's voice breaks my concentration on Hildr.

I hold my breath and glance down. The dark-blue water ripples underneath us as Elan's talons barely miss the dark, looming surface. Suddenly the water pushes up from underneath, surging like a spring, higher and higher.

My heart races, and I clamp my teeth before screaming, "Elan, pull up! What are you doing? Quick! Pull up!"

Jormungundr's gaping mouth charges out of the water only a couple of feet below us, ready to swallow us whole.

Chapter Eight

Elan's enormous wings push down, the tips breaking the water's surface as her body jerks up. The ascent is slow. My stomach lurches to my throat, and my knuckles turn white as I grip her reins. I'm caught unaware and smothered in helplessness. I haven't gathered enough of my magic to throw it at the rising serpent.

The serpent's massive form rises higher, swallowing any distance we manage to create. I grit my teeth and hook my feet tightly in the stirrups. Holding out a palm toward Jormungundr, I clasp the blue rock necklace hanging around my neck with my other palm. Magic shoots out of my extended palm, transferred from the magic stored in the blue rock, and it hits the serpent in the nose.

The serpent writhes and drops to the sea, a strange strangling sound coming from its throat. I shoot another blast at the serpent, draining the last of the power within the charm necklace. The force within the second blast isn't as strong as the first, yet it's enough to sizzle the serpent's skin, causing it to contort some more.

I push the joy of seeing it retreat aside as the scaly flesh disappears under the surface, water splashing out to the sides and coating the other dragons and their riders. I hope I haven't scared it off before Thor arrives. Even though I had no other choice—it had to be done, as Elan and I weren't about to become the serpent's lunch—worry over Asgard's safety torments me.

"Don't ever do that again, Elan!" I scream at her.

Her wings continue to labor, pushing us higher and higher. *Sorry. I just wanted a closer look. Dragon scales! It's quick for such a big thing.*

We rise until we reach the level of the other dragons and hover next to them.

Britta gazes down at the serpent. "Don't you think it's weird that Loki gave us magic? We've used its power against Loki and his children." The wind from the dragons' wings blows the loose strands of her brown hair in her face, and she pushes them back to look at us. "It's rather ironic, really."

I ponder the thought. "I still haven't worked out why Loki gave us magic. It doesn't make sense. If he was planning to bring down Asgard the whole time, then why would he help make his enemy stronger?"

"It is rather weird." Eir pulls at the long braid slung over her shoulder. "Perhaps we aren't seeing the bigger picture. Maybe Loki didn't intend to hurt Asgard, and he had another reason behind raising the dragon army. We never got to see his trial."

Hildr snorts. "Eir, you have got to stop seeing the good in everyone." Hildr spreads her arms in agitation, her voice chastising. "Some are purely out to hurt others. You can't see anything good in that."

Eir raises her chin and flicks her braid over her shoulder. She clutches the strap on Naga's saddle. "I will never stop believing there is good in people and other beings. None of us can be a hundred percent evil or good. Everyone has two sides."

Hildr chuckles. "Yeah, right. All you ever show is a good side. If you have a bad side, you're hiding it well. You even hate hurting a fly."

Eir crosses her arms. "Is there something wrong with that?"

Hildr shakes her head, frustrated defeat altering her features.

Britta answers for her. "No. Eir. Just be yourself. Don't listen to her sarcasm and negativity. I think it's refreshing that you project positivity and see value in everybody."

A red glow on land catches my eye, and I glance over to see Thor on the shore, the sun illuminating his red hair from behind. A monstrous giant about twice his size stands behind him, making Thor's robust form seem puny and ungodlike. The sight brings a smile to my face.

"Haha! Beowulf!" Thor's voice carries across the water, and he punches his fist into the air. He climbs off his carriage, strung behind his two trusty goats, Tanngrisnir and Tanngnjostr.

A loud cry booms from behind Hildr, making the four of us jump. Beowulf shakes his spear, his face filled with excitement. "Thor! Haha!" Beowulf pounds his spare fist on his chest then flexes his arm, pumping it in the air. After his brief display, he thumps Hildr on the shoulder, the sound reaching my ears, then points to Thor. "Fly!"

Hildr glares over her shoulder before commanding Drogon to approach the shoreline, and we follow. Thor tramples across the grass, the giant following not far behind him.

I frown. "Any idea why he brought a giant?" I ask Elan.

Elan chuckles. *Maybe he thinks he's too small to catch such a big serpent.*

Drogon lands a few feet away from Thor, and

Beowulf hastily climbs down, bounds to Thor, and slaps him on the shoulders.

"Good to see you."

"And you," Thor replies.

"It's been a long time." Beowulf eyes the giant warily.

Elan lands a few feet behind Drogon, and I dismount. With my feet securely on the ground, I look up to find Thor studying me, a strange look in his eyes.

"Kara." Thor's voice is firm, his eyes unwavering. "I got your message. So, which part are you going to shave?" He pushes his cloak away from his front and tilts his hips forward, humor dancing in his eyes. "Are you going to shave all of me?"

An involuntary cough escapes my throat, and my eyes drop to the ground as heat rushes to my cheeks. "I had to say something to get Ratatoskr to pass on the message. He refused to carry it unless I sent you an insult."

Thor laughs, his eyes taking in every bit of my blushing face. He slaps me on the shoulder, making my body lurch forward, the pressure easing my embarrassment. "I know. I was having fun. That squirrel takes pleasure in causing others grief."

Finally, he pulls his attention away from me and focuses on his human friend. Noticing Beowulf's gaze, Thor says, "Don't worry about the giant. He's here in peace. This is Tyr's stepfather, Hymir. We're going on a fishing trip."

"You're going on a fishing trip?" Beowulf asks, his voice full of disbelief.

Hildr scans the area. "Where is your boat?"

Thor appears as though this jogged his memory. "Oh. Right. That's in the carriage." The four Valkyries look at each other for answers and frown.

Beowulf follows suit, his voice full of disbelief. "You have a boat big enough to carry you and a giant in a carriage that's pulled by goats?"

Thor shrugs. "Of course. Where else would I keep my boat?" He reaches into the carriage and pulls out a large bag before walking to the side of the ocean.

We follow, watching him pull a material out of his bag and unfold it from a compacted parcel. It grows more extensive with each unfolded section until eventually the soft material firms and forms into a large boat. He pushes it deeper as the last bit expands over the water's edge.

Beowulf's mouth sits agape. "Is this an illusion?"

An amused smirk shines from under Thor's burly red beard. "Why would you think that?"

Beowulf stares at Thor with astonishment. "You carried this on a cart that is pulled by goats. Not only that—it unfolds from a small package into a massive ship."

"Oh, that." Thor chuckles. "Of course. This is Skidbladnir. It was made especially for Frey by the dwarves, and he has loaned it to me. It's rather nifty. Not only are the dwarves crafty, but they have also forged it with magic and other witchcraft." He smiles proudly while observing the ship. "It's rather convenient, don't you think?" He pushes the boat into deeper water and climbs on, holding out his hand to the giant. "Are you coming, Hymir?"

Hymir climbs on the boat bobbing and wobbling on the water, and the color drains from the giant's face.

"Is it going to hold him?" Britta calls.

"Of course." Thor looks offended.

Unconvinced, I add, "Are you sure it's a good idea to go fishing in that boat? The serpent is rather large. The whole boat could probably fit inside its head. Trust me. I've seen it firsthand."

"Oh, Kara. See? I knew I had you around for a reason." He walks down to the end of the boat and turns a knob. Instantly the boat starts to grow, as does Hymir's confidence that the ship will hold his weight. The wobbling slows to a controlled pace.

I shake my head in disbelief. I can't believe they are planning a fishing trip while we're all here to help with the Midgard Serpent. Although the boat is impressive. "What are you fishing for?" I call.

Thor's smirk is barely visible under his burly red beard, but his eyes dance with mischief. "Jormungundr, of course."

Beowulf runs to the ship. "I'm coming."

Thor chortles. "I wouldn't expect anything else." Thor reaches down to help him up, calling back to me at the same time, "Don't worry! I've got my belt and hammer. Everything is under control."

I place a hand on Elan's shoulder and lean against her side. "Yeah, I've heard that before," I say sarcastically.

- Chapter Nine -

As I watch them float farther out to sea, I call to Thor. "What are you going to use for bait?"

Thor holds up a decapitated head of a cow. "I harvested this off one of Hymir's favorite cows just before we came."

I screw up my nose and say the opposite of what I mean. "Lovely."

He threads it onto the end of a long line tied to the ship and throws it over the edge into the water. Directed by Beowulf, they sail out to the spot where we encountered the Midgard Serpent. The water is still. Not one ripple rises from under the surface.

Remaining on the water's edge, I press my tongue to the roof of my mouth. I hope I haven't scared the serpent away by shooting it with my magic. I analyze the still water, hoping for some sign of the monster. My spirits lift when the water ripples slightly only to be crushed when I realize it was caused by a large gust of wind.

My nerves are firing, the sparks intensifying with each uneventful moment. It's best if Thor captures the serpent now rather than wait until it becomes any bigger. Worried, I climb on Elan's back, dig through the pack attached to the saddle, and pull out my dragon-scale cloak. The sun glistens off the golden cloak made from the shed scales of Elan's family. I thread my arms through the cloak's sleeves, covering my quiver and sword slung on my back, and pull the hood over my head. I take special care to cover my legs and every part of the saddle. It's a ritual I have practiced many times. Not long after I made the gown, I learned that if the scales of the cloak are touching Elan's scales when she turns invisible, then the cloak and everything underneath its protection also turns invisible.

Once confident that I am covered, I gaze out over the ocean, searching for any sign of Jormungundr without success. "Perhaps we should do this while we're invisible. Maybe the monster will rise if it can't see us. It might be hiding after receiving a bolt of my magic."

Elan's scales disappear from underneath me along with every part that is covered by my golden-scaled cloak, leaving me with the sight of my hands grasping the straps attached to the saddle. Elan projects into the air, taking us higher with each flap of her enormous wings. The sensation of floating in midair fills me. It's a feeling that took time to become accustomed to. Every time she goes invisible beneath me, it's almost like I am the one flying, without the expelled energy.

Elan circles the area, the ground she's covered growing wider as the search proves fruitless. Eventually, a ripple rises from the depths of the ocean about a mile from the ship. My hopes rise again when I hover over the spot, and I'm rewarded with a glimpse of scales.

Elan tilts to the side and circles the area. *Did you see that?*

"Yes."

Without further instruction, Elan flies to the ship and hovers over Thor.

"It's not far away, Thor. It's still here," I call down to Thor, smiling to myself when he searches unsuccessfully for me. "But at the moment, it's lying low, probably because I shot it with magic not long before you arrived."

He scowls. "You did what?"

"I didn't have much choice. It was going to eat Elan and me."

"You know I would have saved you," Thor says, grinning toward the sound of my voice.

"That's not something I was willing to bet on. You'll find it about a mile northeast." I pull on the straps attached to Elan's neck. "Come on, Elan. Let's join the others."

Her body flips, and we fly back to land next to the other three dragons and my friends.

Elan turns visible, catching Hildr's attention immediately.

"What's going on?" Hildr asks.

"The serpent's lying low. I think I scared it off when I shot it with magic. It hasn't gone too far. We'll have to stand by in case Thor needs our help."

Britta groans. "I wish it would hurry up. I hate fishing. It's such a time waster."

I climb off Elan's back and lean against a tree, my eyes remaining fixed on the ocean. Something touches me on the shoulder, and I jump. Pushing the hood off my head and spinning, I find myself face-to-face with the red squirrel. Ratatoskr leans up against the trunk, his arms crossed and one leg hooked over the other, a smug look on his face.

"Ratatoskr! What are you doing here?"

He dusts his claws on his furry white chest, looks at them, then picks something out of his teeth. "Since you're on my radar now, I have a message to deliver."

"Oh. What is it?"

"Loki says you're a treacherous, grounded Valkyrie and you deserve the lot life has delivered you. He's disappointed in you. After giving you powers, all you did was use them against him."

I gasp. "What? He's the one who attacked Asgard." My voice is shrill.

The squirrel shrugs. "Hey, don't yell at me. I'm just the messenger." He scurries up the tree.

I scream at the squirrel while thumping the tree trunk. "Come back here, you little rat! I'll give you a message to deliver to that conniving Loki."

The tree stops shaking, and Ratatoskr pauses on one of the branches. He gazes down, his head tilting to the side, his expression curious. "And what would that be?"

I thought for a minute then yelled, "Loki is the treacherous being! He is the one who acted like my friend and betrayed me in all different forms." I cross my arms. "Pass that on to him."

Ratatoskr's furry brow bunches, and he crosses his arms, glaring down at me. He shakes his head. "That's not a good enough message to pass on to Loki. It has to be a better insult than what he called you."

My mind whirls. I'm not used to thinking of insults, yet after what he did, there's so much I want to say to Loki and haven't had the chance. "You tell Loki if he's so crafty and smart, then how did he father illegitimate children that turned into monsters? If he was clever, he wouldn't have had them in the first place."

The squirrel briefly screws up his tiny face then shrugs. "I guess that'll do. It's not the best one I've heard." He scurries up the branches, ignoring my astonished openmouthed glare as he disappears.

Elan nudges me from behind. *Are you okay?*

"What mess has Thor gotten me into? He has made me initiate contact with a squirrel that won't pass on messages unless it's insulting. Just what I don't need." I shake my head. "I thought I was finished with the mess Loki created. Now I'm dealing with his children, and not only that. He's haunting me from the depths of the cave he's tied up in."

Elan shows off her teeth in a gesture I have learned is a smile, although it's somewhat intimidating. *Would you like me to eat the squirrel next time it comes down?*

The thought brings a smile to my face, yet I shake my head and place a palm on the trunk of the tree. "As much as I like that idea, I think it's probably best not to. I think this terrible little squirrel has some oddly important role in Asgard and at the world tree."

The tree shakes, and the ground around it vibrates.

Elan's eyes widen. *What was that?* She cranes her massive head to try to get a better look as she stares up the tree.

"Ratatoskr probably just passed on an insulting message from the eagle to the dragon. He seems to take pleasure in annoying people. He told me when he tells the dragon, Nidhogg, something insulting from the eagle, the dragon gnaws at the roots of the world tree, trying to knock the eagle off Yggdrasil's top branches."

"Is the squirrel trying to kill the world tree? Doesn't he know that we need it to thrive in order to survive?" Eir interrupts our conversation.

I frown. "I wouldn't think Ratatoskr would want to kill the tree. He seems to love it."

The tree and ground shake some more, followed by a splash.

"What's going on?" Britta asks.

I gaze out to the ocean, noticing a swell growing in the water. "The rumbling of the ground and the shaking of the tree must be aggravating Jormungundr."

The murky-colored scales on the serpent's head

rise briefly out of the water as it thrashes some more. The boat drags forward, and Thor stands to check his line and see if the serpent is attached. His shoulders slouch when he realizes his rope is slack. Nothing has happened. Disappointment covers his face, then the rope in his hand tightens. Suddenly the boat pulls in the opposite direction, the rope attached to the cow's head going taut. The nose of the ship tilts toward the ocean before leveling then tilts again and rocks from bow to stern several times.

Beowulf and Hymir stand beside Thor, watching the line. Hymir's face blanches as the ship is dragged across the water. Thor straps on his belt for strength and grabs ahold of the rope.

- Chapter Ten -

The serpent dives and swishes so hard it drags the Viking ship several feet. Donning his metal gloves, Thor pulls on the rope, drawing the serpent above the water. Jormungundr opens its mouth, ready to swallow the bow of the ship.

Elan calls, *Jump on!*

Without a second thought, I swing onto her back, and she launches into the sky. I yank my sword out of its sheath then pull my hood on and close the edges of my dragon-scale cloak as we turn invisible.

With its mouth wide, the serpent rises higher, drawing the ship toward its mouth. Thor pulls on the rope as though reeling in a fish. I'm not sure what he's thinking. Between his pulling and the serpent's yanking, the ship is being sucked right into its open mouth. Thor's efforts might have been a good idea if the Midgard Serpent weren't trying to eat them.

I fling my sword at Jormungundr, lodging it deep in the flesh on the serpent's nose. The serpent cries, jams its mouth shut, and thrashes, the movement pulling the ship lower in the water. The waves splash up the sides and onto the deck.

Thor grabs Mjollnir and tosses his hammer directly at my sword, knocking it farther into the serpent. The monster cries again, flinging its head away from the ship and filling it with more water. Thor holds out his hand, calling to his hammer until it flies straight into his grasp.

The ship rocks and sways with the waves created by the serpent. Hymir frantically scoops buckets of water off the deck, tossing them back into the ocean to no avail. Jormungundr's frantic thrashing grows, pushing the sea up onto the land, exposing a section of the ocean floor.

The ship snags on the waterless ground, and Beowulf jumps over the edge and grasps ahold of the rope. This only makes the monster more agitated, and the thrashing increases. The water subsides more, and I notice that the walls of water are holding. Puzzled, I look up to see Britta, Hildr, and Eir sitting on their dragons and holding their palms out as though they are retaining the water with a massive wall of magic.

The bottom of the ocean is bare. Beowulf seems to notice what the Valkyries are doing, and he releases the rope, scoops up his spear, climbs a nearby boulder, and launches himself onto the serpent's back. His leather-strapped shoes slip on the scales, and his arms fling to the side, his spear held horizontally, until he regains his balance. The Midgardian runs along the serpent's back and onto its head.

Sensing something foreign on its back, the serpent lashes out some more. Nimbly, Beowulf runs to its head and slams the spear between its eyes then slides off its side. The rope tied to the ship yanks, pulling the ship closer to the serpent, dragging it along the dry seabed. Thor's body launches from the force.

I notice the giant is missing then spot Hymir crouching in the back of the ship, his face pale and his eyes wide. He pushes himself back onto his feet, trying to back farther into the corner and into the false sense of safety. I huff. It goes to show that bigger doesn't mean tougher. This is a perfect example.

As the serpent continues to slash, I call to my sword. The tiny wings on the hilt flap rapidly, trying to dislodge the blade from the monster's nose. I coax it some more, and at the same time, I gather my magic, letting it build, storing it in my necklace for another emergency.

An arrow shoots past me, careening directly at Jormungundr's eye. The serpent wriggles, and the arrow narrowly misses its target. I turn to see a bow in Britta's hand before she tucks it aside to hold out her hand to reinforce the wall of water.

With Hildr on his back, Drogon nose-dives straight toward the serpent. I grit my teeth. This maneuver could go wrong at any second, and I worry for Hildr. Suddenly, Drogon flips upside down, and Hildr points her sword at the serpent. A bolt of something shoots past her head as she flies forward.

Something crashes into the serpent, and within moments, the serpent halts its slashing and flops to the ground, unmoving. I glance up. Eir's hands are pointed in the direction of the serpent. She must have placed a stunning spell on it and is struggling to hold it.

Suddenly Britta yells, "Eir, work with me!" I realize that Britta has been left holding the walls of water, and they are crumbling at the sides, water breaking through the edges.

Eir glances at Hildr, who's almost at her target, then glances at the crumbling wall, assessing which is more urgent. Eir drops her stunning spell and helps Britta contain the water before Hildr can strike the serpent with her sword. The two Valkyries hover on their dragons, backs to each other, pressing their palms out to the water, holding it in place.

The serpent rears, pulling the ship closer. Drogon and Hildr swerve away from the attack, and Thor jumps down to Beowulf's side, lifting him onto the serpent's back to retrieve his spear. Thor tries to climb onto the serpent but slips to the ground when his feet can't find enough grip.

Giving up, Thor approaches the front of the monster, hammer in hand. Jormungundr snaps at him, black venom dripping from its fangs. I cringe when it snaps at him again, barely missing him. Beowulf slides off the serpent's back, giving up the pursuit of his spear.

Still invisible, I ride Elan, and she flips, granting me access to the spear's shaft sticking out of the serpent's head. I reach for it as we fly over but only manage to loosen it slightly. I groan as I'm unsuccessful in retrieving it from the serpent's flesh.

As Thor holds his hammer high, his face turns blank, his eyes unfocused as he stands fixed to the spot. Moments pass before thunder rumbles through the sky above. Eventually, lightning shoots across the sky several times before forking to the cleared ocean floor.

The walls of water cave slightly, and I fear anyone nearby will be electrocuted by lightning if the water reaches the strike spot.

Hildr joins Britta and Eir in holding the water walls with their magic, all three faces lost in concentration.

Britta groans. "I don't know how much longer I can hold this."

Giving up on my sword and the spear, I line up next to Eir, helping her with her wall of water while Hildr turns her full attention to Britta's side.

Displeased yells and groans reach our ears along with hisses from Jormungundr as it continues to inch its way toward the boat.

Thor stands again with Mjollnir held high, calling to the thunder and lightning. It rumbles and crackles, and light bolts across the sky. I sneak a peek. This is a sight that will never grow old. A bolt of lightning shoots down, hitting the hammer in Thor's hands, shoots up to the sky, then zaps the serpent close to its tail. After expelling a cry, the serpent thrashes some more.

Thor calls to the lightning again, this time using its force to lift him into the air, the hammer acting like a hot-air balloon. Suddenly, he thrusts the hammer at the serpent's head. His body drops as the hammer slams straight into the spear, embedding the shaft deeper into the serpent's flesh. The serpent's eyes widen with the impact, and it yanks itself backward, dragging the ship and the king of giants closer to its mouth.

When the serpent stops thrashing, it lowers its head to the ground until it realizes it isn't far away from the ship. Exposing its dripping fangs, it hisses. Hymir, crouched in the back of the boat, turns ghostly white, almost becoming a pale shade of blue as the serpent pulls him closer again.

I'm amazed that Jormungundr is still thrashing. The only answer I can think of is that the spear must have missed a vital spot.

Thor catches his hammer on its rebound then calls to the sky, releasing another bolt of lightning, hitting the serpent on the head. The muscles in the serpent's body tense before the serpent lashes to the side, striking Thor in the movement.

The god of thunder is tossed to the side and crashes against the side of the ship with a thud. Thor moans, and he takes a while to gather the energy to move, settling for a slow crawl.

Frantic thoughts whirl through my head as I assess the next best move. The serpent slithers forward, thankfully slowed by its massive form. On the ship, Hymir trudges forward, dagger in hand, his face still pale white. He reaches the bow, and shakily he saws the blade across the rope's fibers. The serpent lunges forward, rocking the ship, and the giant almost drops his dagger. Jormungundr yanks its head backward, dragging the attached boat closer until the final strokes of the dagger slice completely through the fibers, dropping the ship's hull to the ground.

Hildr cries, "Beowulf, grab Thor, and get out of there! We can't hold this much longer."

I feel the drain on my energy from exerting so much magic, but I was the last one to join them. It's then that I notice each of my friends' faces are covered in sweat.

Thor's face clouds with anger as he glowers in Hymir's direction. He grabs his hammer and dodges the serpent's snapping jaws as he and Beowulf charge to the ship and help each other onto the deck.

Thor stomps toward Hymir, his feet thumping on the wooden deck, his face full of anger and his hammer held high as he directs his failure to capture the serpent toward the giant.

Slowly, the Valkyries release the walls of water, lifting the boat up evenly and submersing Jormungundr's body. The monster lashes out at the ship one last time.

Noticing that Thor is too distracted by his anger

toward the king of giants to see the threat from the serpent, Beowulf grabs Hymir's discarded dagger from the ship's deck and tosses it blade-first into the monster's mouth. The point lodges in its tongue. Jormungundr rears back and circles away from the boat.

- Chapter Eleven -

Thor stomps toward Hymir, his hammer held high and his face fuming. "We're supposed to stop the serpent, not let it go. You know the prediction. It could cause Ragnarok and be the end of Asgard."

Hymir's face remains pale, and despite his size, he cowers from Thor's raised hammer. "I wasn't about to become the serpent's meal."

Thor scowls, his eyes barely visible under his bushy red eyebrows. He throws the hammer into the water in the serpent's direction then waits, with his hand outstretched, for its return. "It's not about one being or god. It's about the whole of Asgard and stopping anything that may cause Ragnarok."

Mjollnir launches out of the water, and with a wave of his hand, Thor directs the hammer at Hymir. It hits the giant in the stomach, knocking him overboard. Instantly, the hammer returns to Thor's outstretched hand, leaving the giant struggling in the ocean. Ignoring Hymir's cry for help, Thor steers the Viking ship back to shore.

"Elan, turn visible, please," I say.

She obliges, and we fly down to level with Thor.

"You can't just leave him there." I gaze past the ship to see Hymir splashing awkwardly in the background, trying to swim and sinking fast.

Thor growls and places his hammer on the ground. "And what good is he back home? He let the serpent go."

I spread my hands out to my sides. "He was scared. Everybody gets scared sometimes, despite our size and abilities. Clearly, his size doesn't amount to his courage. I get that you're annoyed with him, but don't just leave him in the deep water. We'll have another go at catching the serpent later."

Thor crosses his arms over his chest. "I'm not turning around."

Elan flaps her wings with a mighty whoosh, showing her displeasure and blowing Thor's bushy red hair in a minitornado.

My mouth gapes in disbelief. This a side of Thor I haven't seen before, not that I've been in battle with him until now. I already know I don't like this side. "Don't you think your warriors will worry that you will leave them in battle if they get scared?"

Thor lifts his chin. "We choose the bravest of warriors from Midgard. They won't do that." He gestures to the Midgard beast slayer. "Just look at Beowulf. He didn't cower."

"He specializes in destroying monsters. Others from Midgard might get scared, depending on what they have to face in battle. Not all warriors can stand up against the beasts. Beowulf is an exception." I click my tongue against the roof of my mouth. "Look. I know you're angry right now, but you can't leave him stranded."

Thor huffs loudly. "If you want to get him, go get him. I won't stop you."

I thought Thor would give in eventually, which is why I persisted. He's usually one of the more understanding gods, but now I'm in a dilemma. "And how do you expect me to carry him? Elan is strong but not strong enough to carry a giant plus me."

Hildr and Drogon line up next to me. "We'll help you."

I gaze at Drogon, and he nods once, tilting the horns on his head forward. His brown form is smaller than Elan's, although more robust than the other two dragons'.

Elan rises, heading in Hymir's direction. The giant is barely visible on the wavy surface of the ocean. His head disappears underwater for a moment before breaking the surface and sucking in an exasperated breath. His arms fly and flop in all directions, clearly indicating that the giant can't swim. Dull-colored serpent scales skim the water's surface behind the giant, bringing with them all kinds of dangerous scenarios. I clamp my teeth shut and swallow the lump in my throat. I hope we get to him before the serpent decides to eat him.

Elan's strong wings carry us to him with several strokes, and Drogon follows closely behind. She swoops down and grabs the giant's hands, and I can feel her struggle with the added weight as she drags him higher. Drogon catches hold of Hymir's feet as Elan pulls him out of the water. Together they carry him away from the sea, his massive form swinging uncomfortably between them.

Elan grunts, a sound indicating she is struggling with the weight. *I'm so glad you're helping, Drogon. I couldn't do this on my own.*

Their flight wavers, and they drop toward the ocean, barely missing Thor's ship. My heart jumps to my throat.

Naga flies next to us. *Let Naga help. Kara, hop on Naga's back. It will lighten Elan's load.*

"Good thinking, Naga!" I call.

With Eir on his back, Naga swoops down below me just underneath Hymir's arms. I jump, the air catching my dragon-scale cloak, causing it to billow and flap. I spread my legs, trying to straddle Naga. My backside thumps onto Naga's back, and his flight path dips and swerves as we career toward the water, skimming its surface. Eir embraces me, stopping my fall as my body tilts to the side. Naga's wings pump as he labors to carry us higher, away from the ocean and to the shore.

That helped heaps, Naga. Thank you. Elan already sounds less strained.

Tanda circles around us and catches Hildr, lightening Drogon's load. Hildr slips on Tanda's mound, which looks similar to that of a one-humped camel, her body built differently than the other dragons, and she falls toward the red dragon's tail. Tanda extends her tail and tightens the muscles along its length, trying to support the wingless Valkyrie before she falls. Hildr quickly reaches for Britta's hand. The strain on the Valkyrie's arms is evident in her flexed muscles as Britta clasps her strap with one arm and Hildr with the other. Hildr yanks and claws her way to the edge of Tanda's one-person saddle shaped to fit her hump and wraps her hands around Britta's waist. Thankfully there is only a short distance to the shore to relieve the pressure on the dragons and Hildr's grasp.

Naga lands, followed shortly by Tanda. Elan and

Drogon gently set the soaked Hymir down and land with a thud not far from the other dragons, their breathing heavy from the weight of the giant. They tuck their wings close to their sides.

By the time the ship sails to the shore, the dragons are recovered, and Hymir slowly stands. Thor jumps out of the ship, Beowulf not far behind him, helping Thor drag the boat to the shore. Thor folds the ship up and places it in his bag, a feat I don't know why I struggle to believe. After all, the Asgardians get mead out of a goat.

With brooding faces, Thor and Beowulf approach us, their warrior's chests broad and their muscular arms swinging by their sides.

Hymir blocks Thor's path, his giant body rigid with tension. "I'm so sorry. I got scared. It's stupid, I know. I acknowledge I'm not worth more than Asgard's future. I came because I thought I'd be helpful, but instead, I was a hindrance." He looks at the ground, dejected and sad.

Deep lines crease Thor's forehead as he approaches the massive form. At first, I'm not sure whether or not Thor is going to punch him until the god places a hand on Hymir's arm. "I understand. I'm sorry I threw you in the water. I let my anger get the better of me. But next time, stay away."

Thor leaves the baffled giant and approaches his

100

carriage, rubbing one of the goats that pulls it behind the ear as he passes. He waves to Beowulf. "Until next time." After climbing onto the carriage, he grabs the straps and appears as though he is about to leave without the giant.

A moment passes before he calls over his shoulder, "Are you coming, Hymir?"

Without a word, the giant runs toward the carriage and sits next to Thor, his face still bearing the signs of regret and disappointment.

As they leave, I turn to Beowulf. "Are you seriously the one who slays the monsters on Midgard?"

"True to my word." He pushes out his chest proudly.

"The next time you see Jormungundr, can you send word to us so we can try to defeat it together?"

"And how am I supposed to do that?"

I stare at him in disbelief. "Haven't you sent word to Thor before?"

"No. We always just run into each other when he's on Midgard in the middle of a battle and I'm tackling some monster."

I gaze at the still waters of the ocean, my mind whirling. I can see only one solution, and I'm not that fond of it, but it may work. "Have you met Ratatoskr?"

He looks confused. "Who is that?"

"It's a squirrel that lives in Yggdrasil, the world tree."

The creases in his brow deepen. "I've seen lots of squirrels. What are you talking about?"

"I don't mean squirrels of Midgard. I mean the squirrel that runs up and down the world tree carrying messages."

He shakes his head. "No."

I let out a long breath. "Okay. I'll show you where to call him. I only met the squirrel today, but he's a very feisty little thing." I approach the world tree branches where I met Ratatoskr earlier. "Here goes." I raise my voice and call up the tree. "Ratatoskr!"

Within moments, I hear scurrying, and his little red face peers out of a hole in the tree. The squirrel's nose twitches, and his beady eyes fall on Beowulf.

"Ratatoskr, this is Beowulf. If he calls you, can you come?"

The squirrel's eyes narrow, and he screws up his nose as he stands straight on his two back feet. His tail flicks from side to side. "What am I, a servant?"

"I know you're not a servant. However, we need someone who can carry a message from Midgard to Asgard, and you are the messenger of the world tree."

The squirrel huffs, crossing his arms over his chest as he narrows his gaze on Beowulf.

"If Beowulf needs to get a message to Thor or to me, can you please come down when he calls you?" I plead.

Ratatoskr runs down the tree and up Beowulf's body. The warrior cringes with each scratch the cheeky messenger leaves on his skin. The squirrel scrambles around his shoulders, flexing and pulling on the warrior's bulging muscles in his arms and torso before drawing back and staring straight into Beowulf's eyes.

"I guess he is a fine specimen for a Midgardian." Ratatoskr turns to me. "Have you told him about my conditions?"

"No, I haven't. I wasn't sure if that was something you asked of everyone or just me."

The squirrel tuts then faces Beowulf. "I only carry messages that are insults." He then scurries down Beowulf and up Yggdrasil before disappearing into the hole.

"That's an interesting little creature." Beowulf's eyes are fixed on the hole Ratatoskr disappeared into, and he looks confused.

With raised eyebrows, I nod. "You don't have to tell me!"

We ride into Asgard and separate, going our different ways. I have a sudden urge to visit Odin and see if he's okay. It seems like a long time since I saw him that night outside the entrance of Yggdrasil leading to Mimir's well. The thought has me chuckling. It was only a couple of years ago that I would never have considered visiting Odin of my own free will. But he's changed since the colossal attack on Asgard. I guess some of his stubbornness broke that day.

An image of a crumpled Odin flashes in my mind, reminding me that something broke him this time as well and not in a good way.

After leaving Elan in the large courtyard at the side of the palace, I skim the steps, taking them two at a time. Both sides of the entrance are manned by two guards.

"Greetings, Valkyrie!" the guard on the left calls.

His small chin barely holds the strap of his helmet and contrasts with his large, pointy nose, making his normal-sized eyes seem small in comparison.

"Greetings, Birger!" I call before reaching the top of the steps.

His face spreads into a broad smile.

"Greetings, Gorm!" I call to the guard on the right.

A glimmer of appreciation passes through the eyes of the guard with the large chin divided by a cleft. "Who are you coming to see today?"

It was only a couple of years ago that they would do anything to stop me from getting inside the palace. How times have changed. "I've come to visit Odin. Is he here?"

"We haven't seen him leave," Gorm says.

They open the doors to the palace, indicating for me to go through. I enter the large, open corridors lined with marble and massive pillars. The extravagance is impressive and far from the state of my residence and the Valkyrie Academy. My shoes scuff loudly on the floor from my open and unafraid steps.

So many times in the past, I had to hide when I passed through these halls. It's a nice change, not having to hide behind every pillar to avoid the guards as I weave through the palace.

A guard stands outside the throne room, and I

enter through the double doors unhindered only to find it empty.

I exit, bearing a frown of confusion as I glance at the guard outside in the hall.

His spine is rigid and tall as it presses toward the wall. His horned helmet overwhelms his head, and his curious blue eyes meet mine as he gazes down at me. "Greetings, Kara. Why are you here?"

"I've come to see Odin."

"He is unwell. He hasn't been to the throne room today."

I push my mouth to the side in thought. "Yes, I heard. I've come to see how he is and update him on some news."

The guard nods once. "I will escort you to his chambers and see if he wants to see you."

"Thank you, Den."

It was only a couple of years ago that Den was dragging me back to the Valkyrie Academy, far away from Odin.

He clicks his heels together and nods once, then marches down the hallway, his sword swinging by his side, the hilt clanking against his armor. I follow him until we reach another set of large, decoratively carved, wooden double doors.

Den stops and speaks over his shoulder. "Wait here. I'll check if he wants to see you."

Before I can answer, he yanks on the sizeable golden handle and pushes into the room, shutting the doors behind him. Muffled voices, too soft to decipher, seep through the thick wood.

The golden handle jolts down, and the door cracks open. Den's face peers through the space. "Odin says he'll see you."

He pulls the door open, and I slip past the guard. Ample burgundy folds of material drape from the canopy over Odin's massive king-size bed. The god is lying on a mattress that appears to be several layers thick, his back propped up by an extravagant number of cushions.

With my eyes fixed on Odin's pale face, my boot catches on something. I glance down and gasp. The top of my boot is stuck under an uplifted scale of a golden dragonhide spread across the floor like a decorative mat.

"Oh. Don't mind that. It was my father's." Odin sounds apologetic. "It's centuries old. I haven't had it removed yet. To be honest, I'm not in my room often."

I glance up at the pale-faced god almost swallowed in cushions and buried in blankets. He looks so frail compared to a few days ago. A haunted eye gazes at me, and for now, I push aside my disgust over the dragonhide. I unhook my boot from the scale and sidestep the floor decoration as I approach him, noticing his staff propped against the wall next to his bed.

"Kara, thank you for visiting." The god's voice is husky, a shadow of its former strength.

"I had to see how you were, great Odin."

I move closer to his bed, taking in his hollow cheeks and the dark ring around his eye not hidden behind the patch. Odin pats the side, indicating for me to sit. I do as instructed, feeling out of place sitting on the god's bed. Even though he isn't himself, his eye doesn't shift, making me uneasy even with his weakened state.

"I'm sorry you had to see that the other night."

I push away my discomfort. "Great Odin, everybody has their moments of weakness. I won't let it spread that you had one too."

A massive sigh of relief pushes out of his lungs. "Thank you. I appreciate it. If others on Asgard hear about my..." He pauses, his expression pained. "Weakness, it may cause unrest and anxiety."

I place a hand on his bed, closer to his body, wanting to add comfort but not wanting to touch the god without permission. "That is why I have kept it to myself, and I'm sure Eingana will do the same. I believe it's important to keep this quiet. Asgard doesn't need to worry about its leader falling apart."

"That's very wise, young Valkyrie. Some might not be able to handle knowing their leader has a meltdown occasionally."

"I understand."

I jump as the door suddenly crashes open against the wall and Thor's large form enters, his eyes wild and face burning with concern and worry. "Forgive me, Father. I have failed."

Odin's brow creases in a frown, his eyes falling to me as though looking for answers.

"As I promised, I told Thor about what you said about Loki's three children from his giant mistress and how they need to be contained."

Odin nods. "That was a wise move." He turns to Thor, gesturing to the chair next to his bed. "Sit."

Without a moment wasted, Odin's ginger-haired son obeys.

Odin's dull gaze assesses Thor. "How have you failed?"

Thor throws his head in his hands and rests his elbows on his knees as he stares at his lap. "I took Hymir the giant to help me catch Jormungundr, thinking his size would be of help. Except Hymir buckled in fear and cut the rope when I nearly had the serpent."

Odin nods. "Ah, yes. It was foretold that would be so," he says in a calm voice.

Thor glances up from his lap, his eyes boring into Odin. "And is it foretold that we will catch Jormungundr before it wreaks havoc?"

"No. It is foretold that the Midgard Serpent will be part of Ragnarok and will be part of Asgard's downfall as well as your own." Odin holds up a finger. "But prophecies aren't set in stone. They can be changed if we take a different path from how it was foretold."

"I hope you're right because not even Beowulf is willing to tackle the serpent by himself. It has grown so big. If it gets any bigger, it will be much harder to handle. A simple fishing line or rope will not withstand its weight."

"I understand," Odin says. "What about Fenrir? Did you manage to contain him?"

"No. We didn't," Thor says. "We tried. We chained him with the chains that we used on the dragons, but he broke out within minutes. He is so strong."

Odin nods. "Yes, that was also foretold, but we must not panic."

"He still seems mostly the same, a happy pup." Thor's shoulders soften as some of the stress leaves his body. "But if the prophecy says he is dangerous, then we should take measures." Thor's gaze lands on me momentarily before he continues. "There haves been some reports that he has moments of aggression. We will keep working on restraining him."

Odin nods once. "And Hel?"

"I haven't seen any evidence that Hel is on the rise. I will leave her alone for the moment and try to settle these two—unless something changes."

Odin's face looks distant and slightly scared before he responds. "I believe Fenrir is our most significant risk at the moment. I know it is hard to believe, but try to contain him soon. I can see his anger burning."

- Chapter Thirteen -

Thor and I leave Odin's room and exit the palace.

"I'm going to find out how the gods and forgers are going making a stronger chain for Fenrir. You can come if you like. Otherwise, you're relieved of your duties. You've worked hard today."

A memory of Fenrir as a pup flashes into my mind. He was so adorable, his fur soft and his nature loving. It's hard to believe he's changing into something dangerous. Deep anguish churns in my stomach. I shake my head. "I think I'll sit this one out and have some time by myself, or with Elan. I don't like thinking of Fenrir as something dangerous, and it upsets me seeing living creatures chained when they haven't done anything wrong."

Thor's blue eyes survey me. "You didn't seem to mind with the Midgard Serpent."

"Yes, but Jormungundr was a monster from the start. Fenrir used to be a cute, loving pup."

Thor yanks on the base of his tunic and wriggles as though making it more comfortable. "I understand. I'll see you later." He leaves me, heading in the direction of where the gods train for battle and the place Fenrir will likely be sleeping by Tyr's side.

I make my way to the courtyard, where I left Elan next to the palace. When I round the corner to the courtyard, she is nowhere to be found. I halt then spin to search the area only to see Birger standing by the palace door, a broad smile plastered across his face.

I follow his line of sight to find Gorm walking with exaggerated steps, a look of excitement on his face as he throws handfuls of dirt. I watch him do this a few more times. He halts twice, his body rigid and his eyes on full alert.

I call to Birger, "What is he do—"

A shocked yell comes from Gorm, and when I look, his body is floating, and laughter explodes from his mouth. I raise an eyebrow as Elan becomes visible with Gorm clasped in her talons, and she gently lowers him to the ground.

We're playing hide and seek. Elan's voice answers my unfinished question.

"I see." I smile and shake my head. My dragon is like a big kid, and she has found some playmates. I would never have envisioned this a couple of years ago when Gorm and Birger were making my life difficult.

"Come, Elan. Stop playing with the grown man."

With a look of disappointment, Elan sinks to the ground, making it easier for me to climb onto her saddle. I grab the reins and stroke her shoulder. "I can't believe you're supposed to rule the dragons one day. You're the biggest child of them all."

What's life without a bit of fun? She exposes her teeth in what is supposed to be a smile. "That's where you can rule your herd in a completely different way than your mother."

She pushes off, flapping her enormous wings. The breeze pushes the dirt into clouds, and pebbles scatter noisily across the courtyard floor. We rise above the palace, and Elan asks, *Where to?*

The rocky mountains of Asgard spread out before us. I rub my tongue behind my top teeth. "I think I'd like to see the old cave, the one where Gilroma used to stay. Well, Loki."

Really? Elan doesn't hide the shock in her voice.

"Ah, huh. My magic hasn't grown since he's been locked up. There's no one to teach me." Absentmindedly, I clasp the blue-stone necklace around my neck. Slight nostalgia courses through my veins. "To be honest, I miss those days. I still find it hard to believe he's completely evil and working for the opposite side."

I drop the necklace, and my brows pinch together as Elan veers toward the mountain.

"I don't understand why he stole the dragon eggs to raise an army and why he did what he did, but I do miss the education he gave me."

When we reach the mountain, she circles and lands outside the long tunnel.

I gaze into the darkness, rawly aware of the lack of light in the passage I'm about to enter. "Elan, can you please breathe fire on the linked torches on either side of the wall?"

Elan chuckles. *It does look a little spooky down there.*

She stretches her neck and expels a controlled flame from her mouth, igniting the first torch in line. The fire follows the oil path to the next sconce, lights it, then continues past the extent of my vision. She does the same to the other side.

Musty, stale air assaults my nostrils as I follow the long tunnel down the center of the mountain, and eerie sounds echo off the enclosed walls. I had forgotten the hair-raising feeling I felt the first time I discovered the tunnel. The sensation dimmed in the trips afterward, when I knew I had Gilroma to call on if something went wrong. He was nearly always down at the other end, hiding in his cave.

I haven't been here for quite some time, probably before the last attack on Asgard, when I thought this was a friend's cave. I shake the thought from my head. If the sentence given to Loki is accurate, I was mistaken. Still, even if he's guilty, I'm sure there's valuable information in the books he was hoarding here.

The wind blows from behind me, bringing fresh air and something else. I breathe deeply, trying to work out if it's an odd smell on the breeze, and I come up with nothing. Even so, a strange feeling brushes my skin, giving me the sudden urge to look around. My search remains fruitless, and I push forward to the small rooms at the end, my eyes wide with anticipation as I round the corner. Eerie shadows creep along the stone walls. The flames of the sconces dance on the breeze, and a faintly rancid smell leaks from the burning oil. No one must have visited here after Loki was put away.

My footsteps warn the room I'm entering as I pace straight for the large pile of books neatly stacked in the corner. I run my fingers over the cover of the first book, leaving streaks in the dust. My leather pants creak as I plunk my backside on the stone bench, pulling the top book onto my lap and dusting the cover with my hand. The pages are illuminated by the light from the sconce over my shoulder.

My fingers tremble as I flick through the pages, excitement pulsing through them as they glide over the pages. Dark elves' magic is written in these pages, something I haven't touched for a long time. My magic is so limited, especially since Gilroma can no longer train me.

Yet, as I flick through the pages, my excitement diminishes. The book is written in the language of the dark elves, a language I can't understand let alone read. It looks as though I'm going to have to learn another language. I may have to go back to the library in the academy and see if they have any books on this.

Different elven symbols cover the pages with not one word in a language I understand. It is going to take an immense amount of time to learn this. With disappointment coursing through me, I close the book and set it aside before grabbing the next. Again the pages are filled with a language I don't understand. I work my way through each book in the pile until, finally, I toss the last book aside with a disappointed sigh. A substantial weight pushes on my shoulders.

Besides myself, I have three friends who can do magic, but we're almost entirely untrained. This needs to change. Even though we helped defeat the dark elves that invaded Asgard, there are still threats of another attack and perhaps Ragnarok. My brows pinch together, my mind deep in thought as I stare at each of the unique book covers.

Suddenly, Elan's voice pierces my thoughts. *Kara, wherever you are, don't come out. I hope you're way down in the middle of that mountain.*

My frown deepens. "Why do you say so, Elan?" I know her hearing is good and that she should be able to hear me, but she doesn't answer. With my curiosity piqued, I leave the cave and work my way down the long tunnel. When I'm about halfway, I ask again. "Why do you ask, Elan?"

You're louder. You better not be coming down the tunnel, Elan scolds.

"You didn't answer me before, so I was coming out to make sure you heard me."

Her voice rises, panic lacing the words. *You better not be coming down the tunnel. You better be doing what you're told you. Go back into the cave, Kara!*

The sound of rocks toppling and quick movements echo down the tunnel. I tilt my ear toward the entrance. If I'm not mistaken, there is scuffling just outside accompanied by a growl, deep and long. Shivers run down my spine. That didn't sound like Elan. I quicken my steps, pushing toward the entrance.

You better be retreating to the end of that cave, Kara. Those better not be your footsteps I hear approaching. If they are, I'll never let you live this down. I'll make you pay one way or another.

Suddenly her tail enters the tunnel, slashing as her body writhes. Her long golden tail swings from one side to the other, knocking anything in its wake.

"What are you doing, Elan? Are you fighting something out there?" I move as close to the edge of the tunnel as I can, avoiding her thrashing tail.

She stops wriggling, and I move closer to her as my eyes catch a spot I can slip through, only to jump back to dodge another swing. I wait, tethering my impatience, for a chance to go outside to help her. As though reading my mind, in a split second, she backs up, blocking the whole entrance with her backside. I hear another muffled, deep, and menacing growl.

I stomp my foot, frustrated over feeling helpless. "What is going on, Elan? Let me help you."

No, Kara. Stay where you are. This is not a fight you can help me with.

An ear-piercing scream splits the air, making my

heart skip a beat. Elan flicks her tail again, narrowly missing me. I edge my way up the tunnel even though it's still blocked by her backside.

"What is that? Let me help you, Elan."

No, Kara. Stay where you are. This is nothing from Asgard.

Chapter Fourteen

My interest piques. "What do you mean?"

Elan doesn't answer.

"What is it?"

A tremendous growl reaches my ears, and I press close to Elan's backside, trying to avoid her thrashing tail.

I screech, "Elan, let me out! I want to help you."

No. I told you to stay there.

A grunt travels through her mind speak, followed by a groan so filled with pain I almost think I'm the one who was struck.

"Elan, are you all right?"

She groans, this time with frustration. *You weren't meant to hear that.*

I stomp my foot. She's being overprotective. "Well, I did. So let me out to help you."

No.

Another moan travels through a small crack

between Elan's butt and the side of the tunnel. It isn't loud, as most of the sound is muffled, yet it still sets my nerves on edge. My hands curl into tight fists, my nails biting into the flesh of my palms. Something is attacking her, something big and powerful. Try as I might, I'm at a loss thinking of a creature that is bigger and stronger than a dragon Elan's size. I can't piece together what could be attacking her.

Growling followed by Elan's sudden movements of her backside only make my fear for my dragon rise. My heart pounds in concern for Elan facing whatever monster this is alone. More dragon cries seep into the tunnel and echo down its length, chilling me to the bone. I have to get out there.

A loud roar filled with pain bursts from an unfamiliar creature, and inwardly I cheer for Elan.

Suddenly, Elan jerks forward, and another unknown creature's roar follows. Elan's body lurches to the left, and a larger crack opens between her backside and the side of the tunnel. I contemplate running through the opening, yet I'm also aware that if Elan jerks quickly to the right, I could be squashed. I work up the courage only to have it crushed when suddenly she flings back, covering the gap. I badly want to get out and help her.

My heart pounds so rapidly that it thrums in my ears, making it harder to hear. Thankfully it blocks some of Elan's cries of pain. I'm ready to stick my head out of the new opening she has made, when suddenly Elan's hip slams to the right, her scales narrowly missing my face as she closes the gap. I jump back and try to escape her tail swinging in my direction.

"Elan. You've got to let me out."

No! She sounds as though she's hissing through clenched teeth.

I huff with disapproval. I've got to get out there somehow. She needs help whether she'll admit it or not.

Another dragon cry pierces the air, and she suddenly flings to the left again. In a split second, I run toward the crack, narrowly skimming past, only to have her slam to the right again just after I scrape my last limb through the opening.

My stomach lurches to my throat. That was close. Her foot suddenly flies in my direction, and I narrowly dodge it. Elan concentrates on the beast as she prepares to take it on again.

I move around the side of her, and I'm confronted with the face of a hideous beast. Fire seems to burn in its eye sockets. The creature opens its mouth, exposing flames within the depths of its throat. Unlike a dragon, it doesn't seem to have the ability to breathe plumes of fire. Instead, its insides appear to be made of molten lava that burns deep within its stomach to its very core. Each time it opens its mouth and eyes, they fill with the glowing red flames.

My jaw drops. I have no idea what this is. It's like nothing I've ever heard of before. Its body is black, and horns protrude from its skull, like a dragon, yet it has no wings.

I scan its shape, my eyes traveling up and up as I crane my neck to see its face. It's hideously tall, taller than Elan when it stands on its two legs, its long arms dangling from its sides. I haven't seen anything like this in the books I've read in the Valkyrie Academy library. If we survive this, I will have to revisit the unique monsters section to search for this beast.

Pushing aside my shock, I steel myself. I'm not going to let Elan fight this alone. I press my back against the rock wall of the mountain, strangely finding some comfort in the solid form at my back. The creature swings its arm, and long claws protrude from its fingerlike digits. It rakes its claws up Elan's side, striking against the flow of her scales, hooking into the soft flesh hidden deep beneath them.

My face twists as I imagine the agony she's experiencing. My horror deepens when she expels a pain-filled roar.

With an openmouthed stare, I ponder the best

way to tackle this. This beast is way too big for one Valkyrie and her loyal dragon. We thought the dark elves and frost giant that invaded Asgard earlier, threatening to bring on Ragnarok, were bad enough. I need to stop and assess the situation so I can work out how to tackle this massive monster. The only problem with thinking it through is it will use precious time I don't have. As much as I need to, I don't have the luxury of sitting back and assessing. I have to act now, or this will be the end of Elan and undoubtedly myself not long afterward. My feet shake in my boots as I think of what I might need to do. Even so, it's not the first time I've had to battle a monster.

The monster shifts one of its feet, drawing my attention. Its foot is almost the size of Elan's enormous head, its tall legs reaching halfway up her body if not higher. The legs lead to a long thin frame and spindly arms and a head that's bigger than Elan's. The mouth is similar to a wolf's. I shudder at the thought of what could happen if that mouth came anywhere near me. As I work hard to contain my fear, it dawns on me that the thing doesn't have wings.

Elan lurches forward, horns first, aiming straight for the creature's stomach. The beast's mouth opens wide as it lets out a roar, revealing its lava contents.

Elan twists and flicks her head, one horn ripping at the monster's torso. It throws its head back, releasing a cry of agony.

Elan pulls back then charges forward again, this time using the horns from both sides of her head. Quickly she flicks her head down, releasing her horns from the brute's body, showing off the two fiery holes that she dug.

The beast's arms flail wide before raking up Elan's back. Her screech cuts to my very core as the lava monster rakes its claws up her sides, stopping before it hits the saddle, narrowly missing Elan's wings. Blood trickles down Elan's sides.

I've watched enough horror befalling my beloved dragon. I must think of a way to help. I study her wings, my heart leaping with hope when I notice that they look intact. I have an idea, but I must get on Elan's back first, and I can't distract her from the fight. That might be fatal. I also know that she would be most upset with me if she realized that I was out of the protection of the tunnel and would probably knock me back into it and block me in there again. At least if I were already on her, it would be harder for her to entrap me in the tunnel. I have to get onto her back without her help.

Keeping an eye on the monster, I assess the area and the situation. I must dodge this massive beast and its swiping dark claws. Thankfully, Elan has been keeping it busy, and I don't think it has seen me yet.

Elan's tail remains pressed into the tunnel's entrance. She must think that I'm still trapped within its confines. Amusing as it is, it's also hindering her movements to defend herself. I must get on her back and let her know that I am safe so she can move away from the tunnel, giving her more freedom to flip and move.

On the mountainside, I spot a ledge and a rocky, jagged path that might be possible to climb. Quickly, I head to the rugged track, grasping the rocks on the cliff face and pulling myself up as hastily as I can. I lunge for a difficult spot, clasping a small ledge, only to lose traction. My hands, elbows, knees, and face scrape against the rough rocks before my hand manages to find purchase on a lower ledge. My arms and legs feel weak. My heart pounds in my chest as I tackle the fear of knowing I could have slid to my death. I peer between the rock face and my armpit, taking in the distance to the ground, confirming my suspicions. It's not too far but still far enough to injure me enough to be useless.

Controlling my breath, I focus on my mission and brace my emotions, toughening up. I yank myself upward, drawing my weight higher before hooking a leg over the ledge. I gaze over my shoulder to monitor the position of the beast. The glowing red eyes seem to be looking at me, but I'm not sure. They don't have any pupils, making it hard to know exactly where it's focusing. Quickly, I yank myself up and turn around to assess the situation from my new viewpoint.

The beast flings its arms in my direction. I'm not sure if it's aiming for Elan or me. Elan dodges the strike, and the claws swing over Elan and scrape along the rock wall at the height of my legs. I jump as high as I can, managing to avoid its hand. As though it hasn't spotted me, the monster continues to attack Elan, her backside still pressed against the tunnel. Maybe the swipe was always intended for Elan, and it just missed.

I study the height of Elan's back. It's still too high for me to jump on. I have to climb farther. I struggle up another level before facing the backside of my best friend and dragon, assessing the distance between us. I ready myself, moving my legs into a sturdy position, and lift my arms before leaping off the ledge. I fling my arms behind me to try to gather more speed before reaching forward and clasping onto the saddle on Elan's back.

She jumps, unaware of my position, and her wild golden eyes glance over her shoulder. *Kara, what on dragon's scales are you doing out of that tunnel? I told you to stay in there.*

"I can't let you fight this alone. You need my help, and you need to stop protecting that tunnel. It's hindering your fighting ability."

Her eyes narrow, the disapproval evident in her glare. Suddenly, something black flings in her direction.

All emotion drops from my face. "Look out, Elan!"

E lan whirls just in time to see the monster's claws careening toward her. They rake up her scales along her face, and she cries out in pain, the scream projecting into my mind. The weight of her distress weakens my limbs. She lurches back, and I manage to cling onto the straps just enough to stay on.

The sudden jerk awakens my purpose. "Elan! Use your wings! Push into the air!" I screech.

Elan swings sideways, away from being pinned to the tunnel, blood seeping from her scales.

With a groan of pain, she lurches forward two bounds before springing at the monster with her head down. Her horns ram straight into the creature's abdomen, knocking it backward as she pushes with all her might.

I groan. She ignored my advice.

The monster folds over the top of Elan and stares

down at me, shadowing me in blackness and molten lava. I grasp the power that's been welling inside of me, ready to help defend, and aim my hands directly at the creature's face. I'm not sure if this is going to do anything. This creature looks like a creature of magic. I cling to hope as my power hits it in the face.

The lava monster straightens and staggers backward, a strange look passing over its hideous features. The movement dislodges it from Elan's horns, and a shudder runs down her body. She groans in pain from the wounds all over her body, and lethargically, she pushes into the air.

Seeing Elan's progress seems to revive the creature from its setback. Regaining its strength, it shifts forward, its footsteps pounding on the ground. A long black arm reaches for Elan, claws extended.

At the last second, Elan swerves to fly away from the monster, narrowly avoiding the strike. The creature roars its frustration, sending shivers down my spine.

Elan peers over her shoulder, and I follow her line of sight, spotting the horrid black arm striking out again. Elan furls her wings, and we plummet just in time to dodge the strike. The wind from the attack blows on my face as the extended claws miss me by a foot. I retaliate by sending another bolt of magic at the creature's face, and it topples onto its backside.

Elan unfurls her wings, catching the breeze and carrying us from the monster's reach before it strikes again. She flies several more yards, no longer needing to dodge the monster's attacks. Now that the immediate threat is reduced, I notice her usually controlled flight seems to waver. I concentrate on her and fret. She seems to be struggling underneath me.

"Are you all right?"

Exhaustion and pain reverberate through the words that enter my head. *Not really.*

Worry fills my every pore. Her safety is paramount to me, yet there is a monster still lurking on Asgard. We can't stay and fight. Elan is in no condition to continue. I glance over my shoulder, finding the beast still on its backside, but it won't be for long. I don't know what to do. I can't call the others, and we don't need this thing causing any more havoc.

"Can you make it back?"

Maybe.

My heart sinks. Flying is still the quickest way back, and I can't do that for her. She needs help as soon as possible. I rub my hands together, focusing on my magic, then inject all the strength I can into her. Hopefully, it will help heal her, but I don't like our odds. She looks terrible.

We fly a little way, and I spot two forms in the air heading toward us.

"Who's approaching?" I ask, unable to see them in the distance.

The weariness in her voice shatters me. *It's Drogon and Tanda with Hildr and Britta. I called them when I was fighting... whatever it is. They are coming to assist me.*

I steel my emotions. "Thanks, great thinking, but I don't think two dragons are going to be enough to defeat that thing."

I told them as much, Elan says, sounding more exhausted with every word that projects into my head.

The distance between the two dragons and us closes, and I indicate for them to land. At least Elan can have a brief rest while I update the others. We circle down and land on a rocky plain.

I call to the others, "I don't think two dragons will be enough to fight that thing."

Hildr climbs off Drogon's back, her boots crunching on stone as she approaches. "That's why Naga's not here. He's gone to the dragon wasteland to fetch the other dragons."

"Don't try to attack that thing yourselves," I warn. "It is way too big for just two Valkyries and two dragons, even with magic on your side. We can't turn around and help. I don't know where it came from or what damage it has done to Elan. She needs medical help."

"I can tell." Hildr gently strokes Elan's nose, her concern-filled eyes traveling over Elan's bloodied body. "Don't worry. We have others coming to help. We were all coming to help Elan defend you, but now we will change our plan." She looks at Britta. "We'll circle the monster out of its reach and keep an eye on it. We'll make sure it doesn't come toward the populated areas while waiting for the army of waste-land dragons."

Britta nods. "From what Kara's been saying, it sounds like a good plan."

With one worry taken care of, I prepare to leave. "Great. I'd love to stay and help, but I need to get Elan back. I can feel her weakening, even though she's not admitting it."

Hildr and Britta nod in agreement. Hildr climbs back on Drogon, and I spot Drogon and Tanda staring at Elan, worry filling their eyes. Just from the way they stare at her, guilt and worry swirl through the pit of my stomach. I wish I could transport her back without her having to do all the work.

"Come on, Elan. We have to get you back to Anita and see if she can work some magic on you."

Every beat of Elan's wings fills me with worry as we head straight to the academy to seek the healer's care. Anita is an excellent healer for gods and

Valkyries but has also extended her service to dragons since they decided to join our side.

With the academy in sight, Elan lowers. Her front legs buckle under the pressure of the landing, and we almost crash face-first into the dirt outside. I jump off her back, and my boots hit the ground with a loud thud. They crunch with each hasty step toward her face. Her head collapses on the ground, and I stroke the side of her face, staring into the tiny slits of her golden-brown eyes. "Are you all right while I get Anita?"

Her nose lifts up and down once in the slightest of movements followed by a blink. It's as though speaking to me telepathically is too much effort, confirming my worst fear. I bolt inside the academy, ignoring the wide eyes of the students, and I run through the halls.

"Out of my way! Coming through!" I call as I dodge the large white wings of the winged Valkyries, finding it easier to bypass the wingless Valkyries.

As I crash through the soft white feathers of the winged Valkyries who didn't move quickly enough, I almost collide into Mistress Sigrun. Flashbacks of how mean this woman was to me swamp my thoughts as I stare into the uniformed mistress's hard face. My days in this academy were made very difficult by this woman.

Her voice booms, "Who's running through the academy halls?" Her steel-blue eyes catch sight of my face, and her expression changes. "Oh, Kara. What are you doing here?"

My tension loosens when I remember that things have changed between us since then. "I'm coming to get Anita. Elan has been attacked by a strange monster seemingly filled with lava. The beast was between the mountains not far from here. Drogon and Tanda with Hildr and Britta are keeping watch. Elan needs urgent medical attention, so I have to go. Can you send your Valkyries? They will need all the help they can get. Naga is calling the dragons from the wasteland. I don't know how long it will take them to get here."

Mistress Sigrun's face suddenly turns to business mode again. Her voice projects. "Right, Valkyries. Let's go find this monster. Gear up! Asgard needs us."

A young Valkyrie protests, "But, mistress. I haven't had enough training."

"You are Valkyrie not a human. It doesn't matter how much training you've had. The more of us out there, the more intimidating we are. Suit up!"

Her voice chases me as I run down the hall to the entrance of the healer's room.

Anita's back faces me. Her curly auburn hair is

tied into a ponytail, and she leans over a bench on the far side of the room. A wounded Valkyrie lies on her white wings on top of a gurney table. The Valkyrie's perfect face distorts in pain. Her broken limbs are evident at first glance. She thrashes in discomfort, messing her blond hair against the pillow. From my time in the academy, I know that her injuries were probably acquired by training practice.

With a furrowed brow, the wingless healer turns to her patient, her spatula still stirring the setting paste she's prepared to plaster the wound with after she's set it. After that, the Valkyrie's natural healing powers will take over and heal the break quickly. Just by Anita's casual actions, I can tell it's a menial job for an experienced healer, and although painful for the injured Valkyrie, it's not life-threatening.

"Anita!" I call.

The healer looks up, her face filled with surprise. "Kara." Quickly, her green eyes scan me as though searching for an injury. "What are you doing here?"

I'm breathless, but I push the words out as clearly as I can between pants. "It's Elan. She's been attacked by some hideous beast. It ran claws right up her scales. She needs help."

After dropping the setting paste on the bench, Anita packs a bag and charges down the corridor.

- Chapter Sixteen -

Anita's feet pound down the hallway behind me, dodging through the bustling Valkyries preparing for battle. Following her closely, I charge to the front door of the academy and my dragon's side.

Elan lies sprawled out, her head drooped, her unfurled wings flopping to the ground. Blood pours from underneath her scales, and my heart sinks to my feet. Worry sludges my stomach. I hope she's not mortally wounded. I don't know what I'll do without her. We have become so close over the last few years. Elan's eyes remain closed, and she's unresponsive. I muster every ounce of my energy and project it into her nose, the softest and most receptive part of her body, hoping it will help her heal.

She remains still, showing no sign of coherency. I kneel and sit on my heels, bending over her snout. My long dark hair falls on either side of my face, shielding my distress from the outside world. Her skin is cold to the touch as I clasp her nose between my hands. I shudder. Never is a dragon cold. Their fire always warms their blood.

Horrible thoughts run through my head. Panic surges inside of me. *She hasn't died, has she? Has my nightmare been realized and is manifesting? No! This can't be.* Fear wraps its talons around my heart and sinks into the flesh. It's a fear stronger than any I have felt in a battle to the death. The pain in my chest is so intense, I wonder if my own heart has stopped, refusing to push the blood through my veins. I squeeze my eyes shut. She can't give up. It would kill me. She can't be dead. Determined to manifest my wish, I hold my hands in front of her nostrils, hoping for something, some sign that she is alive and breathing, even if she's just slightly there.

"It's not good." Anita's voice leaks from the background, threatening to rip my last strand of hope away. I want to put my fingers in my ears and block it out. "These scratches have some kind of magic in them. The magic could be pulsing through her body, making it harder for her to heal."

I squeeze my eyes tighter, a movement I regrettably can't do with my ears. I attempt to ignore Anita as I concentrate only on Elan for any sign of hot air, even just a tendril of breath, to come out of her nostrils to prove that she is alive. I wait and wait. It seems to be an eternity with nothing happening. Finally, a big gush bursts out of her nostrils, pushing deep from her belly. I'm smothered in hot breath. Sweat forms on my skin. I relish it until panic clamps onto my heart, digging in its talons farther. Perhaps it's her last breath of life. I've heard that when a person dies, the last thing they do is release one large gush of air, emptying their lungs.

I hold my breath as I wait all over again for a sign of life from my beloved dragon. Another gap of time is chewed up as nothing happens. Tears well in my eyes, threatening to fall down my face. The golden scales on Elan's snout dig into my forehead, but I ignore the discomfort, waiting, hoping for her to show she's alive.

Exhausted from the emotional stress but unable to leave her side, I curl up, circling the front of her nose. I grip her snout and place my forehead in front of her nostrils. I don't want to miss any sign of life.

I whisper to her, my words catching in my emotion-clogged throat. "Elan, breathe, please." A tear trickles out of the corner of my eye and into the dirt. "Please breathe, Elan. Please. I will be nothing without you." My voice is choked with emotion, no longer sounding like me. "You will leave a gaping hole in my heart if you don't come through." My body shudders at the thought, and I curl up tighter, bringing my knees almost to the side of her nose, both of my hands still touching the tender skin. "Please, Elan. Ple—"

A massive gush pushes against my face then is sucked back into Elan's enormous form. The breath is slow and is drawn out and stops, causing my heart to skip a couple more beats. Eventually, another gush exits her nose, the flood of warm air bordering on hot, coming from deep inside Elan's belly.

My tears of sadness turn to happiness as I rejoice over the progress. "That's a girl, Elan! You keep doing that. Keep breathing," I encourage, passing on anything that may help motivate her fight through this.

The clattering of boots on the hard ground and the flapping of wings pulls my attention away. The Valkyries exit the academy and take to the sky, their white wings lining the blue, reminding me of fluffy clouds. The wingless Valkyries break into a jog toward the palace or perhaps the dragon enclosure. I wish them luck, hoping none of them will be severely injured, and turn my focus back to Elan. I should be helping protect Asgard, but I can't with my heart here with my special dragon friend.

It takes me some time before I can sit up. I've been so crippled and distraught, my brain and body struggle to move. I gather any magic left in my body and shoot the healing energy into her body, pushing it through any soft skin I can touch under her scales. My body drains wholly, and I find it hard to rise to my feet.

Eventually, I manage to stand and follow Anita around Elan. "Come on, Elan! You can do it! Fight this! Give it everything you can. You must survive this." I push more energy into her from my already-drained magic source, hoping to help, until eventually I crumple to the ground in front of her snout, resting on my back, exhausted and unable to drum up any more. I hold my hand on the soft part of her nostril. Hopefully, if she can smell me and feel me, it will bring her encouragement—a drive to go on and comfort to know that someone who cares for her is near.

The soft crunch of Anita's footsteps breaks into my consciousness as she circles Elan, plastering healing salve on her wounds, working some of her healing magic into her.

I remain next to Elan, slowly gathering my energy, my thoughts lost in scenarios on how to help her. I try to break through the clouds of exhaustion crowding my brain. I need to find someone on Asgard who has the power of healing magic. Gilroma said that he had taught Anita healing magic, but did he teach her everything? I'll have to wait and see. I remain next to Elan's nose, the steady soft breath the only thread of hope I feel.

Anita works quietly in the background, her brow knitted together and worry filling her eyes. Eventually, she collapses next to me with her legs crossed. She tucks a strand of dark hair behind her ear. "Are you all right, Kara?"

It takes all of my effort to nod.

Concern fills her eyes, and her gaze looks unconvinced as the creases on her forehead deepen. Her flawless face scrunches up as she pouts her lips. "I've covered every wound with a special potion. It's a potion that Gilroma taught me. I'm hoping this will heal her along with the little healing magic I know. My knowledge isn't extensive." She stares into the distance. "If it doesn't work, then we'll have to find someone else to help her."

My throat is dry, and I struggle to talk. I croak out the words. "Is Gilroma's healing magic stronger?" I attempt to push myself up from the ground and prop my body up with my elbows. Failing, I flop back down, my arms sprawling out to the sides. "Is he able to heal wounds as bad as this?"

Serious eyes gaze down at me. "That depends on what kind of magic this creature used. Do you know what this creature is?"

I shake my hand. "No. It's something I've never

seen or heard of before. I'm planning on visiting the library to see if we have any records of it at the academy." I try to swallow to moisten my dry throat but receive little relief. "This creature is enormous. Extremely big, and it is black all over with feet bigger than Elan's head. When it opens its mouth and eyes, they are full of a lava type of flame, burning red and bright. When Elan gouged its torso, the same kind of flames showed through its wounds. It looks pure evil and nasty. Have you heard of something like that before?" Slowly, I prop myself up then collapse again.

She shakes her head. Her eyes fill with sadness again. "Then, I don't know if my magic will help."

Tears threaten to burst from my eyes. "If your magic isn't enough, then who can we call?"

"We can always visit Loki." Her face looks distant and sad as she says this, her gaze falling to the ground. "After all, he and Gilroma are one and the same."

A sudden burst of energy shoots to my core, and I attempt to sit up again, pushing off my elbows. This time I succeed in getting halfway up and prop myself there. "I wouldn't trust a word that came out of that god's mouth."

"I know." She shrugs. "But he may be someone

who has answers. He holds powerful magic when he's in the form of Gilroma, and he trained me."

Despite my disgust for how he treated and deceived me, along with the rest of Asgard, he marked me with his magic. Absentmindedly, I stroke the scar on my shoulder, where the zmey struck me. It spikes the memory of the pain that coursed through the scar before my magic manifested. Not only that, he also marked my friends with the same magic. He was training all of us before he betrayed our realm. Which makes it harder to comprehend where his loyalties lie. Knowing all of this, it still makes it impossible for me to like Loki. The last act of deception created so much distrust, I can't move past it.

"Is there anyone else we can ask?" I search the healer's face for some glimmer of hope.

Anita hesitates. "There is someone else or another race that we can ask."

"Who?"

"The light elves. They know the magic of the dark elves. They know just as much magic as Gilroma did."

"But I thought the light elves are peaceful creatures that do little more than be happy and focus on the light."

Anita huffs in amusement. "The dark elves that

invaded Asgard are light elves that turned bad. The true dark elves are more like the ones that represent what some humans call dwarves. They live deep inside the mountain, and the light elves live on top, close to the light and sun. The light elves that turned, which you know as dark elves, live somewhere else entirely. Even the purest of souls can be turned if they have darkness in their hearts."

I groan. "I'm so confused. I thought what invaded Asgard were dark elves." I stare at Anita, flicking the dirt underneath my hand with my fingernail.

"That was a misconception. In any case, the point we are trying to cover is that the light elves should know the same magic as Gilroma." Anita looks into the distance again. "Except, to reach the light elves would be an extensive trip, and Loki is local. I'm not sure how long Elan will last. You need to get her healed quickly."

"I really don't want to see Loki at the moment, maybe even ever again." I expel a large sigh. "I'm not happy, but I guess he's my best choice at the moment."

- Chapter Seventeen -

I wait, hoping Elan will get better soon. If she doesn't show any improvement in the next few minutes, I'll have to leave. Her large eyes remain sealed shut, and her head still slumps on the ground. I hug her snout and rest my cheek on her scales. "Come on, Elan. Get better and wake up. You can do it. Fight this magic, and push it out of your body."

A soft, comforting hand rests on my shoulder. I peer up to find Anita bending over me. I was so focused on Elan, I didn't know she stood up.

She rubs my upper back gently in a circle. "I'm going to do another round and check on her wounds."

I nod, not bothering to push past the lump in my throat to answer her.

Anita walks around Elan's enormous form, investigating every wound and every magical poultice she's applied to them. There are so many wounds on her vast body that it takes quite some time. Several minutes pass before she finally returns to where I sit.

Clinging onto my final hope, I gaze into her green eyes, searching for confirmation of improvement, but they are clouded with sorrow and regret, crushing any optimism I hold.

"They're not getting any better. You're going to have to find someone with stronger magic."

I cringe, my stomach churning. Elan's going through all of this because she was trying to protect me. If only she had turned invisible and hid from the lava monster instead of standing against it alone.

A loud roar, answered by dragon roars, echoes through the valley toward the academy. Shrill cries of Valkyries pierce the air, followed by another roar. That has to be more than a couple of dragons. The dragons from the wastelands must've arrived. This lifts my spirits slightly, but they're crushed again when I gaze back at Elan's unmoving form.

A moment later, the rumble of a carriage draws my attention, and I see Thor passing, his carriage pulled by his goats, Tanngrisnir and Tanngnjostr. The sunshine illuminates the red in Thor's unruly hair and beard as he charges past the academy, heading straight toward the fight scene. The goats' speed is impressive for such tiny creatures. Behind the carriage, an extensive line of gods follow him, their muscled bodies intimidating as they jog in a group toward the battle. Each god that passes raises my hopes of destroying this monster.

Minutes later, lightning flashes from the sky, darting down to Thor's hammer then back into the sky. Thor is warming up Mjollnir, ready for battle. Surely they must have a chance against this lava monster.

By herself, Elan had no chance. I don't know why she took on this monster alone. It's not like her to take foolish chances. Maybe she didn't have a choice because it appeared out of nowhere.

When I look back at Elan, her lack of movement breaks my heart all over again. I turn a questioning gaze toward Anita. She shakes her head, sorrow filling her eyes. My insides turn to mush as the defeat of Elan's recovery takes over my body. The only hope left is to travel to the light elves, a trip that could take too long, or do the unthinkable. Either way, I can't leave Elan the way she is.

With a heavy heart, I brace my out-of-control emotions and ask Anita the inconceivable. "Do you know where I can find Loki?"

A pang of guilt gnaws at me. I haven't visited the unruly god since he was chained under the serpent's venom. On the other hand, I'm proud that I haven't visited the god who acted like my friend then deceived me and, to some degree, left me feeling as though I was the reason Asgard was put in danger. It hurt me to think that he was my friend in many forms, yet each friendship was a big fat lie.

A strand of curly red hair falls out of her ponytail, and Anita slowly hooks it behind her ear then nods. A strange kind of sympathy flashes through her eyes, as though she read my thoughts, as though she could see deep down into the pit of my soul. "He has done much to me, too, Kara. I know where you're coming from, and I know how hard this is. But it may be Elan's only chance."

I cringe from the fate of those words—to be so desperate that I must rely on my enemy.

"He is trapped in the dungeons deep underneath the castle."

I frown. "The dungeons aren't that deep. I've been there to rescue Elan."

"The normal palace dungeons aren't deep, but they are not the ones I am talking about. These dungeons reside deep within the confines of the realm, buried well within the rocks." Anita's shoulders cave. "It's not a pleasant place. If you thought the palace dungeons were bad, this is almost like living with the undead. I have been once to supply him with salve to help heal his flesh from the burns of the venom. That's all. I don't think he deserves any more than that." She runs a hand gently over Elan's golden scales, love and care radiating from her face. "I can't come with you."

I nod my understanding.

"It's going to be dangerous going down to visit Loki. I was accompanied by guards because my visit was approved by Odin. There are many creatures down there that may attack you. Do you know anyone who could go with you?"

The lava monster roars, and chills run down my spine. The shrillness of the Valkyrie cry follows along with the roar of the combined dragons. Lightning illuminates the sky, and dark, intimidating clouds cluster over the battle.

"Probably everybody I know is in the battle right now, and I don't want to take anyone away from defeating that monster. Asgard's safety is also important."

"I can't come with you," Anita says again, this time almost a hushed whisper. "I wish I could. But I have to stay here because I'm the main healer. There may be many who will need healing from the battle."

I nod. "I understand. I wouldn't expect any more from you." I take another long look at Elan, contemplating what I'm about to do. I ready my weary body, exhausted from pumping every bit of energy into her. It has slowly been recharging but not fast enough. I can only hope it is restored before I reach the dangerous area on my journey. Even if it doesn't, I'm doing this for Elan whether I'm ready or not.

Behind me, something thuds on the ground. I spin to face Naga with Eir mounted on his back. Both their faces look distraught as they observe Elan's state.

"Oh, Vanir!" Eir says. "What happened?"

"The lava monster got her. The creature imbued some kind of magic in her wounds. She's not healing."

"Oh, Kara." Eir climbs off Naga's back. "Is there anything I can do?"

I shake my head. "I've pumped every bit of power into her that I can. I'm drained, and I don't think it's done any good. Anita has applied a magic salve, and the wounds are still not healing. It looks as though I need the magic of the dark elves. I need Gilroma's magic to help Elan."

Eir's hand freezes over Elan's scales, her face stunned. "How can you do that?"

"I'm going to have to visit Loki. Whatever happens from there will happen."

Eir's mouth drops open. "You're not going to set him free, are you?"

"No! There's no way I'm going to set him free." My voice is high-pitched. I sigh, and my shoulders droop. "To be honest, I don't know what's going to happen. Whatever happens, happens, but I must keep a close eye on him because I don't want him to go unpunished. I just know I have to get his magic to Elan. If he can't transport healing magic through me, then I must get it to her somehow."

Naga and Eir will come with you. Naga's big blue compassionate eyes melt my heart. I stroke Naga's snout, and he leans into me, closing his eyes briefly before glancing up at me with that heartwarming expression.

"I would love that, Naga, but I don't know how I'm going to sneak a dragon past the guards at the castle. They will let me in and possibly Eir also, but I don't think they will let a dragon in, even a smaller one. I think they will become suspicious if we try to get you in as well. They may stop us from entering."

Naga's big blue eyes flicker with understanding. He nods once. *Then Naga will stay with Elan. Naga will watch over her.*

"Thank you, Naga." I expel a sigh, happy to know that Elan will have a dragon for company. I gaze at Eir. "Are you sure you want to come?"

Eir's peaceful face breaks into a smile. "Of course. I'm helping a friend. That's a good reason to cause a little mischief."

Leaving Naga by Elan's side, Eir and I make our way to the palace, the opposite direction of the battle with the monster. Without our dragons, the progress is slow, and we break into a run. Each step I take is difficult without my full strength, but my concern for Elan pushes me on, our warrior-trained bodies devouring the distance quickly.

When we arrive, I press my back against a building, my chest heaving, and I peer around the corner, assessing which guards stand at attention at the palace entrance. I wipe my brow, relieved to see Gorm and Birger aren't on break. Still, I know it might take a bit to talk my way in when everyone else is at the battle.

My energy hasn't returned to its full potential, but I don't have the luxury of waiting. I speak over my shoulder. "I'm going to have to talk our way in. Let's go."

Our footsteps echo against the walls as we approach the front door, portraying the air of urgency.

We march up the steps, and Gorm holds out his hand. "Halt!"

My teeth clamp together, and my heart thumps rapidly against my rib cage. Hopefully, I can pull this off.

"What are you two doing here? The battle is on the other side." The guard points in the direction of the different dragon sounds and the monster roaring. A bolt of lightning flashes down from the sky as though pinpointing the location.

I put my weight on one leg and toss my hand, expressing disbelief. "Thor forgot something and sent me back for it."

Birger huffs. "Typical. What did he forget?"

"He forgot his belt. Would you believe it?" I roll my eyes to emphasize the point. "He will need every bit of energy to defeat this monster."

Birger's eyebrows rise, and tension grips my throat as I worry that they won't believe me. "That's a strange thing to forget, but he definitely needs that."

Gorm indicates Eir. "And what's she doing here?"

I can feel the blood drain from my face, and I turn

away from them, hoping they won't notice as I try to conjure the reason Eir is with me.

Eir's sweet, smooth voice brings me hope as she explains, "Kara lost a lot of energy throwing magic at that monster. I'm here to help her carry the belt. Have you ever felt how heavy it is?"

Gorm shakes his head. "No. Although, I've heard it's rather heavy. I don't know how Thor carries all that heavy weaponry all the time."

Birger calls to Gorm, "Let them go. They must be in a hurry. Thor needs that belt." He stands aside, and Gorm follows suit, letting us pass.

I smile, trying to hide my relief. "Thank you. I'd hate to go back empty-handed."

We hurry inside and down the corridors, passing through the passageways and quickly out of Gorm's and Birger's sight. We check swiftly for any guards when we reach the entrance to the lower levels. It would be impossible to explain to any guards that I took a wrong turn to Thor's room when they know I've visited Thor a lot over the last couple of years.

We follow the white marbled hallways farther down, trying to contain the noise of our hurried footprints and staggered breaths that bounce off the stone walls. It's an effort not to run when Elan's life is hanging in the balance and we need to get Loki's help as soon as possible.

I'm reminded just how important it is to observe every direction when two guards march down the next corridor, heading our way. I grind to a halt. Eir slams into the back of me, almost pushing me into the open. Quickly, I back up, and we press our backs against the wall, hoping they avoid our corridor and march straight to another part of the castle.

The footsteps approach, closer and closer, causing my heart to beat harder. I ball my fist, trying to steady my nerves, my mind running through a million different excuses. I need a logical explanation to tell them if they find us. My breath hitches as the marching footsteps approach then continue down the corridor, missing our turn altogether. My legs turn to jelly momentarily. I know how close we came to being caught.

From then on, I pause at every corner before entering another room or level, making sure no one is watching us. Eventually, we pass the kitchen and scullery and move deeper beneath the palace into the dungeons. This area is familiar to me, as I snuck down here when Elan was held prisoner by Odin. It was a horrible place then, and it's an awful place now.

Different creatures and people peer at us through the bars of their locked cells. I can't help checking every dungeon to make sure there are no dragons or anybody who shouldn't be there. Although Odin seems to have changed over the last couple of years, I still wonder at times if it's just a face. Now is the perfect time to check. To my satisfaction, every prisoner seems to be legitimate. At the same time, I check to make sure that Loki hasn't been brought up to this level. Anita hasn't visited him since the early days of him being imprisoned.

Different creatures snap at us through the bars as we walk past, and dark elves stare at us eerily, their hands bound by some kind of magic-dampening cuffs. They must be some of the warriors that attacked Asgard a couple of years ago.

After covering most of the dungeon, I haven't spotted any way out other than the entrance. A monster's snout sticks through the bars and snaps its jaws at us. Eir and I dart to the other side, careful not to back into another snapping creature in the cell behind us. Our footsteps grow less confident as we come up empty-handed, yet determination pushes us on. Anita wouldn't have lied to us. We reach the farthest corner that lurks in the dark, and I'm surprised yet happy to find a door hidden in the darkness.

A silent exchange passes between Eir and me. We know this has to be the entrance to the lower levels. I clasp the handle, yank it down, and pull the door open. Stairs descend immediately from the door, leading down into darkness, occasionally lit by the dull light of a sconce. A creepy feeling travels up my spine to the base of my skull. We haven't even entered the area. This isn't going to be fun.

Eir's face drains of color when I motion for her to follow. Her eyes fix on the darkness below.

"I know," I whisper. "I'm not looking forward to this either."

Despite manifesting her fear and the desire to withdraw, she tiptoes behind me, and we descend the stairs. Each time my boot hits a hard step, the noise seems to explode through the small enclosed area, spilling into the space below. I cringe, trying to make each step softer. We have no idea if there are guards or monsters below.

We go farther down the stairs that seem to never end until finally, they stop. I halt, peeking around the corner before we enter. The layout of the room appears to be designed to give the occupants the upper hand. They have an opportunity to ambush the new arrivals before the new arrivals know of their presence.

After surveying the room, I face Eir. The whites of her wide eyes glow in the sconce's mild light. Even though I couldn't find anyone in the room, I feel the same as how Eir looks about going into the room. Despite her fear, she nods, indicating she is ready to go. I grapple for my sword, taking some comfort in knowing it's by my side, and I face the direction we need to go. I'm about to step into the room when suddenly Eir grabs my shoulder and yanks me back. My sword scrapes against the rock.

Puzzled, I turn to look at Eir. I hadn't spotted anything moving. As our eyes connect, she shakes her head and points to my sword before circling her hand in front of her.

She whispers, "Magic."

I lift my eyebrows at her.

"We don't want to injure anybody," she whispers again.

I contemplate the idea for a moment. My body still isn't fully recovered from giving Elan everything I have. I feel for my power and how much I think I have available to use then nod and slide my sword back into the sheath on my back. Together we pause and gather our magic. When Eir indicates to me that she is ready, we move forward, our hands lifted in front of our torsos, prepared to block or attack.

The room borders on dark, the limited dull light making it hard to see. My senses are on full alert until my eyes adjust better to the obscurity. Every corner of the room screams eeriness. Only the center is illuminated with a dull light. I can't see anything a foot in front of my face, but I press forward, an image of Elan's unmoving body spurring me on.

My eyes take too long to adjust, and I feel sick with insecurity as I press farther into the darkness, afraid for my life and Eir's. If guards were down here, I would think that they would have accosted us by now, but none have approached.

Holding my breath, we shuffle farther forward, unsure if we should move into the light or stick to the darkness just in case the light aids some creature in attacking us. Then again, it might be a creature that can see in the dark. That thought does not bring me peace. Hopefully, if something is waiting to attack, we have been quiet enough to sneak in.

I opt to stay out of the circle of light, knowing the passageway we need to find to the next room is not lit. It takes too long for my eyes to adjust to the darkness, and I curse under my breath. A strange, dense, musty odor mixed with something else assaults my nose. I'm not quite sure what it is, although it reminds me of the corpse smell that clings to the angels of death. It's something I haven't smelled in a very long time, not since I went to Midgard with the winged Valkyries. Thor has had other plans for me lately instead of reaping souls. The smell intensifies with each shuffle forward through the dark. Suddenly, my foot knocks something on the ground. I freeze.

- Chapter Nineteen -

Clasping Eir behind me, I squeeze her hand with so much pressure that I can feel her apprehension manifest.

Her hands grasp my arms, and she pulls close, whispering in my ear, "What is it?"

I hiss my response. "There's something on the ground."

"Maybe it's what's causing that horrid stench." Her breath tickles my ear, sparking my sensations and causing me to shudder.

"Whatever it is, I don't believe this is where Loki is."

"I don't think so either. I don't know that there's anything alive in this room. And that smell..." She sniffs then chokes, expelling a muffled cough. "May be something dead."

"I need to see what's at my feet. There may be more on the floor, and somehow, we need to find the door in this darkness. There must be one in here leading to Loki's area. Not to mention, I would love to see what we are dealing with."

I think I hear her chuckle. "Then, I guess now is a good time to show you the new trick I've learned."

"What do you mean?"

She lets go of my arm, and if it weren't for the incredibly dull light in the middle of the room, I would have felt disorientated. The light doesn't even illuminate our skin.

"Watch," she whispers.

I wait in the darkness, apprehension gnawing at my stomach. Suddenly, a ball of flame from the dimly burning sconce in the middle of the room shoots toward us. Thinking I'm a target, I dodge to the side, trying not to move my feet because of the thing on the floor. The light veers to my right at the last second and straight onto Eir's outstretched palm. It hovers over her cupped hand as though drawn to it.

My wide-eyed gaze slides between her illuminated face and the flame. "When did you learn to do that?" I whisper, not sure why as I'm certain that if anything were in this room, it would know we are here by now, especially after the display of light.

Her eyes flick up from her creation, pride filling her expression. "While you all have been practicing war moves with your magic, I've been practicing things that might be helpful for a peaceful environment, like accessing light and moving the light source when needed." She shrugs. "I had fun with this one."

I'm so happy, I want to hug her, but the pressing issue of what's on the floor still haunts me. Eir holds the light close to the ground and creeps around me. Her light reveals a person's foot then crawls up its leg to a fully clothed body. My stomach heaves as I take in the decaying form, the skin on its face clinging to its bone. Whoever it was, they've been dead for a while, and they're wearing a guard uniform.

Eir gags. "This isn't good. Whatever killed them could still be in this room or below."

"Yup. I realize that, but if we are going to help Elan, I have to press on." I swallow my fear and disgust one final time and follow Eir as she searches for the opening of another door with her illuminated palm.

We slowly make our way around the walls of the large room, our senses on full alert for any other corpses or any other disgusting or dangerous things.

Finally, I spot another door on the far back wall. With her palm held high, Eir opens the door, the hinges squeaking from lack of use, and we gape into the darkness.

Eir whispers over her shoulder, "This must be the way."

I nod, not wanting to speak, and we press forward. I clasp the back of her belt wrapped around her black leathers, making sure I don't lose her. I hate the thought of my peaceful friend going first. I feel as though I'm putting her in more danger than myself, but I have no choice. I don't know how to do the little trick with the light like she does. So without protest, I keep close as we press forward, keeping my eyes peeled for anything that moves.

Our progress is slow as we creep farther into the depths of the darkness. Our leather fighting clothes creak and scratch as they catch on rocks in the tiny tunnels. Eir's sheathed sword clangs against the rocks, and we both jump, pressing on as soon as we realize the cause of the noise. I gather my magic, ready to combat anything that may be lurking in the darkness that's ready to attack us. The trek through the darkness seems endless as we go through another level and another room. Finally, we come across a small pocket of light that glows dully up ahead.

I tap Eir on the shoulder and point in its direction. She nods, and we aim slowly for the light, checking the floor to make sure nothing will sink away and drop off into a chasm or some other kind of nasty surprise between us and the light. I don't like this one bit, but with the image of an unconscious Elan in my head, I press on. I must make sure my dragon survives and things get back to the way they should be. Not only should I be out there fighting this monster, but I should also be by Elan's side.

My nerves are firing as we approach. Strange noises echo back to us, not helping my heart to settle. We reach the entrance, and slowly, ensuring our footsteps are silent, we creep around the corner into the room.

My jaw slackens. Not far in the distance, Loki is strung in place under a sizeable hanging serpent. Poison drips from its fangs. His wife, Sigyn, holds a bowl under the serpent's head, attempting to catch each drop of poison before it drops onto Loki's bare skin.

I had heard whispers that when she pulls the bowl away to empty the contents, the consistently dripping venom would land on Loki. The god would writhe in pain, causing the earth to shake with a violent earthquake as his howl of pain and distress rumbled throughout the land.

I search the room, only finding Loki and his wife, and I press forward, with Eir following. Slowly, I move to stand in front of Loki. The dark-haired god is in his Asgard form and stripped to his underwear, undoubtedly a ploy to leave much of his skin exposed to the venom, inflicting as much pain as possible. The punishment looks cruel, way beyond how anyone should be treated, whatever they have done. Disgust churns in my stomach to know that this is what the gods of Asgard have done to him. I can understand the hatred, but this I cannot. Even though I no longer trust him, it seems rather extreme.

Sigyn follows our progress with a strange look in her eye, her face deadpan and unemotional. Loki must catch the stiffness in her body and glances up at her before following her line of sight.

I halt in shock as I take in his sunken eyes, difficult to see between the dark rings that circle them. It looks as though he hasn't slept for the last two years. His face is drawn, and his body is frail. He doesn't look like the god that he used to be up above, full of life and mischief. I worry about his strength and his ability to heal Elan in his frail state. I hope he has enough energy to transfer his healing power to me.

"Kara. Eir. How nice of you to come and visit," Loki drawls, low with an undercurrent of spite, a tone that I understand after seeing the way he's been treated.

Hesitantly I press on. "This isn't how I imagined the gods would punish you, Loki. I never thought they would be this cruel. Despite what you've done to them, Asgard, my friends, and…" I inhale deeply, trying to release some of the pain before I say the truth. "Me. You were like my best friend in many different forms. For quite some time, I confided in you things I never expressed to my true friends, and you deceived me."

Another drop of venom drips from the serpent fangs, and I watch as Sigyn just manages to catch it in time.

I continue, "Yet, I never would have thought of this punishment in a million years."

One side of Loki's mouth lifts in a sarcastic smile. "They thrive on punishing in terrifying ways. The gods of Asgard have vivid imaginations when it comes to torturing people or things."

I press my tongue to the roof of my mouth. I don't like the way they treated him, but at the same time, I still have a deep rage burning through me over his deception.

Noting our silence, Loki continues, "I was working for Asgard, you know. I realize a lot of you don't believe me. In fact, all of you don't believe me." He huffs. "And to think I went through so much for Asgard." He shakes his head.

I growl. "You brought the dark elves to our land. You split the dragons, stealing their eggs and turning their babies against their mothers and family. How was that for Asgard?"

Something flashes through his eyes. "You wouldn't believe me if I told you."

I shake my head, attempting to clear away his taunting and his baiting, trying to remember precisely why I'm here. An image of Elan enters my thoughts, and instantly I remember. I blurt it out before this unpleasant conversation progresses. "I need you to help me."

His dark eyebrow arches. "And what's in it for me?"

- Chapter Twenty -

"What's in it for you?" I almost yell at him. "You deceived me in every way you could. You don't deserve anything for that. You should want to help me and make amends for everything you've done." I place all my weight on one leg and cross my arms over my chest.

Sigyn stares at us, her face distressed as she contemplates what I've said. Suddenly Loki cries out in pain, and he starts to shake. His limbs pull on his restraints. The rock walls shudder and vibrate. Small rocks clatter from the ceiling to the rock floor.

With wide eyes, I survey the room, hoping that the walls will hold and it won't cave in on us.

Horror washes over Sigyn's face as she realizes that she has moved the bowl and missed the last drop of venom. She quickly moves the container underneath the serpent's head, stopping the poisonous liquid from dripping on Loki's skin again.

It takes a while for Loki to gain control over his body, allowing the walls of the cave to stop their shaking, leaving a wake of scattered rocks on the floor. He glares at his wife, and she cringes.

"I'm sorry." Her voice is small, weak from the exertion of constantly holding the bowl to protect him and knowing she failed for the briefest of moments, causing her husband pain.

Loki closes his eyes slowly, each breath gradual and controlled as the anger eventually washes away. He nods. "It must be hard holding the bowl still all the time. Your arms must be aching."

A sadness envelops her face. "It is hard. But not as much as you bearing the snake's venom on your skin." Her concerned eyes skim to us. "Perhaps you should help them, Loki."

Loki gazes at us, then his gaze travels up to the snake hovering over the bowl. As though watching his every move with a malicious interest, the serpent moves its head directly in line with Loki's face. Sigyn quickly shoves the bowl between them as another drop of venom leaves the serpent's mouth, and Loki returns his gaze to us.

"Fine. I'll help you. What do you need help with?"

"Elan has been injured by some kind of lava monster." A lump rises in my throat, and my voice cracks as I struggle to get the words past it. "She could die if we don't heal her." I swallow, trying to clear the emotional blockage that threatens to make me cry. I must be strong for Elan. "Anita can't combat the unfamiliar magic that travels through Elan's veins, inhibiting her from healing."

Loki nods in understanding. "I should be able to help you, but there's one problem. I can't do anything from here. I have to be touching the dragon, and I know you can't bring her down here." He tilts his head toward the small entrance of the cave. "She's too big, and if she's as bad as you say, she won't make it."

I gape at him. "I can't break you out! Can't you pass some magic on to me that I can carry to the surface or teach me some magic to perform on her?"

He shakes his head. "I'm sorry. I can't. It's too complicated to teach, and it's not transferrable. To be honest, I could use a day trip."

I scowl. "Odin won't allow it!"

A smirk spreads across his face. "I know you say you don't want to go against Odin's rules, but I don't believe Odin would let anybody down here to visit me." He gives me a sly look. "I'm guessing you've bypassed him."

Unintentionally, I gaze down at the ground. That's all the acknowledgment he needs.

"I assumed as much." He tries to sit up but fails, slumping back to the ground with annoyance. "I like your dragon. She has spunk, and she must be in a bad way if you came all the way down here, breaking rules, to see me." His pale and clammy face loses all pretense. "But I simply can't do it from here."

Loki's voice is genuine, and it stirs all kinds of emotions through my gut. I don't know where else to go for Elan in such a short period, and I can't take him to the surface without Odin's permission. Looking for answers, I glance at Eir.

"I don't like the sound of this," Eir whispers. Her face is drawn, and her concerned eyes flash to Loki. "But I don't know what else to do."

I follow her gaze, contemplating my next move. I don't like the sound of it either. It's twisting my stomach into knots, disrupting every bit of peace within me. If I take him with me and I'm caught, I'll be in so much trouble, I don't know if I'll be able to redeem myself.

The image of Elan lying still, her eyes closed, shoots into my vision, and I squirm. That dragon is dear to my heart. I can't let her die like this.

I fix my earnest eyes on him. "Elan was struck by something. We don't know where it came from or what it is. This creature is black, taller than her. When its eyes or mouth open, it looks as though it's filled with lava. Do you honestly think you can heal her from this creature's wounds?"

"I cannot guarantee such a thing, but I do believe that Gilroma's magic will give your dragon the best chance in the shortest amount of time. One thing I can guarantee is that her recovery time is crucial. To seek out anyone else to help heal her will take too long."

I gnaw my bottom lip, weighing my options. Eir shrugs when I cast her a worried look.

I hold up a threatening finger toward him. "No funny business!"

"I would never." An innocent smile spreads across his face, and I cringe.

I don't have much choice. I know it would be best to ask Odin for permission to transport Loki to see Elan and for his help in securing the mischievous god while he is out. Except, Odin hasn't been the same since he received that vision. He would never grant permission for Loki to roam, even to help one dragon who he holds in high regard. With sweaty palms, I reach for my magically blessed sword and begin cutting at the ties that bind Loki.

"You'll have to be quick," Loki says. "These ties alert the guards that I've escaped. They'll be here within moments."

I cringe, slicing my sword across the binds faster.

The damage is already done. "You could've told me that before I started." His hand slides free, and I work on the second binding.

"I have an idea to help buy us some time."

I release Loki's second hand from its ties, and he rubs his wrists.

"Do you have some parchment and a pen?" he asks.

"I do." Eir fishes in her leathers to pull them out.

After squatting by Loki's legs, I give Eir a strange look. It's an odd thing for a Valkyrie to carry.

Eir holds the items out for Loki and catches my expression. She smirks and shrugs. "You like to read. I like to write."

"Thank you." Loki clasps Eir's items and scribbles on the parchment while I work on releasing his feet. His legs slide free, and he jumps up, ducking away from the serpent's head and placing the parchment on the spot where he was sitting.

I read the contents.

I'll be back shortly. Just taking a short trip. Thanks for the pleasant accommodation. Loki.

I lift my eyebrows at him. "Interesting. But I don't think this will excuse what we're doing."

Loki shrugs and smirks.

We charge up the levels the way Eir and I arrived, working our way through the entrances as quickly as possible and assisting Loki when he looks frail. The passage through the horrible room with the dead guard is much quicker than on our way down, and I'm glad.

A rumble of voices echoes through the darkness. We find a gap large enough for us to press against the wall and watch the guards charge toward Loki's room. When the guards are gone, we press on, trying to reach the top of the palace before being discovered.

Light streams through a door, and I'm grateful for the assistance. I push it open, checking every direction before entering the dungeon.

A cloak lies on a table in the corner of the room, and Loki grabs it, sliding his arms through the sleeves. "It's so nice to finally have some kind of clothing. I'm a little tired of always being in my underwear."

I screw up my nose at the reminder and push it out of my thoughts. "Shh. I have to focus," I hiss.

Eir passes me, indicating with her hands that she'll scout ahead and check for guards. Hiding just inside the entrance of the dungeon, I watch her tiptoe across the floor, dodging the vicious animals in their cells, her boots silent on the stones. She reaches the far side and, after peering around the corner, motions for us to follow. We make it to the ground level of the palace, and I cringe as I eye the guards at the front door. I see no way to sneak past the two guards.

"There is a back way, you know," Loki says.

I stare at him in disbelief. "And you're telling me this now? What're we waiting for? Let's go."

Loki leads us in the opposite direction, and we escape out the back doors of the palace. Despite looking frail and starved, Loki manages to keep up a good pace to the academy.

My heart skips a beat when I spot Naga curled up next to Elan. With his head resting on his talons and his body turned our direction, he watches us with concerned eyes as we approach.

Hearing our footsteps, Anita spins. Relief floods her face when she spots me but is replaced with a look of ice when she sees Loki. "You helped him escape?"

"Not escape. He'll be going back. I ran through several scenarios. There was no other way to do it. He needs access to Elan to be able to heal her wounds."

The respected wingless Valkyrie healer pauses for a moment, processing the information, then nods. "Yes, that would be true."

Anita's eyes narrow as she stands back and watches Loki transform into Gilroma. The resemblance to Loki is nonexistent. All signs of hair disappear from his head, leaving a bald scalp, the forehead inked with prongs resembling a trident. Glowing yellow eyes land on me.

My skin crawls. As though sensing it, Anita wraps an arm around my shoulders, a reminder that I'm not the only one who has suffered at the hands of Gilroma.

Slowly, Gilroma circles Elan's unmoving body and investigates her injuries. I can't pull my eyes away from the tattooed lines down his cheeks and the inked points showing the way to the scars that run all the way to his thin mouth. Gilroma tugs at the double-looped earrings on the lobe of his pointed ear before he runs his hands along the damaged scales. His touch is a caress as he senses the magic that lies within her wounds underneath her scales. Gently rubbing his hands over the wounds in a circular motion, he mutters incantations as he paces ever so slowly around her body, addressing one injury at a time.

I cross my fingers and my toes, looking for reassurance from Anita, hoping and praying to the gods that this will work.

·

Perspiration gathers on my forehead, and I wring my hands on my lap as I wait for Loki to finish. I tune into each movement Elan makes, assessing every breath, hoping for a flicker of an eyelid. Gilroma's healing is taking too long for my aching heart.

Elan shows no sign of healing, and I slump down to my knees and embrace her snout. Wet tears well in my eyes and drip down my face, falling onto her golden scales. "I hate seeing you this way, Elan. Please, get better. Please," I plead.

Gilroma's footsteps move behind me, circling my body as I lean against my precious golden dragon's snout. His mutterings and incantations follow him as he continues his rounds of the enormous emperor dragon, his hands continually touching her wounds.

On both my sides, rocks clatter as two warm bodies crumple next to me. Soft hands caress my shoulders and back. In my grief, I lose count of how many times Gilroma circles Elan. Many or few, I don't know. My mind is lost, focusing purely on Elan. Right now, nothing else matters.

My concentration is broken momentarily as Sigyn announces, "I'm going to get my hair done. I've been stuck down there for so long."

I don't bother to respond, and I don't know if anyone else acknowledges her before her footsteps rattle through the rocks as she backs away.

I snuggle into Elan's snout, begging for her to heal and wake up. I have violated the sacred trust of Odin and Thor by breaking Loki out, yet this means nothing in comparison to Elan's health.

Hot steam bursts from Elan's nostrils, and I push away from her. Eir and Anita do the same, and we narrowly miss scalding our skin.

Elan's eyelids flutter rapidly until, eventually, they pause half-open, and her pupils focus on me.

Hello you. Why are you looking so glum? Elan's voice sounds groggy in my head, but I can hear the dampened cheek.

I raise an eyebrow and don't bother hiding my sarcasm. "Maybe because I'm worried about a certain dragon."

And what dragon would that be? she continues, her

voice sounding croaky even in my head. *That particular dragon wouldn't be me, would it?*

I smile and knock my fist softly on her snout. "Of course it's you, silly. I would be lost without you." I wipe away the wetness on my cheeks and gaze at her through moist eyes.

Naga jumps to his feet and trots excitedly on the spot. *Naga's happy to see you, Elan. Naga's so happy to see your eyes open.* Naga nudges Elan in a place that wasn't injured.

The relief through my body is euphoric, and I can't take my eyes off her moving form.

So, did we beat the monster? Elan asks.

I straighten my spine, sitting on my heels, and turn in the direction that I know the fight would be taking place. I had completely forgotten about the monster and the battle to defeat it. Lightning doesn't pierce the sky, and air lacks the war cries of the Valkyries and the roar of the dragons. I swallow. "I hope so, but to be honest, I wouldn't know. I was so worried about you and running down to get Loki."

Loki! Elan gapes at me like I'm insane. *Why would you need him?*

"To heal you, silly." I nudge her again. "Anita's healing magic wasn't enough, so I had to get more experienced help quickly. Gilroma was the only one I could think of."

The scales buckle in the middle of her forehead as she frowns. *That was risky.* Lazily she looks around, her eyes surveying the area. *So, where is he now?*

"What?" I jump to my feet and circle her. She's right. There is no sign of Loki anywhere. "Oh, Vanir! That lying, deceiving god!"

It takes me a long time to see past my burning anger, every curse under the sun racing through my head. The blood drains from my face, and my legs start to quiver. All the happiness over Elan's safety washes away in a matter of seconds.

Eir, Anita, and Naga help me search, each of us coming up fruitless.

"Where do we search now?" The tension causes my voice to rise in pitch.

All of us turn several times, five sets of eyes scanning for any movement over the horizon.

"Oh, this is bad." I can almost hear the tremble of disappointment, anger, and fear of Odin's wrath in Anita's voice.

"I'm responsible," I say.

Anita's eyes fill with sadness. "It's kind of my fault also."

I shake my head. "No. I'm the one who released him, and I'm the one who's going to take the punishment." I growl. "And these last two years have been spectacular having Odin and Thor's trust. I have to find him soon, or I could be the one chained up underneath the mountains with venom dripping off *my* face, or worse." I chortle nervously.

In the distance, a flock of white flies our way, and my heart skips a beat when I realize it's the winged Valkyries heading back to the academy.

Eir claps her hands. "We must've won. They wouldn't be coming back together if we didn't."

I rub my arm as I watch their majestic flight. "Surely, they will spot Loki from their height."

Anita shrugs. "Maybe. But they might not recognize him, especially if he shapeshifts into something they haven't seen before or even into a Valkyrie."

"Is that possible?" I realize my stupidity as soon as the words leave my mouth. Of course I know it's possible. He posed as a wingless Valkyrie when I was at the academy. Another sense of dread travels through me as I watch them come in. I hope they'll pick up on him on the way back.

Mistress Sigrun is the first to land not far from Elan. She pulls at her tan leather fighting jacket, snapping it together. "I see you've healed the dragon." Her eyes travel to Anita. "You've done well with this one, healer."

Anita's throat moves awkwardly as she undoubtedly swallows away her nervousness, fighting the urge to tell the mistress the truth. Instead, she inclines her head. "Thank you, mistress." Gratitude fills her voice even though she knows that she's not responsible.

The mistress nods her approval.

"Did you defeat the monster?" Eir asks.

The mistress's chin lifts. "Of course. How could it succeed against all of us and Thor's lightning and hammer? One monster against the majority of Asgard's fighters doesn't have a chance."

I worry my upper lip before blurting, "Did you see any other unusual beings or foreign threats on your way back?"

The mistress chuckles. It's a strange sound from her and something I never heard in my years at the academy. "Like what?"

I toss a hand dismissively. "You know, like frost giants or dark elves?" I try to sound blasé.

The mistress chuckles again. "No. We didn't see any more threats. If you don't mind, I'm going to get cleaned up and ready for class." She disappears into the academy, and my brow pinches into a frown as I watch her vanish into a cloud of winged Valkyrie Academy students. When she's out of earshot, I face my friends and the healer. "What are we going to do? I have to find Loki. If the Valkyries didn't see him, where has he gone?" I groan. "I'm officially wrecked. My life as Thor's respected dragon rider is over."

. . .

THE END

~~~~~

If you enjoyed Safeguard, please takes a few minutes of your time to review it on Amazon. Reviews help to grow my readership.

FREE SHORT STORY

Fenrir's Journey to Asgard HERE (https://dl. bookfunnel.com/8glo62ay9e)

KATRINA COPE

PURSUIT

THOR'S DRAGON RIDER

BOOK 2

EDITORIAL REVIEW

Thor's Dragon Rider
Book Two

PURSUIT

"Fans of the Thor's Dragon Rider series will be pleased with *Pursuit* as Kara returns on an urgent mission to track down the trickster god, Loki. With the assistance of Sobek—the brother of Kara's beloved dragon, Elan—Kara must lead a squad of Valkyries into the icy land of Jotunheim, where they are tested by danger and treachery." Kelly R., Line Editor, Red Adept Editing

❀ Created with Vellum

*To my readers - may your life be as happy as the gods &
einherjar after drinking Heidrun's mead.*

- Chapter One -

A robust fist slams the table, and I jump. The wooden legs squeak their protest at the force. The muscles on Thor's arm twinge, and every fiber of his being expresses his anger. Gradually, his blue eyes rise to mine, his bushy red eyebrows furrowing together like an angry storm approaching from the horizon.

"What on Asgard were you thinking, Kara? How could you let Loki go?"

I swallow, desperately trying to remove the lump clogging my voice box. "I didn't let him go. I promise. I was only releasing him for a moment so he could heal Elan. Nothing else was working, and she… she…" I take a staggered breath, and my lip quivers. "Was dying." My shoulders cave.

His thunderous eyebrows separate slightly as a flash of understanding travels through his eyes. He expels a loud breath. "I understand you needed to save your dragon. I like Elan. I would miss her greatly. But this is Loki." He pushes off from the table and paces. "How could you let Loki out?" The god of thunder pauses, and his eyes land on me again. "There must have been another way you could have healed her." He resumes his pacing, clasping his hands behind his back. "And you've waited this long to let me know!"

I cringe at the disappointment radiating from his body and tone. Guilt twists into my heart, yet deep down, I know I wouldn't have done anything differently.

I flail my arms. "I wanted to let you know. But first, I wanted to at least try to recapture the deceitful god and put him away. I thought I could secure him. I know several of the places he hid before he was captured." I clasp my hands before myself and squeeze tightly. "I thought maybe he would go back to them. I hoped I could return him before anybody would even notice he was missing. I've been searching for him ever since I knew he had bailed."

Thor grunts and slams a fist against a marble wall. The hall is empty, leaving us to have the conversation in private, which was what I hoped when I asked Thor to meet me here to confess my error. Odin's capability to run Asgard remains stilted as he gathers his strength. Even so, his son hasn't been giving me an easy time over my error, and I know I deserve it.

"That's a whole week! We could have helped you search for him. A whole week he's had to escape and blend into his surroundings or flee to another realm." His boots' hard soles clack against the marble floor, silencing when he slumps into a chair next to the throne. His elbow digs into an armrest as he props his head in his hand. After a moment, he slams against the backrest and scratches his bushy red beard. "Loki has caused enough trouble in Asgard. He's probably gathering his forces, getting ready to start another battle. Vanir! He could even be coercing his children."

I rub my upper arm. "I thought his children were the ones causing havoc because Loki had been captured and restrained. Maybe now, we can go to his children and tell them that he's free and they don't need to attack Asgard anymore."

Thor runs a hand through his red hair and struggles when his fingers get caught in the strands. "I like your train of thought, but I don't think his children are that understanding. For one, I know we cannot negotiate or reason with the Midgard Serpent." He loosens his fingers and relaxes his arm on the armrest. "Two, Fenrir is on the borderline. His agitation grows every day. And three, Hel takes pleasure associating with the unworthy dead. In my eyes, that doesn't indicate a pleasant personality." He runs his fingers along the grain of the wooden chair. "Let's anticipate that we sort this mess out before Odin regains his strength and goes back to Mimir's well."

My cheeks turn clammy. I don't need Odin finding out about Loki's escape. As much as I've let Thor down, I know he's more understanding than Odin would ever be. Even so, the disappointment falling from Thor's shoulders causes my heart to sink into the floor. The only way I can look him in the face is by remembering why I did this in the first place. I could never have stood around doing nothing when my loyal dragon was dying. In fact, I couldn't have done nothing if *any* of my friends were in that position.

I hold my head high, certain I followed my moral beliefs. "I will continue my search for him. I promise. My intention was never to set him free. He escaped when I was distracted by my distress and then excitement when Elan's health improved." My feet automatically splay into position, ready for a fight, instinctively displaying eagerness to act. I gaze directly into Thor's eyes. "I will recapture him again, one way or another. He should be captured for the trouble he caused." The image of Loki stripped to his underwear and strung up flashes into my mind. "But do you really think he should be contained the way he was? To me, it seems excessive to have his bare skin exposed to a serpent's searing venom."

The edges of Thor's mouth quirk as he appears deep in thought. "It wouldn't be my idea of punishment. But you have seen what my father is like when somebody upsets him. He can be quite unreasonable at times."

I huff. "You think? It took me ages to get him to treat wingless Valkyries the same as the winged and to look after the dragons rather than treating them as something to fight against." I rock my weight onto one leg. "The last thing I need right now is for Odin to find out."

Thor's expression is clouded with disappointment and annoyance, which shoots straight at my heart, yet at the same time, understanding barely glimmers in his eyes.

"What do you suggest we do, then?" I ask.

The god tosses his arms out to the sides. "We have to continue to protect Asgard. Fenrir is still angry, although he seems to view the game with the chain as fun. So far, he has broken through every binding the gods have placed around him."

"But is he angry because of his father's capture or something else?"

"I don't know. Tyr can't quite understand why he

has suddenly changed from a cute pup to a large hound with a grudge on his shoulder."

I smirk. "Maybe Loki's children are dealing with the hormones of teenagers."

Filled with disbelief, Thor's eyes level with mine, and I swallow my amusement. Showing disrespect to my understanding leader isn't the best response. He's nothing like his father. He didn't deserve me going behind his back and making things worse. The last thing I should be doing is joking about these things.

I straighten my black fighting leathers and nudge the marble floor with the toe of my boot. "Look. I'm sorry that I have let you down. Although I have to be honest and say that I would do it again if any of my friends were in danger and on the brink of death. Like I said, I never intended for Loki to go free. I had every intention of returning him to where the gods had put him, as much as I disagree with the punishment." I toss my hands high. "But I'm not the ruler of Asgard nor its judge, to uphold the law."

Thor rests back in his chair. "No, you are not. And Loki cannot be left to run free. Until he has served his sentence or learned his lesson."

Worrying my bottom lip, I stare at him with apprehension. "Are you certain that Loki was going against Asgard? I know it's a long shot, but things don't add up."

"I know some things have come to light that may make it appear so." Thor crosses his legs, the leather in his pants squeaking. "But Loki must be recaptured, and then we can discuss what exactly his intentions are." He fixes his eyes on me. "Your actions must be fixed, Kara."

I nod. "How can I make this right?"

"You can find him by whatever means."

"Like what?" I frown. "What do you mean 'by whatever means'?"

Thor's eyebrows push together. "You work it out. If Loki is in Asgard, we'll find him. If you think he's not in this realm and you need to leave Asgard, come back and let me know. In the meantime, I'll warn my close circle to be on alert for any odd behavior. Fix this quickly, or I'll be the laughingstock of the gods."

"But *I* did this!" I exclaim. "Not you."

Thor's glowering eyes are crowded by bushy eyebrows, red and threatening, as he fixes his gaze on me. "Yes. But your actions reflect on me. I'm the one held responsible for them."

- Chapter Two -

My head buzzes with an electric charge. Thoughts dart through my mind, of what was covered in my meeting with Thor. Trying to keep up with the shape-shifting god's mischievous doings was going to be difficult. Blessed with a life of immortality, he's had many years to perfect his twisted ways and betrayals. I, on the other hand, am only a youth. Even though Valkyries live for a very long time, my life has only begun, hopefully. Glancing over my shoulder, I gaze up at the palace windows, spotting the room of the leader of Asgard, and I cringe. If Odin finds out about this, my life might be considerably shorter.

Rapidly, I skim the steps, keen to see Elan. A while has passed since I've displeased the gods. After wingless Valkyries were deemed equal to their winged counterparts, I've been settled and keen to serve Asgard under Thor's instruction. It would be a shame to lose it all. I've worked hard for my achievement of serving under Thor and changing Odin's mindset over wingless Valkyries and the dragon alliance. Now, I need to work equally hard to keep it. I hope Loki has remained in Asgard. He would be easier to find. Then again, his ability to transform into any creature or being is going to make that a difficult task, let alone his ability to travel to any of the nine realms. If he has left Asgard, my task could be nearly impossible.

I pass the hall of Valhalla, and a gust of wind pushes me from behind. The rustling of leaves grasps my attention. I realize I'm not far from the World Tree, and the sound reminds me of the terrible little squirrel I met on Midgard. If anybody knows where Loki is, it would be Ratatoskr. To be good at his job, he would have to be able to find just about anyone.

Taking a detour, I head toward the trunk of Yggdrasil. Maybe I can get the squirrel's attention and ask him.

I scan the branches of the tree towering over me and forking into smaller limbs covered by leaves. I'm so focused on finding Ratatoskr that I stumble over a rock and struggle to right myself. Asgard is such a rocky, hard place. After having seen Midgard, I'm surprised we've survived here for so long, a feat accomplished only by harvesting food from other realms. It's strange to think that the gods' realm relies on the lands of humans to survive.

I travel through the area where Elan and Thor held their eating competition only days ago, surprised how things have changed for Elan and me in just a couple of days. Merriment and joy have twisted into catastrophe and strife. The Valhalla hall is quiet. The day is early, and the warriors most likely training. The einherjar fill each day with perfecting battle skills to combat Ragnarok, celebrating their efforts by night.

The noise of trickling liquid travels through the leaves of Yggdrasil, and passing under the branches, I follow the sound. The trickling falls silent, and a furry brown face peers at me through the green leaves. A long tongue sticks out and wraps around the leaves before the jaw clamps and chews noisily.

"Heidrun. There you are," I say as I stroke the bridge of her nose.

Her lips smack together as she chews the broken greenery. With more trickling sounds, golden fluid pours out of her udder into a large bowl.

"You've done well. Your mead looks exceptionally good today. The bowl is over half full. The einherjar will be pleased tonight."

She pushes her head into the rub I give her behind an ear, and she bleats.

"Good job for working so hard for the warriors."

I smile to myself. If the warriors didn't have her mead, there would be protests. My thoughts turn to Thor, and I wince. He will most likely miss the celebration tonight, probably spending his time trying to recapture my mistake.

The rough bark of Yggdrasil sends vibrations through my fingers as I trace the grooves, searching for a hole in the trunk. The place that Ratatoskr would exit to visit this area must be nearby. My knowledge of the squirrel is low, although I assume he travels the different realms through holes and branches of the World Tree. Surely, he would have looked for a warrior at some stage, meaning there should be evidence that the squirrel has exited here to visit this area.

Slowly, I circle the trunk, feeling the vibrations up my arm from the coarse bark scraping against my skin. Unable to find a hole, I slap the side of the trunk with my palm. The sound is barely audible, so I knock on the surface with my fist. Frustration shrouds me when my knuckles burn from the impact, yet the sound remains too soft even for my ears. After grabbing a rock from the ground, I smash it against the bark, only slightly satisfied when it creates a more audible sound, yet after several minutes, the squirrel still doesn't show. I slam the rock against the trunk, calling up the rough surface.

"Ratatoskr!"

I wait, hoping the squirrel has heard. When he doesn't come in a few minutes, I call out again.

"Ratatoskr! Ratatoskr!" I scream.

I'm confident that the whole of Asgard will hear me before this squirrel does.

Waiting, I hope to see a sign of that orange-red face with a black snout and pointy ears. It's not the pleasant company I'm looking for, but the hope that he'll surprise me and help me find Loki. He might be smart enough to know that the devious god needs to be found and punished.

While completing another circle of the trunk, I gaze up into its branches, looking for any sign of that little red face, only to be disappointed. "Ratatoskr!"

Then his little red face pokes through the leaves, landing beady eyes on me, his claws digging into the bark. He scurries down the trunk headfirst, tail pointing to the sky, until he pauses at a fork in a branch not far from my head. Standing on his hind legs, he leans against the tree trunk and crosses his forelegs, blocking some of his white furry chest. As though agitated, he flicks his bushy tail from side to side as he points a little claw at me. "Look at you. You seem pale and down. What happened to you?" Not an ounce of sympathy infuses his voice, the lack of empathy confirmed when he shoves his little paw back into his folded arms.

I waggle my head, making sure the sarcasm flows through my voice. "Nice to see you too!"

"Yeah, yeah. Enough with the niceties. What do you want?" He scratches the back of one ear with a hind foot then leans against the tree trunk as though returning to his favorite stance, his arms crossed.

My eyes narrow. "I was hoping you would help me."

His body language displays a lack of friendliness, and he huffs. "Since when do I help people?"

When I inch closer, he straightens his back, knocking away some of my confidence in my plan, but I press on anyway.

"I was hoping it would be different with me. I thought we've built some rapport."

He pushes off the trunk with his furry elbow and paces the small branch. "Valkyrie, love. I thought you would have learned by now that I have rapport with no one."

Acknowledging his condescending tone, I give a little back. "But you know everyone's location, right? Because, you know, you're the messenger. And to be a good messenger, you'd have to know where everyone is."

He waves a front foot at me. "I can find the receiver eventually. But that doesn't mean I know where they are all the time."

I arch an eyebrow. "So that would mean you would be able to find Loki. Right?"

"Pfft. More than likely." He stops pacing, stands firm, and lifts his chin.

"Then can you tell me where Loki is? Please," I add when his face looks set and unrelenting.

He plants his paws on his hips. "You of all people should know that I don't pass on messages without an insult. And I haven't heard any insults aimed at me laced into your request." Setting his claws on the trunk, ready to climb, he calls over his shoulder. "So I'm going to go now."

"But you're not carrying a message," I protest.

"You have requested something from me. Therefore, the message is for me, and I have refused to accept the message because there is no insult included." His words are painstakingly slow, as though explaining to the simpleminded. He pulls himself up on the trunk, his back legs planted, ready to scurry up.

I reach for him. "Wait!"

He pauses.

Glaring, I retort, "You're nothing more than a rodent."

Ratatoskr lets go of the trunk, landing on the branch. "Please. As if that one hasn't been used before." His claws return to the trunk, hooking deeper.

Dumbfounded, I look at him. He's going to make me work at my insults—something I'm not used to doing. I try my luck. "But isn't that an insult for a squirrel?"

He calls over his furry red shoulder, "Of course it is. But it's definitely not original. It's been used so often I'm used to it. If you want me to carry your insult, think of something original. If only I had a dollar for every time someone used that one. I'd be a rich squirrel... Claws! Even if it was only a dime, I'd still be a rich squirrel." He shakes his head, leveling his beady eyes on me. "Don't you think people have tried to get information from me before, without passing a message? Pfft! What am I? A traitor? Not a chance. You can't use me to find out everyone's secrets." He scurries halfway up the tree.

I call up to him. "Wait! I have an insult for Loki."

He huffs loudly then scurries backward, returning to the branch. His black eyes narrow. "What is it, then? It better be good."

As I pause, my mind whirls, trying to think of something to say. "Tell Loki... that he's a lying, evil, conniving god, and he's a disappointment to Asgard."

Ratatoskr presses his back against the tree and crosses his arms before shaking a claw in my face and tutting. "Didn't you use that one last time?"

Frowning, I try to remember. My shoulders slump. "I guess I did. But please wait—I'll think of something," I blurt out quickly, attempting to hold the squirrel there. My brain hurts with trying to do something that doesn't come naturally. "All right. Then what about this? Tell Loki… his last act of disappearing was the lowest thing he has done to me yet. I put my trust in him, giving him another chance. Just because he helped my dragon doesn't pardon him from his punishment, bestowed by the gods of Asgard. Tell him that he is the lowest scum—that his actions place him underneath the Midgard Serpent in the dregs of the bottom of the ocean floor—a scum that should never see the light of day."

Ratatoskr scratches his cheek. "Hmm. I guess that'll do. He might be insulted by that… Maybe." He scurries up the tree, his bushy tail disappearing within the leaves of the World Tree.

"Tell Loki that he needs to bring his butt back here!" I yell.

- Chapter Three -

My mind whirls as I try to work out my own intentions, gazing at the spot where the fluffy tail disappeared. I've confused myself. Seeing that Ratatoskr didn't cooperate and tell me where Loki was, I pulled at strings, desperate to get Loki back. But when I think about the insult I sent, I don't know what it will achieve. Loki won't give himself up and return to Asgard to be enslaved deep beneath the palace. I guess I was just saying whatever came to mind at the time.

My shoulders slump in defeat, and I tear my sight away from the tree, wondering what to do next. This isn't news I want to deliver to Thor. I need to create some hope and good news to rectify what I did to save Elan.

Slowly, I trudge down the hill and across the rocky plains, alert as I scan the landscape between the rocky mountains and the academy where I left

Elan. Although Elan is recovering, she still has a lot of healing to do before she regains her energy and strength. The magic that the lava monster infused in her wounds was potent. I'm glad that I have access to an accomplished healer like Anita so that I can leave my dragon in her care while cleaning up my mess.

Within a few hundred yards of the academy, several wingless Valkyries are mounting dragons on an open plain. I recognize the dragons. They were once chained in the mountain, enslaved by Odin and the academy for practicing warfare. A shiver runs down my spine. Those weren't pleasant times. At least the dragons, once sacrificed for the alliance between the dragons and Asgardians, are no longer being mistreated.

The dragons, once mounted by Valkyries, lunge into the sky, and my heart warms. My bond with Elan and my relationship with Eingana had a hand in the change of attitude. Only a couple years ago, wingless Valkyries were treated as slaves, while dragons were injured by the winged Valkyries as they practiced their fighting skills against the magnificent beasts. Now, the dragons that used to be held captive have agreed to stay and work as the wings and fighting companions of the wingless Valkyries.

One of the young Valkyries from the academy leans forward, her long black plait falling down the back of her black fighting leathers. She strokes her dragon in the soft spot under its scales along the back of its neck. I recognize the yellow dragon as one of the babies that had been taken by Loki.

The rider cuddles into the dragon, and from my own experience, I imagine the sharp points of the scales digging into her skin. Even so, as she rests against them, her expression is soft and caring, as though she is cuddling the softest animal in the realms.

A warmth grows in my stomach. I know that feeling. It's the bond between dragon and Valkyrie—a connection I've shared with Elan since I met her.

In many ways, the yellow dragon breed is a similar build to the emperor dragon, Elan's breed, yet slightly smaller and less intimidating. The other dragons are also different—each color having a different build. In front of me, the small group consists of one of each of the dragon breeds that have bonded with my friends. A smaller blue dragon, just like Naga, stands next to the yellow. Its big blue eyes survey its surroundings, and it furls and unfurls its wings several times, showing off white stars on the undersides of its wings when it stretches them to the sky. The white stars seem to help this breed of dragon blend better into the blue skies when seen from underneath. The next dragon in line is a red. Intimidating, fiery red eyes survey the area. These dragons have a hump in the middle of their torsos resembling a camel's. It's an odd shape for a dragon and probably slows it down with the interrupted aerodynamics, but the glaring red eyes alone would make prey want to run in the opposite direction. The last dragon in line is brown, just like Drogon. The breed's size is thinner than many of the others, and the wings are attached to the front legs, making it an excellent glider, a talent resembling a bat's. Any opponent is often scared away just by looking at the array of horns covering the head and upper neck, almost as thick as a porcupine's quills. No emperor dragons like Elan are around. That breed is larger and lays fewer eggs, making it rarer. The dragons and Valkyries practice taking off and landing. The chance to learn how to stay on the back of a dragon is a privilege I missed out on, and I certainly didn't have a saddle when I first rode Elan.

Pressing forward, I round the corner of the towering mountain splitting the academy away from the dragon training ground. My happy thought of the dragons and Valkyries bonding is heightened when I spot my golden emperor dragon lying with her head resting on her front feet and her eyes closed. She looks peaceful, curled up with her tail wrapped around the front of her body. The light beautifully bathes the golden scales of my favorite dragon in the world. All the distress of the morning is shoved to the back of my mind as I observe her body, which looks robust again. Her sharp horns somehow appear unthreatening even though she is from the breed of the most ferocious dragons in the area.

I plunk down next to her nostrils and place a hand softly on her snout. I can't help touching her even though I don't want to disturb her rest. She needs all she can get. Weakness plagues her robust form. The only thing that keeps me going is that she seems to be healed of the magical poison from the lava monster.

Gently, I slide my hand down her snout to the soft part of her nostril and inject some of my magic's strength into her, hoping to speed her process. A hot puff of steam exits her nostrils, warming my legs through my black leather pants, and I gaze up to her eyes. Her eyelids slit slightly wider than her pupils— enough for her to peer through. Seeing her alert and responding to me again is a relief. Thinking she was going to die was too much to bear. And as I said to Thor, even though I know getting Loki out without permission was wrong, I would do it again to save my best dragon friend.

Her telepathic voice hums in my mind. *Hey, you.*

I smile. "Hey to you too. It's good to see you in the land of the living."

Her large mouth expands with a yawn, and she stretches her front legs, narrowly missing me. *I'm not quite there yet, but I'm feeling a bit better today. Just really, really tired. I feel like my mind is stuck in dreamland.*

"I can imagine. You have been through a lot." I rub my palms together, regathering any magic and letting it well between my palms and fingertips. "I hope this helps." With her soft nose between my palms, I again release into her all the power I've gathered. "Does this help?"

The edges of her mouth tilt up slightly, and she yawns again. *Ever so slightly.*

My forehead furrows. "Really? That was as much energy as I could give you in one hit."

Disappointment swamps me, and I slump. If that's all my entire magic energy does when she's feeling better, it's no wonder my injecting energy and healing power into her when she was really sick didn't do anything.

She nudges me lightly with her nose. *You have to remember you're a lot smaller than me. In case you haven't noticed, I have a much bigger form.* Her words are sluggish and her speech slow, almost like she's drunk. She rests her chin on her front talons again. *It would take a lot of your energy to make any difference to this form.*

Sitting tall, I say, "Yes, you are big. I certainly can't carry you when you're injured."

Unusual sounds exit her mouth, almost like she's giggling but too tired to execute it properly. She garbles, *That would be a sight to see.*

I smile, picturing it in my mind. "Yes, it would be rather funny. Although I don't think you would be able to see me."

Elan lets out a big puff of warm air. "No. You would be squashed." She chuckles.

I chuckle with her, resting a hand against her scales, unable to resist the urge to touch her after the ordeal of thinking I'd lose her. "It's so good to see you getting some of your humor back again. You must be feeling better."

I'm getting there. Her eyes close for a moment as though chuckling had taken too much energy. I play with some loose rocks circling my body, flicking them in different directions.

Her voice enters my head again. *What's up? You look sad and worried.*

"Yes and no. I'm glad you're looking better, and I wouldn't do anything differently, but I'm in a lot of trouble. Thor is extremely upset with me, and I can't work out how to fix this mess I've created."

Is he disappointed in you?

I nod. "I don't really blame him. I did kind of let Loki go. Definitely not on purpose."

Elan's mind seems to sharpen, and she lifts her head slightly to stare at me with astonished eyes. *Does he know why you did it?*

"Yes, and I believe he understands, but I still need to find Loki somehow to make it better. He must be brought back. Thor's glad that you're better and that Loki could help you. I think the only reason he hasn't told Odin yet is because I brought him out to heal you." I flick another rock aside. "So hopefully, I can find Loki and get him to return before Odin knows anything about this."

What about Loki's children? Won't they settle down now that Loki is free? She momentarily sounds a little more coherent.

"You would think so, except the Midgard Serpent is still causing trouble, and Fenrir is still angry. Who knows if Hel is going to send any more of those lava monsters or something similar from her realm?"

Was it Hel who sent the monster?

"We believe so." I hug my knees to my chest. "Where else would a monster filled with lava come from? From Fenrir and the Midgard Serpent's actions, either they don't know Loki is free, or they don't care and want to wage war on Asgard anyway.

Although I must admit, other than being a little grumpy, Fenrir hasn't really done anything yet."

Have the gods managed to secure him in a chain yet?

I get up and stretch my legs. "No. Fenrir still breaks every chain they make. Even the one that the gods designed, which needed several of them to carry it over and place it around his neck. He's one powerful hound, and I'm not surprised the gods are afraid of him."

Then perhaps you should go see their mother. Maybe you can ask her to control her children and get them to settle down.

"But that's not finding Loki." I wipe my hands over the backside of my pants.

True. But maybe the mother will know where Loki is. Even if she doesn't, if she can control her children and stop them from attacking Asgard and Midgard, what are you going to lose? That way, Odin will still be happy with you if he finds out about Loki's escape.

Deep in thought, I push my mouth out to one side. "That might work. I must discuss this with Thor. He said he didn't want me to leave Asgard without telling him where I was going first."

- Chapter Four -

E lan's right. This plan is a long stretch, but it's all I have to work with. The mother might have control over the children, and she might know where Loki is. Even so, the trip could be dangerous. The last I heard, the mother lives in her native realm, deep in Jotunheim, the land of the frost giants. That's another reason I need to confide in Thor. Perhaps he will come with me.

Standing tall against the wall of the entrance, Den guards the doors to the hall. "Greetings, Kara. You're back so soon?" His blue eyes are serene as he surveys me.

I stick my head into the room where I met with Thor. It's empty. "Yes. I need to speak to Thor. Do you know where he went?"

"I believe he's practicing his battle skills against the other gods and einherjar."

My apprehension dulls. To know that Thor has

had the opportunity to work off some of his frustration since we talked is a relief. A solid workout, especially practice fighting, cures all kinds of annoyance and gives the mind reprieve. "Is that in the usual sparring spot?" I ask.

"I believe so."

"Thank you."

Grunts of effort synchronize with the clanging of swords before I can see the sparring ground. I pause at the edge of the battlefield, gazing down into the open area resembling an arena, and watch the gods and warriors battle. Several pairs of warriors are scattered throughout the flat ground, and I search each sparring couple until I spot Thor in the distance.

A gruff voice sounds behind me. "What are you doing here, Valkyrie?"

Taken aback, I spin around to face Fenrir. His lips pull back, showing off his vast display of sharp canines—the expression looks more like a snarl than a smile.

"Oh, Vanir!" I hold a hand over my heart. "What are you doing sneaking up on me?" Since the hound has been more irritable these days, I lean toward caution and retreat slightly. I'm not keen on a confrontation with Loki's animal child.

His large brown eyes stare at me in a way that

makes the skin on my neck crawl. "I could ask you the same thing."

Not for one moment do I take my eyes off him. "I was looking for Thor." I motion toward the sparring field with my hand. "And I've found him." I try a friendly approach. "Thanks for asking, Fenrir. I'm glad you would've helped me if you could." I make sure my voice hides all emotions and slowly take another backward step.

His fangs protrude a little more, and I retreat farther before turning to leave and almost sprinting to the sparring field. Casting a last glance over my shoulder, I make sure the massive hound hasn't followed me. I sit on a seat on the edge of the field, mesmerized by Thor's battle skills. I'm not in a hurry to interrupt him. Only on rare occurrences have I had the chance to watch Thor sparring. I'm surprised at how quickly he can move his bulky form.

Moving with strength and assurance, Thor dodges a sword that swings his way. He retaliates with a swipe of his own sword at Balder. The blessed god maneuvers, his shoulder-length blond hair swishing to the side. The strands covering his skin fall away, exposing the radiant glow and kindness expressed on the god's face. No wrinkles of worry line Thor's brother's face as the god of thunder slices his sword across his abdomen. It bounces off his torso without a nick to his skin. The move should have spilled his guts on the ground, but as usual, the promise made by everything to not harm Balder rings true.

It seems like such an unusual request from all things, yet not really. His mother's love must be incredibly strong, and because she holds the power of a goddess, she used it to protect her son. That's a power I wish I possessed, to protect my friends. Then I wouldn't be in this mess in the first place. Yet I am merely a Valkyrie, not a goddess.

Thor jabs his sword at Balder's open side. Once again, the strike is true, but the edges of the sword seem to turn to foam just as it touches the handsome god's body, bouncing off him and leaving him unharmed. Balder shrugs and smiles, light radiating off his well-defined face. His eyes catch mine, and my heart skips a beat. For an instant, I understand where Britta's fascination comes from. I shake my head, clearing the strange sensation.

Balder's distraction makes him too slow to avoid the next strike. I would hate to think what would happen if he lost the gift and things were able to harm him. Then again, if something was able to hurt him, he would probably practice better and dodge anything thrown his way. Balder refocuses on his battle and circles his opponent, turning his back toward me. Thor follows to face Balder, moving into a position to face me. He catches my eye for a split second then brings his sword down, left then right. Balder dodges to the side, missing the strikes. Thor then adjusts his grip and jabs straight at Balder's torso and connects, the tip of his sword bouncing off the bright god's abdomen, and Balder moves to the side, unharmed.

Thor pauses. "Okay. That will do for now." He slides his sword back into its sheath hanging from his belt and marches to my side.

Pushing myself off my seat, I'm greeted by the smell of sweaty leather when a gust of breeze blows from behind Thor.

He wipes an arm across his forehead, removing the sweat trickling into his eyes, his breath slightly uneven and recovering from the spar. "Kara. What is it?"

"I've been talking to Elan." I push my mouth into a straight line. "Well, actually, have been talking to Ratatoskr and Elan."

"Yes." His face is blank, his tone unimpressed.

"Ratatoskr wasn't helpful when I tried to locate Loki. Although I've managed to send an insult. If Loki has any kind of conscience, he'll come back." When disappointment tarnishes Thor's features, I hold up a hand. "I know it's a long shot. But after that, I talked to Elan. She suggested that I go to Jotunheim and talk to Loki's mistress and see if she will help us. Maybe Agrboda will hold her children back from attacking Asgard."

Thor rolls his head back and closes his eyes.

"I-I…" I stammer. "I know it is not impressive, but it's something. Maybe she knows where Loki is, and I can ask her while I'm there."

Thor looks at me, his face softening slightly, almost to the expression he usually held before I broke Loki out. "I doubt it'll work, but it may have potential. At least you should be able to search Jotunheim while you're there."

Slight apprehension travels through me. I had hoped he would offer to accompany me. "Would you like to come? I know this has the potential to be a dangerous mission."

Breath hisses through his nostrils. "I have to stay here, Kara, in case the children attack."

His gaze passes my shoulder and up the hill, and I turn to spot Fenrir, sitting on his hind legs, his gaze fixed on me with narrowed eyes. The hound's scruffy fur shows signs of personal neglect.

Thor continues, "Fenrir's current stance confirms that I need to stay here and make sure the children can't attack Asgard."

The skin on my back crawls as my eyes connect with the large hound's. Facing Thor, I nod.

"Why don't you take your Valkyrie friends and their dragons? Surely if the four of you stick together and keep your heads on, you'll be able to stay out of trouble. You're all trained battle maidens with dangerous dragon allies to help."

"But I can't take Elan." I can hear the disappointment in my own voice.

Thor places a hand on my shoulder, his gaze soft with compassion. "I know you have a special bond with her, but surely there must be another dragon you can ask to go with you. After all, you have managed to make them into our allies."

I groan softly, rolling my shoulders to relieve some tension. "It's not my favorite option, but you're right. I have to find another dragon."

"I have faith in you, Kara. That's why you were sent to help me. You have initiative, and with your trained Valkyrie friends, you should be fine. After all, you've been to the land of the frost giants before." His one eyebrow rises, and I see the loveable brute again.

"Yeah, but it wasn't by choice. It was another of Loki's strange plots."

Thor chuckles. "At least this time you have the opportunity to take some warm clothes."

"Like I had a choice last time," I say sarcastically.

- Chapter Five -

Collapsing to my knees next to Elan's face, I rest my head against her snout. She still hasn't moved from the spot next to the academy. "You were right, Elan. Thor wants us to go and visit Angrboda."

She lifts her head to look at me, gently knocking me back. *That's awesome! I'll prepare to leave.* She pushes on her front legs to stand, and her knees buckle, flopping her back to the ground with a grunt.

After squeezing her snout in a hug, I stand. "You're in no shape to come with me. You have to stay. As much as I don't want to go without you, you're not going to make it in your condition."

She narrows her eyes at me. *There's no way I'll let you go alone. I'm coming with you whether you like it or not.*

"I'd love you to come with me, but you're still regaining your energy. You have nowhere near enough to get us there and back."

She lowers her golden eyes to the level of mine and glowers.

Not wanting to see her disappointment, I gaze down at my hands clasped in front of me. "Thor suggested I take another dragon. Do you have any ideas?" I meet her stare. "I don't want to. I'd rather take you."

Her mouth seems to droop at the sides, and sadness fills her golden-brown eyes. I rest my hands on either side of her snout. "You know it's true. You don't have enough energy."

She lets out a puff of steam, the sides of her rib cage collapsing inward with the release of pressure. *I know. But it kills me to think you're going without me.* She gazes at the mountains, toward the area where the dragons used to be chained. It's been converted to a base and a home for the dragons befriended by the wingless Valkyries. *You can ask one of the young ones and see if one of them wants to go with you. Although you'd probably also have to ask the Valkyrie they are bonded with. Or you could go to the dragon wastelands and ask some of the dragons you know there. Maybe even someone from my family will go with you. That would make me feel better than taking any random young and inexperienced dragon. Please tell me you're taking your friends as well and Drogon, Naga, and Tanda. I don't want you to go alone.*

"That is the plan if they are willing. Thor suggested I take my Valkyrie friends and their dragons." The edges of my mouth turn down as sadness washes over me. "I really don't want to take a different dragon, but you're not strong enough."

A shadow passes over us, and I glance up to see the underbelly of the brown dragon. Its front legs are spread wide, the membranous wings connected between the wrists and two-thirds down the torso, stretched to catch the wind as he glides through the air. Hildr's cry of excitement follows the shadow. Not long afterward, another brown dragon flies over, and I realize that Hildr, Britta, and Eir must be training the new dragon riders.

I smirk. "I guess I know where to find them."

I would feel much safer if you take them with you. They are excellent warriors, and I trust those three dragons completely.

I lean into her golden scales and slide a hand underneath the hard exterior to the soft flesh underneath. "Get better, Elan. I might not see you again before I leave, so this is my goodbye."

She nuzzles me, pushing me lightly to the side. *You're the one who needs to take care. I'll just be lying down, hanging around the Valkyrie Academy. Not my favorite place to be, by the way. To top it off, my thoughts every second of the day will be worrying about you.*

I gaze into her eyes. "I'm going to miss you."

And I you.

With a heavy heart, I leave her behind and approach the training base where I saw the four dragons and their wingless riders before. They must have been waiting for Hildr, Britta, and Eir to train them. I wait only a few minutes on the open rocky plain before Hildr passes over then circles Drogon around to land.

She climbs off Drogon and lands with a thud. Her boots crunch on the gravel as she walks toward me, running a hand through her spiky red hair to straighten it with her fingers. They momentarily catch in a small wind knot. "Hey, stranger. I was wondering when you would drop by. Have you come to help train the new dragon riders?"

I shake my head. "I wish I could, but not today. Where are Britta and Eir?"

Hildr points into the sky. In the distance, I can barely make out Naga's draconic form against the sky. His extended blue wings with the white star markings underneath are only slightly darker than the sky. I can almost make out Eir's figure sitting on the saddle on his back. Behind him is another blue dragon, practically identical to the sweet blue dragon, carrying a small speck of a Valkyrie, a new dragon rider. The two blue dragons and their riders circle over us.

"Where's Tanda?" I ask, unable to spot her yet.

"Over there." Hildr points in the opposite direction just as a red streak shoots through the sky.

The red dragon lowers and flips, and Britta clasps her saddle straps while mounted on the peak of her dragon's hump. Imitating Tanda a second later is another red dragon and a new rider on its back, whose face is ghostly white after the daring nosedive.

I chuckle. "Is there a yellow dragon? I saw a yellow dragon take off earlier as I passed through."

"It's over there." Hildr nods in another direction behind us.

Heading in our direction, close to the ground, is the yellow dragon. The dragon rider flops from side to side, face pure white with terror.

A small smile creeps onto my face. "Doesn't the rider know the dragon won't let her fall?"

Hildr harrumphs. "She hasn't learned to trust the dragon yet, and because of it, her confidence is lacking. I was hoping you would be able to help train that one. The yellow dragons are much the same as the emperor dragons, and it would be easier for her to learn from Elan and you and how the dragon moves."

I shake my head in disbelief. "I can see she needs help. We didn't get any help when we rode our dragons. It was trial and error."

"I know. But some don't learn as quickly as others."

"I can see that. I would help, but right now, I need to complete a mission for Thor. Maybe after that."

Naga circles above us before lowering and landing next to Drogon. The trainee dragon and rider land next to Hildr's trainee. In a few moments, Eir flips her leg over the blue dragon's body and slides down, hustling to greet me.

"How is Elan?" Eir suddenly squats to the ground, screaming, "Look out!"

The yellow dragon passes over our heads to land, so low that we have to duck. The new rider slides and hurtles unceremoniously off the side.

I quirk an eyebrow before pulling my attention away, returning to our conversation. "Elan's still regaining her strength. At least she's improving. Do you know if Britta is landing soon?" I search the sky for the red dragons and spot them still high in the air.

"When she sees that we've landed, she'll probably join us," Eir says. "Why do you want to know?"

"I have something to ask you three as soon as she lands."

"Let's hurry her up then." Hildr slips a forefinger and thumb into her mouth, and a high-pitched whistle pierces the silence of the sky.

Eir waves her arms, motioning Britta and Tanda to land. Moments later, Tanda takes a sudden turn and drops, followed by a confident trainee rider steering her red dragon toward the others at the last second.

After sliding to the ground, Britta straightens her black fighting leathers. "Hey, Kara. What's up?"

"I have something to ask you three," I say.

"What is it?" Eir asks.

"Thor is sending me on a mission to Jotunheim. He suggested I take you three and your dragons. But I'm not forcing you. It could be quite dangerous, and I only want you to volunteer if you want to come."

"I'm in," Hildr says about hesitation.

My jaw drops in disbelief. "You don't even know what the mission is yet."

"I'm in too," Britta says.

I shake my head. "I appreciate it. Even so, you should know what we're in for before you decide to come."

"What are we in for?" Eir's tone indicates she's coming as well.

"I need to go and see Loki's mistress. I'm going to see if we can convince her to get her children to settle down."

"Do you think it will work?" Eir asks.

Splitting my ponytail in half, I secure the band closer to my scalp. "I don't know, but we're also hoping she'll know where Loki is and tell us."

"It sounds like a long shot." Britta shrugs. "Are you taking Elan?"

I shake my head. "Elan isn't strong enough to go. I'll have to find another dragon." Suddenly, a loud thump sounds to our side. Starting, I face the noise—one hand grabbing my sword and the other clasping my necklace—ready to shoot the magic stored inside.

- Chapter Six -

In the corner of my eye, I spot my friends mirroring my actions, their hands grasping their weapons and preparing their magic. My eyes sharpen on the figure before me, a golden emperor dragon slightly larger than Elan.

The dragon pulls its head back. *Dragon claws, ladies! Is that the way to greet an old friend?*

That voice is familiar. I peer at the dragon, taking in every feature. Besides being the same breed, so much about this dragon reminds me of Elan. I haven't visited the dragon wastelands in a while, but one dragon's name pops into my head.

"Sobek? Is that you?"

Of course it's me, girl. The big dragon grins, showing off too many teeth, a look that would appear more threatening to someone who wasn't a dragon rider. *Who else would I be?*

"Sorry. It's been a while since I've seen you. It's

great to see you again. What are you doing in this part of Asgard?"

I've come to see if my sister is still alive and kicking. I just flew over and spotted you guys. So here I am. I thought I'd come and say hello. He extends his wings in a grand gesture, reminding me that he had sheltered me once from the prying eyes of dragons determined to kill Valkyries. That happened just after Elan bonded with me. Things have changed so much since then.

I hadn't seen him much, other than in the last battle, protecting Asgard from a dark elf invasion. Even that was quite some time ago.

"Let me take you to Elan so you can say hello," I say.

Pfft. Sobek brushes his wings out to the sides. *I'm not that close to my sister. I know she's alive, and that's all that matters. I could see that from the sky.*

"I can feel the love." Ridicule oozes from Britta's voice.

Sobek smirks and shrugs. *Sibling love. Maybe you know how it is. It's all good, though. I can tell Mother she's fine.*

I don't remember Sobek being quite so jolly, and he seems more open and relaxed. "Then what can we do for you?"

Sobek tilts his head to the side. *You mean, what can*

I do for you? I thought I overheard that you needed a dragon to ride.

I lean on one leg, assessing him. "You *do* have good hearing. In fact, Elan recommended that I take one of her family members. Are you keen to go to Jotunheim? It could be quite dangerous."

Of course I'll go with you. Anything to protect my sister's little dragon rider. Sobek lifts his chin. *You'll be better off with me, anyway. I'm broader and bigger than Elan.*

"That would be spectacular, Sobek. Thank you." I clasp my hands in front of me, excited to find a willing and vicious dragon already. "And the cloak I made from golden emperor scales will blend in nicely with your hide."

Sobek smirks. *Probably half the scales you collected were mine.*

I chuckle. "Probably. I did collect them from the area you and your family reside."

So. When are we leaving? His scales bunch over one of his eyes as though he's lifting an eyebrow.

I gaze at my friends. "Are you fine if we leave as soon as we gather supplies? It could be a long trip. I know it was a quick trip when Loki kidnapped me, but I have a feeling this could be a bit longer. It might take some time to find her."

"That's sounds good. I don't see a problem. Do

you?" Hildr looks from Britta to Eir, who both shake their heads.

Drogon moves closer to Hildr, listening to the conversation.

"What about you, Drogon?" I ask.

I want to stop these beasts. I don't want the same thing happening to the other dragons as what Elan went through. I'm willing to try the peaceful approach. Drogon's dark-brown eyes are serious. *I don't speak for the other dragons, though.*

Naga slips next to Eir. *Naga goes anywhere Eir goes.*

"Of course I'm going." Eir cuddles into Naga's neck, and Naga wraps himself around the peaceful Valkyrie.

Tanda joins us, standing next to Britta.

"How about you, Tanda?" I ask. "You have a say as well."

Tanda's bright-red eyes focus on me. Before she became a friend, they were quite terrifying. She nods. *I will not let Britta down. I will go with her to help and to protect her.*

After explaining to the student dragon riders that we could be away for a few days, we travel to our rooms with the dragons following. Because we got along so well, we decided to live together. The accommodation is similar to the dormitory we shared at the academy, but we have separate bedrooms and a living room. A couple of soft blue leather double lounge chairs section the open room off from the dining area consisting of a small round dining table and four seats.

I grab my pack and my saddle, hoping it will fit around Sobek's broad body. Carrying my cloak, I sling my sword, bow, and quiver of arrows onto my back. Then I grab another bag and fill it with water and whatever food would travel well, most of which I've stashed from my trips to the palace. Thankfully, I grabbed enough snacks for a few days. Dragging the large saddle along the floor and out the door is a struggle. A strange look passes over Sobek's face momentarily but washes away before I can ask.

He squats down to the ground as though he's a natural at having a rider on his back. As he hunkers down, I toss the top of the saddle over his back, flinging the straps over the other side. The buckle of the main belt barely reaches the other end, making it a mission to connect them across his chest. I secure additional straps under his wings, where they join his body, and hook some at the connection where his legs join his body. I make sure each additional scale I'd attached to the leads faces out, ready to turn invisible with Sobek if the situation requires. I toss the reins over the top of his head and clasp it with one hand, the other hand grasping the saddle as I pull myself up.

Something suddenly occurs to me. "Sobek. Have you had a rider on your back before?"

His voice seems amused. *No. I haven't.*

Suddenly my stomach twists into knots. "Do you think you're going to handle it?"

Of course I will, he scoffs.

"Perhaps you should fly a quick round first," I suggest. "Let's jump to the sky and do a couple of circles overhead. That way, we can get a feel for each other and create some understanding so you know exactly what I want when I ask for it."

Sure thing. Without warning, he pushes off into the sky, and my stomach lurches. I didn't have time to prepare my body for the sudden jerk, and his spring from the ground was faster than Elan's. After the escalation stops, we tilt to one side a little. My backside skids that way, and I clasp firmly onto the reins, trying to prevent myself from sliding off.

"A little warning would be nice next time."

Oh? I thought you would be used to it. Sobek's wings rise and fall in a steady motion, taking us several yards higher. Suddenly he nosedives and twists to one side, his body gliding sideways, and I struggle again to stay on. I squeeze my legs into the saddle as close to his body as I can. My knuckles turn white as

I grip the straps. He straightens, and when I gain control, my clamped jaw relaxes. "Can you give me a bit of warning before you do that?"

You need warning even over that? Surprise sounds in Sobek's voice. The golden dragon straightens and flies higher, continuing his climb for a few minutes and gaining a lot of height. Suddenly, he flips upside down and furls his wings by his sides. The feeling of falling shoots bile to my stomach, and I long to throw up. I drop from the saddle, my knuckles ache from clasping, and my feet slip out of the stirrups. My whole body flips and dangles, the ground calling me to a harsh death below, leaving me hanging with my feet below, the wrong way from the saddle. My only savior is my white-knuckled grip on the reins hanging around his neck.

- Chapter Seven -

"**S**obek!" I scream.

He flips back over. My stomach lurches to my feet from the force, and as he rights himself, I'm flung to his other side, slamming against his flank. My arms sear with pain, and my hands burn from clasping the straps. Drawing from my core, I launch one leg over his back and pull while using my leg as a lever, flipping myself to the top and finally sitting upright.

His body shakes underneath me, accompanied by a strange sound. It almost sounds like a chuckle.

"Sobek. Did you do that on purpose?"

Of course. His chuckle broadens, reverberating in my head. *I have to keep you on your toes and see what you can handle.*

I tap his scales playfully. "Stop it!"

What's the problem? Don't worry. If you fall, I'll catch you.

"And why do I not feel comforted?"

Just trying to make sure you're paying attention. I'd hate for you to go into the land of the frost giants and forget to concentrate. I think my sister has been too soft on you.

"Hmm." I push my lips to one side. "I think I'll be fine without your antics, thank you. I'm starting to think cheekiness runs in your family."

I don't know what you mean. Mother is ever so serious.

"Yes, she lacks the mischief that you two have. After all, she is the leader of the dragons. You would think some of her sensibility would rub off on her children."

He smirks over his shoulder. *Now, where's the fun in that?*

We fly a few more rounds of the area, these trips much smoother than the first, leaving me with no trouble staying on. Sobek lands next to my friends and their dragons. Wasting no time, I climb off his back and sit on the solid ground. Never have I been so glad to sit on hard earth.

Eir sits next to me on a large rock. "It looks like you had quite a rough ride. It looked kind of scary, actually."

"Yes. Apparently, Sobek was just keeping me on my toes, trying to make sure I won't get distracted on our mission." I shake a fist at him, and he chuckles, showing off his broad array of dangerous teeth.

I dust off my clothes, pulling at the hems to straighten them as though this would calm myself after such a rough ride. When I stop fiddling with my clothes, my breath returns, bringing a small amount of peace, clearing my mind, and enabling me to think. I frown. "I just had a thought. I haven't taken a dragon anywhere but Midgard. Does anyone know the best way for dragons to travel to the other realms? The Bifrost is out. It only travels to Midgard."

Blank faces stare back at me, and I'm at a loss. I can't think of anyone who knows how to get them there. I'm starting to believe we have failed before we begin when Sobek's voice enters my head.

We can go through Yggdrasil. When I look at him, confused, he shrugs. *I thought it was common knowledge.*

Astonished, I gaze at him. "The branches are big enough for humans and some smaller giants, but not for dragons."

"Then how did that lava monster get in?" Britta asks.

I push my tongue against my teeth and frown. "That's the thing. I don't know."

Sobek slowly paces my way, his long golden legs regal. *It is true that most of the World Tree only allows smaller creatures and beings through, and it isn't big enough for dragons of my size. But the main trunk of Yggdrasil is vast and can carry several dragons in a row.*

That finally makes sense. "So that's how Loki got all those dragons back to Asgard when he attacked."

Sadness flashes through Sobek's eyes but disappears quickly. Perhaps he remembered the day they had to fight against their own kind. *Yes. That would be how he got all those dragons into Asgard at the same time.*

"Do you know where it is?" Eir asks Sobek.

I don't understand. I thought it was common knowledge. The scales above Sobek's eyes crumple together in a frown.

Not to us, it's not, Drogon says.

Oh. Sobek looks puzzled.

"Can you show us the way, Sobek?" I ask.

Sure. Just climb onto my back, and let's go. He stoops down again, and I climb back on, securing my feet in the stirrups and fasten the extra strap around my ankles before hanging on tightly to the reins. I glower at the back of his head. "No funny games, Sobek."

I'll see what I can do. The cheek remains in his voice.

The flight across Asgard to Yggdrasil's main trunk, where it was large enough for the dragons, wasn't as quick as I hoped. We pass several of the small branches of the World Tree, where Ratatoskr had peered through holes and rested on smaller branches.

Sobek leads us to the middle of Asgard. The bright sun burns against our skin, acting like a wall of heat pushing us away, making us labor to the end.

After a few hours of flight, Sobek glides gracefully to the ground, landing at the base of an enormous trunk growing almost at the center of Asgard.

The trunk's width is impressive, and I don't doubt it will allow the passage of several dragons.

Thankfully, the trip is graceful and steady, absent Sobek's antics. As I climb off his back, a flash of red scurries along the bark of the World Tree, grabbing my attention. It almost looks like the colors of Ratatoskr. By the time I can focus on the area, no red is to be found, and furry, snarky critters are definitely absent from Yggdrasil's branches. However, I wouldn't be surprised if the little squirrel is up to something.

Thumps of the other dragons landing sound behind us seconds after we land, and Eir and Hildr dismount their dragons.

"What a lovely, huge tree." Eir shamelessly approaches the massive trunk and wraps her arms around it as far as they can go. She pulls back and runs her fingers over the bark, her hand jerking from the roughness of the dips, and rises. Her face is passionate and peaceful, filled with love as she gazes up into its branches dreamily. "I wish we had more trees on Asgard like there are in Midgard. It would be much more beautiful."

"Agreed." Britta climbs off Tanda, struggling slightly with the height that Tanda's hump creates, compared to the other dragons. With her feet firmly on the ground, she tucks some loose strands of brown hair behind her ear and circles around the broad trunk of the World Tree. She pauses and calls back, "Is this the entrance?"

Sobek wanders over to her, and all the riders and dragons follow. We gaze at a deep hole in the trunk, big enough to allow a dragon the size of Sobek, if not bigger.

Sobek sticks his head into the hole, his voice echoing through the void. *That's the one.*

"Jeez. It's no wonder the big lava monster got through. This hole is huge." Eir hangs on to the side of the gap, peering over the edge.

Hildr screws up her nose. "Still, the lava monster would have a challenge to fit through the hole, although it wouldn't be impossible."

I gaze into the hole. Light is pushed away by darkness, giving the impression that it dominates the whole way through. "It's hard to tell exactly how big it is, although the void is rather impressive." I observe Sobek, assessing his size and the expanse of his wings. Fitting through would be tight for him, but he talks as though he's done it before. Turning my gaze upward inside the trunk, I'm met by darkness again and maybe a hint of light in the distance. Seeing is going to be impossible. I'm glad we have dragons. They can see much better than us in the dark.

Turning to the other dragons and my friends, I say, "Well, this is it. It's the last chance to pull out before we leave Asgard."

As if muttered at once, I'm met with a jumble of similar words. "Not likely to happen."

I tighten the straps of my bag over my shoulders and secure my quiver, bow, and sword firmly in place on my back. Then I close a flap over my quiver to keep the arrows from falling out before turning to the others. "Let's do this."

- Chapter Eight -

Standing at the edge of the hole in the World Tree, I creep a little farther over the edge for a final look into the dark abyss, searching for some sign of light or a hole that would act as an exit into another realm. With the exit remaining hidden, I grasp a small lip inside the trunk and peer over the edge a little farther. My feet slip, and suddenly, I'm hurtling over the edge and into the darkness of the abyss, my hands grasping for anything, struggling to find purchase. I dangle over the edge, barely grabbing hold of the inside of the trunk. Fear pulls the strength from my fingers and weakens my arms, right when I need the energy the most. Still weak from Sobek's earlier antics, my fingers slip. I squeal and grit my teeth, tightening my grasp and mustering enough strength to pull myself up.

Something grabs my arms and wrists, securing

them firmly. I look up to find Hildr and Britta hunkering down and dragging me up the rough surface to the ground.

"Oh, Vanir!" Hildr exclaims. "What are you trying to do, fall to your death?"

Using their strength, I scramble to the ground and lie flat, panting. "I was trying to find the next exit out of the tree. I can't see any above or below." My chest heaves, and I lie still for a few minutes, thankful for the solid surface under me. My racing heart takes a while to settle. "Does anyone know their way through the World Tree to Jotunheim?"

I do, of course. Sobek plunks his backside next to me. *If you asked me, I could have told you and saved you some excitement.*

Heaving myself up, I assess him with a furrowed brow. "Have you been there before?"

He flicks his golden wings before furling them against his golden body. His gaze drops to the ground for an instant then back up, a conniving smirk on his face. *I may have traveled down there to have a look around—you know, to see what they were doing with the young dragons stolen from our herd. I needed to find out how the dragons were being treated and their living conditions before they returned home.*

I plant my hands on my hips. "Huh. I had no idea Eingana sent anybody down to have a look."

Sobek's gaze is sheepish. *That's because she didn't send me. I had a look on my own.* He presses his chest against the ground and lifts a scaly eyebrow at me. *Are you going to climb on, or what?*

I duck underneath his extended golden wing and climb onto the saddle, hooking my feet in the stirrups and clasping the reins.

Okay, Valkyries and dragons, it's time to go. Sobek stands and charges into the hole, diving off the edge with his wings tucked down at his sides. My stomach rises to my throat, as though I left it in Asgard, as the freefall takes over my body and we careen endlessly down.

The pressure of the wind forces my cheeks up toward the hole we exited. After a moment, I gather the strength to spin my head to look behind us and see if the others have followed us through the hole. Far in the distance, small specks are blocking the tiny ray of light from our exit. Then my hair whips over my face, blocking my vision, and I flick my head around to face the front, which pushes the long strands behind me again. A chill bites into my fighting leathers, and I clasp my numb fingers tighter around the reins. I never know when Sobek will decide to test my riding skills again. Even though Sobek protected me in the dragon wastelands when Elan left me in his care, he isn't Elan, and riding a different dragon feels strange.

The fall continues beyond an extended, comfortable timeframe. I thought this direct route would be quicker than the way the abducting frost giant took me. Surely, climbing down individual branches of a tree would take longer than a freefall. Then again, perhaps I was paranoid.

The strange feeling takes over my stomach, and I close my eyes to wish the sensation away, only to find that makes it worse. I pry my eyes open, glancing into the darkness, disappointed when we pass a patch of light without stopping.

"What was that?" I ask.

It was just one of the exits. The indifference in Sobek's voice annoys me. *It's not the one we want.*

"How can you be sure?" I ask. "We didn't even get to look inside."

"Because I've been here before," Sobek says. "There are many more of those to pass before we get to Jotunheim."

We continue freefalling, and a bug flies into my mouth. I clamp my jaw shut and attempt to spit it out. A few more patches of light flash by, then suddenly, Sobek extends his wings, and we flip and reel straight into the light. My brain slaps against my skull, giving me a headache, the feeling intensifying when Sobek slams his feet down. We skip across the ground, Sobek's tail bumping behind us, and his wings extend to capture the wind like a parachute.

I want to thump him for the lack of warning. When we finally come to a halt, my wind-whipped hair swings around my face, getting caught in the wet trails from my nose and mouth. My body rocks back in the saddle, and my hands are frozen from the cold and lack of movement as I'm too scared to release my grip on the reins. After a few moments, my nerves settle as my eyes focus on snow-tipped mountaintops surrounded by a frozen river. The river snakes through the deep valley crusted in ice, and I'm confident we've arrived in the land of the frost giants.

Three soft thuds sound behind me, the landings entirely different from the one I just endured. When I turn, I'm greeted by the peaceful faces of my friends, who appear to have been on a carefree flight.

"That was a fast fall, Sobek." Eir shoots him a curious look as she casually climbs off Naga.

Kara wanted to get here in a hurry. So I did as she wanted. I live only to serve. Sobek folds a wing across his chest and bows, his golden eyes mocking me over his shoulder as he bends his front legs.

I slide down off his back, my feet landing on the hard, icy ground with a crunch. After a few steps, I work out the wobble in my walk, my nerves refusing to settle. I stumble over my feet, and Eir catches my arm, preventing my fall.

"Thanks," I breathe to Eir.

"No problem." Her eyes peer toward the horizon as she searches the icy tips of this land, which appears absent of all life. "Are we in the right place?"

"Yes. It looks how I remember it." I rub the chill from my arms.

The cracking of ice behind me announces Britta's approach. "Which way do we go now?"

"I don't know. Last time I was here, the frost giant dragged me to the tunnel straightaway and placed me in a cave. There was no time for sightseeing, and Loki only had me here for a little while." I face Sobek, surprised to see peace and contentment on his face, almost as though he loves it here. "Do you know where to go, Sobek?"

Sobek lowers his nose down to my level. *No. But I'm happy to look around.*

"It looks like that is the only option we have," Britta says.

Hildr joins us, standing by Eir and observing the mountain peaks. Hot dragon breath warms our backs as they gaze over our heads.

"What do we have here?" a strange voice says behind us. "Did you hear me calling for you, my snacks?"

Standing behind the dragons is an enormous blue-skinned frost giant.

T he big blue giant towers over us. "Hmm. Scrawny. Not much of a snack." He rubs his beard, a contemplative expression on his face.

Broad shoulders, approximately six times the width of Thor's, slope away from his head. Thick arms, about twice the thickness of an Einherjar, frame either side of his thick torso. The blue-skinned giant's legs seem tiny underneath the vast body, yet they're still several times the average man's height.

Disbelief plagues me—just our luck to be discovered the second we arrive in Jotunheim. I forgot how lucky I was the last time I was escorted in frost giant country by Loki. His shape-shifting form alone guaranteed safe passage through this land.

If I was sitting on Sobek's back, it would raise my position to about the height of the giant's groin. I forgot how big these giants could be. After all, some time has passed since we fought the frost giants in

Asgard. This specimen would tower over the dwarf giants Loki used for his army. Compared to this frost giant, the dwarf giants were more like large humans. This giant is so big that it's ridiculous. I hope this guy is friendly, but something deep inside is crushing all that hope. Frost giants are renowned for disliking Valkyries, and he's looking at us like we're food.

The giant's voice booms down at us. "You look like battle maidens, but you don't have wings." He rubs the bald patch on top of his head, circled by a loop of golden-blond hair falling in straight strands past his shoulders.

Cupping my hands around my mouth, I yell up to the giant, "Yes, we are! But we come in peace! We're not here to fight like the winged Valkyries would be!"

A loud rumble exits the giant's mouth in a husky laugh, and his belly wobbles as he holds it. "Do you think I'm worried about four little women?" He tugs at the end of his long mustache and wipes the corner of an eye.

Climbing onto Sobek's back, I stare up at him in disbelief. He's laughing at us. Anger warms my insides as I assess the other three Valkyries. Hildr's face burns red at the insult, and her hand twitches over her sword hilt.

I need two large breaths to calm my anger. When I think I can project a calm voice, I call up to the giant, trying a slightly different tactic. "We're not here to cause trouble. We're here to look for Loki's mistress, Angrboda."

The giant's laughing subsides for a moment as he bends over to peer down at me. He rubs the base of his beard, braided against his chest. "Is that so?" Stale breath blows over my face.

A cough stems from a strangled gasp, and I splutter away, turning my head momentarily. After regaining composure, I gaze directly into the giant's eyes as he remains bent over gawking at me. "Yes, that is so."

"Then let me take you to her." The giant swipes his hand at Sobek and me, his fingers constricting as he attempts to grab us.

"Move, Sobek!" I yell.

The golden dragon jumps to the side, narrowly dodging the giant's hand, and pushes up, flapping his wings, attempting to take to the sky. The giants swipes a hand left, then right, narrowly missing Sobek. Groaning with frustration, the giant aims a little higher, attempting to clasp Sobek's feet or body. The dragon's movements are jagged, knocking my position in the saddle, and I struggle to maintain my hold on Sobek's reins and stay on his back. The attempt uses all my concentration.

As the swipes grow closer, I shriek, "Keep dodging, Sobek! Zigzag up into the sky."

Sobek follows my orders, and the bumpy, awkward ride continues. I gaze over my shoulder and see the three other dragons are doing the same. The giant continues swiping at Sobek and me, his giant hand swiping every direction. Finally, Sobek manages to fly out of the giant's reach. After missing his opportunity with Sobek, the giant suddenly swipes lower, trying his luck with the others.

"Stop!" I scream when he narrowly misses Drogon and Hildr.

With a questioning gaze, the giant peers at me.

"You don't need to grasp us to show us where Angrboda is."

Disbelief covers the giant's face. "Where's the fun in that? I've always wanted to hold a dragon."

His hands work at Drogon. The dragon spreads his wings and dives, gliding rapidly toward the ground before suddenly swerving up, the maneuver taking advantage of his batlike wings.

With a face blanched whiter than a ghost, Hildr glances over her shoulder. When she realizes she is out of the giant's reach, the color returns to her cheeks. Seconds later, a rumble rises from the ground, and a scream rings out. The giant breaks into a jog, his face beaming with excitement and arms flying, like a child chasing a butterfly. I watch in horror as the giant takes another swipe at my friends, the ground rumbling its protest with each monstrous step. Each step is several wing paces for a dragon as our scaly friends attempt to fly up and away.

Tanda's slower form struggles more than the others to get out of the giant's reach. The stocky blue hands swipe at the red dragon and Britta, and my friends barely manage to swerve away.

Reaching over my shoulder, I retrieve my bow and nock an arrow from the quiver to shoot at the giant's hand. The arrow digs into one of his fingertips, looking as big as a pin in a human hand. The giant pauses midswipe, opens his hand, palm up, and stares at the arrow sticking out of his finger pad.

Confusion washes over the blue face, and after a brief pause, his voice booms, "But you said you come in peace." His mouth drops open as he stares at me, his eyes filled with hurt.

I square my shoulders as Sobek remains out of the giant's reach. "We do come in peace, but we do not come as your playthings." The distraction gives my friends time to rise beyond clasping distance. "You can show us where to find Loki's mistress without handling us."

Sadness swamps the giant's face. "You don't want to be handled by giants?"

Hildr screws up her face in disapproval, pushing her freckles together. "You got that right."

"But you're so cute, and your dragons are adorable. I want to hold one in my hand." The giant opens a hand as though imagining a dragon resting on his palm.

I shake my head. "I'm afraid that's not going to happen without permission."

"It's definitely not!" Britta yells over Tanda's side.

"So how can I show you the way?" the giant asks, looking lost and confused.

"You can walk that way, and we will follow," Eir calls as Naga lowers and hovers in front of the giant.

When I see her position, my heart thumps against my rib cage. She's too close. I swear she's too close. The sweet, ever-trusting Eir believes that things will listen to us and our words and do as we ask. Sometimes her peaceful mind can get us into a lot of danger.

My jaw tenses as I call between clenched teeth, "Eir. Join us up here."

She peers up at me with a smile. "He's listening to us."

"Please, Eir." Panic strains Hildr's voice. "Come join us up here."

Eir sighs audibly, sounding disappointed. "Okay." She pulls on Naga's reins, directing him to turn. His big blue eyes land on me, filled with compassion, almost a reflection of Eir's most used expression. They are a good match for peace, but not for situations like this.

Something moves behind them, and a large blue hand flings in their way. "Awww. I like blue dragons. It's my favorite color." The giant's hand continues to swipe.

"Look out, Eir!" Britta screeches as she whips out her bow and nocks an arrow. "Oh, no, you don't. Not on my watch," she mutters into her poised hand, releasing the arrow straight into the giant's hand. This time, the giant doesn't stop. Instead, the hand moves closer and closer to Eir and Naga. The size of it would swallow them up within the confines of the hand. Britta releases another arrow. The aim is true but, at the last second, narrowly misses the giant's hand, failing to stop the swipe accelerating toward Naga and Eir as it moves in a slightly different direction.

Chapter Ten

"Noooo!" Britta screams the word, dragging it out into a howl.

Jumping, I toss the bow into my left hand and reach for my sword with my right. Sliding metal scrapes as I retrieve my sword from its sheath on my back. When I feel the sword's freedom, I twist the angle and fling it straight at the giant's hand, swiping for Naga and Eir. The sword glides and straightens as though tossed like a dagger, my magic steering it straight toward the giant's wrist. Hope rises in my heart as the aim flies true.

The giant grunts, a displeased expression filling his face as the point of the sword digs deep into his skin, yet his hand doesn't stop. His fingers wrap around Eir and Naga.

Grasping Naga's legs between index finger and thumb, the giant holds him in front of his face, with

Eir clasping onto Naga's reins. "I like dragons." The giant pulls my two friends closer to his face, Eir's knuckles white from the strain of holding on. "And this one is just an itty-bitty one. It's cute." He twists Naga's body in different directions, displaying Naga's terrified face and circled mouth. "Look at those big blue eyes." The blue monster chuckles, hitching up his long brown pants, which slipped down his backside while he jogged.

Hildr cups her mouth. "Douse him with fire, Naga!"

Naga's eyes widen as he stares from the giant to Hildr, looking stunned.

Using his spare hand, the giant plucks the sword out of his skin and tosses it over his shoulder then clasps Naga tightly in his hand as Naga peers through the gaps of the fingers. Even if Naga wanted to shoot fire, his lungs are probably squashed and unable to suck in enough oxygen.

Using my magic, I call to my sword, the wings on the hilt growing and flapping their way toward me. Blood spills down the giant's arm, and momentarily the giant looks put out. Then he shrugs.

His big blond brows furrow as he peers at us. "Seeing you battle maidens aren't going to play nice, I'm going to take this little blue dragon and its rider and go play with them. They seem like the nice ones." He closes his entire hand around Naga and Eir, hiding them from view. The giant's jaw rises. "And I'm not going to give them back."

For a moment, I stare at the giant's back in disbelief as he marches in the opposite direction. I study the size and shape of the giant and the long leather pants he wears under his potbelly. I'm dumbstruck that he's simply grabbed another living being—two, in fact—and carried them away. Ice shatters as the large footsteps pound their way through the valley.

As I sit in a daze, a distant voice hails me. *Kara. Calling Kara.* The words bounce against the soft walls of my brain, only vaguely registering. *Kara. Calling Kara. Hello-o-o, Kara. Come in, Kara.* Suddenly my seat drops away from underneath me.

My mouth drops open as I'm jolted out of my stupor. The reins rip across the skin of my hand, and I instantly feel the burn. Wind gushes up from underneath me, blowing my hair to the sky. I'm falling.

I glance down at the dragon beneath me and scream, "What are you doing, Sobek?"

His wings push out horizontally, catching the wind and halting our fall. *You're welcome.*

I growl at the smug tone in his voice.

He chuckles. *I was shaking you out of your trance.*

That giant is taking off with your friends, and you're doing nothing about it.

I shake my head, trying to clear it. "You're right."

Silver glints in the light and catches my eye. I clasp the hilt of my sword after realizing it followed me in the dive. As soon as my hand wraps around it, the extended wings retract back into their metal shape, and I slide it back into its sheath. Wrapping both hands around the reins, I sit forward in the saddle. "Let's go, Sobek. After that giant!"

Sobek accelerates, flapping as fast as he can. Drogon and Hildr join us on the left-hand side and Tanda carrying Britta on the right, their smaller frames struggling to keep up with the emperor dragon. As I grip the reins more tightly, my nails dig into my palms, and I will Sobek to fly faster. The distance between us and the giant is increasing. Disappointment grows within me with each enormous step the giant takes. Sobek's wings flap faster, yet the gap extends in moments. To make things worse, fresh snow is falling, covering the tracks of the giant.

"Fly faster, Sobek!" My high-pitched scream grates in my own eardrums. Still, the distance grows.

Panting sounds in my head, followed by a voice filled with disapproval. *What do you think I'm doing?*

I groan in frustration. I wish I had enough magic

and knowledge to encase the giant in a stunning spell. Instead, I'm cursed to watch the gap between my friends and us extend. I can't lose Eir like this again, plus Naga too. I know Sobek is flying as quickly as he can, but I still can't help saying, "I swear Elan flies faster than this, and she's smaller than you."

A low growl radiates through my head, deeper than Elan's ever could. I've insulted Sobek, and I don't care. All that I want is my friends back.

Tanda's red form slowly disappears behind us, her strangely irregular shape struggling to keep up with the speed of the emperor dragon. On the other side, Drogon pumps his wings faster, his body bigger and leaner, making his progress better than Tanda's, yet he still struggles to keep up with Sobek.

Sobek pushes himself harder, attempting to close the gap to the massive blue giant. Drogon's movement disappears from my peripheral vision, and I turn to locate my friends. Their progress has slowed dramatically, their bodies unable to keep up with the larger form of the emperor dragon.

"It's just you and me now, Sobek." I return my gaze to the front, and my eyes widen. The frost giant has disappeared.

"Where did he go?" My heart beats rapidly with panic.

Don't worry. I'm on it. Sobek pants, pushing his wings even faster. *Don't you have a cloak?*

"Why do you ask? I'm not cold." My blood is pumping so hard that my body hasn't had a chance to get cold, even surrounded by snow-capped mountains.

Seriously. That's your answer?

Dumbfounded, I sit still for a moment before I realize what he means. He's talking about the dragon-scale cloak. "Of course." I curse my own stupidity. Unlatching the flap of my saddle pouch, I pry it open over the saddle, pull out the cloak, and slide my arms through the sleeves before raising the hood over my head.

Sobek disappears underneath me, giving the impression that I'm flying on my own. For a moment, it rattles my nerves. It's a sensation that I've felt many times with Elan, but she's a familiar dragon that has my complete trust. I squeeze my fingers tightly around the reins, square my shoulders, and shake off my nerves. I'm being ridiculous. This is Elan's brother. He's trustworthy, even if he tried to prank me initially. He's protected me in the past.

Suddenly we flip, and my body flies horizontally as we round the corner of a mountain. Large frosty clumps stick out of a mountain near my head, and I have to duck to avoid the collision. Small waterfalls run down the mountainside, developed from melting snow. Sobek unexpectantly flips again to an upright position, and my body slides in the saddle. The wind from his wings brushes against my leather pants, reminding me of the effort he's exerting to speed forward.

Squinting, I catch sight of the frost giant's back in the distance, barely visible through the falling snow. At least Elan's brother has managed to keep up with him so far.

"Good job, Sobek." The words shoot from my mouth before I consider that this probably sounds condescending. "What I mean is keep up what you're doing." I try to correct myself but end up sounding like a schoolteacher talking to a young student.

Sobek's wings pump harder underneath me, and the cold from the snow bites into my skin. Even though Sobek has managed to keep track of the giant so far, the distance is growing between us, and the fear of losing my friends twists massive knots in my stomach. Worry is starting to wear at me, the fear escalating when the frost giant rapidly turns and runs behind a mountain.

"Hurry, Sobek!"

I'm sure Sobek is cursing me under his breath. Even so, his wings pump harder. The distance to that mountain tears at my nerves. Suddenly, Sobek flips to glide around the corner, lurching my body side-ways and leaving me flying horizontally again. After a moment, he straightens then halts, and we are confronted with an empty plain. The frost giant, Naga, and Eir are nowhere to be found.

S obek circles the plain, covering its boundary with the snow-capped mountains. Every gap is scrutinized as we check for an enormous blue figure. It's hard to believe that something so massive could disappear like this. But this frost giant has indeed managed to vanish, taking my friends with him. With our invisibility hiding us, he doesn't even know Sobek and I have followed him. After the first round proves unsuccessful, Sobek tries again. He hovers at the entrance to each channel between the mountains, searching for any sign of life.

My heart aches. "Where did they go, Sobek?"

I don't know. So much regret rings in those words. *I'll circle around again just in case he's hiding in a nook somewhere.* Remaining invisible, we check again, this time slower than the last two, making sure our haste hasn't caused us to miss something vital.

Each empty valley we observe causes my heart to fall further into my stomach.

We're back where we started, hovering at the spot, when a scream grabs our attention.

My eyes widen. "What was that?"

I don't know. Let's check it out.

We fly back the way we came, our eyes peeled, searching for Hildr, Drogon, Tanda, and Britta. Snow falls rapidly, obscuring our vision past a few yards. The lack of clear vision accentuates the tension running through my limbs. The empty countryside is eerie in the wake of danger. Sobek veers to the right, back onto the original path, and we almost collide with Drogon. My spirits rise when I spot Hildr on his back, my hands straining with the effort to hang on as Sobek struggles to dodge them and right ourselves.

"Stop, Sobek!" I screech.

Sobek circles back and hovers by Drogon's side. I yank my hood off my head, exposing myself to Hildr. She jerks with a start, her face pale and her eyes wide until she realizes it's us.

"What was that?" I ask.

"I don't know. I think it might have been Britta. I can't find her and Tanda anywhere. They must've been snapped up by another giant. You would think a red dragon is easy to spo—"

I slap a palm on my forehead as dread fills my stomach. "Of course. A red dragon in a frosty blue atmosphere will be easy to spot. How could I be so stupid? I should have told them not to come."

"It's not your fault," Hildr says. "Besides, I'm sure they would have come anyway."

"But I could have insisted that they stay behind. I'm the one that has been here before. I should have remembered the realm is a dull blue and filled with ice. It's suitable for the frost giants and not a place you take a red dragon if you don't want to be found."

"That may be so, but we're on a search mission for Loki's mistress. We hadn't intended to be hunted by the frost giants."

In frustration, I slap my thigh. "Then we're stupid. We're four Valkyries, for goodness' sake. We're trained to fight. We should have been smarter about it."

"And I'm telling you Britta wouldn't have stayed behind anyway. We'll find them. We've just got to keep looking." Hildr searches in the direction we just came from. "Did you find Naga and Eir?"

I shake my head. "We had run out of options and wondered which way to go next when we heard the scream."

Drogon suddenly spins and heads in the opposite direction.

Hildr clasps her reins more tightly. "What is it, Drogon?"

I can smell Tanda.

"You can smell Tanda?" Hildr frowns.

Of course. I can smell dragons. Haven't I told you that?

Sobek and I follow as they pursue Tanda's scent.

Hildr's voice trails back to me. "No. You haven't told me that."

Drogon looks over his shoulder, his pointed horns poking out in every direction from his head and neck. *I guess I didn't think it was necessary before. But the brown dragons have a heightened sense of smell, especially when it comes to other dragons.*

"That's good to know. And what a time to bring it up," Hildr says.

The falling snow tapers off into a light dust, clearing a longer visual distance. Sobek increases his speed, lining us up with Hildr and Drogon.

"What do you know about frost giants?" I ask.

Drogon peers sideways at me. *Who are you asking?*

I shrug. "Everyone."

Hildr shakes her head. "Not much. Other than they're considered enemies of Asgard."

"What about you, Drogon?" I ask.

They aren't my favorite beings, Drogon grumbles.

"Sobek?"

Some of them are known to be nasty.

"No kidding!" I say. "I think we've worked that out."

But there are a few pleasant ones, Sobek adds as a last-minute thought.

"Only a few?" Hildr tilts her head.

Yeah. Just a few.

"You aren't making me feel better, Sobek." I tap his scales near the saddle.

Oh? I didn't realize that was my job. A displeased snort travels through his mind projection. *I thought my job was to give you an honest answer about what I know about them.*

Expelled air whistles through my teeth. "You're right. Although I was hoping for some good news."

We follow Drogon around a few more corners until we eventually spot the back of a frost giant in the distance. This giant is lean, unlike the giant that captured Eir and Naga. His torso is bare, his ribs slightly visible through his blue skin. The giant rubs his bald head, and his stance almost seems uncertain.

"Did that giant come from our way, Drogon?" Hildr asks.

Drogon lifts his nose, and his nostrils cave slightly as he sucks in a deep breath. *I think it did. The scent leads me that way.*

We pursue the frost giant, Drogon's nostrils twitching in the wind. The frost giant presses forward, slow and steady, then pauses, gazes downward, and hunches over something in its hand. The distance between us closes as the frost giant is unaware of us closing in on him.

My hope rises slightly, but at the same time, I'm apprehensive about what we're about to face. I embrace my inner warrior, ready for whatever may come.

When we near, I pull the hood of my scale cape over my head. In our invisible form, Sobek and I circle around the giant's front, catching a glimpse of what's in his hand.

My neck stiffens, and before I can stop myself, I mutter, "It's Tanda and Britta."

The giant turns, searching for my voice.

Good one, bright spark, Sobek retorts. *He heard you.* Sobek backs away from the giant, giving us some distance from any swinging limbs.

The giant continues to search, confusion growing on his face. Several lines are etched in grooves in his face, giving him a freakish appearance.

Tanda's red legs and head poke out from the hand, her red body framed by his fingers, which are spread to grasp the dragon. It's hard to believe that something as significant as a dragon can look so small in comparison. The giant pinches Tanda's legs between his forefinger and thumb and opens his hand farther, exposing Britta sitting on her back, the Valkyrie's jaw set in determination.

Despite her predicament, Tanda continues to fight for herself and her rider. She flaps her wings, hovering in place, her secured leg stopping her from traveling. A plume of fire expels from her nose at the giant's face. Swiftly, the giant pulls back, tuts, then clasps his hand around the dragon. Terror flares in her red eyes, dulling with hope when she spots Drogon and Hildr hovering behind the giant.

"You're a pretty red dragon. You're so cute," the giant says. "But what do I do with you? And why are you flying in our lands? Perhaps I'll be able to eat you."

"Oh no, you're not." Britta shakes her fist at the giant. "Not on my watch."

The giant snorts with amusement, and the gust of wind pushes over Britta's face, flicking her brown hair behind her shoulders.

Nothing is holding Britta in Tanda's saddle. She can leave her dragon as soon as she has an opportunity, yet she remains on Tanda's saddle, firmly clasping the reins. Flicking her palm at the giant, Britta releases a pulse of magic at the giant's face, landing it on his nose.

Sweat gathers on my forehead in anticipation. Ever since we lost our magic trainer, Gilroma, our magic has improved very little. Britta has had less training than me, and after pumping all my magic energy into Elan and seeing very few results, I fear Britta's magic would do nothing to the giant. If anything, it would probably annoy him.

The giant's nose bunches into a strange shape, then his head flings back then forward in a rapid motion as he sneezes all over Britta and Tanda, covering them in snot.

Ewww! That's just wrong! Disgust fills Sobek's voice.

Screwing up her face, Britta wipes the gooey mess out of her eyes and off her face, curling her lip. Tanda flaps her wings, taking advantage of a slightly loosened grip, and the goop flings off them, her fiery eyes glaring at the giant.

As I suspected, Britta's magic wasn't enough to hurt the giant. However, it did give me an idea. I need to get a message to the others somehow, but we can't yell to communicate. That would alert the giant to our next move. Even if Sobek and I flew to their side in our invisible form to speak to them, the giant would probably hear us.

Pulling on Sobek's reins, I direct him away from

the giant, hopefully out of earshot. "Sobek. How far can your mind speak travel?"

Fairly far. Why?

"Can you talk to the others from here?"

He scoffs. *Well, yeah. They're not that far. Hasn't Elan told you how far she can speak?*

"It's not exactly something I've needed to ask her before. Although I do remember her talking to me through the academy walls even though we couldn't see each other." I growl. "Anyway, we need to coordinate our magic attacks."

But you just saw how that went for Britta. If you want to be covered in snot, you're on your own.

I cluck my tongue. "That's not what I was aiming for, and you know it. I can't believe you're making jokes at a time like this. Elan likes her jokes, but she still knows when it's time to be serious." I dig a boot into his side.

There's no need to get nasty. Sobek growls. *I can't believe you're going to stoop so low as to compare me with my sister.*

"I wouldn't have to if you did what I asked."

Just remember I came here to help you on my own accord. I didn't have to do it.

I yank at my cloak, pulling it tighter around me. "You're right. I'm sorry. But I really need you to focus right now. My friends—and also some of your dragons—need our help."

Then what are we waiting for? What's your plan?

I shake my head. As much as I appreciate Sobek's help, he's not Elan. I miss her terribly.

"I need you to talk to all of them. Maybe if the three Valkyries gather our magic and use it together, it may have enough of an effect against the giant."

- Chapter Twelve -

Remaining invisible, Sobek and I hover above the giant.

"What can we do, Sobek? We need to come up with a plan." I keep my voice in a whisper, hoping we're out of the giant's hearing range. Just in case, I remain alert, ready to shift if the giant searches for the origin of the talking.

I'm open to ideas. The cheek in his voice rings loud and clear, and I groan with frustration. He just doesn't know when it's inappropriate.

I clamp my teeth together to stop myself from giving a biting response. A vast void expands beneath me, giving me the feeling of floating on air as my gaze passes through Sobek's invisible form to focus on the giant. He doesn't respond in facial expression or movement, and I keep hoping we're out of his hearing range.

Tanda's red eyes remain wide with fear at being

trapped in a hand big enough to secure a dragon. Britta's jaw is set in determination, her Valkyrie training kicking in. The concentration is clear on her face as she's continually assessing the situation and possible escape options.

As my brain whirls with options, trying to develop the best plan of action, an idea rises. "Sobek. I need you to pass on the message. I need Hildr, Britta, Tanda, and Drogon to hear this as well. That way, we all know what's going on."

Okay. Here goes. Sobek clears his voice. *Um. Hi, everyone. This is Sobek.*

Tanda raises her head, her eyes searching frantically for Sobek.

Remain still, Sobek commands. *Act as though you can't hear me. Any movement you make should be slow and aimless, as though everything is as it seems.*

Both dragons, Britta, and Hildr, casually spin their heads, searching for Sobek, before refocusing on the giant.

That's better, but you won't find us. We're invisible. Kara wants me to pass on a message. We may have a chance to help Tanda and Britta escape if we all work together. Hildr and Britta, gather your magic. Let it well as large as you can. Sobek pauses, the silence piercing through the distress of having two of our own captured as we glide down to hover next to the outside of the giant's hand. *Okay. Now brace your-selves. The three Valkyries are going to shoot your magic at the giant. The magic you hold isn't enough to take down a giant of this size, so together, you're going to shoot it at the hand securing Tanda. Hildr and Britta, aim for the fingers. Tanda and Britta, get ready to flee. Let's hope this will work. On the count of three. One. Two. Three.*

All three Valkyries shoot their magic. Suddenly, the giant's hand twitches and flings open, an auto-matic reaction from aggravated nerves. The expected cry of pain doesn't happen. Instead, the blue giant gazes at his hand, confusion plastered on his face. Tanda scrambles to her feet, wings flapping urgently, as she pushes off and takes flight. Her unusual humped form isn't as agile as the other dragons', and she struggles more than usual with the added weight of Britta. My teeth clench, and I silently wish her luck.

The giant's reaction is slow, his massive head apparently absent of a fast-thinking brain. The puzzled gaze travels slowly over his hand, his mouth dropping open after realizing that he has released the red dragon. Slowly, his hand swings at Tanda.

"Fly left!" Britta cries.

Tanda dodges to the side, and the giant's stroke barely misses the humped dragon. Britta twists in the saddle, keeping an eye on the giant's movements.

When the giant swipes again, Britta calls, "Go right!"

My heart is beating rapidly. Tanda's rise is extremely slow, and the giant's reach barely misses her.

After searching his empty hand, the giant braces, ready to strike again. He extends his arm, raising his hand and lifting it close to where Sobek and I are hovering. Using my additional welled magic, I shoot at the back of the hand. I curse as the large amount of saved magic I release doesn't cause even a grimace on the giant's face.

The massive blue man reaches up, grasping for Tanda.

Britta screeches, "Forward!"

Tanda's wings double their pace, and she follows her rider's instruction, narrowly missing the clasp of the giant. The giant swipes his right hand, aiming for Tanda, and I clench my teeth, hoping for the best.

Britta yells, "Left!"

Tanda dodges to the left then up, and the blue fingertips narrowly miss my friends as they fly just out of reach. Drogon rises, under Hildr's instruction to greet Tanda and Britta, and I join them. Relief washes over me, and I clap, echoed by Hildr.

Dragon scales! Drogon's rough deep voice trails our clapping. *That was close.*

You don't need to tell me. Tanda's wide eyes peer below, a slight hint of triumph covering her face.

Britta gazes over Tanda's side at the large blue man, her body shaking visibly. "Let's get out of here."

Wide eyes stare up at us, and the corners of the blue mouth turn down, the sad expression on his face growing as he watches us fly higher, into the cover of the clouds. Once out of his vengeful stare, we hover, catching our breath.

Britta pulls at the bottom of her black leather top, straightening a few wrinkles, almost in a nervous gesture. "Thank you, guys. I couldn't have done it without you. Well, really, we couldn't have done it without you."

Sobek turns visible, and we hover next to them. "How did the giant catch you?" I ask.

She shrugs. "The giant appeared out of nowhere. We were searching for Naga and Eir, and before I knew it, an enormous hand clasped around Tanda from below, encasing most of us in the hold. The grasp secured me for a little while then released me slightly as he secured Tanda more. I might have been able to escape, but there was no way I was leaving Tanda alone." She rubs the red dragon under the scales in front of her saddle. "Not only do I need her, but she's also become a good friend."

Tanda's wide eyes soften, and she cranes her neck to nudge Britta's leg.

"I know what you mean." I stare down at Sobek. Many of his features are exactly the same as Elan's, except for his size and personality. Still, my heart sinks with sadness. I miss my beautiful dragon friend. Sobek's been helpful, and I know I couldn't complete this trip without him, but he's not Elan. I push the thoughts aside. My feelings toward him aren't fair. Perhaps one day, he will become a great companion for a dragon rider.

Hildr and Drogon lower to Tanda's other side, and Hildr offers a warm smile as her shaken friend's pale, freckled cheeks fill with warmth. "I'm glad we could help you. It was something the three of us had to do together. I tried throwing magic at that giant many times, and he didn't even flinch."

"Me too." I pull the cape off my head, and the cold air numbs my ears. "I stung him with magic many times, and he didn't even flinch at all. I don't think he even felt it." I scratch an arm under the golden dragon-scale sleeves. "I don't know if I should feel insulted."

Britta peers at the clouds above then circles her head, searching the area, before her eyes land on me. "Where are Eir and Naga?"

Lowering my eyes, I fiddle with the straps

attaching the saddle to Sobek. "I lost them. The giant took off so quickly that even Sobek couldn't keep up. We were doing okay until he turned a corner. By the time we got there, we couldn't find where he'd gone. The fresh snow covered his tracks. " I lift my gaze, meeting Britta's. "We have to find them. I hope the fat giant just wants to play with them and not eat them. I feel terrible that I haven't found them yet. When I heard your scream, I was in the middle of trying to find a trace of them."

"It's not your fault," Britta says. "Eir and Naga put themselves in danger."

"Yeah," Hildr grumbles. "That's Eir. Always seeing the good in people and things. Little does she think that it puts herself and others in danger. Not everything has a good heart. I love that about her, but it makes me so angry that she doesn't think otherwise."

Drogon snorts and shoots steam out of his nostrils. *Naga isn't much better.* His horned covered head turns as he lands determined brown eyes on me. *But we must find both Naga and Eir. I will miss the poor little guy. He is my little peacemaker. Always open and friendly.* He displays a long row of sharp white teeth, his draconic smile looking more threatening than friendly. *Very unlike me.*

I look from Drogon to Hildr then back to Drogon. They are well matched in personalities and trust issues, and most likely, that's why they bonded so quickly, growing mutual trust.

Breaking my thoughts, Britta says, "Let's go search for them. Perhaps if we fly at this level or just below the clouds, we might have a better chance of finding them." She pushes her long strands of hair back into place. "Now that my heart has stopped racing, I'll be able to concentrate more. I'm astounded how much my vision tunnels when my heart races."

I grin. "I think it's that way for everyone. Panic tends to make it difficult to focus." I pull my hood over my head. "I like your idea. We should leave now. They need to be found quickly in case the giant has something more sinister planned for them. There must be a reason why dragons and frost giants have been enemies for so long."

A roar reverberates up to meet us in the sky.

Startled, I peer over Sobek's side, checking for the disappointed giant expressing his frustration, only to find clouds below.

Sobek glances over his shoulder at me, one scaly eyebrow raised. *Jumpy much?*

Glaring at him, I'm only edged further into annoyance as he reciprocates with a playful gleam dancing in his golden-brown eyes. I stick my tongue out and tighten my cloak around my waist, straightening it to cover every inch of the saddle and my legs.

While still visible, I address the others. "Sobek and I will turn invisible and drop below the clouds to get our bearings. Wait here out of the giant's sight. We'll be back in a minute."

Sobek raises both his wings and drops beneath me as he phases into invisibility. My stomach lurches to my throat, and my heart thumps against my rib cage as I'm again flooded with the sensation of falling to my death. The wind pushes up, blowing my hood from my head. My teeth chatter from the cold and the adrenaline as I clamp one hand around the reins and grasp for the hood with the other. When we break through the cloud cover, Sobek extends his wings, and we jerk to a halt, my stomach slamming back into my abdomen.

"Thanks for the warning," I mutter to Sobek.

I can see the edges of his toothy grin from my saddle. My nerves calm after a couple of deep breaths, allowing me to get my bearings and establish the giant's location. Within a few minutes, I spot the cluster of mountains surrounding a plain in the distance. The snow had made it difficult to see where we had been before.

Pulling on the reins, I spin Sobek in that direction. "Is that the mountain cluster we were at?"

It certainly is. I'd recognize that anywhere. It's a strange formation for mountains to be that close and circling a plain. Without instruction, he ascends to meet the others. The rise is much smoother than the descent, and as we near the group, Sobek's visible golden form appears beneath me.

Indicating the direction of the mountain cluster hidden below the clouds, I say, "We're sure the giant took Eir and Naga that way. I think we should stay above the clouds for a little way. The thin giant that held Tanda and Britta remains not far from here."

Sobek leads the way over the mountains. I shiver and pull my cloak tighter around me, pulling the hood to cover my ears. Every time I use this cloak, I'm thankful I made it, especially in climates like this. I feel for Hildr and Britta, wearing only their fighting leathers. After flying for a while, Sobek gradually drops through the clouds, allowing the others to follow.

A bird's-eye view of Jotunheim spreads below us, and Sobek spreads his wings, gliding just below the clouds. I scan the area, searching for any giants or signs of our friends. The giant we left behind is too far to spot, and I see no sign of other giants in the area. The two dragons with Hildr and Britta follow. Silence encompasses us, everyone deep in thought while scanning for any danger or our peaceful friends.

The golden dragon slows his pace, allowing the others to catch up, and they spread out slightly, widening the search. The icy land's blueness makes it harder to spot the threat of blue giants and a similar-colored dragon.

Glancing over my shoulder, I notice the others have fallen behind. I call over my shoulder, pointing down at the familiar plain stretching before us. "This is where we lost them. The giant headed off into this plain. By the time we reached it, he had disappeared. I'm assuming he went down one of the gaps between the mountains." I pull on Sobek's reins to slow him, and the other dragons labor to catch up. "We searched down every single gap between the mountains, but we didn't see any sign of the giant or evidence of where he had traveled."

Drogon reaches Sobek's side first. "We should spread out around the circle, concentrating on individual sections, and see if we can spot anything farther out," Hildr suggests as Britta and Tanda join us.

We part ways, and I travel straight across the plain to the far side of the mountains, while Hildr and Drogon part to the left and Tanda and Britta search the right. The terrain in front of us remains void of evidence that any giant, dragon, or Valkyrie has passed through.

"Sobek, can you contact the other dragons to see if they've had any luck?"

Only a moment later, Sobek responds, *No. They haven't seen anything, either, the riders or their dragons.* He veers slightly to one side, and we search the mountains below.

Dragon communication is such a useful thing, I muse, wishing communication with the other Valkyries was that easy. "Can you call Naga and see if he can hear you? If he's close, maybe he will be able to direct us to their location."

Sobek groans. *Why didn't we think of this before? It would have saved so much time.*

"Dragon speech isn't my first language. It doesn't come naturally to me to expect others to hear me over a mile away," I say mockingly. "More likely, why didn't you think of it?"

It's not exactly my first language, either.

I frown, but before I can ask his meaning, my thoughts are interrupted by his call dragging my attention back to the task on hand.

Naga? Sobek's voice echoes in my head.

I wait patiently, hoping for an answer.

Naga? Can you hear me, Naga?

The silence eats at my nerves as we fly farther, searching.

As minutes pass and more distance is devoured underneath us, Sobek keeps calling out, *Naga? Can you hear me?*

Tanda and Drogon join in the calls, their voices sounding in my head, the distance making them fainter than Sobek's. With each dragon calling for Naga, I hope one of them will be close enough for Naga to hear us.

The combined effort is invigorating, and I long to

join in and call out for Naga and Eir, but I resist the urge. My efforts would be fruitless, compared to the dragons'. My voice would be lost in the icy breeze, which cuts through every gap in my cape. At least the dragons have voices that can't be affected by outside elements, although they are possibly dimmed by the thickness of the rocks. I kick myself at the thought. Mountains are filled with rocks and caves. Even the dragons' voices were probably dimmed.

"Sobek, can you fly lower and circle each mountain in the area while calling out to Naga? If we spot any caves, you might need to descend and call through the entrance."

But Naga should be able to hear me from here. Sobek sounds confused.

"Yes, Naga should be able to hear you, but the rocks and the mountains would be dense and harder for your voice to break through even though it is done telepathically." I'm puzzled that this didn't occur to Sobek, but I push the thought away when I observe the actions of the other two dragons. They aren't lowering and calling into every cave either. "Isn't that right?"

Even though Sobek is flying, his shoulders slump forward slightly. *Yes, it is right. It makes sense now.* He descends and flies closer to the mountains, his voice projecting every time we see a gap or cave. His calls for Naga grow more agitated every minute that passes without progress. *Naga? Naga, where are you?*

We pass another mountain.

Naga. Naga, can you hear me? Sobek flaps his large golden-membraned wings, aiming for the next mountain and calls again.

A small voice echoes back in my head. *Yes. Yes, Naga can hear you.* The sound is music to my ears—so soft and frail yet still sweet.

Sobek's wings halt, almost reversing, before he circles to the previous mountain and calls again, *Naga? Where are you, Naga?*

Naga... Naga don't know. His broken English sounds slightly louder. *The giant took us somewhere. Naga couldn't see. Big hands were wrapped around Naga, blocking Naga's eyes by his massive fingers.* A soft grunt of frustration sounds through the telepathy. *I shall ask Eir.* We were left in silence for a few moments until Naga came back. *Eir doesn't know either. She says we have been brought to some mountain. She doesn't know which one. They all looked the same, and we passed so many, and the giant covered the distance quickly.*

The vulnerability in Naga's small voice pulls at my heartstrings as Sobek flies around the mountain, looking for an opening big enough for a frost giant. Abruptly he halts outside a deep tunnel into the closest mountain. It's quite large, probably big enough for a giant to travel through.

Sobek turns invisible, and we land in front of the entrance, his talons soft against the stone. We peer deep into the tunnel, shocked by the depth at which the hole sinks into the mountain and disappears into the earth below.

"I don't like this, Sobek. There could be anything down there. It's a big enough tunnel for any frost giant come through. I don't know how we didn't see it before." I shift nervously in the saddle. "I think we should let the others know where we are first before we go down. We might need backup."

Suddenly, we push off into the sky. The golden scales appear underneath me, and Sobek raises his head before projecting his voice. *Are you guys ever going to catch up? You need to come this way. You will find us at the end of the plain, off to the right. We've followed Naga's voice, and hopefully, we've tracked it to the right place.*

No need to be rude about it. We're on our way, Drogon grumbles, his voice sounding closer.

We need you to come help out, in case we're ambushed. I thought you guys would have been here already. Surely, you would have heard me talking to Naga. Sobek's sarcasm surprises me. *Where's the red dragon?*

I'm with Drogon, Tanda says, also sounding annoyed. *We'll be there in a few minutes.*

Peering over my shoulder, I spot both Drogon and Tanda heading in our direction. Without waiting, the golden dragon sinks and lands at the tunnel entrance, followed moments later by the other dragons.

About time you guys got here.

"Sobek!" I scold. "That's rude. We could hardly hear Naga. How do you expect them to hear him?"

Glowering, Drogon lands with Hildr frowning on his back. His restraint is admirable as he ignores Sobek's comment and lifts his nose, sucking in a large breath, his nostrils constricting from the pressure. *I can small Naga. He is down this hole.*

"Great!" I say sarcastically as Tanda lands next to Drogon.

"Just what we need. Another enclosed area that's possibly a trap." Britta sighs.

Mounted, we slowly descend the tunnel, the dragons laboring to keep their footsteps silent.

- Chapter Fourteen -

Darkness encases us as we progress down into the tunnel, setting my nerves on edge. My eyes take a long time to adjust, and I'm thankful the dragons have better night vision.

"Where is Eir with her light-making abilities when you need her?" I murmur quietly to my friends, hoping my voice won't be heard any farther past their ears.

"What do you mean?" Hildr's whisper is barely audible.

My brows push together in a frown. I'm surprised Hildr doesn't know this. I've hardly seen Eir, compared to Hildr and Britta. "Eir has mastered how to hold light in her palm. It came in handy when we were looking for Loki."

"She's full of surprises, isn't she?" Hildr turns to Britta. "Did you know that?"

"No. But I did know she was working on magic that was more peaceful than what we would use."

Hildr huffs. "How do you know more about her than I do?"

Britta shakes her head. "I wouldn't say I know more about her. But I probably listen to her peaceful ways more than you."

"What do you mean?" Offense laces Hildr's voice. "I like Eir. I listen to her all the time."

"But you tune out when she talks about peaceful things." Britta chuckles softly. "You're too busy wanting to fight everything, always grabbing for your sword hilt."

I chuckle with Britta, knowing it to be the truth. "Clearly, you guys have been busy while I've been under Thor's guidance."

"Yeah, busy fighting." Britta glares at Hildr, the look only barely captured in the light fading from the entrance.

Hildr spreads her arms. "We don't fight much."

"What are you talking about?" Britta's eyebrows rise in surprise, along with her volume. "Eir doesn't. But we fight all the time. You just don't see it as fighting because it's not the way you prefer… with a sword or sparring."

"Shhh!" I try to quiet them, the request falling on deaf ears.

"I don't like to fight all the time." Hildr plants her fists on her hips and faces me. "Do I, Kara?"

I pull at the leather around my neck. "Well, I haven't hung around with you lately. But you do like a good confrontation, whether it be in battle or with words." I try to keep my voice a whisper.

"Fine!" Hildr huffs. "Take Britta's side." The leather of her uniform squeaks as she folds her arms, the motion barely visible from the almost extinguished light.

"You're biting well today, Hildr." Amusement sparkles in Britta's voice. "A little bit more argumentative than usual."

A large grumble sounds from down the tunnel, breaking up our conversation. The only sound remaining is the soft patter of the dragons' paws gently stepping on the stone as they progress through the tunnel. I feel the pressure of Sobek's wings tucking closer to his body, and I try to move with the sway of his movements to eliminate the squeaking of my leather uniform and saddle.

The noise from below sounds again, and with it, I imagine the giant scattering boulders and clashing them into each other—my nerves fire, stretching them to their limit.

The soft noise coming from our group still feels too loud. I wouldn't be surprised if the sound escalates as it travels farther down the tunnel. Straining my eyes, I try to see more in front of us, only to be disappointed. With my sight failing to pick up anything, I'm left feeling glad that the dragons can see in the dark.

After several more steps, the dragons round a corner, and a dull light glows in the distance. Eventually, my vision improves, revealing the three dragons' outlines and eventually Hildr's and Britta's faces. Sobek disappears from my sight, and I set to work making sure my dragon-scale cloak completely covers the saddle and me. Peering out from under the hood, I catch sight of Hildr. Her jaw clenches, and the muscles along her neck and jawline ripple with force. She looks as though she is steeling her emotions. On the other side, Britta seems slightly more relaxed.

Sobek's voice projects through my head. *Naga?* After a short pause, he tries again. *Naga, are you in this cave?*

A little squeal sounds in my head. *Yes. Naga and Eir is here in this cave. We are here with the giant. Naga started a fire for him. The giant asked Naga to.*

A combined sigh of relief escapes my friends. Naga would have sounded more panicked if things weren't right. I smile. Naga's language skills have improved significantly over the last couple of years, but he still refers to himself in the third person. Suddenly, a chill runs down my spine. Although Naga sounded positive, a deep fear fills me as I think of the fire Naga happily started for the giant. Maybe it was intended to cook them later.

My thoughts are interrupted by Naga's voice. *The giant's happy for the fire Naga made. He can warm his hands.*

A curse escapes Britta's lips, and I study her pale face as we continue forward as slowly and as silently as possible. I can't help wondering if Britta's thoughts match my own.

Loud banging from the end of the tunnel interrupts my thoughts, and I stiffen as a soft, panicked voice that sounds awfully like Eir's cries, "What are you doing?"

Absent an answer, more loud bangs follow, like large logs of wood being thrown on the fire.

The giant's voice booms. "I'm stacking up the fire. It must be strong and burning. It's the only way I can cook my dinner."

The tunnel fills with more sounds of logs thrown on the fire.

"And what are you going to cook?" Eir's voice remains tense, almost at a level of panic.

I nudge Sobek to move faster. Knots twist in my stomach as I wait for the giant's answer.

When it doesn't come, Eir continues, "I don't see anything in here to cook."

A deep belly chuckle lined with an evil tone reverberates down the tunnel, and my cheeks turn clammy.

"Why, after I finish playing with you, I will eat you. You can go first because you will cook quicker and stop me from being so hungry. But I will enjoy the dragon better. He will fill my tummy much more. You're too bony, and your body doesn't hold much meat. I have a big belly to fill."

The following cackle doesn't ease my nerves. My fear has come true.

Did you hear that, Sobek? Naga's voice, soft and scared, fills my head.

We all heard that, Drogon answers before Sobek can. *We are coming. Don't worry. We'll be there soon.*

Please do. Eir looks very scared, just like Naga feels, and Naga can't stop him. He's big. You need to be here now. His fire is burning bright. Oh, what has Naga done?

A rumble sounds down the tunnel, like rocks scattering.

An internal squeak sounds from Naga. *He's getting up. He's walking toward Eir.*

A tremendous growl reaches us from deep in the tunnel, the strange, menacing sound of a ferocious dragon, but the only dragon that we know of in the tunnel is Naga, who doesn't usually sound like that.

Naga will not let you have Eir. Naga's voice sounds oddly aggressive, a deep, low growl. It's extremely out of character, but the peaceful dragon has no other choice.

Drogon throws his large spiky head forward, expelling a loud roar that echoes down the tunnel. I shoot an impressed look toward him, but it's missed entirely because all I spot is his behind as he charges forward. He seems to have taken charge of the dragons since Elan isn't here. Usually, this would be a task undertaken by another emperor dragon—not a role Sobek has seemed keen to uphold even though he's directly related to Elan and Eingana, leader of the dragons. Before I know it, Tanda sprints after Drogon with Britta egging her on.

Frustrated by Sobek's lack of response after a few seconds, I kick his sides then jolt magic under his scales, enough to get the message through. "What are you doing, Sobek? Go! We have to help."

Without another word, Sobek breaks into a run, following the other dragons' lead.

- Chapter Fifteen -

Tanda struggles to keep up with Drogon. The brown dragon's talons scrape over the rocks as he charges straight toward the light at the end. All attempts to sneak up are tossed away in seconds. The giant will be fully aware that we're coming now.

The light from the fire frames Drogon's intimidating horned head as he springs to ram it straight at the enormous giant. Hildr screams her Valkyrie cry. The high-pitched sound is disturbing as it echoes down the tunnel. The noise intensifies as Britta joins Hildr, holding her sword in one hand and the saddle straps in the other. The longest of Drogon's horns barely pierces the giant's abdomen before the giant swings a fist in an undercut at him. Hildr sees it coming and pulls on his straps, yanking his head back, dragging the horn across the giant's tunic and leaving a long tear. Blood seeps through the damage, and the giant cries out in pain and frustration, his fist narrowly missing the brown dragon. Britta circles the giant on Tanda and jabs her sword into the giant's butt cheek. The massive hips jerk forward as he cries out in disapproval.

Sobek and I follow the others into the cave, our pace slower as we use the guise of invisibility to assess the situation. Naga and Eir remain at the back of the cave, their mouths wide as they observe the commotion. Using Hildr and Britta's distraction, we veer to the right and use the fire's light to observe the giant's captives, checking them for any injuries. My heart soars as they seem unscathed, and my attention quickly turns to the attack on the giant.

Sobek charges to the fire and leans over it. I'm puzzled at his sudden interest until I hear a sucking sound and see the red-and-orange flames dwindle away. The embers sputter for a brief second before recouping, but not before Sobek shifts underneath me and we rise from the ground. The movement feels as though he's stretching his neck up. Flames shoot from the spot I imagine his mouth is, straight at the frost giant's face. The giant recoils from the fire, ducking and releasing a cry of shock as the plume shoots overhead from an invisible source. The giant's shrieks echo down the tunnel, twisting knots in my stomach. Even though the giant wants to hurt my friends, I hate the thought of inflicting pain.

Sobek's body lowers underneath me and trudges to the fire. Once again, the flames flicker as an enormous amount of the bonfire disappears with a sucking sound. This time, after a pause, a strange vibration runs down his neck then recoils. His head jerks forward, and he regurgitates embers at the giant's hands then feet. This fire seems thicker and more than what usually comes out of Elan. It has more volume, and the stream appears longer—perhaps it's a combination of dragon flame and the fire from the bonfire.

Drogon springs off the ground, and Hildr screeches a Valkyrie cry accentuated by the enclosed walls of the cave as she clings to the reins with one hand and her sword in the other. The brown dragon flaps his wings, rising then spinning to pummel his spiky tail into the blue giant's face. I cringe as the spikes pierce into the blue cheek. Drogon recoils, and Hildr bends to the side, slicing the other blue cheek with her sword.

The giant sweeps his hands, trying to avoid the long mace-like tail, only to be distracted by the cut from Hildr's sword. The brown dragon's tail careens straight into the large eye, embedding deep into the socket. My stomach convulses, its contents rising in protest over what the three dragons are doing to the giant. His screeches overpower the high-pitched

Valkyrie cries. A huge blue hand covers the injured eye when the spiky tail is removed. Tanda lines up to join Drogon as Hildr and Britta set to work, shooting magic in unison at the giant's hands and eyes, changing targets when they think of another weak spot.

The giant shrieks, falling against the wall before hoisting himself off the hard surface, arms flailing and feet stomping, narrowly missing the fire as he scrambles down the tunnel. Cries echo as he stumbles and trips over large boulders that block his way, the hand not covering the injured eye fumbling along the walls as he tries to get out of the cave.

Drogon braces himself on all fours and roars after the giant.

The giant's cry answers as his voice echoes behind him as he continues to bungle his way to the entrance. "I don't like dragons anymore. They're not cute. They aren't fun to play with. Stop it, dragons! You're hurting me."

Sobek's invisible form bounces to face the fire, and I gasp as the flames halve then splutter and cough in protest.

The sickness in my stomach churns. "Stop it, Sobek. Surely, that's enough. The giant is running away, screaming. We have defended Eir and Naga. We don't need to attack him again."

But his noise may alert other giants. You must stop him, Sobek says.

Sobek is right. I know he is. I swallow, pushing the contents of my stomach back down and straighten my shoulders. I'm a Valkyrie. I need to toughen up. A lack of battles has softened me. We're fighting for our lives and the lives of our friends. This mission can't fail, or lives on Asgard will also be in danger. "All right! Let's make sure that doesn't happen."

As Sobek sucks in more flames, Eir's face falls in horror. Her hand reaches for his invisible form, and she screeches, "No! Stop! You don't need to go any farther. We're safe." She runs to the tunnel, holding her arms out wide, attempting to stop any more attacks on the giant.

Slowly, Tanda approaches and stands over the top of the peaceful Valkyrie. The dragon's glowing red eyes gleam down at Eir, and her voice, cold and laced with disapproval, travels through our heads. *The giants must be punished for what they did to us. A giant was going to kill Britta and me as well. You should be stronger. You're a Valkyrie.* The red dragon puffs out a mixture of smoke and steam all over Eir. She flicks her long red tail, sending the white tuft of fur on the end flinging around the room. The brilliant red wings spread wide as though she's contemplating taking off after the giant even against Eir's disapproval. Suddenly, a brown streak flies past the red dragon, gliding down the tunnel, releasing a roar of warning toward the fleeing giant. The spiky brown dragon seems unstoppable with his war-hungry Valkyrie on his back, sword drawn.

No. Drogon, no. A sweet, innocent voice fills our heads as we watch Drogon disappear. *Stop doing this. This is not nice. You make Naga sad.*

I search the cave until my eyes land on Naga. His big blue eyes are drooping with sadness, and my heart wants to break.

Sobek's feet grind to a halt, and a thump sounds down the tunnel, followed by the clacking of rocks.

Drogon appears on the other side of Eir, a strange mixture of emotions running over his scaly face. *Sorry, Naga. I was caught up in rage. That giant threatened to eat my friends.*

Eir lowers her arms, and Tanda joins Drogon.

Sobek appears underneath me and pauses before passing the peaceful Valkyrie and gazing over his shoulder. *Come, Naga. Let us leave.*

Naga's little round face nods once, and Eir climbs onto his back. Contemplation covers their faces as they follow us in silence.

Tanda circles around Sobek and approaches Naga, nudging Eir then Naga with her head as she walks along beside them. *I'm sorry.* She focuses on Eir. *Fear for myself and for my friends took over. We're all sorry. We were frightened for you both, and we wanted to make sure this giant left. Perhaps after the scare we gave him, he will tell the other giants to leave us alone.*

Naga cranes his neck to gaze up into Tanda's fiery red eyes. *Naga was scared—this is true. And Eir was too. But we live in peace. There is no reason to act like you did.*

Drogon snorts. *But the giant was going to eat you.*

Naga's eyes widen with fear. *Yes. The giant did try to eat Eir and Naga. We are grateful that you saved us.* Naga bows his head in a display of respect to their rescuers. *He is gone now, and we are safe. Let's leave him alone. He is already hurt, and this makes Naga and Eir sad.*

I gaze at the blue dragon and his rider. Both want peace and honor among dragons and Valkyries alike. Their love for other creatures is bountiful. We could all learn from them. Even after their life was threatened, they still want to uphold peace and the hope that good exists in other beings.

"Oh, Vanir!" Hildr's voice echoes down the tunnel.

I spin to see what's wrong. The entrance of the tunnel frames Drogon and Hildr with a background of nothing but darkness.

"How did it become night so quickly?" Hildr throws her arms out at the sides, disappointment covering her face. "I swear it was daylight less than half an hour ago, without a hint of nighttime coming."

Sobek joins them at the entrance, his nostrils working overtime, trying to pick up scents and assessing the land before us. Hovering slightly over the horizon, the moon shines dully, the light just touching the land's surface.

The little blue dragon stops next to Sobek, and his big blue eyes appear larger in the faint light as he gazes at me then at the golden dragon. *What are we going to do?*

Britta groans. "Great! We're stuck in Jotunheim at night with hardly any moonlight. It's impossible to see."

Tanda surveys the horizon from behind my shoulder. "So what's the plan?" Hot breath covers my head and neck, a welcome warmth to my body, which is riddled to the bone with cold despite having donned my dragon-scale cloak.

I observe the countryside, taking in the extent of darkness, pondering what to do next. "I wasn't expecting darkness to settle so quickly. I didn't realize we had taken so long to find Eir and Naga after rescuing you and Britta. I was so preoccupied with finding them that I lost track of time."

Eir gasps. "Wait. You had to rescue Tanda and Britta too?"

I nod then realize she probably can't see me. "Yes. That's another reason why Tanda was so upset, but that's a story for a different time." I rub my upper arm, missing the warmth of Tanda's breath. "It's too dark for the Valkyries to see. Either we rely on the dragons to lead the way, or we rest here and hope the frost giant doesn't return."

Drogon snorts. *Oh, the frost giant won't be returning. I'm pretty sure I sent a clear message.*

"I'm pretty exhausted." Eir yawns audibly. "That took a fair bit out of me."

"I think it took a fair bit out of all of us," Britta agrees.

The decision weighing heavy on me, I roll my shoulders then my neck, attempting to ease the tension and clear my mind. "We need to leave Jotunheim as soon as possible." I gaze down the tunnel, remembering the warmth of the fire in the distance and the cave's shelter from this harsh land. A chilly breeze catches me from outside, and I return my gaze to the darkness covering the frosty land. "But I don't like the looks of it out there. Unless the dragons can read a map, maybe we should stay here for a bit and wait for the moon to rise enough to shine some light over the land."

Nope. I definitely can't read a map, Drogon answers.

"Then we need to wait for more light so I can read the map. If I don't follow Thor's directions, we'll probably get lost, and it's going to take us longer to find Angrboda."

Sobek drops to his haunches, and I climb off his saddle, the clomp of my boots echoing down the tunnel. Another gust blows from the land, and I shiver, tugging the edges of my cloak closer together. "Let's move deeper for a while and have something to eat." The cold breeze encases my hands as I reach for the saddlebag and carry it to the middle of the tunnel. "Here should be far enough inside the cave to give us some shelter from the wind yet also allow the dragons to keep an eye on the entrance for any giants."

Unpacking the supplies, I hand each Valkyrie some food then sit on the hard stone floor, resting my back against Sobek's warm body. "I think it's best for us to rest for a while in the cave." I take a bite of the dried meat, the shock of its saltiness causing my tongue to recoil until the taste spreads through my mouth. "You three and your dragons can rest around the fire."

Hildr starts to protest, and I cut her off.

"It's no use all of us being tired. I'm sure Eir and Naga could use some rest, as well as Britta and Tanda. You and Drogon can be the last line of defense if anything gets past Sobek and me."

Sobek snorts out steam. *What about my rest?*

"Are you for real?" I ask.

I'm tired too. Hot, smoky breath washes over me as I imagine him yawning.

"Then you can sleep near me at the entrance of the tunnel with half an eye open. That should be enough for a dragon to regain their strength. I need you close in case I need backup." I prop myself up to stand and feel for the cool firm roundness of apples in my pack. Then I fumble around the circle in the darkness to hand one to every Valkyrie. "These are fresh from Midgard this morning—courtesy of Thor." I then hand out chunks of bread from the palace kitchens.

"It must be nice to be able to eat from Thor's supplies," Britta says, followed by a loud crunch into an apple.

My thumb strokes the firm skin of the apple in my hand, my mouth watering in anticipation. "I must admit it's nice having my meals cooked for me by the palace cooks. This is a perk, but you guys keep it real for me. After all, I still live with you in our humble accommodations."

"Aw! I pity you," Britta chimes in.

A small ball of flame races in midair down the tunnel from the cave. When I brace myself to move away from the attacking light, it suddenly halts and slowly moves to hover over the middle of Eir's upraised palm.

I watch her fondle the flame, mesmerized how she appears to be caressing it like a favorite pet. Eventually, I blink, bringing my attention back to the conversation. "Well, it's going to be worse if I don't fix this mess with Loki. I might have all my privileges cut off. Then I'll be eating back with you as well. I may even have to cook for myself."

Sobek scoffs, his lips blowing an unintentional raspberry.

"Hey!" I say with feigned hurt. "That doesn't seem nice. What's your problem?"

Eir giggles. "And we all know how bad your cooking is." Her eyes gleam with mischief in the light of the flame.

I glare at her, adding as much malice as I can, only to be rewarded by her chuckle growing louder, joined by Hildr and Britta.

"It's funny because it's true." Hildr holds her stomach.

"Your cooking isn't much better," I retort.

Hildr waves a hand at me dismissively. "Do you think I care?" She wipes the edges of her eyes. "The specialty that I focus on is not cooking—it's fighting. You should know that by now."

"Yeah. Thank goodness we have Eir to cook." Britta puffs, regaining some air.

A loud clatter of rocks reverberates down the

tunnel, and we fall into silence. With wide eyes, we look at one another. The ground vibrates slightly as the sound of giant footsteps comes from outside. I reprimand myself as we wait in anticipation, knowing we were too noisy.

Several more footsteps echo down the tunnel until they slowly fade away.

"We have to keep it down," I whisper. "We let our caution slip and made too much noise. I think it's time to break up. You lot go down into the cave like we discussed and get some rest. Sobek and I will head to the entrance. At least if you talk down there, it won't be so loud. But try to get some rest. I'll keep an eye out here and let you know when we have enough light to read the map and see the land."

Quietly, the Valkyries pack up, and we part ways, the dragons following like personal bodyguards, the sway of their hips outlined by the dull light in Eir's hand.

"Come, Sobek," I whisper before creeping quietly to the tunnel entrance. I pull my hood over my head and tighten the cloak around my body, securing it to stop the chilly breeze from seeping through my clothes. I park myself on the cold, hard stone ground on one side of the entrance with my back against the rock, watching the darkness and waiting for any sounds.

The cloak keeps out most of the cold breeze and traps enough warmth that I'm not disappointed when Sobek sits on the other side of the tunnel. The whites of his golden-brown eyes barely shine under the dull moonlight as his eyes search the surrounding area.

Sinking my teeth into the juicy apple as slowly and quietly as I can, I tear away a mouthful. At the crispy sound, I cringe, hoping the noise doesn't carry too far. I keep my eyes and ears peeled for any attraction to the noise.

By the time I've finished eating, a small rumble comes from the other side of the entrance. Quietly, I approach Sobek to find his eyes closed and his head resting on his extended front talons. When I brush my hand over his nostrils, he works his mouth then stretches, extending his legs farther and tucking his tail around his body. He seems to be in a deep sleep. The speed of his slumber surprises me, yet I leave him to rest. The day has been long for all of us.

Circling back, I slump against the cold stone wall and let my knees crumple beneath me. The sleeping golden dragon's scales glimmer dully in the faint moonlight. The sight sparkles in my peripheral vision as I keep watch. His steady breaths slow to a monotone beat, dragging out and setting off a slight rumble deep in his throat with the sound of intense sleep.

Leaning back against the cold stones, I adjust my cloak, making sure every gap is covered. The leather-lined golden-scale cloak traps the warmth I need, making me grateful for the time I spent making it. My boots stick out the bottom, and a chill travels up my legs. I hug my knees to my chest, covering them with the cloak. Warm, I stare out into the darkness, and time seems to stand still. The moon's ascent is slow. What little it illuminates catches my attention until I know no threats are out there. As hardly anything moves and nothing needs my attention, the boredom causes my alertness to fade and my eyelids to grow heavy, weighing down my eyes until they shut.

My body convulses, and I start, realizing that my head fell to the side with a jerk that woke me up. I fling my eyes wide and stand, stretching my body, then pace the entrance. Angry with myself for falling asleep, I push the hood of my cloak back, allowing the cold air to flood my face, waking my senses. I'm supposed to be guarding everyone, not sleeping on the job.

A noise sounds around the right corner of the entrance, and I halt in the middle of the cave. I attempt to peer around the corner while trying to stay hidden, twisting my body into an awkward angle, but I can't spot anything amiss. Not wanting to face whatever it is alone, I search for the sleeping Sobek, only to find the spot empty. My heart stops beating. Thoughts of him being nabbed by a giant run through my head, which would all be my fault because I fell asleep, leaving the place unguarded. Elan would be so disappointed in me. I rub my temples, attempting to drum up reason. Keeping my steps silent and trying not to alert whatever was around the side of the tunnel, I approach the place I last saw the dragon. Perhaps he turned invisible for added protection because he was worried his golden scales were glimmering too brightly in the moonlight. With my arms out, I search for an invisible sleeping dragon. Maybe I'll wake him up by falling over him. The thought sparks a slight amusement and lack of empathy. I shrug. It's time he woke up.

Sweeping my feet forward, I take cautious steps, determined not to fall flat on my face into a scaled dragon side or the hard stones. I continue until I reach the far side of the entrance and my hands land on the cold stone wall, unobstructed. A deep chill sets into my bones. Sobek's gone.

Chapter Seventeen

"Sobek!" My voice is a hoarse whisper. "Sobek. Are you around?"

Pausing to concentrate, I hope for some dreaming noises or a dragon voice in my head, confirming he is nearby in his invisible form. Remaining alert, I peel my eyes, hoping for a golden dragon to suddenly appear in front of me. No matter how hard I try, I can't think of why he would leave, but then again, I don't know him that well. I thought I had only dozed off for a couple of minutes. Now that I can't find Sobek, I'm not so sure.

Quickly, I pad through the tunnel, softly calling Sobek's name, hoping it's quiet enough to not echo out of the tunnel and into the lands of Jotunheim. The large tunnel is eerie in a different way from the one that leads to Gilroma's cave, and the hairs on the back of my neck stand on end as I pass through the darkness. I reach the cave at the end. All the other dragons and Valkyries are resting peacefully against their partners, their bodies relaxed in a deep sleep. I see no sign of the golden dragon anywhere.

Quickly, I race back to the entrance of the cave. The last thing I need is for something to sneak into the cave without me knowing. My trek lacks a golden dragon, and I call again, "Sobek!"

Only the whistling winds outside the cave answer me.

"Sobek, where are you?"

Lacking a response, I step outside the cave, and my nose instantly freezes in the icy breeze. Despite the wind, I leave the hood slightly back, making sure it doesn't block any part of my vision. Tugging at the ends of the sleeves, I bury my hands within its protection. Moving away from the shelter of the tunnel, I land in the light of the moon, and my heart sinks. The dragon scales covering my cloak are glowing in the moonlight, basically calling out to any giant to come and find me. With sincere regret, I untie the belt and shrug it off, folding it and tucking it in the bag that held the food. My body aches, screaming for the cloak's comfort and protection from these cold winds, but I press forward, trying to ignore that.

Hunching over and rubbing my forearms, I scan the sky for a golden dragon. No shadows pass above, and no golden scales glimmer in the moonlight. My search continues on the ground as I survey every spot of the land more visible in the stronger moonlight. We probably should be continuing our journey, but we can't go without Sobek. Elan wouldn't forgive me if I left him here even if he left without me knowing.

I'm conscious that I am still the guardian of my friends, and keeping an eye on the tunnel proves challenging while I'm searching for a rogue dragon. I pass the edge of a mountain, and something golden catches my eye. The breeze stills for a moment, and I hear chuckling. I frown. That's not the sound I was expecting in the middle of the night, and the noise doesn't sound like a frost giant. The gold glimmers.

"Sobek?"

The dragon twists to look at me, the scales on his face twisted in an expression of curiosity followed by amusement. Over his shoulder, something red catches my eye, and I frown as my eyes connect with the beady eyes of a squirrel, glaring down at me over his pointy nose.

"Ratatoskr?" I ask. "What are you doing here?"

The squirrel's body shakes as he climbs off the icy mountainside and onto Sobek's shoulder and tucks his little feet under one of Sobek's scales and against the soft skin underneath.

"Oh, Sobek. You're so warm." The squirrel's high-pitched nasal voice sounds strange in the silence. "I can finally feel my toes."

"Ratatoskr. What are you doing here?" I ask again.

"Oh, Kara. I didn't see you there," the squirrel lies, making me clench my jaw. "Sobek and I are having a little chat."

I eye them both suspiciously and cross my arms. "Sobek is supposed to be guarding the cave to help protect my friends and me. Why are you out here, Sobek?" I raise an eyebrow.

Ratatoskr runs along Sobek's back and whispers something into the dragon's ear. Sobek snorts with laughter, and the squirrel returns to his original spot on the dragon's shoulder. I glower, only to be met by Sobek's mischievous grin, which irks me. I shove the annoyance aside. Clearly, I need some sleep. I'm getting agitated over stupid things.

I heard a little noise, and I went out to investigate. Imagine my surprise when I spotted Ratatoskr freezing his little tail off, here in Jotunheim. I've only been here for a moment.

"But I've been looking for you for the last ten minutes, at least." I spread my arms in frustration.

It took me a moment to find Ratatoskr, Sobek retorts cheekily.

Pulling my eyes away from Sobek, I observe the squirrel with a glare. "And why are you here, Ratatoskr? You still haven't answered me."

The red fur ball moves to the top of Sobek's head and leans against a horn, tucking his feet back into the dragon's scales, then plants a hand on his hip. "Actually, I was looking for you."

Sobek attempts to gaze up at Ratatoskr, confusion and amusement written on his face.

The squirrel continues, "I have a message for you from Loki."

"Oh." Bewilderment flushes through me as my gaze scans Sobek then Ratatoskr, thinking they look way too chummy to be looking for me.

"Yeah. I have a message for you from Loki," he says again, nodding as though satisfied with his answer.

I think I catch amusement on Sobek's face, but his expression changes before I can read it.

"Yeah," the squirrel repeats as though trying to convince me. "That's right." He crosses his arms over his chest.

I scratch the back of my head. "Have you found Loki?"

"Of course. I wouldn't just be making up his

message." The squirrel manages to look offended. "It wouldn't be worth my while."

Shrugging, I wait for the message to be delivered, bracing myself for an insult. "Well, don't just stand there. Tell me."

"Yeah. All right. Here goes. Loki says that if you really wanted to find him, you already would have."

Gasping, I spread my arms out to the sides in frustration. "How am I supposed to find him? He disappeared, running away when he was in my care, leaving me to take the blame for his actions. Having success in locating him is like finding a needle in a haystack. He can turn into any form he likes. I can't believe he said that!" I throw my head back in frustration. "You give him a little, and he takes a mile," I rant, unable to help myself.

Ratatoskr raises a furry eyebrow. "Well, he says that he's been in your face the whole time. You could have found him, but you're too complacent. He said that the number of opportunities he's given you is ridiculous, and he's starting to wonder if there's anything in your brain." The squirrel passes on the message with such conviction that it's insulting.

"Ergh! I'm not stupid. Loki hasn't been near me. If he has, the shape he took on would have made it impossible to tell it was him." I flail my arms. "He could have been in any form."

The smirks grow on the squirrel's and Sobek's faces.

"You hear that, Sobek? She says he could have been in any form."

They both chuckle, Sobek's belly jiggling with laughter.

Crossing my arms over my chest, I lean on one leg. "I'm glad you two find it funny. You're no better than me, Sobek." I return my glare to the squirrel. "At least we're here to seek Loki's mistress and the mother of his monstrous children. We've come across nothing but trouble on this trip. It is Loki's fault that we're here, trying to see if anyone can control his wayward offspring. They want to attack Asgard because they're angry at all of us for locking Loki up." As Sobek continues to laugh, I glare and throw in an insult. "If Sobek was as good as his sister, we could have returned home by now."

Ratatoskr elbows Sobek's head. "You see, Sobek? These are the sort of messages I like to carry. The reactions are priceless! Especially with people like Kara." The squirrel runs off of Sobek and charges away without carrying any new messages.

I can almost feel smoke coming out of my ears. My eyes narrow on the golden dragon. "Sobek, are you coming back to guard the entrance, or what?" I plant my fists on my hips. "In fact, we should have been on our way by now, and it's because of you that we haven't started traveling yet."

Yes, ma'am! Sobek's chuckle continues to rumble through his ample belly.

I growl, "I can hear you, Sobek."

"So what were you two talking about?" I ask. "You and Ratatoskr seemed quite friendly. I thought he didn't speak to anyone unless he's delivering an insult."

An amused gleam passes through Sobek's eyes. *It was nothing that interesting.* He looks thoughtful for a moment then shakes his head. *No, just small chitchat.*

I grumble softly. "You're rather frustrating at times. Do you know that?"

Sobek bows mockingly. *I'm glad I could be of assistance.*

I huff. "You two suit each other."

We reach the cave and find our friends still asleep, the Valkyries curled against the warmth and protection of their dragons.

"Let's wake them. We have to go. You start with the dragons, and I'll wake the Valkyries."

Sobek's grin looks cunning. *With pleasure.*

Pausing, I raise an eyebrow at him. "You know, I have to say I don't remember you being so cheeky when I stayed with you in the dragon wastelands."

He shrugs. *I've relaxed around you. Back in the wastelands, I had to protect you. Now... well... you're just my sister's friend, perfectly capable of taking care of herself.*

"Nice! I thought you came on this trip to make sure your sister's friend stayed safe."

Sobek pokes Tanda with his nose, the prodding taking a few attempts before the red dragon opens her eyes. She climbs to her talons, nudging Britta in the process.

Starting on the right, I shake Hildr softly by the shoulder.

Slowly, she rolls over on all fours, eventually pushing herself up to standing, and stretches. Yawning, she rakes her fingers through her short red hair, pulling it into the spiky design she likes. "Is it time to go?"

Clasping Eir by the arm, I softly shake her. "There's enough moonlight to read the map. We should get going. I want to get out of this land as soon as possible."

Eir yawns and holds a hand over her mouth, eventually prying her eyes open. She wipes out the ducts then climbs onto Naga. "Let's get going.

I hope we don't get kidnapped by giants this time."

Britta climbs onto the saddle and hooks her feet into the stirrups. "I suggest we fly higher than the giants' reach this time."

Strapping my feet into Sobek's stirrups, I say, "That was the plan."

Britta turns to me. "Do you think you can see the land properly in the moonlight from that high up?"

"I think so. If not, then I'll fly lower with Sobek invisible, and you lot can stay above. If we have to use this method, I'll reappear now and then, and the dragons can communicate so that you know where we are."

After shrugging on the dragon-scale cloak, I pull the hood over my head, and the dragons pad softly toward the cave entrance. The frosty breeze brushes our skin, and moonlight bathes the icy landscape before us, giving it a fairy-tale appeal. The second we reach the exit, Sobek turns invisible.

"Wait here," I call to the others while scanning the area around the cave from the ground to the sky. "We're going to do a quick check to make sure all is clear and you can exit the cave safely." I stick my fingers under Sobek's scales just in front of the saddle, touching the soft, warm skin underneath. "Are you okay with that, Sobek?"

"Of course," Sobek says, sounding as though he's feigning confidence and importance.

His changing character throws me into uncertainty, and I frown. He's suddenly acting sensible and reliable. We lunge into the air, the beat of his massive wings jerking me as we climb into the sky. The increase of altitude brings a crispier cool breeze, and my eyes water in discomfort. My face stings, and any skin exposed to the elements turns numb after a few moments. The ground falls away underneath me, and in his invisible form, Sobek circles the area several times, surveying the cave and the other mountains within the vicinity.

After making certain that no threats lay hidden, we wind farther until something catches my eye in a corridor of the distant mountains. I pull on the reins, directing Sobek's head in that direction.

"Over that way, Sobek. I see movement."

I'm on it.

Tilting his wings, he steers us that direction, and I relax the pull on his reins, letting him take the lead. He keeps our altitude level for quite some time, his eye on the movement. Suddenly he dives toward the ground, and a scream stops behind my clenched teeth.

"What are you doing? We don't need to fly this

low to see what it is. We're flying in the danger zone."

We're invisible. He sounds conceited, making me want to slap him. *Whatever it is, it won't be able to see us.*

A growl sits in my throat, but I refuse to release it. It would probably just encourage him, knowing that his sudden dive set my nerves on edge. Our flight stabilizes as he glides, using the wind to his advantage as he captures it within his membranous wings. Eventually, we near the moving object, and we dip slightly closer to the ground, riding just over it. Sobek flaps his wings a few times, raising us higher, then circles the area twice.

I'm having trouble working out what I'm looking at. It appears to be an animal that I haven't seen before. "What is it?"

No idea. It must be an animal native to Jotunheim.

The thing scrambles around a tight spot, its face down as it devours something. Sobek sinks to a level just out of the animal's reach, gliding in a circular motion. It doesn't look up even though it might have felt the breeze from Sobek's wings. My impatience grows, and I yell. The animal looks up, and I'm confronted by a piglike nose. The rest of the body is covered with long white fur that spreads all the way down its legs, stopping at the trotters. The design of the animal is perfect for the cold weather in Jotunheim.

Satisfied, I say, "It looks like only a pig. It shouldn't be dangerous to us unless it has the temperament of a boar. Let's fly up. Let's go back to the others."

Yes, ma'am, Sobek says. *But we shouldn't get complacent. Maybe everything in this land is dangerous to us.*

"We'll keep an eye on everything."

Of course you will. The presumption returns to his voice.

I roll my eyes, not that he could see. "I didn't think your seriousness would last long. You seem to thrive on being cheeky." I push my mouth to one side. "And not always in a good way."

You're welcome, Sobek says. *This little trip would have been boring without me.*

"Yeah." I pile on the sarcasm. "Because rescuing my friends from frost giants isn't exciting at all."

In a few minutes, we return to our friends.

"We only found something like a wild pig. There don't seem to be any frost giants hanging around. However, while saying that, I suggest we keep away from anything that moves," I say.

Hildr's grip around her reins tightens. "Lead the way."

The dragons take to the sky and rise as planned until they are high enough to be out of the reach of any giants. Above the cloud cover, the moonlight shines on the map I pull from my cloak. I turn the map one way then the next, trying to find a location that reflects the markings on the map. "Thor's drawings are rough, certainly not the effort of an artist." I twist my mouth to the side. "But clear enough for recognizing landmarks. It's been several years since Thor and Tyr traveled here to retrieve Loki's three children—Jormungundr, Fenrir, and Hel—from Angrboda." I twist the map in another direction. "After looking at the drawings on the map and the landscape, it's possible that his memory has faded as well." I spot a set of mountains drawn on the map. "Thankfully, it might not have faded too much."

Britta moves next to me on Tanda's back. "I hate to be the bearer of bad news, but you know there's no guarantee that this is where the mother is going to be. No one, other than Loki, seems to know where she moved to after losing her children. She might have relocated to a completely different location."

Sobek scoffs. *Frost giants are creatures of habit. She'll be there.*

"How would you know?" I ask.

I just do.

I shake my head. "Somehow, that doesn't bring

me comfort. So let's hope she's still there." After finding a couple more bearings on the map, I roll it up and tuck it back into my cloak. "I think I have enough information. Let's go." I direct Sobek with the reins, and the others follow. The dragons fly in a diamond formation, Sobek leading the way and Naga tucked just behind in the middle.

- Chapter Nineteen -

After flying several leagues, Sobek and I turn invisible and drop below the clouds, and I pull out the map and study it in the moonlight. The wind whips at the edges of the parchment, threatening to rip it from my hands, and I tighten my hold. The last thing we need is for it to be lost in the wind. I study each section of the map. A sickness grows in my stomach as I struggle to find any of the landmarks.

Groaning in frustration, I say, "Pull up, Sobek. I need to find my bearings. I don't want to travel any farther until I'm sure we're going the right way."

Sobek makes us visible and circles the other dragons, giving me time as my companions' curious eyes observe me.

"I can't find where we are on the map. I need to reassess it for a moment," I say in answer to their unvoiced questions.

"Let me have a look." Britta holds out her hand, expectantly.

"The coast is clear of giants." I roll the map tight and hand it to her, refusing to release it until I'm certain she has a firm grasp.

We drop below the clouds and hover, waiting for Britta to test her navigation skills. Her brows furrow, and her lips flatten into a line as she pulls the map closer to her face, studying certain areas more closely than others. The dragons hover, waiting for her decision, occasionally watching her as she angles the map in new directions in the moonlight. Her frown deepens, and she peers over the side of Tanda, glancing past the hovering wings.

"Ah." She points down at the spot below her. "There it is." Her expression turns to excitement. "There's one of the icons. We're not far now." Then she points over to the right. "It's just a little farther that way."

A welcome relief washes over me. "Awesome! Can you lead the way?"

"Of course." Britta rolls up the map and tucks it into her jacket. "Follow us!" she calls over her shoulder before directing Tanda and leading the group in the right direction.

We remain high, just below the clouds. The hood drags off my head, pushed by the force of the wind.

White noise fills my ears as the wind thrums against my eardrums, making it hard to hear anything but its constant beat.

We pass several large buildings, and after having seen only a frosty countryside during my past visits, finding that the frost giants live in communities seems strange.

The moon begins its descent, aiming for the horizon in the west, and a rising shine on the far side indicates the sun, determined to start a new day. We pass several more buildings and aim for the cave where Thor and Tyr found Loki's children.

Britta slows Tanda, giving us time to reach their side. "The coast seems clear!"

"It seems that way," I agree. "But stay alert, just in case."

After a final circle around the mountains, we land not far from a cave resembling the one marked on the map. It doesn't look much different from the one we slept in except for a river flowing nearby, surrounded by greenery. After dismounting Sobek, I loosen the straps holding my cloak together. Although the wind still holds a chilliness, it isn't as cold as the temperatures we've encountered in Jotunheim before. I gape at the greenery and notice a thick tree trunk forking out into smaller branches covered in deep-green leaves. I run my fingers under some of the lower leaves, green tips flicking across my skin. "There's even a few trees in this area." I study the branches and leaves. "Some of those leaves appear to be like the ones on the World Tree."

Of course they do. Sobek shakes his head as though in disbelief. *The branches of Yggdrasil spread out wide even if you can't access the tunnel. If you're small enough, you'll be able to travel along the branches of the World Tree. They spread far among every realm. How do you think Ratatoskr finds all these people?*

"I've never thought about it."

Sobek shakes his head. *He can't run too far from the tree. He's only a small guy.*

"I hadn't really thought about it," I repeat. "I guess I assumed that he scurries the lands until he finds the person or creature he needs to talk to. That would be the best way to listen to rumors of where his target is residing." I shrug. "It's not like you can ask him these things."

Sobek snorts. *I think you're wrong about that. I find the little guy quite approachable.*

I shove a finger at his nose. "See. I thought you two had something going on." The soft flesh bends away as I jab it. Pulling away, I indicate another tree. "This tree looks different from the Yggdrasil."

Sobek shrugs, looking indifferent.

Grumbling to myself over his lack of response, I

gaze at the entrance of the cave. "Anyway… We must get going and do this quietly. She isn't expecting us." After taking a few quiet steps, I add, "I'm not sure if she's even here. But naturally, we need to eliminate as many risks as possible."

"Then I think it's best if we all gather our magic," Eir says, "and not rely on eloquence."

"That's a strange thing for you to say, Eir," Britta whispers. "Are you feeling all right?"

Eir frowns. "Yeah, Why?"

Britta feels for her sword, hanging by her leg, then her quiver on her back. The shafts rattle as she runs her fingers over the feathers. "You're usually against anything to do with hurting anything."

Eir groans and reties her long light-brown locks into a ponytail, securing all the loose wavy strands. "I know. I don't plan on hurting anyone, but I think it's wise to be prepared. We've already had enough excitement on the trip. At least if our magic is ready, it may give us enough to help us escape if needed."

I place a hand on Eir's shoulder, the soft leather in her black fighting uniform bending under my touch. "Whatever the reason, it is probably the best way to protect ourselves at the moment. Our tiny little swords or arrows against huge frost giants are just not enough."

My footsteps turn into tiptoeing as we slowly

enter the tunnel, doing our best keep our boots silent on the hard floor. Our breaths are shallow and soft, yet the sound reverberates back at us from the tunnel walls. The dragons' talons scrape on the stones, and I flinch at the loudness.

I whisper over my shoulder, "I think you dragons should stay here for now." When answered by confused looks, I continue, "Your talons are too loud, and the noise might alert her of us coming. Just remain alert in case we call for you. If there is anyone down at the end, we want to surprise them until we know what we're dealing with. We don't want to be ambushed the second we get down there."

The dragons plunk themselves on their haunches and wait, bored looks plastered on their scaled faces as we leave them behind.

"I have no idea where Angrboda lives," I say.

"Do you think there's a chance she'll be down here?" Eir's light-brown eyes are clouded with apprehension.

"To be honest, it would seem strange that she would remain here. I don't think I would like to remain in a place my children were taken from. It would be depressing."

The tunnel darkens, the deeper we travel. Beside me, Eir's leather uniform squeaks before I hear a sharp crack. A glow ignites in her hand, and a faint waft of smoke greets my nose.

I gasp. "You brought a flint striker! Way to go!"

A satisfied smile spreads across her face as she calls the flame to her open palm. The fire hovers over her hand, and she shoves the flint striker back into her fighting leathers. A soft incantation whispers through her lips, and the flame on her hand dances, jumping higher and growing in volume.

Hildr's eyes are wide, the whites shining in the light of the flame. "That's a cool little trick you've got there, Eir."

"We told you she was working on another type of magic, Hildr." Britta's face glows in the light next to Hildr. Despite her words, wonder covers her face. "This is one of the things she can do."

"It's one of the peaceful things I've been working on, while you've just focused on fighting and battle skills, Hildr." A simple matter-of-fact tone frames her words.

We push forward. The flame flickers over Eir's palm as we progress, each step drumming up a slight wind, causing it to continue dancing.

We progress toward the end of the tunnel, searching for the cave Thor described to me. My hopes dwindle as the width narrows without any sign of Angrboda and almost disintegrate when we run into a solid rock wall. It's the end of the cave.

With her palm leading the way, Eir circles the area, her flame illuminating the room, and flickers its light against the walls, revealing an empty cave.

Hildr's shoulders slump. "It looks as though it's a dead end."

"Where to now?" Britta asks.

"I don't know." I try to push down the frustration that chews on my nerves. "After we leave this cave, we'll circle the area, looking for somewhere that might resemble something that she lives in."

Suddenly, Drogon's voice enters our heads. *Ah, Valkyries... You might want to come out here. There's somebody that wants to see you.*

Chapter Twenty

Concerned glances pass between the other Valkyries and me, and we break into a run toward the entrance of the tunnel, all attempts to be silent smashed. The dragons' backs face us as they focus on something outside. Magic fires under my skin, loaded and waiting to be released, and my fingers twitch, longing to unleash my weapons.

We slow not far behind the dragons and cautiously approach their sides. Using Sobek as a shield, I duck behind a front leg and peer into the light.

Long brown leather pants cover towering muscled legs stand before us, the waistline hiding under a long tunic tied at the waist and cutting off midthigh. Leather straps with silver buckles dangle from the belt, and a silver sword sheath is suspended from the waistband. As it sways, its metal clangs against buckles and studs.

When I follow the long white hair falling past a waist in a thick braid, my mouth wants to fall open. A pale-blue giant stares down at us, her determined eyes focused on us from a face lined with blue zigzagging tattoos trickling down her cheeks. Something about them reminds me of some of Gilroma's tattoos even though the markings are different. Perhaps some of the strange dark elf's markings stemmed from the frost giants. I push aside the odd coincidence to focus.

Secured in a steady stance, a nocked arrow points directly at our small group, and the giant's blue fingers are poised, ready to release the string. I pull my attention past the fierce blue eyes and take in other features. Despite her size, her face is elegant, almost beautiful. As though sensing my wonder, she points the tip of the arrow directly at me, and I straighten. I feel incredibly small and insignificant, and I can't help wondering what such a large arrow would do to someone my size.

I silently whistle a puff of breath and steel my nerves. Without dropping my gaze, I secure my dragon-scale cape to cover more of my body. Yanking at the straps to tighten them in place, I hope the tough scales will withstand an arrow that size. Then I realize it doesn't matter. The pressure of something that big hitting my body, even through the cape, would pummel my organs and probably do too much damage. Gathering courage, I move slowly from around the security of Sobek's leg and approach her. Even though a fair distance still separates us, I crane my neck to focus on her eyes. They narrow, turning as hard as icicles as they glare down at me.

With each step I take, she adjusts her arrow to aim straight at me. I gulp, trying to swallow the lump stuck in my throat. My fingers fiddle nervously with the straps of my cloak, and I push my palms together, wrapping my fingers to secure them in place, in an effort to squash the hesitancy in my steps.

"Halt!" the frost giant calls. Her voice is strong and deep, almost as low as a male's.

My steps falter, and I do as instructed, forcing down my fear and staring straight into her face.

She lifts a blond eyebrow as though pleased with the result. "What do you want here? Why are there dragons here and four Valkyries?"

Bracing myself, I call out from the depth of my diaphragm, trying to make my voice bigger. "We're searching for someone."

Her brows furrow, and suspicion creeps through her expression.

I continue, "We come in peace. We do not want to cause any trouble."

The female frost giant huffs a laugh, sounding

unconvinced. "When do Valkyries ever come in peace?" Her face turns cunning. "If you come in search of my children, then you're out of luck. They were taken by the gods. You should know that, for they were taken to Asgard and distributed to different realms." She raises her chin. "There's been nobody residing in this cave since my children were taken. There is no reason for you to be here."

My jaw drops. She said her "children." I brace myself for mockery, but to me, that seems the only explanation. "Angrboda?"

Her face twists before it quickly flattens again.

"Is that you?" I try again.

Something firm presses me from behind, and golden scales catch the corner of my eyes. Sobek leans over me, and hot breath falls over my shoulders. His eyes remain fixed on the female giant.

His face beams, almost dreamy, as he says softly, "Can't you tell? Look at those gorgeous blue eyes."

I nudge him with my elbow. "Sobek. Get a hold of yourself." Afraid to take my eyes off the giant for too long, I return my gaze just in time to see her determination waver with a moment of softness in her blue eyes as they focus on Sobek.

Her gaze returns to steel as her attention turns toward me. "Who wants to know?"

Placing a hand slowly on my chest, I say, "I'm

Kara, a Valkyrie and mostly a peacekeeper. These are my wingless colleagues and their dragon companions." I wave a hand around the group. "We just want to talk to Angrboda."

"Then you're looking for me. I am Angrboda, also known as Loki's mistress." Her brow furrows, pushing together the blue lines that streak down her forehead. "Why would you be looking for me?" Keeping the arrow nocked, she drops the point away from us.

Eir moves forward, placing her peaceful face in the spotlight. "We just want to ask you some questions."

She chuckles and sits on the ground, crossing her long thin legs. Even at her reduced height, she still towers over us. "What sort of questions would drag you into the dangers of Jotunheim just to search for me?"

Confused by the sudden ease infused in her manner, I twiddle my thumbs behind my back. "Do you have any pull on how your children behave? We were wondering... and hoping... if you could control your children a little bit."

"Why?" She raises her nose, looking slightly annoyed yet amused. "They're teenagers. Nobody can control teenagers."

"Are you saying you have no influence over your children?" Britta asks.

Angrboda's blue eyes flash a warning as she stares Britta down. "For one, the gods pinched my children years ago. They haven't been in my care for quite some time." She flicks a dismissive hand out to the side. "Why would you think they would listen to me after all this time? Can't the gods control them?" She eyes us individually. "If they took my children, they should learn how to control them."

Eir's places a hand on the giant's knee. "Did you want them back?" A strange, hopeful sound fills her voice. "Perhaps they would be more settled if they came back to their mother."

The mistress's laugh is so high-pitched that I have to cover my ears. She slaps a hand against the ground, and smaller stones around her jump and clatter a short distance. "That's a funny one." She thumps the ground a few more times. "As if I want my wayward children back. They have a power that you will never under-stand. Besides, have you not heard? They are monsters."

Annoyance whirls and raises its ugly head within me, and I push it down with a frown. "Yes. That is why we're here. We hoped that you would help us control them. It is essential for Asgard, and for many other realms, that they are controlled."

Hildr stands by my side and crosses her arms. "How did you manage to have three completely unique monsters with one god, anyway?"

The mistress slaps a hand over her mouth as she chuckles. Eventually, her laughter grows so loud that she can't contain it anymore. Rocking back, she holds her stomach and laughs boisterously until she finally regains her composure. Wiping the laughter tears from her eyes, she sits up and stares down at Hildr before gazing at all the Valkyries. "You are young Valkyries, yes?"

Hildr stands on one leg, her arms remaining crossed. "We are still young as far as a Valkyrie is concerned. What is your point?"

"That perhaps you are too young to understand."

When we stare at her with confusion, she continues, speaking slowly and emphasizing her words, "Loki is a shape-shifter. Think about it." When our expressions don't change, she adds, "Perhaps you should go back to the academy and learn some Baby-making 101 skills."

I feel my cheeks redden and turn away, trying to hide my face. An awkward silence taints the air, broken by the clearing of throats then Angrboda's laughter.

In one way, I'm glad for the distraction of her laughter so I can regain my composure. When she finally quiets down, I add, "We need all the help we can get to stop your children. They have been causing trouble ever since they learned of their father's demise."

"Ha. Then let him go." She says this so simply and matter-of-factly that it shocks me.

I take several steps back, running into Sobek. "We can't just do that. He has caused so much trouble on Asgard, and he's extremely deceitful."

"But my suggestion may be your only answer." Placing her palms on her knees, she leans forward as though plotting a conspiracy. "Or have you lost him?" Her eyes narrow on me. "I've heard rumors that he has escaped. Is that what you're not telling me?"

My gaze drops to the ground, and I fiddle with my fingers before pulling my gaze back up. "Yes, it's true. He's no longer held in captivity by the gods. He has run away somewhere."

- Chapter Twenty-One -

After recovering from my embarrassment over my failure, I look up. Angrboda is beautiful compared to the other frost giants I've seen, and I understand to some degree how Loki could fall for her. After all, he was also part frost giant and a shape-shifter. However, I didn't want to think about how he managed to create different types of monsters as children. They aren't the only unusual children Loki sired. I heard that Odin's eight-legged horse, Sleipnir, was created because Loki shape-shifted into a horse to lure another away and ended up having a baby with it.

"Then can you help us to find Loki?" I stare up at her with hope. "I must redeem myself before the gods."

She rests her elbows on her knees and leans forward, staring down at me. Even though her movement isn't aggressive or threatening, her massive form towering over me is daunting and makes me feel small and insignificant.

She raises a white eyebrow. "Have you not found him yet?"

Sobek makes a funny sound in his throat. Glancing at him, I'm surprised by his expression. It appears to be riddled with love and adoration, his eyes soft as he gazes at Angrboda, his face about to melt with passion. He said she was pretty, but this is ridiculous.

Shaking my head, I return my attention to the mistress. "No. I haven't found him. If I don't find him, I'll be in lots of trouble."

Amusement grows on her face.

My jaw drops. "Do you know where he is?"

"Maybe."

"I know I can't expect any favors from you, but if you tell me where he is, I can rectify my mistake, and I'll make sure he'll get treated better than last time."

Still towering over me, she gazes at me intensely with her big blue eyes then over my shoulder, taking in my golden mount, before returning to me. "No. I cannot help you find him. You must rectify what you have done on your own. If he is chained up, I will never get to see him, and that is simply not good enough." She sits straight. "But if you do capture him and make sure he is treated nicer than before, I may put in a good word for you with our children." She crosses her arms and gazes at me curiously. "You know he's a shape-shifter, right?"

"Of course I know that," I say, almost insulted. "Besides, you mentioned that only a little while ago, plus I've seen him in many shapes since I've known him."

The edges of her mouth tilt up in a smirk. "Well then, you know he can take on any form. So good luck with that."

I resist the urge to stomp my foot and glare at her. "We have traveled a long way and dealt with much danger to ask you these questions. Can you please help us out slightly? At least give us some help with the children."

"Hmm. You have been somewhat pleasant to talk to even though you're a Valkyrie and work for Asgard." She rests her chin on a hand. "I guess I'll think about talking to the children anyway."

I breathe the words, "Thank you." Then I add, "Any help will be appreciated. This isn't only for Asgard's safety."

"I don't know if my chats will be that helpful." Levering herself off the ground, she stands then bends to look at me. "Seeing you know that Loki is a shape-shifter, you must know that he could be anywhere... or anyone. Perhaps he is closer than you think." She turns to leave and calls over her shoulder, "Oh, and take note, if you follow me, I will kill you."

From the warning in her eye, I wasn't going to test her threat.

"And that goes for your friends and the dragons too." After facing us, her glare lands on each of us and finishes with Sobek. She bends over and frames his golden snout in her hand.

I move back, observing her. It's such an unusual thing to do. Sobek's scales glimmer in the light of the early morning.

Lightly, she shakes his jaw, gazing straight into his golden-brown eyes. "You're a beautiful dragon, aren't you?" She kisses his forehead then strokes his body from the top of his head, down his back, avoiding the saddle.

Sobek moves into the stroke, his face soft with adoration.

Her eyes land on me, observing my surprised expression with humor. "Emperor dragons are magnificent creatures, aren't they?" Without waiting for an answer, she straightens.

A thunderous rumble breaks the silence, and a crack of lightning follows, forking into silver lines and splitting the sky. Surprised, I stare at the icy blue sky. The clouds there didn't indicate a storm.

Angrboda growls, and the tunnel shakes with a

different kind of thunder. She glowers at me. "You said you come in peace."

"We do," I stammer.

She extends her long arm at the sky. "Then why did you bring the horrid god of thunder?"

"What?" Open-mouthed, I stare at the sky again, and another rumble of thunder sends vibrations through the ground, followed by another crack of lightning, forking in two directions.

"You have lied to me. I will not help you now. There is no chance I'll help you find Loki, nor will I try to convince our children to stop attacking Asgard and your gods."

I try to argue. "But—"

My words are cut off by the sound of sliding metal as she unsheathes her sword.

Lightning forks from the sky, hitting the ground only a few yards away, and everyone in the cave jumps, but no one as much as Angrboda. A determined snarl replaces all pleasantness in her face. She repositions her feet in a firm stance and raises her sword.

Suddenly, something shoots from the sky and lands with a thud right where the last bolt of lightning hit. The ground shakes from the impact, and a figure of a man rises from a squat. Dressed in brown leather topped with a tunic and a long fur cloak, Thor stands with hair burning red in the sun's light, an enormous hammer in hand.

"Wow!" Hildr exclaims. "That never grows old." The sound of metal slides as she yanks her sword out of her sheath.

I grasp her arm. "Wait!" When met with a frown, I continue, "I don't understand why he is here. Maybe he's just here for a chat."

"Uh, I don't know how you don't already know this, but if Thor arrives in this fashion, it's always because he's coming to fight." Hildr indicates Angrboda. "Even she knows this."

"But why would he be coming to fight when there is no need to?" I ask. "We weren't in danger, and she was sort of cooperating."

Angrboda charges for the god of thunder, her large legs covering the ground in seconds, her sword held high. Casually walking her way, Thor holds Mjollnir to the sky, and lightning forks from the hammer into the sky and hits the ground right before Angrboda's next footstep.

She grinds to a halt, her foot raised, before placing it back down cautiously. "You'll pay for that."

"And you'll pay for mistreating my Valkyrie and her companions." Thor swings the hammer and releases it. It charges straight at Angrboda, slamming into her torso and sending her reeling backward past the cave entrance. Pebbles fall from the ceiling of the cave as a loud thud rings out and the ground shakes. Thor holds out his hand, beckoning Mjollnir, and is rewarded only moments later when the hammer's helve slaps into his palm.

What is he doing? Concern fills Sobek's voice.

"I don't know." I shake my head. "I don't know why he's here. It doesn't make sense."

"We have to stop him." Eir shifts to leave the cave.

I grab her arm. "I'll do it."

Solemnly, she nods.

Pebbles sting my head again as heavy footsteps charge past the entrance. A loud cry cuts the silence as Angrboda swings her sword at Thor.

Thor ducks, pivots, and releases Mjollnir in the opposite direction, directing it with his hand to fly back with added momentum directly at Angrboda. It slams into her stomach again and pushes her several yards away from him before landing in his extended palm.

His boots crunch on the realm's stony surface as he paces toward the female frost giant.

I charge out of the cave, waving my hands. "Thor. Stop!"

His expression is curious when his eyes land on me.

"Look!" I wave my hands, pointing to my body.

"I'm unharmed." I indicate the cave. "My companions are safe. Angrboda was not attacking us."

He frowns. "But Ratat—" Understanding fills his face. "Why that dirty little rat."

I groan. Clearly, he has been misinformed.

With a smile, I say, "Well, it's good to know that you will turn up if you hear I'm in trouble."

"That is true, Kara. But this time, it appears I've made a grave mistake." He nods to the giantess, who is rising with a promise to kill written on her face. "My apologies, Angrboda. I was misled." Twirling his arm, he swings his hammer and lets himself be carried away by the momentum, out of sight.

Taking in Angrboda's face, I groan. "Thor thought you were hurting us. I'm sorry."

Completely risen to her feet, she growls and leers over me. "Your apology for your stupid god is not accepted. You can forget receiving any help from me. You're lucky I don't kill the lot of you now. You're nothing to me." She straightens and stomps off.

When she's gone, I groan. "What are we going to do now?"

"That was a waste of a mission," Eir says.

"You don't have to tell me." I check the straps of the saddle on Sobek, tightening any loose belts. "We came all of this way for nothing. She's not going to help us the slightest bit, even if it is also for other realms." I expel a massive groan and stomp my feet. "Now I have to return to Asgard with nothing. This is embarrassing and a disappointment."

Britta rests a hand on my shoulder. "At least you can blame Thor if he gets testy over a fruitless trip."

Hildr slides her sword back into its sheath. "That has some truth to it. She was going to cooperate with you a little bit. I don't know if it would have been much help."

"I guess. Really though, I don't think she was going to help us. It was going to be a pretty useless trip."

It wasn't all bad. Sobek sits next to me, his eyes soft with admiration. *After all, you got to meet Loki's mistress.*

"Sobek. Get over it. She's just a frost giant in a female form, an enemy of Asgard, Valkyries, and dragons alike." I shake my head. "No amount of beauty is worth that much trouble."

But I'm sure she liked me. Didn't you see? Sobek swoons. *She even kissed me and rubbed my body.*

"Probably because you stared at her with adoring eyes," I say. "You looked like you were about to smother her with love kisses."

Well, she is gorgeous. Sobek drools.

I groan. "Let's go. We didn't get anywhere, and I want to go home to contemplate my next move before Odin finds out." Sobek sinks onto his chest, and I yank myself up onto the saddle. "Take me straight home, please, Sobek." My body slumps over in defeat. "Take me home as quickly as possible. I want to go back to safety and away from this dreaded land filled with frost giants."

- Chapter Twenty-Two -

Sobek extends his wings, and we glide down to the apartment Hildr, Britta, Eir, and I share. The golden dragon lands on the ground with a soft thud. I climb off and immediately unbuckle the straps. With a slight tug, the saddle slides off his back and down his side. Hunkering down, I drag it to the apartment as the three soft thuds from the other dragons sound behind me.

"This is it." I circle to the front of Sobek and face him. "Thank you for your assistance, Sobek." I purse my lips. "It's been interesting, but I couldn't have done it without you."

Sobek puffs out his chest. *I know you couldn't have done it without me. And you would've been bored if I didn't come.*

"Without Elan, that might have been true... although I'm sure I'd find all dragons interesting." I stop myself, realizing I sound ungrateful. "Still, thank you for taking me." As the other three Valkyries remove the saddles from their dragons, I rest a hand on his snout. "Are you going to visit your sister now?"

No. We've only been gone for about two days. I'm sure she's fine, and I need to get back to Mother to tell her that my sister is okay. When I gaze at him in disbelief, he continues, *We're not that close, you know.*

I shrug. "I'm going to see Elan as soon as I can. I want to see how she's doing. Don't you want to come with me?"

I'll see her next time. Sobek pushes off into the sky, flapping his enormous wings. Dust and dirt billow from the ground, surrounding me. Sheltering my eyes, I blink up at his spectacular form.

"Elan's brother is rather… interesting." Eir stands beside me, her chest heaving as she catches her breath after having moved the saddle.

I cross my arms. "You don't need to tell me. Elan has her humor, and it's often mischievous, yet it's different from Sobek's. Even so, I couldn't have made the trip without him."

Hildr and Britta pull at their dragons' saddles, which land on the ground with a thud. A trail cuts through the dirt as they drag them toward the apartment, next to mine, exhaustion riddling their faces.

"What are you guys going to do now?" I ask.

"I'm beat," Britta says. "I'm going to rest for a while."

"Me too." Hildr's face looks drawn, making her red hair seem brighter. "It was a tiring trip. I'm going to rest for a while, seeing nothing urgent needs addressing."

Drogon and Tanda curl up near the apartment.

Eir strokes the side of Naga's face as he nudges into her hand. "I'm going to stay with Naga for a while. Are you happy to rest here with me for a while, Naga?"

Naga nods and slumps to his stomach, and Eir stretches within his forearms, leaning back against his chest. She presses her palms together and nestles her hands under her face, almost as though she's ready to curl up and go to sleep. She looks at me with sleepy eyes. "Are you going to visit Elan, Kara?"

"Yes. I want to see if she's okay. I'm keen to find out if she is feeling any better."

Eir yawns. "Okay. I'll see you later, then."

Naga circles his head around her, resting his chin on his front talons. The blue dragon and my peaceful friend look adorable curled up together.

The trip has been a big one, and I'm not surprised the others need rest. Even though I'm exhausted, my rest can wait until after I've seen Elan. Not bothering to remove my quiver and sword, I take off to see her.

I'm so used to the weapons being on my back that I'm almost oblivious to the added weight.

When I reach the academy, I pause to catch my breath, only to find the spot where I left Elan empty. My heart speeds up, worry niggling at my core until I remind myself that she's probably healed and moved on.

A shadow passes over me as a yellow dragon glides over the academy and circles back to the training field. Legs dangle over its sides, the rider sitting firm, not flopping from side to side, unlike the last time I saw them. A few seconds later, another shadow passes over as the massive form of a dragon flips and golden scales glimmer in the sunshine. My heart leaps with joy. I would recognize that dragon anywhere. Elan glides behind the yellow dragon and rider. She must be helping them learn.

With a smile, I immediately sprint to the dragon rider's training field, ignoring the screams of protest from my exhausted body. Nothing is going to hold me back from seeing my beautiful golden dragon and best friend.

The yellow dragon lands smoothly, and Elan follows her. Even though I'm not included in Elan's projected words, I can see the excitement in her reactions as she dances on her back feet and extends her wings. Joy beams from her golden face as she communicates with the yellow dragon and its rider.

The wingless Valkyrie tucks a hand underneath the yellow scales, connecting with the dragon's soft flesh and expressing the growing trust between the dragon and its rider. As I approach from the side, I can see a broad smile on the Valkyrie's face. The improvement is remarkable, with a little guidance.

My running footsteps alert Elan's sharp dragon ears of my approach. She spins, her face stern until she catches sight of me and flashes a toothy grin.

Kara! You got home okay! She rears, and her talons move in a happy dance before she charges forward, not slowing until I slam into her nose. I grunt from the force and wrap my arms around her.

Before I can speak, the other dragon rider sneaks up behind Elan, her yellow dragon following. She runs her fingers through her dark shoulder-length hair, looking almost bashful. "Thank you, Elan. We're going to leave you to catch up with Kara. Thank you so much for your help," she repeats before turning to lead her dragon away without waiting for an answer.

Anytime! Elan calls after her, with a voice full of enthusiasm. *I'll see you later.* As they disappear into the distance, she turns her attention back to me. Her beautiful golden membranous wings spread with excitement and wrap around me.

My heart melts with satisfaction. "It's so good to see you up and about, Elan. You must be feeling better." I pull back. "Look at you."

Her chest puffs out. *Of course I'm feeling better. My best Valkyrie friend has returned, and she's in one piece. Which dragon did you take?* She peers from under a raised scaly eyebrow.

I chuckle. "You're not going to believe it."

Believe what? she asks. *What am I not going to believe?*

"Well, Sobek dropped by just after I saw you, and he offered to take me. He said he was checking to see if you're okay so that he could pass the news on to your mother. It had been a while since I talked to him. I didn't know he had such a weird sense of humor. I didn't notice that when I was with him in the dragon wastelands." I gaze up at her face, surprised to see a frown scrunched into her dragon scales. "What's wrong?"

What do you mean by Sobek?

My jaw drops. "Your brother, of course. Your brother offered to take me to Jotunheim. He was the one that took me all the way there and back." I frown up at her confused face.

And when did you get back?

"Just a few minutes ago. Why? I came straight here."

Elan's face is grim. *Sobek visited me early this morning.*

I gape at her. "What do you mean?"

It's simple. My brother dropped in early this morning to see if I was okay. He brought me some food and had a quick chat with me before returning to the wastelands.

Frowning, I spread my hands out at my side. "But Sobek was with me."

Elan shakes her head, her eyes somber.

"Then who took me to Jotunheim?"

She drops down to her front talons and lies on her stomach, leveling her eyes with mine. *Who is an expert shape-shifter that can take on any form he chooses?*

My knees buckle beneath me, and I flop to the ground, my legs crossed. The answer escapes in a hissed whisper. "Loki!"

Elan nods, slow and melancholy.

I flop onto my back and groan, ignoring the uncomfortable weapons rattling underneath me. "How did I not get it? It makes so much sense now. The unusual humor, the mischief, the ogling over the mistress." Growling, I hit the ground with my fist. "I'm so mad at myself. Loki was literally within my reach the whole time. No wonder the dreaded Ratatoskr was a little brat. He knew it was Loki. He even told me that Loki was closer than I thought. The mistress said the same thing." I slam my palm on my forehead. "How could I be so stupid?" I groan loudly before sitting upright and grasping Elan's nose in both hands, resting my forehead on her snout. Long dark hair shields both sides of my face from the world around me, and my focus narrows on my stupidity. "No wonder he didn't land to say hello to you. You would have known it was him because of the way he acted."

It's a strong possibility, yes. Elan huffs hot steam, which warms my body. *Don't beat yourself up so much. He is a master of disguise and a trickster. We will get him. Don't worry.*

After sucking in a big breath, I ask, "Can you at least tell me—have Loki's children stopped attacking Asgard and causing mischief since his escape?"

It's only been about two days since you left. I haven't heard anything much. I believe the gods are still trying to make a chain strong enough to secure Fenrir. He's been acting up, but I think that's mainly because he's an aggravated teenager. It's only threatening because he's so big. As per usual, the Midgard Serpent is always causing mischief, but nothing more than usual. As for Hel, I don't know. I haven't seen anything other than the lava monster coming up from Helheim to cause damage to Asgard.

From behind Elan, I hear a strange sound, and I push against her scales, gazing over her body. Instantly, I jump to my feet. "Get up, Elan! I thought you said nothing was coming up from Helheim. Get up!" I yell again.

Elan springs to her feet, but she's too late.

A large black hand scoops down and secures her and me within its grasp. The dark claw closes around us, pushing us together. I peer through the cracks between digits, my face pressed against the black forms, smothered in a heat warmer than a normal hand. My eyes widen as fear fastens a hard knot of helplessness in my stomach. Peering down at us secured in this grasp are two eyes set in a coal-like exterior, the contents burning red and hot like lava.

The End

~~~~~

If you enjoyed this book, please takes a few minutes of your time to review it on Amazon. Reviews help to grow my readership.

KATRINA COPE

ENTRAPMENT

THOR'S DRAGON RIDER

BOOK 3

Thor's Dragon Rider
Book Three

ENTRAPMENT

"Kara the wingless Valkyrie and her beloved dragon companion, Elan, find themselves in deep trouble once more. Stuck in a swelteringly hot realm of molten rock and fire, they are outmatched and isolated. *Entrapment* is a claustrophobic roller-coaster ride for fans of the series!" Kelly R., Line Editor, Red Adept Editing

Entrapment

Ebook first published in USA in November 2020 by Cosy Burrow
Books

Ebook first published in Great Britain in November 2020 by Cosy
Burrow Books

www.katrinacopebooks.com

Published by Cosy Burrow Books

❀ Created with Vellum

To my readers - I'd like to apologise for the cliffhanger in the last book… right after the apology I receive from all the other books and TV series that left me hanging off the edge, begging for more.

Protecting friends is deadly.

It's happened. Hel has sent her minion to attack Asgard, or so Kara thought. She and Elan are entrapped and dragged into the depths of Muspelheim, the land of the fire giants, bringing a whole new meaning to "warm welcome."

In an attempt to retrieve the information Kara holds, creatures that live only in nightmares surface, threatening Kara's freedom and life.

- Chapter One -

E lan's golden scales crush against my chest as the lava monster's grasp tightens, squeezing us together against its palm. Extending my body is a struggle as I'm pressed flat against her scales. I have just enough room to gaze over my shoulder and peer through a crack between the dark digits.

The finger cage traps in the heat, raising the circulating temperature. Sweat breaks out on my brow and trickles into my eye. The hard surface of the lava monster's skin is warm from internal heating. Combined with the stress pumping adrenaline through my veins, it makes the enclosure almost as hot as a sauna.

A soft puff of colder breeze sneaks through the crack as I observe our surroundings, my mind racing to find a way out.

The scenery changes, and my stomach flops to my torso floor, only to rebound, tightening into a knot as an eye of red lava stares at the hand confining us. I let my magic well up. Having had no luck against the frost giants, I don't know how to combat this monstrous beast. The lava monster is just as big as the frost giants and maybe more vicious. I don't know how we're going to get out of this predicament.

"How are you feeling, Elan?" My voice is muffled against the large hand.

A little squashed. But I'm fine, other than it's my worst nightmare come true. I don't understand why it's not attacking us. It's just grabbing us. Even though her voice is internal, speaking directly into my mind, it still sounds strained. That's probably because of the pressure against her head. *How are you feeling?*

"My heart's pumping a hundred miles per hour, and the heat is causing me to sweat. I can feel it gathering in the leather down my thighs." I attempt to shift my hands to rub my legs, only to find I can hardly move them. "Other than that and being cramped, I'm fine."

Observing what little I can through the crack, I attempt to work out where we are.

"It's weird for it to be just grabbing us." An itch grows on my stomach, and I'm desperate to scratch it, with no success. "Why would Hel be targeting us? If anything, we should be safe because I accidentally let Loki go."

The hand tightens, and Elan groans. *I don't know. It doesn't make sense.*

The hand loosens slightly, and I suck in the fresh air. "Do you have any ideas on how to get out of here?"

Nope. I have no idea. She squirms to get comfortable, only to press me farther.

I grunt. "Stop moving! You're squashing me."

Her body goes deathly still. *Sorry.* Her chest expands a couple of times as she takes some breaths. *Except for the massive horn sticking out of its head, it's much like the lava monster from earlier that injured me badly.*

Slightly shifting my head enables me to see somewhat more through the crack, and I catch a brief glimpse of the monster's face. Glowing red-and-orange lava fills gaping holes resembling eyes. As I gaze into them, the sensation of death assails me. I worry my lip but halt when a flash of lightning fills the sky behind the monster's head. A booming clap of thunder reverberates the surrounding area only seconds later.

My heart skips a beat. "Is that one of Thor's electrical storms?"

Another flash of lightning forks through the sky.

I don't know, but I sure hope it is.

Something thuds. Suddenly, we jerk to one side

before being overcome by a strange feeling of floating on air, still enclosed within the giant hand. I peer out the crack, attempting to focus on the land streaking past.

The giant hits the ground with a thud, and the fist holding us slams against the solid surface. The impact reverberates through my body, banging my body harder against Elan's scales before slapping me against the palm.

The sliver of a crack between its clenched fingers opens wider. I peer out in time to see the ground bounce underneath us, and something careens through the sky. Focusing on the flying object, I see Mjolnir charging through the air and landing right back in Thor's hands.

I gasp. "It is Thor!"

He stands with his feet splayed shoulder distance apart as he releases Mjolnir again and braces for the hammer's impact, and his shoulder jerks backward when it slams back into his hand.

I can see. Excitement fills Elan's voice.

My breath catches as he launches the hammer at the giant, bracing for another hit. His movements are so fluid and quick that the giant doesn't have time to rise to its feet. Even so, the impact flings the giant lava monster across the ground, the hand around us refusing to release its grip.

Mjolnir yanks free from the giant's abdomen, returning at Thor's call, the head of the hammer glowing golden red as though it had been embedded in a fiery lava pit. The color changes back to silver as the metal cools before it slams back into Thor's hand. The hammer must've gone straight through the lava monster to make it glow like that. I'm astonished that the lava monster is still clasping us.

A strange groan fills the air, and the monster's body shudders as it rises to its feet. In a muffled and unnatural voice that's barely decipherable, it says, "I have no quarrel with you, Thor, God of Thunder. I'm not attacking Asgard. There is no reason for your attack on me."

With his hammer raised and feet splayed, ready for a fight, Thor narrows his eyes. "Besides being on Asgard without invitation, you have captured my Valkyrie and her dragon. This action alone has instantly made you my enemy."

The giant releases a displeased grunt. "I will not release this Valkyrie and dragon." The monster bends low, releasing words filled with determination that sound like they are being gargled through a bubbling lava stream. "I must return with this Valkyrie and her companion. It's my command to do so or not to return at all."

Thor pulls the raised hammer back, his voice

deep and loud as he matches the monster's intensity. "Then you shall not return at all." His shoulder thrusts forward as he releases the hammer straight at the lava monster's face.

My heart skips with hope and ripples with cheer, thankful that Thor is on my side. Unsuccessfully, I attempt to clap my squashed hands as the hammer careens straight for the monster's face.

Disappointment grips me when the monster jerks, and Thor's face twists with disappointment. The beast must have shifted its head to the side, causing Mjolnir to miss. The lack of any jarring fuels my assumption.

Quickly, Thor wipes his failure off his face when his hammer lands back in his hand, and he holds its massive form high. Lightning cracks through the sky, and thunder booms, rumbling the ground and shaking the monster's enormous form. Several more lightning bolts shoot from the sky to the hammer before charging back up then aiming for the beast. The lava monster jumps aside, and the lightning narrowly misses the giant's form and singes a black patch on the ground.

Twisting my palm around, I release my stored magic, trying to give the lava monster a jolt of pain on its hand. I cringe as the fingers curl, and the gap around us tightens. Instead of releasing us or opening its grip farther, the magic shock causes the hand to constrict rather than retract.

What just happened? Elan grunts, thankfully remaining still.

Grasping my next breath to answer is a struggle. "I just tried magic to get the monster to open its grip on us. It appears to have had an opposite effect."

Then maybe you should keep your magic to yourself, Elan gripes.

I grumble. "Sorry. But at least I tried."

Another crack grabs our attention as Thor holds Mjolnir high, lightning splitting the sky in all directions until it redirects and aims at the lava monster. The beast twists at the last split second, causing the lightning bolt to miss it again. I'm shocked that something so big can move so quickly. Either that, or it's just dumb luck.

Disappointment and frustration cloud Thor's face. He spins and releases his hammer, using Mjolnir's projection to fly his body straight at the monster's feet, knocking the beast to the ground. The jolt shoots through the whole body, including its hand, as its backside hits the ground. I wish all this jerking and jumping would cause the lava monster to release us, but my wish goes ungranted, and the hand doesn't release its grip, although it does loosen enough to give us a clearer view of our surroundings.

A view of Thor getting pummeled by the lava monster and knocked away shatters my hopes. That wasn't the image I was hoping for. His body flips and rolls before grinding to a halt. Almost immediately, the monster's empty hand swipes at Thor with claws extended, ripping a hole in his pants.

Through clenched teeth, I cry with dread. *That can't be good.* Scratches like that infected Elan, rendering her unconscious and almost killing her. Getting over that injury and the magic held within the lava monster's claw marks took a long time.

Despite the pain covering his face, Thor climbs to his feet and swings his hammer, releasing it at the lava monster before staggering awkwardly. Already, his actions seem more sluggish, and the lava monster has more time to move to one side, sending Mjolnir careening past unhindered.

A massive black fist swipes at the staggering Thor, pummeling him again and sending him flying several feet in the other direction with a final hit. Thor's body flops aside like a plush doll and thumps to the ground, unmoving.

I clasp at the crack in the fingers with both hands, trying to pry them farther apart. "No!" I scream, dread riding my voice.

Elan's tail twitches beneath my feet. *What is it?*

"Thor's been scratched by the monster. He's tried to continue fighting, but the scratch is already affecting him. He's being thrashed and thrown, and he won't get up." I stare at his unmoving body, willing him to move.

Elan gripes, *Well, that's it, then. We're doomed.*

"I know it's not looking good. But we can't give up."

Hmm. I disagree. The monster hasn't released us yet, so we're officially damned. She attempts to swivel, probably to see out of a crack.

"Stop moving, Elan. You're squashing me. If you keep it up, I'm not going to be able to breathe."

Sorry. I was attempting to help, but that's useless. I can't bite the stupid monster because it's squashing my face.

The vision of Thor's lifeless body is ripped away as the lava monster swivels. Vibrations rattle us, matching the walking giant's pace as the grasp on Elan and me tightens.

- Chapter Two -

My heart sinks—not only for myself and Elan but also for what happened to Thor. The last I saw, he was sprawled on the ground, unmoving. I hope he's all right. Asgard needs him, and he is also becoming one of my friends.

My body jerks with each giant footstep the monster takes, the reverberations traveling through its enormous body. The constant shaking rattles my bones, vibrating up to my neck and head and giving me a headache. For a moment, the movement stops, giving me a reprieve, which is shattered when the giant monster shoves its hand into a large bag and drops Elan and me into the center, swinging within the material.

The dark fabric completely blocks my view, especially when the monster seals the opening shut and swings the bag. The uncomfortable feeling of floating through the air comes to an abrupt halt when we slam into something hard and warm. The monster must have tossed us over its shoulder in the sack. My assumptions are confirmed as we sway roughly from side to side, swinging out then slamming into something solid again. My headache grows, along with additional bruises as I continually slam against the hard surface, sometimes unlucky enough to be squashed under Elan's form.

Elan grimaces. *Sorry. This is uncomfortable enough for me, but at least when you collide with me, your weight isn't unbearable.*

I groan, gritting my teeth, bracing myself as we swing out, and Elan's body pummels me again, squashing me against the monster's back. My vision seems blurry inside the dim enclosure, and I feel like I want to pass out. A slight depression creeps up on me. *Here I am, trapped again.* I was going to find out ways to learn more magic and make it stronger. Instead, I've been captured by a giant monster, and I can't do anything about it. My magic isn't big or strong enough to help protect me, Elan, or Thor.

My thoughts trail off to Thor again as sadness encloses my heart. I hope the monster didn't hit him too hard, and lethal magic hasn't filled its scratch, as with Elan's injuries. The sack enveloping us swings from side to side, and I wonder why this monster hasn't tried to kill me. I don't understand why it's carrying us.

Elan groans.

"What is it?"

This bag is made out of fabric, right?

"I believe so. Why?"

No matter how much I try, my talons won't cut it.

I roll my head back in defeat. "It must be tainted with magic."

Elan huffs, and hot air fills the sack. *That would be the only explanation. These talons have cut through many things stronger than a simple piece of fabric.*

The movement changes, and the swinging motion shortens for a while, turning my headache into motion sickness. I clamp my mouth shut, willing my rising stomach contents to settle. At least Elan isn't being slammed into me. Minutes seem to turn into hours as we swing smoothly from side to side. Unable to see anything to keep my mind occupied, my eyes droop with weariness, and my mind drifts into vagueness, eventually giving in to the pull of sleep.

Nightmares riddle every strand of a dream, carrying with them my concern over Thor and what happened to him, the future of Asgard, and what will become of Elan and me. Eventually, a peace takes over my dreams, only to be jerked away when a warm breeze brushes against my face. At first, I think Elan has expelled a hot breath over me until I open my eyes. Elan is facing the opposite direction, her scales glowing a deep orange-red. My eyes widen with fascination that quickly turns to dread as I scan our surroundings. The bag has fallen away, revealing a landscape made in my worst nightmare. I didn't know a place like that existed in the land of the living.

"Am I dead?" The words were a whisper tickling my circled lips.

Elan bends to look at me, her golden eyes glowing eerily with red. *Nope. This is definitely happening.*

Bile leaks into my mouth. A dark sky looms overhead, smothering ominous tall black mountains dripping with waterfalls of burning orange lava. Only the orange embers' glow illuminates the sky and surrounding land—arid, rocky ground, more mountainous than flat, with glowing orange rivers.

Residential structures are cut into the largest mountains in the distance, with lava waterfalls falling from all sides. A gust of hot breeze brushes my face, and I back up to Elan, pressing my body against her scales, taking comfort in their hard spikiness.

An eruption sounds not far away, and a blowhole

of lava shoots several feet high, firing out splotches of orange clumps. A golden membranous wing loops around me, and I press into Elan's side. Being a dragon, she would have some natural resistance to the heat and burning magma.

The surroundings have distracted me from the lava monster's swooping hand, and it gathers us up and plunges us deep into a hole. Then the hand opens, leaving us on the black rock floor. I don't know whether that is a blessing or a curse until I realize it's placing us in a cave, sheltering us from most of the exploding lava pits. A big gaping hole lines one side of the cave, giving us a view of a large lava river flowing directly from our doorstep.

Elan's protective wing wrapped around me furls as the large hand pulls out of the entrance at the top of the cave, exposing the glowing pits substituting for eyes as the monster peers down at us as though we are the size of small rodents.

This monster is enormous. I'm not surprised Thor had a hard time fighting it on his own. The glowing eyes pull away, and the ground rumbles underneath us at the tempo of its large footsteps.

My eyes remain wide as I survey our surroundings, my arms protectively crossing over my chest. "Where are we, Elan?"

I don't know. But from what I've heard, it looks a lot like Muspelheim, the land of the fire giants.

I approach the lava river and peer over the edge. "It's not Helheim? It looks like part of the under-world, a place fit only for the dead."

The scales above her eyes bunch into a frown. *I'm not sure. But wherever we are, it doesn't look friendly.*

Beads of sweat gather on my forehead and neck, and I yank at the long dark strands of my hair, tucking the wisps behind my ear. The ground shakes in even vibrations again, and I gaze up at the hole, shaped almost like a wide chimney, to see the glowing red eyes of the lava monster have returned.

A feeling of hopelessness swamps me as I gaze into the glowing red pits fixed on us, seemingly fasci-nated by the captives in its enclosure.

I mutter to Elan, "It's certainly diligent in watching us and making sure we can't leave. However, even if it wasn't watching, the only escape route is through that hole or past the lava river." Keeping my voice low and my eyes fixed on the lava monster's, I ask, "What do you think your chances are of flying past the peering lava monster?"

Sadness fills Elan's eyes. *I don't like my chances. The lava monster's hand nearly takes up the whole of the top of the cave. I could do it in an invisible form, but you don't have your cloak, so that kind of defeats the purpose. The monster is undoubtedly taking its job seriously.*

"I still don't understand why we're here."

Elan sits on her haunches then lowers onto her stomach. *Me either.*

Dizziness washes over me, and the arrows in my quiver rattle as I sit, leaning against Elan and taking comfort in the scales poking into my side. She rests her head on her front talons, and I gaze up at the hole only to find the disturbing red eyes constantly glowering down at us.

Frustrated by being watched continuously, I yell, "Why are we here?"

The lava monster remains unmoving, the unblinking eyes staring at us.

I ask again, "Why have you brought us here?"

Met with silence, I groan. "Where even is here? Where are we?" I glower when no answer is given.

After a few moments of silence, the lava monster straightens then turns, and the ground and cave shake as something large blocks the large hole above.

I cringe. "Please tell me it didn't just block the hole with its butt."

Elan cranes her neck, staring at the sealed opening, the scales above her eyes bunching together. Her mouth turns down at the corners. *It appears so. I just hope it doesn't have to go to the toilet anytime soon.*

I shudder. "That's so gross. However, I wouldn't be surprised if the only thing coming out of that is lava. Perhaps we should move to the side."

We do so, and I press against the hard, rocky wall. Within moments, the heat radiating from the rocks has become too much, and I pull away quickly, the arrows in my quiver rattling. Everything seems to have additional warmth in this land, like an internal heat that radiates to the surface, causing everything to burn.

Splashes sound from the lava river, and I retreat into a dark corner as some kind of monster wades through the scorching lava river, thumping its way past the cave entrance.

- Chapter Three -

The darkness enveloping me causes the hairs on my body to stand on end. The shadows bring with them an eerie sensation as I sink farther back into their embrace, watching the four-legged monster trudge through the lava. Hard dark plating similar to the lava monster's exterior resembles black rocks covering the creature's body. That layer looks like the scales of a dragon but lacks their beautiful colors and finesse. Whatever the thing is, it seems to hold off the molten river's searing heat, leaving the monster unaffected.

The lava bends like thick mud around the long legs of the creature as it trudges downstream through the river. The rigid plates around its mouth pull back, exposing a threatening display of teeth. It appears to be enjoying the river's scorching heat, trudging farther and swishing its head from side to side. Throwing its head back, it lets out a roar, opening a mouth filled with burning red magma. Long black spikes trail down its back, along the spine on an animal similar to a hound, except for the burning red eyes peering our direction. Its enormous legs trudge forward, its short tail dipping its tip in the melted river.

The creature sways our way, and my hands instinctively reach for my bow and nock an arrow. Gazing down the shaft, I wonder if it would do any damage at all if I hit the creature.

The doglike creature's tail finally passes the entrance, and I breathe out a sigh of relief. This whole realm, black and glowing with red, seems dangerous and uninviting. I long for the tall marble pillars and stony mountains of Asgard. Despite not being as green and welcoming as Midgard, they are still beautiful to me. Even the lack of Thor's playful taunting fills me with homesickness.

My gaze remains fixed to the last spot the four-legged monster was visible as I pack my bow and arrow away. "What do you think they want from us, Elan?" Briefly, I gaze up at the blocked hole, where the lava monster remains. "Why do you think they captured us?"

Elan steps away from the wall. *I have no idea. And if they were just after you, why did they capture me? Don't they think that I will put up a fight to protect you?*

I smirk. "Don't they think I'll put up a fight to protect *you?*"

She lowers her head to my height, and I grab her horn, tugging at it playfully.

Releasing her horn, I say, "Not that I think either of us has a chance of defending against these things alone. I'm only at the beginning of learning how to use my magic. It's not strong enough to use against these things."

Elan lies on her stomach, and I lean against her, leaving the quiver of rattling arrows on my back. I'm too afraid to take them off, in case we have to move in a hurry. After several uneventful minutes tick past, I rest my head against Elan's side and gaze up at the large backside—or whatever part of the lava monster that is—blocking the hole. The heat is wearing at me, making me sleepy even though my nerves are fully alert.

After a little while, the air pressure around us shifts as the monster moves from above us, revealing a part of the red-glowing sky. A puff of breeze drifts through the cave, and even though it was warm, the temperature drops slightly, bringing some relief from the trapped hot air and removing some of the stench of the heated minerals.

Elan cranes her neck, looking at the hole. *I wish I could see the stars. I miss them already.*

Expelling a sigh, I breathe. "Me too. What do you think the lava monster's doing?"

I don't know, but if that hole remains open, I think I'm going to try to fly out eventually. I'll wait and see. Hearing her voice inside my head brings me comfort, and my spirit soars over the thought of escape. Hiding my emotions takes an effort. The last thing we need is for the monster holding us captive to be able to read my body language.

Elan rests her head back on her front talons, her eyes trained on the hole. *The problem is I can't see if the lava monster is hanging around the outside or if it's gone.*

I pick lightly at the edge of one of the scales on her front leg. "That could be a problem."

We remain huddled together, and the ground beneath us vibrates slightly while rocks tumble from the sides of the cave above us. Our attention is pulled from the gloomy redness illuminating the hole to the cave, and Elan instantly shelters me with her wing. The ground and cave shake in rhythms different from the walking of the lava monster. The ache in my head is almost gone, only to be brought back with each vibration. My weapons rattle against my back, and the ground shakes so much that I have to stand to avert the pain in my bony backside.

With a question in my eyes, I gaze at Elan.

I have no idea. But the closer it seems to be and the

more it seems to vibrate, the more I think it's the pace of a giant's footsteps.

A shudder runs down my spine. "Great! Just what we need."

The shaking of the ground continues, and I pay attention to the tempo. Elan could be right. It could easily be the even pace of large giant footsteps, except these seem heavier, with a longer time between them than the footsteps of the frost giants we met in Jotunheim.

With wide eyes, I meet Elan's gaze. "How big would the giant be to make footsteps that far apart and that heavy?"

I don't know. Even in my head, Elan's voice is a hushed whisper. *I thought the lava giant was big enough. These footsteps seem heavier somehow.*

Larger rocks clatter off the cave interior and drop down, one narrowly missing my hand resting on a tall boulder. I yank it away and snuggle closer to Elan and the protection she offers with her wing. She wraps her wing around me, tucking me close to her hard scales. The heavier the footsteps become, the larger the rocks that topple from the cave's sides, some of them half the size of a human. I fret for Elan. Even with her tough scales, if they fell on her, they could still cause her harm.

As I peer out from under her wing, I spot a large

human-sized boulder toppling toward us, and I send out a bolt of magic, shattering it and sending slivers of black rock shooting in the opposite direction. I'm tempted to hold the rocks in place with magic, but I want to leave as much of my magic stores as possible ready for whatever is coming. Elan's wing tightens closer around me, squishing me against her body and tucking me slightly underneath her.

Unable to see much through the tiny crack she has left, I duck under her body and peer from under her forelegs. "I can't imagine something causing this much destruction to the ground is going to bring us good news."

We will take this as it comes. We have been through much together and will work out how to get through this.

I press against one of her large golden forelegs and inspect the hole above. The slow and steady footsteps approach until, eventually, something passes over. I brace myself, standing under Elan's huge form with my feet hip-width apart and hands balled into fists as the thing passes over. Something long and about the width of two of my arms curves in a seemingly never-ending loop. I haven't seen the beginning or the end. Eventually, it leads to something denser, blocking out the red glow in the sky. I squint, trying to work out what it is until one glowing red eye peers down at us, followed closely by another. The scrutinizing stare ties my stomach in knots. *Some pupils wouldn't go amiss on these creatures with lava-filled eye sockets.* The face alone tells me that this monster is even larger than the lava monster that left us here.

As an automatic response, I reach for the sword strapped under my quiver on my back. The scraping steel groans its protest, echoing through the cave as I yank it from its sheath and fling it upward. The metal gleams golden against the light of the lava, aiming straight for the hole, point first. With my magic, I guide the tip true to the target. At the same time, I grasp my bow and nock an arrow then send it directly at whatever is peering into this cave.

The thing moves, swatting my sword toward the burning lava river as though it was a fly. I call my sword with my magic, coaxing it to use its wings and return to me. I trust this will work as the arrow aims straight at the monster's eye. The monster swipes again, this time missing the target. The giant monster grumbles, and its eyes narrow as it pulls back, allowing the arrow to pass unhindered. A rumbling sound tumbles into the cave, resembling laughter drowned in lava.

Elan lowers her backside and braces her front legs as she roars the loudest and most impressive roar I've heard from her. It echoes up the cave and out of the tunnel. I wait, hoping this will have some effect on the monster. It does, but not the kind I was hoping for. The beast throws its head back, and explosive laughter thunders through the air.

Elan tilts her head to the side. *Dragon scales! What is this thing?*

"I have no idea." I wrap an arm around her front leg. "But clearly, it doesn't take us seriously."

Elan exposes her teeth in a silent snarl. *I know. How insulting!*

Despite myself, I can see the funny side and cackle briefly, receiving a glare from Elan. I shrug. "This thing is huge. How could it be threatened by something as small as us? It could swallow the two of us in one mouthful. Like we think we have a chance against this." I pull away the long dark strands of hair sticking to my sweaty neck. "It was quite pathetic of us."

My humor dissipates as the giant monster raises a sword engulfed in flames.

Distracted by the flaming sword, I almost miss my sword's singing as the magical wings bring it back to me. A high-pitched whistle grabs my attention, and I catch it a split second before it collides with me. Clasping the hilt, I hold it across my front, poised and ready, even if the gesture is useless. I'm never giving up without a fight.

I set my jaw and fix determined eyes on the monstrous beast peering down at us.

Illuminated by the flaming sword, a malicious grin spreads across its face, and its glowing insides shine past a surprisingly broad array of sharp teeth. The head tilts to one side, and an eye narrows at us, having a closer look before pulling away. The added distance exposes the long, curving thing's identity as an enormous horn curling down the massive form to the waist. Several smaller horns, which resemble the impressive horns of a large goat, protrude from the head around the larger one. Exposed, impressively broad shoulders top a bare muscled chest and protruding pecs that would leave any warrior envious. I hoped this was a male, as the chest defined, and the largest of the creatures of this wretched realm.

The strange rumbling continues, growing louder when the creature opens his fiery mouth, and the sound explodes with laughter.

With a voice so deep that it sounds as though it has risen from the depths of the realm, he says, "Did you think that little sword and little arrow would do something to me?"

I scowl, and his grin spreads.

"Or did your dragon think that their roar would scare me off?" His laughter pauses as he observes us then throws his head back. "That's hilarious!"

The ground shakes violently, and I bend my knees to combat the rumbling and avoid more falling rocks. I imagine the only explanation for this destruction is that the monster has stomped his foot while laughing —the destruction growing as the laughter crescendos.

I almost feel insulted, Elan grumbles.

Crossing my arms and glaring up at the giant monster, I say softly into her ear, "I don't know about almost. I *am* insulted. Who does he think he is?

Although admittedly, he is a lot larger than us, so I guess he has a point."

More rocks scatter to the ground around me, and I dodge to the center of the cavern. Unwilling to let them hit my head, Elan towers over me, her protectiveness rewarding her with several stones falling on her body. Her lips pull back, baring her broad array of sharp teeth at the monster.

Annoyed by his continued taunting, I call up to him, "What do you want with us?"

His cackling halts, and I continue, making the most of the silence. "I can't imagine dragging a Valkyrie and her dragon here is your normal entertainment." Huffing, I pull my arms into a tighter cross.

The ground stops shaking, and he peers down at us, a curious expression crossing his hardened grotesque face, resembling both man and monster. "You are not here for my entertainment, mark my words. I wouldn't go through so much trouble to grab you or bring you here."

Not staring at his lava pit of a maw is hard. Every time he opens his mouth to speak, a fiery red burns within, making it hard to concentrate. Still, I control my emotions and splay my legs. "Then why did you bring us here?"

The giant monster straightens his back, showing us his full height with the added distance through the hole, and tucks his chin. The cave entrance frames his face and some of his body, exposing more of his bare muscled abdomen. "Do you not know who I am?"

"No. Why would I? I have hardly even heard of this place. That's assuming we're in Helheim." I lift an eyebrow. "Is that where we are?"

His monstrous hairless brows lower. "No. You're in Muspelheim."

I fail to hide the shock on my face.

"Don't they teach you about this realm in Asgard?" he asks.

"We were taught very little about Muspelheim at the Valkyrie academy. It isn't a place we would normally go. As you probably know, our main focus is on Midgard."

His hairless eyebrow arches, and he waves his sword. "Ah, yes. So you can reap the souls of the brave warriors for Valhalla."

Keeping a straight face takes all my strength. I didn't know that was common knowledge.

He grins. "Don't worry. It isn't a secret. I know Midgard is the place you go because you are after the poor warriors' souls, enslaving them to Valhalla for eternity."

I stare at him. "I wouldn't say that exactly. How do you know so much about what we do?"

The huge male clasps his stomach, his fingers rippling over his six-pack, and lifts his chin as he bends backward, roaring his laughter to the sky. "Your naivete is rather amusing." He chuckles until it mellows into amused huffs. "I can't believe you know so little about me and my realm."

I grunt, unamused that he is finding me so comical and angry at feeling foolish. My thoughts turn toward the Valkyrie academy. We should've learned more about the realms other than Midgard and Asgard. I've learned more about the different realms since serving under Thor than I did during my years at the academy.

Elan's voice interrupts my thoughts. *Don't beat yourself up. He's baiting you. Valkyries aren't meant to be fighting in every realm. They're meant only for only one purpose. You must remember your role changed when you were chosen to be Thor's representative. It's a higher purpose than merely reaping souls for Valhalla.*

"Reaping souls is an important role for Asgard," I argue.

Exactly! You should be proud of that, not ashamed because you don't know everything about other realms.

I pull my gaze from the giant mocking me to Elan, finding her golden eyes gleaming down at me with compassion and pride. Yet again, I'm thankful that this dragon and her mother have chosen to represent me and support my struggles. Because of them, I have turned my services into something more powerful than simply getting wingless Valkyries recognized for being more than just slaves.

"Did I ever mention how much I appreciate your support and friendship, Elan? I thank my lucky stars every single day that you entered my life."

Her head tilts to the side, and a funny little smirk spread across her face. *No. You haven't actually said that.* She lifts a scaly eyebrow. *But I know, and the feeling is mutual.* She quickly shoves me with her nose, affection in her golden eyes.

Despite our situation, I smile. "All those things wouldn't have been achievable if I didn't have the support of you and your family and if they hadn't convinced the other dragons. Even if we don't make it through this, I'm extremely thankful that I lived my short life with you in it."

Her brows push together. *Hey. We can get through this.* She flicks her nose briefly at the giant monster, still staring down at us. *This has got to be another idiot giant with the brain capacity of a nut. I hear they are quite dumb. You must've seen that on Jotunheim.*

Pushing my lips to one side, I stare up at him. "I

don't know, Elan. This one seems to have a few more brains than the frost giants."

Large red eyes zoom in at us as they peer into the hole. "What are you two talking about?" His head tilts, and he seals the hole briefly with one eye as he gets a closer look at us. "Are you planning to escape?" His voice reeks of amusement. "If you do, you will be unsuccessful." He straightens, pulling his face farther away and giving us another a full view of his monstrosity. "Although it would make life rather interesting, you could at least let me introduce myself before you plot to leave. I am Surt, the leader of Muspelheim and the fire giants."

I frown. "I thought this was part of Helheim and under the leadership of Hel."

"Is that what they're telling you these days?" He taunts me again with his amusement. "How little you know about Muspelheim."

"Then educate us!" I snap. "Didn't Hel send one of your lava monsters to Asgard to attack us as a warning?"

Surt snorts, and fragments of molten lava fall to the ground around us, but not before Elan covers me with her fireproof body, protecting me from the burning debris. I think the snort was supposed to be laughter, but I wasn't sure. When the burning embers stop falling, I peer past Elan's wing at him.

His massive lava-filled mouth turns up at the corners in what I guess is a smile. "Oh, how you are wrong. As if I'd send my pet to Asgard for Hel's bidding. For a start, she would have to give me something in return. In order to do that, she would have to speak to me." He rubs his upper arm. "Except for rare occasions, she speaks to no one but the dead." He shrugs. "I'm too alive for her to be bothered with me."

My brow crinkles into a frown. I find it hard to believe that anything that burns internally with lava could be alive. I push this thought aside. That's a consideration for another day. "But a lava monster attacked Asgard," I protest.

Surt shakes his massive head, the long, curved horns swiping at a few floating embers. "No. The lava monster was not attacking Asgard. The lava monster was there to get you."

"What?" I stare at him in confusion. "But that was a little while ago. Why would you send a lava monster to get us?"

"No. I sent my minion to get *you*." Surt's mouth settles into a straight line.

I set my fists on my hips. "So you sent it to attack me?"

"No. You're not listening." Annoyance creases the gap between Surt's fiery eyes. "I sent it to collect you."

"Then why did it attack Elan?"

"Because your dragon is always with you, and I'm guessing she went into defense mode and attacked first."

"It nearly killed her," I growl.

Surt's massive shoulders rise in a shrug. "What can I say? It was defending itself."

The answer doesn't sit right with me, but I didn't

see what unfolded when I was within the tunnel's confines. Although I knew my heart was always going to believe Elan.

He must have read the disbelief on my face. "My pet turned up to collect you. It would have sensed you and followed you. Except your dragon blocked the tunnel you disappeared into, and she attacked it. My pet, or what you call a lava monster, was attacked by your dragon. It was only retaliating and trying to get rid of your dragon so it could get to you."

I cross my arms over my chest. "That's a rather extravagant way to try to collect me. I don't understand how you would even know that when you weren't there."

His lava-filled smile sends a chill down my spine. "I have my ways."

"How?" Raising an eyebrow, I press the point. "How could you possibly know what happened?"

"Let's just say I have friends in places, and I received a message."

Moving out from under Elan's protection, I uncross my arms. "I still don't understand why you'd be bothered to get me. If you're after Thor, he was there trying to stop this monster from getting me. He was protecting me, and the monster could have grabbed him instead."

Surt chuckles. "I'm not after Thor."

I flail my arms out to the sides. "I can think of no other reason why you would want me here."

Surt gazes at Elan. "Despite that you've befriended the dragons and turned them into friends, for not only yourself but also all the other Valkyries and the gods and Asgard."

I need all my might to clamp my mouth shut and stop my jaw from dropping. *Has the result of my small personal quest spread through the nine realms?* "Well, yes. I don't see how that is your business."

He huffs, and light embers shoot out of his nose and float on the air. "That is mostly true. It doesn't involve me. But the reason I've grabbed you is that, for many years, I've been looking for a mate."

Despite my situation, I laugh, shaking my head. "Your mate is certainly not going to be me."

"You." He scowls with disapproval. "No. It's not you. You are too violent and aggressive. You aren't the most beautiful maiden that I have seen."

I lay on the sarcasm. "Gee, thanks. I still don't get why you would want to grab me."

"It's because you have access to the most beautiful maiden in the world." His gaze turns dreamy as he focuses on the lava-lit sky.

My mind swirls, trying to figure out who he is thinking about. Unable to come to any conclusions, I say, "You'll have to help me out. The only maidens I know are Valkyries—and some goddesses, but I have little to do with them."

He leans over the gap above the cave, his burning lava eyes narrowing on me again. "And that is where you are lying."

"What?" I bellow in outrage. "I'm not lying!"

"Hmmm!" He sounds unconvinced. "I have it on good authority that you know who I am talking about and you have access to her."

As though sensing a threat, Elan steps protectively over me, ready to block me from anything he may send my way. I rest a hand on the scales on her chest, a silent thank you before stepping out from under her protection. With nothing to hide, I face him directly. "I honestly don't know who you are talking about. I have contact with hardly any other females, and the goddesses don't pay me any attention."

"And that is where you are wrong." His voice thunders down the hole, and his brows crowd angrily over his burning eyes.

With one swift movement, Elan wraps her wings around me, leaving only my face exposed, giving me room to assess the situation.

Something hits the side of the cave, and rocks drop into the cave, narrowly missing us. "I know you have access to Freya." A threat stains Surt's voice. "I want her to be my wife, and I can never find her. But one day, she will be my wife."

The sides of the cave shake again as more rocks drop around us. I wriggle under Elan's protection to free my arms and blast the falling stones away with my magic.

With an open-mouthed gaze, I find my voice faltering. Pushing past the blockage takes a few moments, but I say, "I don't know why you think I'd know her. As far as I know, she doesn't even live on Asgard."

In truth, I spent time with Freya a couple of years ago. Despite being the goddess who rules over the Valkyries' natural enemies, the angels of death, she helped me protect Asgard. She instructed our known enemies to fight for Asgard's safety against the dark elves' invasion and Loki's army of wild dragons with dwarf giant riders. From my brief encounter with Freya, I learned she is sensual and thrives on love and understanding, the opposite of the fiery abnormality standing in front of me, the leader of the fire giants. He doesn't deserve Freya's affection, and I could never see her giving it to him. Furthermore, because she has been kind to us and helped against the attack on Asgard, I could never give up her location even if I did know where it was—which I don't.

Since my association with Freya isn't a secret on

Asgard, as it's known that I called her for help, I tell him part of the truth. "I don't know where she is. I haven't seen her for at least two years. As far as I understand, her residence is shrouded in secrecy."

He clasps the entrance of the cave with both hands and glowers down at me. "But I have it on good authority that you have been to her residence."

I gulp. Somehow, he has gathered information on me and my movements. "She did have me taken to her location. But I still don't know where that is. I was blindfolded and kept from knowing the location of her camp." And now that I hear this giant demanding her location, I understand the reason behind that secrecy.

More rocks crash around us as his grip of the cave tightens. Elan and I dodge the falling debris until the chaos stills. I stand on a large boulder that landed near me. If he keeps this up, the level of the rocks will lift us closer to him. A growl rumbles down through the entrance, whose shape accentuates the volume, and I clench my teeth, cringing.

His gaze is threatening. "I do not believe you are telling the truth. Would you like to start again?"

"I am telling the truth. I haven't seen her since that time a couple of years ago. I don't know where she is or where she stays."

After another crash, more rocks rumble into the

cave, and I miss deflecting one that rebounds and crashes onto Elan's side. She flinches as it tumbles over the canopy of her extended wings, attempting to protect me, and I flinch as it falls to the ground.

Another loud grumble reverberates through the cave. "I know you know more than you're letting on. You must come clean with me. The sooner you do this, the sooner I'll let you out without harming you… and your dragon," he adds at the last second. "But if you don't come clean with me, this promise is void. I will leave you in here, stewing over the consequences of your silence. You cannot leave this realm without my help or the help of my pets."

My silence only seems to aggravate him more. He pushes off the cave and stomps off, the ground rumbling with each step.

- Chapter Six -

S etting my jaw, I gaze at the last spot I saw Surt. I don't like our situation, but I couldn't give up Freya's location even if I knew. The canopy of Elan's golden wing retracts from over me, accompanied by a wince, pulling my attention back to my friend. The offending rock lies only a few feet away. It's huge.

Rounding her large form, I try to peer at the spot the boulder hit on her back. "Are you okay, Elan?"

She attempts to cover a small grunt that escapes her when she moves to face me. *Yes. A little bruised, but not too bad.*

"You didn't have the saddle to protect your back." Regret nibbled at me even though it was an honest oversight, considering I didn't know we were about to be kidnapped by a lava monster. "I left it next to my apartment after I took it off Sobek, I mean Loki." I growl at my error.

Elan nudges me with her snout. *I'll be fine. It's just a bruise. My scales protect a lot of that, remember?*

"I know. But it still would've hurt. I heard the impact, and it was a huge boulder." I continue to assess her scales. "Any broken bones?"

Kara! Stop fussing. We have to get out of here. Remember, that's the most important thing to focus on. I'm guessing you're not going to tell him where Freya is. She lowers her head, leveling her gaze at me. *Not that I want you to.*

"No. I'm definitely not going to tell him where Freya is. But it's true: I don't know where she is. Even if I did, I wouldn't tell him. She deserves much better than him, no matter what he threatens us with. Besides, I don't give up friends who help Asgard or me."

Elan scoffs. *She can definitely do better than him. That wouldn't be hard!*

Burning with annoyance, I glare up at the hole of the cave. "What is it with the gods thinking they can take any goddess as their wife? So old-fashioned."

Yeah, just like they think they can own all the dragons and control them and make them agree to unfair alliances, Elan says with spite.

"We worked on their attitudes and treatment of the dragons and ended up with a fair outcome. Don't you think?"

Of course. I was just using it as a reference to their selfishness.

"Indeed. Maybe we can work on changing their view on goddesses and thinking they can own them."

Sounds good. Then maybe we can stop them viewing Valkyries as only battle maidens who aren't supposed to get married and settle down and have children. Or if they do have children, it can only be with particular warriors to create more Valkyries.

I huff a laugh. "I don't think it's quite that bad, but close. That view is very old-fashioned as well. Thankfully, they haven't tried to pawn me off to create Valkyrie babies."

They probably think you have a few more good battle years in you before they start using you for breeding.

"I'm not going to do it." I kick a rock, and it clatters across the ground. "There's no way they can pair me off with someone."

Elan tilts her head to one side. *I can see this will be another battle you're going to have to face and try to overcome.*

I glare at her.

Hey! She retreats and straightens her back. *It's not my fault. I completely agree with you. It's another thing we'll work on with the gods and the head Valkyries.*

My chest heaves with a massive sigh. "I know. It's

not something I want to think about. Thanks for bringing it up." I roll my eyes.

Rocks clatter to the side, knocked by Elan's talons as she paces the cave, her gaze traveling to the hole above and the opening toward the lava river. *What do you think? Should I try to fly out of here?*

Happy for the change of subject, I join her and assess the openings available. "I would say our only chance would be past the river," I muse.

Rumbling sounds from above, and the hole above is blocked again, I assume by the backside of the lava monster.

I huff in disgust. "Are we looking at the lava monster's butt again?"

I think so. If it is, it certainly has a strange but effective way of blocking the hole. Although I think it forgets that I have wings.

Something moves over the entrance opening to the river of lava, and disappointment crumples Elan's facial scales when solid black legs dangle past it. The legs don't block the entire entrance yet remain a deterrent and a promise of a warning.

"I guess that's our answer. It hasn't forgotten you have wings. I'd say it thinks it can catch you on your way out." My heart sinks at the thought. "I wouldn't know which direction to go anyway. From what I can see, the land is covered in black rock and flowing lava, giving very few distinctive landmarks, and I certainly can't see the Yggdrasil."

The world tree must be here somewhere. Maybe it looks different down here. It's supposed to touch all nine realms. Elan sits on her haunches. *And I assume the giant brought us down here through the Yggdrasil.*

Anger churns deep within as I stare at the hanging legs that swing once as though reminding us of their presence. I stoop down and pick up one of the many fallen rocks, one that fits perfectly in my hand. I toss it then catch it in the same hand, glaring at the obstacle threatening our freedom before being overcome by temptation. I peg it at one of the dangling legs. A loud clank reverberates through the cave as it collides with the back of the lava monster's calf. The leg flicks forward for a few seconds before swinging back over the opening menacingly.

The walls of the cave rumble as the legs slowly swing wide and more rocks crumble from the inside lining, falling around us. Glowing pits resembling eyes peer over the edge of the river opening at us, the red flashing in a warning that it's still watching us, waiting for us to try to escape.

Instantly, Elan shifts in front of me to block any threat from the monster. Her wings drape around me, leaving me to peer out from behind her front legs. The lack of pupils makes it impossible to tell who the eyes are looking at or if they can see me.

"I guess that answers our question," I say softly.

Elan's protective stance remains unwavering until the monster finally pulls away, taking its fiery red glare with it. The draping legs kick out and swing back into position, partially blocking the entrance to the river. Rocks clatter around us again, and I push them away with my magic, smashing them against the cave walls.

With the threatening pits gone, Elan says, *We're just going to have to wait for our chance. It's not going to be impossible, just tricky. That strange thing works like a dog watching over that hole.*

"Maybe it has more brains than we give it credit for."

Elan spreads her wings and shrugs. *Who knows? I wouldn't be surprised if it can sniff us out like a dog on the hunt.*

I n the dull light cast by the lava river, I collect the arrows scattered over the ground, dislodged when we were unceremoniously dumped in this cave. Only a few had managed to remain tucked in my quiver, ready to grasp when needed. At first, I was surprised that my weapons weren't confiscated, but my wonderment at remaining armed was abolished when I threw my sword and shot the arrow at Surt and he found my efforts laughable, incapable of injuring or harming him. Thanks to his reaction, I hadn't bothered collecting the weapons earlier.

With the talk of escape, a new hope infuses my veins, and I set my mind to gathering my things in preparation. Clasping my sword hilt over my shoulder, I lift it, listening to the metal sing before releasing it with the satisfaction of its accessibility.

Casting one last look around the cave, I'm satisfied that I've retrieved all lost weapons, and I slump down against Elan. Heat radiates through her scales —a warmth I don't need, yet I lean in, resting against her and soaking in her friendship and comfort. It's a welcome relief from this depressing place.

Elan curls into a ball, wrapping her head close to my body, almost in a protective enclosure. Her golden eyes glimmer in the orange glow of the lava river, her face thoughtful. The river's golden light is mesmerizing as my mind swirls with ideas and plots to free us from this entrapment. The warmth from the lava glazes my eyes, and my body thrives in the short rest as I think things through.

I tuck a hand under one of Elan's scales, touching the soft flesh underneath. The simple gesture brings so much comfort. I can even feel her body relaxing into my touch. The connection wipes away some of the stress of being kidnapped and taken to a foreign and dangerous realm.

Elan must be exhausted. She just recovered from the lava monster's first attack, only to be kidnapped, her body thrown into another explosion of stress.

Hot breath shoots out of Elan's nostrils, and she rests her head on her front feet. *Let me know if you come up with any ideas on how to get out of here. My guess is that these mind games aren't going to go away, and our only escape is planning a dash past the legs of the lava monster.*

"Something tells me that you're right, Elan. Although we can both use a little bit of rest to try to recoup energy."

Elan's eyelids close slowly before being jerked open. *Ain't that the truth.*

I wrap an arm around Elan's front leg. "I wish we had our friends here, Valkyries and dragons. We might have more of a chance. The reality is that Thor may still be unconscious, and no one will know where we are. They may not even know that we're missing."

She twists her head to land her sad eyes on me. *I hate to say it, but with the condition Thor was in when we were taken, I don't think anybody will know we're gone. I doubt anyone else saw the lava monster leaving.*

Defeat and disappointment creep into my optimism, taking over my muscles, which go lax, and I flop against Elan, her sharp scales digging into my flesh. I ignore the discomfort, taking solace in knowing my scaly friend remains by my side. "You're probably right."

I assess our surroundings, taking in every inch, and study the access points again to assess if I've overlooked a loophole that will get us out of here. I can't tell when Surt will be coming back, and when he does, if I don't give him the answer he seeks, we may need an escape route, however dire it is.

Minutes, if not hours, tick by, bringing the discomforting feeling of being lost. If not for Elan, I would be very lonely. I've studied every part of the cave, only to come up empty-handed for brilliant ideas, and my gaze returns to the lava lake, my eyes drooping with exhaustion as the warmth lures me to sleep.

A strange scratching pulls my focus upward, and I search for the source. The glow of the lava bathes everything in an orange-red light, making it hard to spot the source of the noise.

The scratching continues, and I squint, focusing within the darkness, higher than the light of the lava. But I fail to catch any movement pointing to the cause of the sound. Looming darkness, thick enough to cut, prevails in the top half of the cave, the hole remaining blocked by the lava monster.

The scratching continues, setting my nerves on edge. Worried that it might be a dangerous creature exclusive to Muspelheim, I continue searching the shadows cast by the orange light behind the jolting rocks. Eventually, something glowing a deeper orange darts across the far side of the cave. I blink. The object is hard to discern in the light from the molten lava river. Perhaps the fire embers are reflecting against something, but then it seems to glow a different kind of red. Whatever it is, it continues to move in a circular downward motion, heading toward us.

Pushing off Elan, I stand to get a clearer view of the approaching creature. My fingers tingle with anticipation, and I gather my magic while unhooking my bow and nocking an arrow to aim at whatever is scurrying along the wall.

In a place like Muspelheim, it could be anything. As Surt pointed out, I've been uneducated about this realm and the creatures it holds, other than my personal experience with the lava monster. Whatever this is, it could be just as dangerous but in a small form.

Elan shifts behind me, and her presence looms over me protectively even though my arrow remains nocked and ready to release, aimed at the anticipated location of the moving creature. As though oblivious to the threat we present, the animal continues to scamper, and its scurrying echoes as it circles around and down, crawling closer to our position.

My eyes narrow, focused entirely on this thing. It maneuvers to a rocky ledge and pauses, standing upright and exposing a furry white chest that burns with the lava river's golden glow. I squint harder. *It can't be*, I think.

"Elan, are you seeing what I'm seeing?"

Do you mean Ratatoskr? She sounds almost bored. *I*

told you Yggdrasil must come to Muspelheim somewhere even if we can't see anything that resembles a tree. He is renowned for carrying messages to every part of the realm.

I gawk at the little thing, my eyes widening as I realize the truth. Elan is right. This is that tiny, annoying rodent. He has followed me even to the depths of the fire giants' realm.

Beady little black eyes focus in my direction, peering over the sharply pointed nose. The high-pitched voice reaches my ears as he crosses his arms and leans against the rock wall. "There you are. I finally found you." He scurries down a couple more levels. "My source was right. The talk on the rumor mill is that you've been taken to Muspelheim."

My eyes narrow at the little rodent. "How could you possibly know that?"

The squirrel waves a paw at me. "You'd be surprised by the connections I have." He looks me up and down. "Clearly, this time, it was right."

He scurries farther down the cave, weaving over the jutting rock surfaces.

For a moment, my heart skips before beating rapidly, and a glimmer of hope rises to the surface as I stare at the squirrel coming my way. "Are you here to help us?"

The squirrel halts midclimb, momentarily freezing before leaping onto the next flat surface and facing me. "Are you serious?" His face is awash with disbelief. "What do you possibly think I could do in a place like this?" He spreads his arms wide and swings them wildly, indicating the blocked hole and the lava river's opening.

The erratic beat of my heart slows as I realize that was a stupid thought. The idea of this annoying, sarcastic squirrel helping us doesn't make sense. Besides his apparent lack of care for others, he's too small. He couldn't do anything against the fire giants.

I roll my eyes and lean on one hip and attempt to be insulting. "My mistake. A self-centered little creature like you wouldn't want to help anyone anyway."

Ratatoskr puffs out his chest, the white fur almost beaming with orange from the lava glow, illuminating his pride. "You got that right. Unless there's something in it for me, I'm not going to do a single thing to help you."

I scrunch up my nose with distaste. "I should've known better."

He nods, and his self-righteousness is hard to miss, coupled with a demeaning tone. "Yeah. You should have."

Glowering, I wish the sulfurous fumes from the lava river would render this little rodent unconscious. "Then what are you here for, little rodent?"

The squirrel poses his head and plasters a smirk on his face while circling a little paw around his temple. "You are a little nuts. I knew there was nothing held up here." He rotates his claw some more. "I seriously would've thought you would know better by now. This isn't the first time I've seen you."

"Right. Of course." I drag the last few words out. "You're here to bring me a message."

He shakes his head in disbelief. "Thank the Vanir! She's finally got an answer right."

- Chapter Eight -

At this moment, I can't conjure the words to describe how irate I am over this little rodent. Only moments before, I'd been longing to see a familiar face that could reconnect me with Asgard. A few short moments spent with this little critter had shattered that hope. Now, all I want to do is push his little face out of my sight.

"So, what insulting message have you brought me?" I ask, leering at him.

Ratatoskr chuckles through his teeth, his breath sucking in and out in short stints of rugged hissing. "Oh, this is a good one. I've been looking forward to delivering this one."

I shove my hands onto my hips. "Then why don't you just tell me? And then you can run on your merry little way."

Elan shifts, reminding me of her presence looming over me, attempting to protect me from harm. Even though Ratatoskr is tiny, his insults have the potential to cause more damage than something physical. My heart warms, knowing that she's here for me, no matter what. I stroke her front leg, taking pleasure in the roughness of her scales under my fingertips.

The beady eyes narrow on me. "I have a message from Odin."

My teeth clamp together, and dread travels through me. I can't help thinking of the last time I saw him sitting in his room, bedridden and weak. He still hadn't recovered from the terrible vision he had at Mimir's well.

Pulling me from my thoughts, Ratatoskr continues, "Although I don't think this is a message I would usually carry." He polishes his claws on his furry white chest. "As you know, I only bring messages with insults. I have a feeling this one carries more truth than an insult." He shrugs. "But I thought I'd bring it anyway because... I do love it!" He stretches his front paws up in the air as though he's worshipping the top of the cave.

I frown at the squirrel's excitement and focus on my concern. "Is Odin okay? Is he feeling better?"

The squirrel chuckles into his paw—his sharp teeth obscured by the tiny claws. His beady eyes torture me with their amusement, and I glower and cross my arms. When Ratatoskr is finished chuckling, he pulls his hand away and stands straight, one eyebrow cocked. "You could say that."

When he doesn't elaborate on his statement straightaway, I press him. "What do you mean?"

"As you know, Thor was injured, and he's in the healer's care. Hearing the news was enough to bring Odin out of bed to check on his son as soon as he could. Before he decided to leave his room, he was granted some final news."

When he doesn't continue, I coax him by saying, "And?" while rolling my hand as an indicator to hurry the story up.

Ratatoskr chuckles briefly into his paw again, eventually pulling it away and standing straight. "And he heard that you released Loki." The rodent's words were sharp and precise, and his mischief-filled eyes never leave me as he waits for my reaction.

A gush of air expels from my lungs, and my shoulders cave. Shame sends my gaze to the ground. "I didn't..." I stammer. "I didn't technically release him. In truth, he escaped from under my guard." I hate myself for looking at him, almost pleading for understanding, as if I could get that from this rodent.

Ratatoskr clucks his tongue. "Oh. Don't worry. Odin's been told that. But..." He shrugs. "It didn't make any difference." The smirk on his face wipes away my fleeting plea for understanding. "You should've seen how deep red his face turned. It could've matched my fur, if not that lava out there." He tosses his head backward. "And the steam coming out of his ears! Phew! I could've sworn he was a dragon." The rodent drags out his words, his tone mocking and emphasizing the severity of the actions.

I cringe, dread running down my spine, and grit my teeth. "And what was his message?" I want to cover my ears and not listen although that would achieve nothing. I have to hear what Odin had to say. I can't do anything to change my actions. I can only face the music and get it over with. Maybe he'll help Elan and me to get out of Muspelheim if I listen.

Ratatoskr stands straight, clasping his claws behind his back and puffing out his chest. "Your message from Odin is…" He sucks in a breath and clears his throat. "You are the most useless Valkyrie he has ever seen. He should have left you and your kind as slaves. He wished he didn't allow you into his mind and heart, giving you access to change the way he deals with your kind. The Valkyries without wings are an abomination and shouldn't be rewarded by serving him and reaping warriors for Valhalla."

"What?" My jaw drops as I gape, analyzing whether this was an insult or the truth. I have to agree with Ratatoskr's earlier statement. It's too close to the truth and how things used to be to think this is just an insulting message carried by Ratatoskr to get my attention.

Ratatoskr holds up a paw, his back remaining rigidly straight. "Don't yell at me. Remember—"

"You're just the messenger," I finish in a cynical tone.

He drops his paw, and amusement dances through his beady black eyes. "Yes. You're finally learning." He adds in a condescending tone, "Bravo."

Clenching my jaw, I ask, "Is that it?"

"No. There's more. That was just a small insult."

"A *small* insult?"

"Yes. I could think of more to add, but that wouldn't be Odin's words."

I can almost feel steam coming out of my ears. "Then get on with it!" I snap.

"Because of your serious mishap of letting Loki free and not catching him again even though you spent over a day with him—"

I interrupt, flailing my arms out to the sides. "That's not fair. He was in the form of Sobek, Elan's brother."

Ratatoskr raises a claw at me and shakes it. "I'm not finished. And I am not the judge and jury. I'm just passing on a message."

I roll my eyes and let impatience seep through my voice. "Then stop wasting time!"

"With pleasure." Ratatoskr puffs out his chest as though preparing for a long speech. "He said that because you let Loki out and didn't recapture him when you spent a full day with him"—he holds up a claw at me again as a warning not to interrupt—"that he now forbids you from entering Asgard. From this moment on, you are hereby banished until you have retrieved the deceitful Loki and have him secured within the mighty Odin's grasp." He lifts his chin and looks down at me. "There. I finally passed on the message."

I hate that I can't hide the hurt on my face from this conniving rodent. "What about all the good things I've done?" My bottom lip quivers. "I've done so much good for Asgard. I'm going to rectify this situation, at least eventually. But I can't do it if I'm stuck here. I don't understand. How am I ever going to get out if he isn't sending me help and is banishing me instead?"

Ratatoskr shrugs nonchalantly. "No idea. That is for you to work out. Goodbye." He scurries up the cave wall, heading toward the top, where the lava monster still blocks the entrance.

My mouth is agape as I stare up at him. "But—"

- Chapter Nine -

Traitor! Elan grumbles, sitting on her haunches.

The rodent scurries up the side of the cave, the glow of the lava river on his red coat unmistakable now that I know what to look for. My heart thumps rapidly in my chest as my brain attempts to process the unpleasant outcome and information dumped on me. I can't believe I've been banished. After a moment, I pull my thoughts together and realize that we're still stuck in the middle of Muspelheim with no one to help us escape this sweltering enclosure. As much as I don't enjoy Ratatoskr's company, my only lifeline and potential help is running toward the top of the cave.

Even though he's out of reach, I extend my arm, reaching for the faraway rodent as though I could stop him. "Wait!"

Ratatoskr pauses on a rock, his glare evident even

from a distance. "What is it now? You always do this —call me back every time I'm disappearing."

"Well, if you didn't disappear so quickly, I wouldn't have to call you back," I retort.

"I'm a busy messenger!"

"Can you please come down lower so we can discuss something?"

"I have nothing to discuss." His gaze becomes pointed with annoyance.

I roll my eyes. "The discussion is about a message I want to send."

"You know I don't discuss things," he repeats through his teeth.

"Okay. Okay. Then I want to pass on a message. Just come down and give me a moment."

He groans loudly before dramatically turning and slowly climbing back down the wall of the cave.

As I watch him, my mind swells with insults I could send to Odin. With regret, I push them away though expressing them is tempting. After all, I'm already banished and too far away to hear his punishment. By the time I see him again, his anger would probably have subsided. Humming, I marvel over the different things rattling through my head. Tempting though they are, I hope to re-enter Asgard someday, and to make that happen sooner, sending insults is probably not the best choice at this point.

The scratching claws grow louder as the squirrel closes the distance, his red form zigzagging down the rocky ledge.

Crossing my arms, I lean against Elan. "Just wondering... Have you seen Loki lately?"

Ratatoskr reaches the lowest ledge and stands straight with his paws on his hips. "What makes you think I would have seen Loki lately?"

"Oh, I don't know." I wave a hand dismissively. "Perhaps it's because you were giggling with him when he was in dragon form in Jotunheim. You could easily have informed me that he was Loki and saved me all this hassle. My friends and I could have plotted to recapture him as soon as we arrived in Asgard."

Ratatoskr tilts his head to one side. "Don't you start with me. I gave you plenty of hints that it was Loki. If you're not smart enough to put it together, it's not my fault." He shakes a claw at me. "I am not responsible for your stupidity." He blows at the bottom of the feet. "Hurry up with the insult. These rocks are rather hot, and it's hurting my paws. What insult do you want me to give to Thor"—he raises a furry eyebrow—"or Odin?"

Shaking my head, I chuckle. "Oh, I am not sending an insult to Odin. You really do think I'm stupid if that's what you think I mean to do."

Ratatoskr presses his furry backside against a wall, taking turns standing on different feet. "Okay then, who are you sending an insulting message to?"

"To Thor."

Ratatoskr straightens. "That could take a while. He's still out cold."

My heart crashes to my stomach. "What?" I wipe the sweat off my brow, my skin cold and clammy despite the heat. My mind swirls with dizziness as I try to think of other options, but I fear I'm clean out. Perhaps I could send a message to my friends. I shake my head at the thought. They might not understand it because they don't know Ratatoskr very well and might take the mock insult as reality.

"I need to get a message to someone, letting them know where I am. It's clear you're not going to tell someone I need help, out of the goodness of your heart."

"Pfft! Sweetie, I don't have a heart." He sits on a rock ledge, letting his fur take the brunt of the heat, and lifts his feet. "Fire away! I can hold the message for Thor until he wakes up. I can't guarantee I'll call in on him every day, though."

I take a deep breath and let it out with a hiss, knowing Thor is probably my only hope. "Okay. Tell Thor it's kind of him to have a little nap and let that lava monster take Elan and me. He could have stopped it. Instead, big, tough Thor, with his light-ning and hammer, decided to play a little sleeping game and let the lava monster take us to Muspel-heim. Now I'm stuck here, in this heated hole, kidnapped by Surt. Thanks very much, Thor."

Ratatoskr cackles. "I love it! You're getting a little better at this." He points a claw at me and winks his approval. "I'll be glad to pass that on when he finally wakes up. Who knows when that will be." With a pleased expression, he gazes at me. "Now, is there any other message you need me to carry? Or are you finished with your messages?"

I nod. "I've finished. But can you please get the message to Thor as soon as possible? I don't know what Surt's plan is for us down here. We could be in a lot of danger. He seems to think that I know where Freya is, and I don't."

"Hmm. Is that so?" His pointy face scrutinizes me. "I thought you had visited her and called to her for the war on Asgard."

"Well, yeah. But that was so long ago, and I don't know where she resides."

"Oh?" he says, sounding unconvinced. "All right. That's it now." He scurries up the side of the cave to the hole, disappearing after the lava monster releases him.

I'm surprised at the ease with which the cheeky

little rodent can travel through the realms, unhindered even by monsters. Eyes fixed on the hole, Elan drops to her stomach, and I slump next to her, wriggling in close and leaning against her scales. My eyes remain fixed on the blocked hole where Ratatoskr disappeared, amazed how something so small could be the most annoying personality I've dealt with.

My gaze drops to the opening to the lava river. The monster's legs remain dangling over the top.

"Are we ever getting out of here, Elan?" I clasp the edge of one of her body scales and fiddle with the pointy edges. "The one person I think can save us is wiped out unconscious, thanks to the lava monster."

She circles her neck around me, resting her head on her talons, not far from my leg. *Don't worry. We'll get out of this soon one way or another. Rest up. You need your strength.*

Stretching my legs in front of me, I attempt to relax, only to have my feet twitch, restless from the fear and doubt churning through my thoughts. I've just been exiled from Asgard. Telling me to rest up is easier said than done. Also, we could do with some help. I don't want to be stuck here and want to get my life back to normal. I need to help Thor protect Asgard from the potential threat of the three siblings, especially after we recapture Loki.

At the thought, my forehead creases, and I mutter, "If the children are only going to attack Asgard if Loki is captured, wouldn't it be better to leave him free?"

Elan hums. *Possibly, but then that would probably leave you homeless for the rest of your existence. Not only that, we don't know what Loki's true intentions are.*

I fold my arms over my stomach and pull my knees to my chest. "You're right. At times, he seems to be working for Asgard, and other times, he seems to be working against."

I shake my head, pushing aside my doubts. My first focus should be getting out of here… after some much-needed rest. Visions of Odin being proud of me again as I hand Loki over fill my head, despite my attempt to clear my mind of all worries. Time passes slowly until my eyelids eventually droop and my head tilts to one side. Pulling my knees in closer to my chest, I snuggle into Elan. The hard scales bring me comfort as they press into my skin, for I know she is near, and I'm not alone. I wriggle, resting my face against her front leg just in front of her chest, and listen to her breathing. The slow and monotonous sound sends me off into a deep, calm sleep, finally pushing the day nightmares away.

Something jerks me awake. I jump as a rock

crashes on the ground, not far from our side. Springing to my feet, I glance up at the top of the cave in time to see a massive hand sweep into the hole, aiming directly for us.

Chapter Ten

The enormous hand lowers, swiping one direction then the next and pushing us back into a corner. The arm shifts as the body attached to it moves to a better position. Something lowers over the top of the opening to the lava river, fixing my attention on a glowing red eye peering over the top. One long, curved horn sweeps down into the molten river and out again, forming almost a full circle.

Elan lurches protectively in front of me, her legs sprawled and her lips pulled back into a snarl, blocking the burning eye's view of me. Undeterred by Elan's efforts, the hand whips across the cave, swiping the large golden dragon out of the way.

Helplessness overcomes me as her large form is flung to the side like a small toy, slamming her against the wall.

A yelp reverberates through the cave, coupled with the thud of the impact.

Yanking my eyes from the mesmerizing lava gaze, I check to see if Elan is okay. A worried frown creases my forehead as I wait for her to move. I attempt to go to her only to have my effort wasted as a hand sweeps over, clasping me around the waist and yanking me upward. Struggling to push my hands down, I squirm but fail to shimmy out of its grasp. The grip is too tight, and no matter what I do, I cannot loosen its force.

My breathing grows ragged as panic weaves its ugliness through me.

I peer over the side of the hand to see Elan climbing to her feet, staring up at me. She looks tiny down there.

The hand yanks me through the hole, away from her concerned gaze. I catch a final glimpse of her golden eyes staring up at me as another hand swiftly blocks the hole enough to prevent Elan from flying out to help me.

I'm lifted farther until I'm dangling in front of a large dark face, eyes burning with lava and two horns that would impress the strongest of goats, shadowed by several smaller horns. The large horns are so big that they appear to be almost useless—ornaments, mainly used for show—whereas the smaller ones surrounding them seem a more practical size and an actual threat.

With wide eyes, I hold my breath as I let my gaze travel up to look at the hideous face now level with my body. Surt's form is enormous, and I flinch when I realize I'm being held in a direct line with the giant's mouth.

Lifting my focus to Surt's eyes takes all my effort. I don't want to be this close to pits filled with lava that act like eyes. I think they focus on me, but that's hard to tell when the eyes have no pupils. They seem more like lava abysses, never-ending gateways to a fiery death I don't want to experience.

The fingers shift, and one clasps me around my waist. I attempt to wriggle out of it but can't, eventually giving up and steeling my fear as I gaze up into the glowing eyes, mesmerized by the lava pits.

The enormous mouth spreads into something like a smile, exposing not teeth but red molten rock. That makes sense—Surt would have no need for teeth when anything consumed can be incinerated. I don't know how this giant can talk. I don't want to be this close to Surt.

"So. You've had long enough to think it over?" His voice is deep, with an edge that expresses how difficult it is to talk through melted stone.

"To think over what?" I ask, playing dumb.

Impatience shows on his hard face as fiery evil

climbs into his voice. "Are you going to tell me where I can find Freya?"

My insides recoil, and I want to curl up into a ball. This giant is huge. After a moment, I pull my thoughts together, reminding myself of what I stand for and why I'm protecting the goddess. I shove away the fear and encase my spine with emotional steel to bring strength back into my shoulders. "I don't know where Freya is. I've told you this." I lift my chin, knowing that's not a lie. "I don't know how you think threatening me is going to make me suddenly come up with something I don't know."

A deep rumble, low and menacing, sounds in his throat. "I have it on good authority that you know where she is."

I cross my arms and tilt my head to the side. "And who tells you I know?"

His eyebrows push into a vee as annoyance washes over his face. "I have it on good authority from Loki. He tells me that you know. He sent me a message through Ratatoskr."

"Then he's misinformed."

Surt shakes his head. "I believe him, not you."

"Hmm. Interesting. Do you know Loki personally? If you do, you should know that he's mischievous. Don't you think he could be misleading you to distract you from something? Please tell me that you have at least considered this. You cannot trust what he says!"

Surt nods his head, expressing a noise of agreement. "I know he's a weasel, but on this, I'm inclined to believe him." He lifts me to eye level. "I don't trust what comes out of your mouth."

"Do you think I'm going to change my story because you're threatening me?" I flail my arms out to the sides. "Why don't you capture and question him like you're questioning me? See what he tells you then."

A strange emotion flickers across his features then is washed away by anger. "Tell me or else."

"Or else what? Are you not listening to me?"

His hand shifts around me, and somehow those massive fingers clasp onto my quiver still attached to my back. He shakes me lightly, my dangling legs and arms whipping in different directions. I drop my gaze downward, thinking maybe I can abandon my quiver and drop to the ground. The idea is quickly shoved away when I see the distance to the ground. As much as I've wished for it all my life, I can't fly. Before I know it, I'm dangling over an open lava pit. Surt has reclined his head and raised me, dangling me over his horrid mouth.

Shivers rock my body as I gaze down into the

fiery pit. Knowing it's a mouth seems to make it a lot worse than just a bubbling pool of molten rock.

His hand pauses, the heat from his mouth warming my boots to the point that my feet feel like they're on fire. I retract my legs, pulling my knees to my chest, and hug my arms around them. Nothing I do is going to save me.

My weight pulling against the quiver forces the straps to dig into my underarms and shoulders. Large beads of sweat form on my arms and forehead, but I'm too scared to move to wipe them away. With one wrong move, I would be Surt's meal, for sure.

The muscles in my arms, abdomen, and legs ache from the pressure of holding them curled against my body. I don't know how long I've been dangling here —probably only a few minutes— yet hours seem to have ticked away. Every little movement of the fire giant's hand sends bolts of fear straight into my stomach. If his fingers open or I slip, I will cannonball right into that lava pit.

Eventually, he moves me away, holding me out to look at me again. "Now… are you going to tell me where she is?"

Releasing my legs, I let them dangle awkwardly below, the straps from my quiver cutting into my underarms and causing them to go numb from the lack of circulation. I stare Surt straight in his burning eyes. Maintaining a steely expression is hard, with fear raising the bile in my throat. "As I said, I don't know where she is."

"But you do know how to call her."

I huff. "I don't know where you get this information from. Sure, I admit, she came once before when I called her. I was lucky. Somehow, I managed to do it, and she came to us during a battle to help save Asgard. I haven't found anything to use to call her since then, and if I did, she probably wouldn't come."

"Why would you say that?"

"She's a goddess!" I exclaim. "She probably won't remember who I am, and if she did, I doubt she would be listening for my call. I've had contact with her for only a couple of hours in the past, and she helped only because she had a hunch that another army was brewing trouble. She requested we stay in contact so we could sort out that battle. The battle is over, and without that threat, we no longer need to keep in contact."

His facial expression doesn't change.

I groan. "When are you going to believe me?"

In my frustration, I shoot magic at his nose. It screws up, appearing almost like rock folding upon rock. The reaction is minor, but it gives me enough incentive to shoot more magic at probably the most tender part of his body. He shakes his head, trying to rid himself of the discomfort and giving me hope that this may be working. Maybe my minute amount of magic is doing something.

I consistently send magic bolts at his face and cry, "Put me down!"

Frustration explodes through my body as he ignores me, yet at the same time, it gives me power to increase my magical intensity. I'm happy that my magic works, and I know I've stirred up some reaction, at least. The energy seeps from my body, leaving each magic attack weaker than the last, and my arms grow sluggish, causing the throws to become sloppy. I fire my last few bolts of magic until his nose wrinkles and he shakes his head.

His head folds back then shoots forward, releasing an enormous sneeze. Hot scalding breath blasts me, loosing me from his tentative grasp on my quiver. My terror rises, matching my speed as I shoot backward, straight toward the river of lava.

- Chapter Eleven -

I scream, my body a projectile through Muspelheim's sulfurous air. Nothing is there to protect me or stop my fall. Surt's massive hand swipes for me—concern flashing briefly over his face. He narrowly misses, leaving my body careening toward a scorching death. I scream again, flailing my arms and wishing I had wings. I know that's a useless wish.

This must be it. This is going to be my end—after everything I've struggled for.

Surt swipes a dismissive hand at me. He's given up trying to save me even if I am the only one he believes can call Freya.

Then my back slams into something, and I'm yanked upward, away from the glowing river. Twisting, I search for whatever changed my direction. The straps of my quiver dig into my underarms, rubbing a deeper chafe along the front of the shoulders.

That's a pain I'll gladly put up with, happy to watch the lava river shrink from underneath me as I rise.

The arrows rattle in my quiver as my legs dangle beneath me while I'm dragged through the air. I search again for the thing grasping me, thinking that maybe the lava monster caught me to help Surt.

The air above me is empty. Nothing is pulling on my quiver, saving me from falling to my death.

Shutting my eyes, I thank the nonexistent rescuer and suck in deep breaths, calming my nerves and clearing my other senses. I rise in patches to an almost monotonous beat, and I realize with each rise, I'm hearing the flapping of wings.

"Elan! Thank you." I breathe the words, keeping my voice soft, not sure how good Surt's or the lava monster's hearing is.

Of course I'm going to catch you! I'm not going to let you fall to a fiery death. Her voice was most welcome in my head. *I've been floating around invisibly since Surt grabbed you. It's easy now that I don't have to worry about you giving us away.*

My flight continues to rise and dip in time with the flapping of her wings, and I welcome the hot breeze pressing against my face. For these few moments, everything is beautiful, almost perfect. Elan's just rescued me from certain death. Even better, I am safe in the grasp of a friend.

Elan flies across the lava river, leaving dark rocky piles underneath us. Searching the land, I find everything in this realm appears to be made of dark rocks or molten lava. The land is desolate—barren and threatening—the red and black heightening the arid land's nastiness. Nothing nice exists in this place.

Gazing over my shoulder, I spot Surt diminishing in the distance, which gives me some hope. The lava river lies between our captors and us. "Come, let's get out of here. I hate this place!"

Carrying you like this is getting rather tiresome. Do you think you can put up with what I did the first time you rode me?

I trudge through the depths of my memory, trying to remember everything we did on that first flight, in the early days. Unable to pinpoint what she means, I say, "You're asking a lot, expecting me to remember. That was ages ago."

Oh well. If you don't recollect, then you're just going to have to deal with it. Brace yourself! Suddenly, she throws me.

As I hang in the air, waiting and hoping her invisible talons will catch me soon, my stomach lurches. My legs and arms sprawl as I drop, flipping and facing the ground, attempting unsuccessfully to glide like a bat as the land below rushes up to greet me. Watching history repeat itself, I'm struck with the memory of the time I fell off the edge of a cliff and she clasped me, tossed me, and caught me on her back. That was the beginning of my very first ride.

With a thud, I collide with what must be her back. Well-practiced, I hook my hands onto her invisible scales and scramble into a sitting position and wrap my legs around her neck.

I purse my lips to one side and push my sarcasm to the front. "Hmm. Thanks for the adrenalizing jump to my memory. I remember now."

Despite my situation, I can't help but smile as her brief laughter fills my mind. *I'm glad I could jog your memory.*

She swerves, missing a smaller mountain. Even without her saddle on, the feel of her massive form underneath me brings me a feeling of security. It's a step closer to getting out of here. Surveying the horizon, I find nothing friendly and certainly no sign of a way out of this realm.

Where to? she asks. *I don't know which direction to go.*

"Me neither. I can't see the Yggdrasil anywhere or anything that would resemble the World Tree."

I peer backward. Surt and his lava monster are lagging, a distance that is closing quickly with every enormous step they take. A sudden wish overcomes me, that I had grabbed my dragon-scale cloak before visiting Elan. If I had it, we could both be invisible. Instead, I'm exposed to the elements and the prying eyes of the fire giants and their monsters.

The warm air brushes against my sweaty skin, cooling me despite its heat. I can almost smell the freedom from Surt's grasp. First, though, we need to find a way out of this horrible realm. With each flap of Elan's wings, my excitement grows, along with my hope.

Movement underneath us catches my eye.

"What's that?"

Dread fills me. The ground appears to be growing. Deep lava pits rise, along with the rock around them, giving the burning holes the appearance of eyes. More rock pries away from the ground underneath us, forming into another creature.

Elan tilts slightly to get a better view of the progress below, her tone suddenly panicked. *That's another lava monster, and it's growing out of the ground.* She swoops upward, twisting, narrowly missing a limb clasping at me from the other direction.

Flinging to one side, I dig my hands between her scales and clasp them with white knuckles. I need all my strength to not fall off. Gritting my teeth, I peer over my shoulder, catching sight of one large hand of this new lava monster, swinging our direction. Its digits hook as it tries to swipe at me and catch us both together.

The lava monsters must be smart enough to know that Elan is invisible below me. At least this time, the claws are retracted, not ready to scrape down Elan's side and embed the magic that severely injured Elan last time, almost killing her.

We are battered from the other side, and Elan flings us in the opposite direction. I glance back and spot the second raised hand of the lava monster. I cling tighter to Elan's scales, the sharp edges biting my flesh. She weaves and swerves, attempting to right herself while heading toward the snaking lava river.

Surt and his minions remain behind us. Each step they take lodges more tension in my spine. I shake it out and return my gaze forward. We narrowly managed to escape the last lava monster's grasp, and before they get any closer, we need to find a way out of here. Despite the lava monster rising from the ground, if we fly higher, we may miss spotting our exit.

Endless stretches of menacing mountains with lavafalls splay before us. Nowhere I look holds any hint of a way out of this realm or shows any of the greenery of the Yggdrasil.

I worry my bottom lip. I'm out of clues.

Elan flies over the lava river. *I don't like things growing out of the land. I'm going to follow the river. Any monster from this land should be highlighted by the glowing molten stone. Keep your eyes open.*

She rocks from side to side, swerving with the curves of the river. We cover a great deal of land, yet every time I glance over my shoulder, Surt and his two minions seem to be catching up.

An explosion bursts from the lava river several yards ahead, and flames shoot into the sky. I shriek, almost letting go of Elan's scales. She veers upward harshly, attempting to avoid the molten geyser. But as I eye the spot the explosion took place, my mouth drops open. The glow rises higher, pushed by the river rising.

I shriek. "What's going on with that river?"

I don't know, but it's something weird.

My eyebrows push together into a frown. The lava appears to be growing out of the river. Right before my eyes, it gathers and forms a shape.

"No way! That can't be!"

Elan doesn't answer, but I can feel her shock reverberate through my mind. The lava in the river is diminishing, reshaping from a flowing river into something else. Two large horns form on the top of a head, a snout growing long under black holes for eyes. When the snout finishes extending, it tapers off under two nostrils and opens, exposing a vast array of pointed teeth. The lava moves around the shape as though the skin is alive with it. The forming creature stretches higher, growing a long neck with spiky scales down its long neck, leading to fiery wings outstretched. It grows within a few seconds, a presence ten times larger than Elan, towering over us. The creature isn't fully formed, yet it's clear what this is.

Fiery dragon scales! It's a lava dragon. I thought they were a myth.

"Clearly not." My spine stiffens in shock.

Fire shoots at us from the dragon's mouth, and Elan dodges to one side. The body emerges farther out of the remaining lava in the river, only a small puddle underneath. Detecting where we are heading, it flicks its tail with the rapidity of a striking snake and wallops Elan on her side, just behind my leg. The heat from the lava seeps through my leather pants. I'm amazed how it knows exactly where to hit Elan, for she's still invisible. The creatures of this realm must be smarter than they look, unless this dragon and the lava monster can sense her invisible form.

Elan yelps as the impact sends her flying to the left with such speed that she doesn't have a chance to regain control. She smashes sideways against a mountain, crushing my leg between the rocks and her scales—my leg throbs with pain from the impact. She flips as we fall, pushing off the side with her talons.

We project into the air, only to be swiped by the lava dragon's front feet. It hits us with the fleshy part in the middle rather than the talons—the impact sends us careening again toward the mountainside.

I grit my teeth as we fly toward the rock wall, and I attempt to scamper away from the impact while still hanging on. The impact is hard as we slam into the mountainside again. This time, I swear I hear the cracking of bones.

Pain screams through my body, almost drowning out Elan's groan in my head. Limply, she slides down the mountain toward the ground.

The dragon made of lava roars, the sound deafening. I cry out in pain as rocks slide across my leg, ripping into my leather uniform. We reach the bottom with a thud, and I slam to the ground and tumble off Elan as she turns visible.

This is not a good sign. She must be unconscious or hurt badly and unable to keep up the ruse. Elan lies unmoving in front of me, and overcome with dread and pain, I slump on the ground momentarily. When I attempt to rise to my feet, the pressure on my left ankle is agonizing, and I cry out in pain. It doesn't feel right. I clamp my teeth and struggle to stand on my right leg. Each hop in Elan's direction jars through my body, sending the vibration through my left leg. Between each hop, I gasp with ragged breaths but continue, determined to reach Elan's side. Seeing her like this brings back recent nightmarish memories, and my heart shatters.

"Elan." My voice breaks. "Elan, are you okay?"

She doesn't answer. My leg pain grows stronger, and I take a brief rest and feel down the injured leg. My hand brushes something hard, and after further investigation, I realize my thigh bone is sticking through the skin. I retch to one side, my stomach swirling with unpleasantness. It takes all my effort to still the cyclone of nerves in my stomach and concentrate on Elan.

A dull orange light shines down, and hot breath blows from above. I gaze up to see the dragon made from lava peering over us, its mouth open in a half grin. Its nostrils flare as it takes in our scent.

I wave a dismissive hand at it. "Go away! You've caused enough damage."

It keeps looming over the top, its black eyes focused on us, watching us as though it's on guard.

The ground vibrates in an even rhythm, and I ignore it, positive one of the lava monsters is stomping over the land. Pushing aside my pain, I stagger up to Elan's nose and tap it with an open palm, trying to awaken her. When this doesn't work, I shake it slightly.

"Elan. Elan, are you okay?" Urgency grows in my voice with each passing second. *Not again. I don't need her to be injured again or worse.* I push the thought of worse options out of my mind, not allowing myself to think along that path.

Shoving my hand against the soft part of her nose, I inject healing power into her. As no lava creatures' claws have struck her, I hope this will help her mend. I repeat this several times, hoping for a result before the ground-shaking monster comes close. Even when I know the beast is leaning over me, I don't stop. I continue injecting the healing power until I'm ripped off the ground by an enormous hand, and pain blasts through my body from the movement of my leg. The ground shrinks beneath me as Elan's eerily still body accompanies me.

Wrapped in the massive hand, we're carried for many ground-stomping paces. The large hand opens, revealing the inside of the same cave and crushing my spirit. We thought we had escaped. We tried, yet here we are, back where we started—trapped inside the cave guarded by the lava monster with no way out. Making it worse, we are now injured. My body screams when we're tossed onto the ground with a thud. Pain soars from my broken leg up to my hip and straight down to my foot. I crush my eyes shut and hiss through my teeth.

The ground beneath me shakes violently at an even tempo. Small rocks break loose as I can only imagine Surt stomping away, surly after we nearly escaped. Eventually, the vibrations fade, and I wrestle with the agony shooting through my body from the shakeup. When I get a hold on my pain, I pry my eyes open only to find Elan's motionless body slumped next to me, which fills me with stress. The rough treatment didn't even wake her.

"Elan! Are you with me?"

Her beautiful golden-scaled body doesn't move, and I struggle to keep my hopes up. I need to get to her, but first, I need to pay a little attention to my own condition. I'm no use to her injured. Being a Valkyrie, I have fast healing powers, but the next part isn't going to be pleasant. I have to do something about this leg.

Rolling up and sitting is a considerable effort. When that round of pain subsides, I grit my teeth and gather the courage to feel down my injured leg again. My hand grazes the broken bone protruding from the skin, and I cry with pain. Amazingly, my leather pants are still mostly intact over the fracture. The lump from the bone is evident through the fabric, with only the smallest hole where a bone fragment sticks through. I grimace. This is going to hurt.

My breath catches as I run my hand over the hole again, feeling the sharpness of the protruding bone. Somehow, I have to get this leg straightened so it can heal. I need something to grasp the other end, and Elan is out cold. At least, I hope that's all that is wrong with her. I shove the negative thought out of my brain and focus.

A dark shadow passes over the cave, drawing my

attention. I'm confident that I'm looking at a part of the lava monster blocking the hole again.

After clenching my teeth, I scream up to it, "Hey, you! I need your help."

The shadow remains fixed over the hole.

"Lava monster. Or whatever you call yourself. I need your help."

It takes a moment, but the monster starts to move, and the shadow pulls away from the hole, replacing it with the lava-filled pits that act as eyes, peering down at me.

"What do you want?" Its voice is obscured just as before, as if it's drowning in lava.

"My leg's broken. I need you to hold my foot so I can straighten it."

The lava-pit eyes narrow. "I'm not helping you. You are a prisoner."

"I get that, but you want information, don't you? Or at least Surt does." I pause, trying to read the monster's expression, then continue, "I can't think, I'm in so much pain like this. Perhaps if you help me straighten my leg to help the healing process, I'll be able to focus more and give you the answers you need."

I'm not sure if my bluffing will work. Unlike the frost giants, this giant has remained silent as it guarded us. Without much interaction, I'm not sure how intelligent it is.

The glowing eyes stare down at me for a while longer, sending shivers down my spine. Eventually, it huffs, filling the cave with breath hotter than the air already in here. "I guess you might be telling the truth. I will hold your foot." The enormous hand weaves through the hole, and the glowing eyes peer down over the edge of the lava-river opening, staring into the cave.

"What do you need me to do?" His voice sounds more gargled, probably from the different position.

"If you can hold my foot steady, that would be good."

He braces my foot between his forefinger and thumb. The squeeze of his fingers on my foot is uncomfortable but is nothing compared to the pain of the broken leg.

Briefly, I inject some magic to clamp the blood from flowing freely through the open wound. "Hang on tight and don't let go." I clamp my teeth together, knowing this will be excruciating, and brace my hands on the warm ground after wiping my sweaty palms on the leather at my waist. "Okay."

With a rapid push of my arms, I fling my body backward, ripping the protruding bone back into my skin and slamming the broken ends together in a straight line. My vision goes black, and my head spins as the pain drags me into unconsciousness.

Sweat trickles over one closed eyelid, welling in the cavity. The numbness blocking my thoughts is slowly edged away by rough stones sticking into my side. Slowly, I pry an eye open, my eyelid fighting against the invasion of the salty sweat as I attempt to focus on the cave dimly lit by the orange lava glow. I don't know how long I was out for, but the stiffness in my body tells me a while has passed.

When my brain starts to piece things together, I pull myself up into a sitting position, careful not to move my leg, the action accompanied by the clatter of my remaining arrows in my quiver.

Gently, I press my fingers over my thigh, feeling for the result of my backyard medical practice. The hole in my skin is mending. From what I can feel of the bone through my thin thigh, the straightening has been successful. Tenderness still surrounds the area, yet it seemed to be subsiding thanks to my Valkyrie healing abilities. It appears to have gone well.

In the dim light, I assess the amount of blood pooled around the leg. The collection is small and coated in a thin crust because of the length of time. A small smile of pleasure crosses my face. The magic to stem the blood flow worked well.

Even though the wound and bone are healing well, I look for something to secure the bone and keep it straight. Being on the safe side is best, in case it hasn't mended enough to handle a little pressure. Finally, I settle on my sword and yank it from its sheath between my back and quiver. I use the tip to cut two strips off my leather uniform around my waist then strap the sword against my thigh. It's an awkward fit, with the blade being too long against my thigh, yet that is needed to stop the bones from moving. My Valkyrie healing ability shouldn't take long to mend it enough that the splint will no longer be needed.

With my leg secure, I push with my arms and slide on my backside across the warm stones toward my beautiful dragon friend. Elan's unmoving form dampens my mild pleasure from my healing and fills me with panic.

I scramble to her front, holding my hand before her nostrils and praying for hot breath to cover them. Within moments, warm breath streams out of her nose as she exhales then reverses as it's sucked back in, weaving over my fingers.

"Good. You're alive. Now, I need to see what's

wrong." I stroke the end of her nose, hoping my touch will awaken something in her.

Since I know she's breathing, I focus on other parts of her body. Her legs are folded awkwardly underneath her, alerting my suspicion that they may be damaged.

Sliding on my backside, I make my way over to the exposed legs, assessing them and feeling for broken bones. They seem to be intact. I maneuver to her far side, pulling on her scales to help me rise to my feet. Grabbing the top wing, I stretch it out, checking the bones and membranes. When I don't find anything untoward, I fold it back by her side. I shuffle around her, using mostly my good leg and skipping lightly on my healing leg.

Blood has gathered around her, and her bottom wing lies in a strange position, partially underneath her body. It looks like she needs help healing, or she won't be able to fly.

I set to work on the small bones in the exposed part of the wing. I straighten the first bone, hold it in place, then allow the healing magic to flow out of my palms and into the damaged area. Each bone mended raises a small smile on my face. Slowly, I work my way around her body, healing any open wounds along with the bones. I don't know where the larger puddle of blood stems from. I hope it is a collection from every injury, not something more sinister hiding underneath her massive form. Just in case, I press more healing magic into her through the soft skin under her scales, coaxing it to slow down any blood loss, buying time for me to get to the wound.

Although healing the small wounds brings me comfort, I know from the position of her wing that her larger bones have a more substantial break. The problem is that I have no way to roll her onto her other side. Her form is too big to budge in any direction, and nobody could drag the broken wing from underneath her massive form without causing it more harm. The yanking might break the wing further or tear a hole in her membrane. Even if I were at my full strength, that would be an impossible task.

With every visible wound healed, I continue injecting healing energy into her through her soft nose until my knees go weak and raising my arms becomes an effort. My energy depleted, I crumple to the ground, draping over a large rock close to Elan's massive form, and rest my head on my folded arms. My eyes remain open, fixed on my recuperating friend's condition, taking in her body, thankful she's still alive. My eyelids droop, and I force them open. Remaining awake is a struggle as I cling to hope that she'll wake up soon to keep me company in this dreadful place.

Jolting awake, I curse myself for falling asleep again. I'm torn between the needs to stay alert and to grab the sleep I need to function. The time we've spent in this fiery realm is undecipherable. Without the sun's rise and the company of the moon, each day or hour blends into the next. The lava-filled fields under the dark sky look the same no matter how many hours have ticked by. One thing is certain: I've spent way too long without a decent night's sleep.

Prying my cheek off the rock, it twinges where a point dug into the flesh. I massage the spot lightly with my fist, stimulating the circulation, before pushing off the stone to rest on one hip. My bones ache with each movement after sleeping in such an uncomfortable position. As I straighten, I study Elan. My concerns dampen slightly with each movement she makes. Her restless stirrings are welcome, giving me hope for her recovery. A clunk sounds as I shift from my hip onto my backside, which drags my attention down to my leg. I forgot about my broken thigh bone until my sword sheath clanked against the rock.

I run my hands along the length of my thigh and stop when I reach the hole in my leather pants. The tenderness is gone, even when I poke the area softly. I finish by running my hand down the leg, concentrating on the bone. Thanks to my Valkyrie blood, the wound is mending rapidly. At the rate it's progressing, I'll be able to remove my sword splint shortly.

My stomach groans with hunger. Not knowing how long I've been down here also means I don't know how long it's been since I ate. A buffet at the palace sounds delicious right now. I'm so hungry I think I could eat the whole display.

That thought is quickly tainted when I remember I'm no longer welcome at the palace. And it doesn't stop there—I'm no longer welcome in Asgard. I rub my crinkled forehead, trying to wipe away the worry and pain of being banished. Thanks to Odin and his unforgiving ways, I'm no longer welcome. I made a grave mistake, but I thought he would've shown me some leniency after everything I've done for Asgard. After all, I kept his little emotional breakdown a secret from everyone. As usual, our relationship has seemed to go one way ninety percent of the time.

Hoping to prove myself once again, I drag my soul out of the depths of mourning the loss of Asgard and focus on Elan again. Slowly, I shift to one knee with my splinted leg straight behind me. Using the rock, I push myself to standing and shuffle toward Elan, placing most of my weight on my good right leg while skipping lightly on the left, and a pleasant surprise fills me. As I step with my injured leg, the pressure doesn't hurt as much as I feared. In fact, I feel barely a tingle of pain. Just in case the bone hasn't adequately fused, I keep the weight on my left leg to a minimum, not wanting to disturb the healing process. My healed leg will bring us the best chance at survival.

My progress is clunky and unrefined, but I don't care. No one is going to see me. All I care about is the golden dragon in front of me.

I drag myself to her nose, where I reach around her snout and rest my forehead on its surface. Touching underneath one of her scales, I feel for the soft flesh and search her face.

Her eyes open slightly, and my heart skips with joy.

"You're awake. That's great!"

She moves slightly and groans aloud. *Barely!* Her

hot breath bathes me, adding to the existing heat of the cave. Groggily, she says, *My head hurts. If it weren't for the rest of my body feeling just as bad, I would think someone drugged me.*

"That's understandable. You were knocked unconscious, and your wing was broken. I've mended some of it, but it needs more mending."

Slowly, Elan rolls onto her stomach and off the broken wing, which causes her to groan with pain and bare her teeth. She looks ready to bite someone's head off. Then her jaw clamps as she struggles to hang on to sanity while forcing down her agony.

That hurts so much! she groans.

Despite myself, I smile slightly with empathy. "That's understandable. I broke my leg too."

You did? I had no idea. She turns her head sharply, her lips covering her gritted teeth while she stares at me, her eyes pausing on the makeshift splint of my sword sheath. *Is it bad?* Despite her own pain, her eyes fill with sympathy.

Stroking the soft part of her nose, I attempt to ease her worry. "It was. The bone stuck through the skin and protruded slightly through my leather pants. With the lava monster's help, I managed to get it straightened." I whistle and shake my head. "Now, that was painful! I passed out."

Elan's lips pucker with distress. *That sounds*

nasty! Her eyes travel over my full leg, stopping at the hole, which exposes a small amount of skin. *I can't see it now.*

I shrug. "You know how fast Valkyries heal. It was a while ago now, and I've already mostly healed. I'm just keeping this splint on and not putting my full weight on the leg to make sure I don't hinder the healing process." I note the pain still in her eyes. "At the moment, I'm more worried about getting you better. Let me look at that wing."

As she straightens taller, allowing me full view of the other side of her body and the broken wing, I shuffle around to her injured side. Each time she groans, I cringe, sympathizing with her pain. Now that I have access to her full wing, I line up the broken bones and heal each one individually. I'm thankful that the Valkyrie academy healer, Anita, spent the time to teach me to do some healing. That wasn't a talent that Gilroma, my magic teacher, had spent time working on.

I set to work on the breaks in the largest bone, holding my hands over the injuries and willing them to heal by my magic, which saps my energy with each fracture. I use the bubbling lava river as a reminder to keep going, pulling more strength from determination until it becomes too much, and I take a small break. The more I heal, the more frequent my rests become, and each successive time, my energy takes longer to recover.

In my weakened state, my stomach growls in protest. I need food to refuel my body. Surt hasn't sent any nourishment to quench my dry throat or still my roiling stomach.

After another round of healing, I collapse to the ground beside Elan. "We need to get out of here," I whisper, watching for any movement at the hole the lava monster is covering.

You don't need me to tell me.

My eyes droop with weariness, and I rub my cheeks, trying to stimulate the circulation in my face and head. "Most of your wounds are healed. I have one last spot to check and inject with healing magic."

She circles me with her head, stretching her neck to gaze down at me, her eyes intense. *What is it?* The echo of her voice in my head gives me some oomph.

"I'm not sure. I can't stay here much longer. I haven't given away anything yet. But the way things are going, we need to find a way to get out of here before I become careless or Surt becomes desperate. I don't want to be responsible for any more bad things happening." I rest my head back against Elan's golden scales, taking comfort in their hardness. "I know Thor's not going to come for us. He's probably still unconscious, or Ratatoskr hasn't checked in on him to give him the message."

Now, that wouldn't surprise me, with that little rodent. I'm starting to think he's worse than Loki.

I look up at her. "You may be right."

Levering myself up again, I set to work on the last of her injuries then check the wounds I've already worked on. Seeing her condition improving lifts my spirits slightly and helps my strength return more quickly, but my exhaustion reflects in Elan's eyes. Healing takes a lot of energy.

"First, we're going to wait for a while, to let us both heal further and regain our energy. It's no use attempting to get out of here when we're in this condition." I cup her nose in my hand, getting a nod of agreement. "Hopefully, we won't get another visit from Surt before we can try to escape."

Are you going to give me any hint of what you're planning? One scaly eyebrow rises as interest dances in her eyes.

I shake my head. "Not yet. I'm not proud of what I'm thinking, but I'm out of ideas. Also, I don't want to say it out loud, just in case the lava monster can hear everything I've got planned. I'd hate to give them a warning and possibly ruin our last chance."

I guess I better get healing then.

Even though I'm nearly spent, I pump the last of

my healing energy into her soft nose for an overall heal then curl up against her side, keeping my healing leg stretched forward. Elan's breathing slows to an even rhythm, lulling her into relaxation.

Fixing my gaze on the lava river, I watch the molten lava flow past. Despite our situation, the orange-red glow holds a certain allure, bringing beauty to the dry, desolate realm. Elan lowers her head closer to my body, resting it on her front talons. I drape an arm over her front leg.

"You know, despite lava being scalding hot and dangerous, something is mesmerizing about that river. To some extent, it brightens this place. Perhaps it's the call of death. I don't know."

Elan suddenly straightens and glares at me. *Dragon scales! What are you talking about? It sounds like you're longing for death.*

I nudge her with my shoulder. "That's not what I meant, Elan. You know that."

B eads of sweat form on my brow and trickle into my eyes, the salty water blurring my vision. I wipe the moisture from my forehead with an arm, cursing this dreadful heat. The realm of Muspelheim lacks the abundance of fresh air, and being trapped in this hot cave with the entrance blocked accelerates my yearning for freshness. Getting back to Midgard, with its large green trees and oxygen-filled air, would bring me great joy. I wipe my brow again, but with the sweat coating my arm, the gesture proves useless.

Elan's gaze bores into me, and I meet her stare.

So are you going to tell me what your next move is? Elan's voice is a welcome distraction, easing the discomfort of the heat.

Bending one knee, I embrace my good leg, leaving the splinted one straight. "To be honest, I can't do anything until your wing heals. No matter what I have planned, I don't think anyone's going to get you very far in your condition... unless a giant rescues us." I chortle softly, my voice remaining in a whisper. "I don't know about you, but I don't know of any giants friendly enough to help us."

Folding my bent leg to the side, I reach forward and jab at my broken leg, testing for any tenderness. Even when I poke my leg roughly where the bone once protruded from my skin, it remains free from pain. After untying the straps securing the sword to my leg, I remove the sheath and tuck it back into its home between my back and the quiver.

Tugging my mended leg close, I rest the bent knee against the other, folding my legs in a zigzag as I lean on my right hip.

Happy that I can bend my leg again, I study Elan. "How's your wing feeling? And don't lie about it. I need to know your proper condition."

She stretches to one side then pushes off the ground to stand. After rising to my feet, I circle her large form to reach the wounded wing.

My fingers trace the bones, feeling for any remaining breaks and studying Elan's face for any sign of pain. I poke a couple of places where I remember bad breaks. "You're looking a lot better. I guess my magic helped because you weren't embedded with whatever magic the first lava monster tainted you with."

Elan unfurled her wings, extending them wide, and flapped them a few times, just enough to test their strength but remaining grounded.

A grin spreads across her face, displaying her nasty-looking teeth. *It feels much better. I'll give it a few more hours before giving them another go with more force. If we decide it's at full strength then, you need to put your plan into place.* A cheeky smirk spreads over her face. *I don't know why you think people can't carry me out of here. I'm only small.*

I quirk an eyebrow, acknowledging her cheeki-ness. "The only thing you're small against is giants."

She stops flapping and lowers her wings, and I take the opportunity to inject more healing magic into her body and old wounds.

Elan hums with pleasure as I run my hands down the joints and bones. *That feels so good. I think I'll be able to fly again very soon.*

My hands buzz with the release of magic. "That's good. But it would be best if you didn't rush it. I want to make sure you feel capable."

Elan stops flapping, drops to her stomach, and rests her head on her front feet. I circle to her other side and drop to the ground, snuggling in against her again, soaking up her company.

Do you think Thor will come? Elan asks. *I was hoping he would be here by now.*

"I don't think so." I shift my weight to my other side, taking pressure off my healing leg. "I think he's still passed out or Odin's stopping him. Secretly, I hope he would go against Odin, at least to help us out of here, but I can't be sure. I don't think Thor would leave me here if he knew we were in danger, but who knows? He's always shown me more care than Odin ever has."

What about Mistress Sigrun? Her attitude has changed a lot over the last couple of years.

I run my hands down my forearms, wiping off some of the accumulated sweat. "Yes, but she also follows Odin's rules, and he's banished me. So I'm pretty sure she won't help me."

Elan straightens, tension hardening her body. *Even after everything you've done? Not even to get you out of danger?*

Heaviness weighs on my shoulders as I shake my head. "I doubt it."

What about Anita? Would she be able to help? I know she would if she could.

"I don't think she would be able to get away

unnoticed. Her healing talent is in demand. Besides, I'd have to get Ratatoskr back. Something tells me he isn't going to visit anytime soon. Unless, by some chance, someone sends me another message."

A loud squawking pierces the eeriness of the fire realm. Elan turns invisible, and I squat low to the ground, peering out the large opening facing the lava river. Something glides across the entrance, the dark form illuminated by the background of molten stone. The creature has long pointy wings and a thin extended neck finished with a long beak. The shape and size of the creature reminds me of a pterodactyl that existed in prehistoric times on Midgard—one of the many animals I read about in the strange creatures' section of the academy library at the time I was searching for information about the zmey. Shivers run down my spine as I remember the lava dragon we encountered not long before, and I wonder what exotic gifts this creature may have.

The birdlike creature flies in a straight line, only pumping its wings every few yards to break up the smooth glide, enough to keep it at the same level. I press farther into the ground, attempting to flatten myself against the rocks. If this creature is hungry, I don't want to be its next meal. If it's anything like the rest of the animals in this land, it's probably also vicious. We keep our eyes on the creature until it finally disappears in the distance.

Elan turns visible. *That creature looks nasty. I could take it on, but I don't need any more injuries.* The scales along her snout bunch together as she screws up her face. *We need to get out of here.*

Pushing against the ground, I rise to a seating position. "I completely agree."

If we get out of here—she catches my scowl—*or should I say, when, where are you going to go? I could sneak you into the dragon wastelands. It's part of Asgard, but I doubt Odin would come to find you there.*

I groan. "I don't know. I have to find Loki, but he could be on Asgard, hiding in plain sight of the gods. That would make it tricky for me to find him." I lean against Elan's side and straighten my legs, crossing one over the other. "I'll work it out when I get out of here. One step at a time, as they say."

She nudges my legs with her nose. *I know for sure that Mother will protect you. And of course, I will too.*

"Thanks, Elan. Let's see how it goes. Maybe Loki has left Asgard by now."

Her concerned eyes study me. *What do you think his plan is?*

Confused, I frown. "What do you mean?"

In one instance, he's giving you the power of magic, then the next, he's betraying you. On top of that, it's happened again. He seemed to help you by healing me. Then he looks as though he has betrayed you again, like in this case. I'm pretty sure that he had Ratatoskr tell Surt that you have access to Freya, putting you in more trouble. Elan stands, leaving me fighting to regain my balance after pulling my support away. The scales on her brow crumple together in a frown. *He helped you on your trip to Jotunheim, but now he's leaving you to rot in Muspelheim, yet you haven't done anything different to him. It doesn't make sense.* She paces in front of me, her talons clicking on the rocks. *Is he on our side or against us?*

I stand, leaning on my better leg. "I don't know. I want to think he's with us, but his actions often confuse me, just like you say. He did help me a lot when I was fighting to prove that wingless Valkyries were worth more than slaves. Yet at the same time, he went through all that effort to raise the dragon army and used them to rise against us. It is confusing." My boots crunch on the rocks as I join Elan in pacing. "Right now, my focus is to clear my name and recapture him if I can't convince him to do the right thing. Then there's the problem of his children. If he's recaptured, they'll probably act up again." I halt and flail my arms in frustration. "It's like Asgard is in trouble either way. But I can't help Asgard while I'm banished. Not properly, anyway."

A dark strand of hair hangs over my face, and I tuck it behind my ear. "We can deal with the children one by one. I'm also confused about their involvement. We thought Hel was attacking Asgard, but so far, she isn't. She didn't send the lava monster."

Elan stops pacing and plunks to the ground, expelling a groan of frustration. *Nope. It seems like Surt sent the monster to attack us.*

Imitating her actions, I rest against her side. "You know, it's pretty pathetic. How are you supposed to win over a bride-to-be by forcing others to give up her location?" I rest my head against Elan's scales and glare at the lava monster's legs, still dangling over the river entrance of the cave.

We sat in silence. Elan's golden eyes stare longingly out the opening until her eyelids grow heavy and she dozes. The sight of the legs keeps burning anger surging within my stomach, and my mind spins as I consider how I got here and ponder my next move. My eyes constrict with determination. I don't want to put anyone else in danger or get them in trouble with Odin and kicked out of Asgard. I only have one plan of action that I think might work, and no matter how I look at it, that would still bring the person into danger if we're not careful—if my call for help would even work.

I long to grasp the thing that could give me a link

to the outside world. It may not work. I know it's grasping at straws, but I'm desperate. The option is my last and final hope. With only two of us against the lava monster and the other weird creatures of Muspelheim, I can't see us successfully escaping this realm alone.

Eventually, Elan's breathing staggers as she yawns then clicks her tongue against the top of her mouth and extends her front legs in an exaggerated stretch. *What did I miss?*

I chuckle. "Absolutely nothing."

She grins, her eyes still drooping with drowsiness. *Good to know I didn't stay awake for that.* Slowly, she rises to her feet, giving me enough time to move off her. *I think it's time to check my wings. They feel fabulous.*

Rising to my feet, I stand aside and watch her stretch her legs in a doggy pose with her backside up and her front legs extended straight forward. She then kicks her back legs behind herself, one at a time, rolling her back feet in slow stretches. After shaking her body, she extends her wings, furling then unfurling them. *Yup. I feel awesome. Nothing hurts. Let's give it a go.*

She flaps her wings several times, flying within the cave and circling the widest part. My excitement rises, and I want to yell my congratulations. Instead, I wait until she lands to whisper them quietly. I don't want to attract the attention of the lava monster.

Softly, I clap. "That's awesome, Elan."

She leans forward and tilts her head sideways, raising a scaly eyebrow. *Okay. Now I want to see what your trick is. How can we get help?*

The arrows rattle inside my quiver as I slide it off my back. Holding it in one hand, I stand close to Elan, who lowers her head to press her ear close to my face.

"We have to do this quietly. Don't get your hopes up too much. This may not work, but it's the only thing I can think of, and it may be our last chance of getting help out of here."

She tilts her head to look at me with one of her golden eyes. *At the moment, I'm willing to give anything a try. If it doesn't work, it doesn't work. At least we've given it a go.*

"Okay," I whisper and back away from her slightly to lower my quiver to the ground. The sword attached to it clanks as the hilt hits the stones, synchronizing with the arrows' clatter. I haven't taken it off the whole time we've been in Muspel-heim. Although it's uncomfortable to wear all the time, I never knew what would happen next. Even though my weapons didn't do any good against Surt or the lava monster, they were like a security blanket, and if by some chance we did escape, I didn't want to leave them behind.

"I don't know if you remember, but Freya gave me this." Keeping my voice as low as possible, I squat, clasping the small charm that dangles from the side of my quiver. The charm covers not much more than a fingertip. I hold it between an index finger and thumb, showing off the shiny silver wings with a horn in the center.

Elan peers down at it. *It's pretty. What does it do?*

"At first, I thought it was just a kind gesture by Freya because I didn't have wings, and I badly wanted to prove myself back then. She gave it to me when she had me kidnapped and taken to her camp."

Elan snorts. *Ah. Not exactly the best way to start a friendship.*

I smile. "I know. I guess it wasn't really kidnapping. Let's just say I was roughly escorted to her camp with Mistress Sigrun's approval."

I remember you telling me about it. That was a terrible act by the mistress.

"As it turns out, she had her reasons and gave me this. This little charm has magical powers. It's through this that I called her when we were in the middle of the battle on Asgard."

Elan sniffs the charm. *I don't remember seeing it.*

"You were too busy fighting to know what I did."

How does it work?

Rocks crumble around us, and I check the hole above to make sure the lava monster isn't listening. When I'm confident that it was just shifting to a more comfortable spot, I continue whispering.

"I'm not quite sure. All I do is this." I rub my thumb gently over the charm a couple of times.

Elan tilts her head to one side, her eyes curious. *And then what?*

"And then we wait and see if it still works. I haven't used it since that day and Asgard. There's been no need to."

Nervous, I busy myself with pacing the cave and checking for any fallen arrows I may have missed collecting earlier. The charm remains between my forefinger and thumb as I slump to my backside in the middle of the cave. Elan's eyes barely leave me as she continues circling, her talons tapping on the rocks with each step.

We wait and wait. Nothing happens. I lower myself to my back, the stones poking into my flesh as I gaze up at the covered hole. Worry twists in my stomach, making me sick. The silence eats at me, and

I need all my willpower not to hurl the charm across the cave.

"Maybe it doesn't work anymore."

Sadness fills Elan's eyes. *Maybe it will take a while for her to respond. As you said, you haven't used it for a long time. Perhaps she's forgotten about it, or whatever helps her hear your call is placed aside.* She shrugs, spreading her wings.

"That's not very encouraging," I retort.

She purses her lips. *I'm trying.*

My shoulders cave. "I know." Staring at the little charm, I lightly brush my thumb over it again. "Maybe you're right. Maybe she's lost whatever it is that can tell her I've used it. I don't know for certain, though. I thought the notification happened in her head."

Elan eyes me strangely. *What makes you think that?*

"Because when I accidentally stroked it in front of her, she said it sent a sharp pain through her head from a loud piercing noise." I continue rubbing my thumb softly over the surface, wishing she would hear it. All my hopes collapse with each unanswered stroke. I reach for my quiver bag, ready to put the charm away, when something clicks inside my head, almost like audio has been flicked on. My spine straightens with apprehension.

Kara. You can stop rubbing that thing, please. An

implored urgency underlines the soft, smooth voice inside my head. *I heard you the first time.*

I cringe. "Sorry. I thought you didn't hear me."

I know. My response took so long because I couldn't work out where you were. I need to locate you to talk to you. Where are you, exactly? Murk disturbed the channel, blocking the direct link to wherever you are.

With my head angled toward my lap, I talk to my stomach, trying not to let the lava giant hear or see what I'm doing. "I've been abducted with Elan."

Upon hearing me communicating with someone, Elan stands over me. "Is that—"

I shush her instantly, holding up a palm. "I'm stuck in Muspelheim, the land of the fire giants," I tell Freya.

Her voice is as lovely as I remember it, if not more so. *You're stuck in the land of the fire giants?*

"Yes. We need help to get out of here."

What about Thor? I hear you're serving under him now.

"Thor was rendered unconscious by the lava monster that kidnapped us. He tried to stop it, but it overcame him. He's only one god. I don't know if he's still unconscious or awake. I don't think Ratatoskr has passed on my message."

I haven't had the best communication success with

that little rodent. Her voice fills with distrust. *He delivers what he wants to.*

"I've only known him for a little while, and I'm starting to think that too. Although if what he says is true, Odin has banished me. That means I'm out of luck, trying to get help from Odin."

Why did he banish you? Was it because... Wait. Don't bother. I can ask you later. I'm guessing you have no one else to contact. That's why you've tried me.

"Yes. Are you able to come help us?" I ask, almost pleading.

I'll see what I can do.

The connection wavers, and I fret she's going to break communication before I've finished.

Quickly, I call out, "Wait! Don't you come." I pause, waiting to see if she's gone.

Why? Confusion laces her voice.

I blurt out, "Surt kidnapped me because he wants to find you."

Find me? Her voice is alarmingly seductive and beautiful yet full of surprise.

"Yes. It's something to do with him wanting you to be his wife."

Her chuckle is priceless, filled with a deep sensuality bubbling from the depths of her abdomen. When she finally regains composure, she says, *That's delirious but also not good news. Leave it with me, and I'll see what I can do. I won't come unless I have to.* The bond in my head severs, leaving me feeling empty, with a blank open space.

I gaze at Elan, feeling slightly more relaxed.

What was that? Elan's voice fills the space in my head.

"She contacted me." I refrain from using Freya's name, just in case the lava monster can hear me.

Elan executes a little happy dance with her front talons. *That's great news! So what took so long?*

"She said she had trouble because the connection was all hazy and she had to push through some barrier. Perhaps Muspelheim is out of reach from where she usually communicates."

Is she going to help?

"She's working on it. Hopefully, that means she'll organize someone else to come and get us—more than one person, I hope. I don't know who she knows besides her army of angels of death. I doubt they'll come—they hate Valkyries. I guess we'll just have to wait and see."

- Chapter Sixteen -

The wait for a rescue party drags on. With each passing minute, the creeping tentacles of worry wrap around me, squeezing every particle of optimism from my pores. Maybe the rescue party can't make it. It probably hasn't been as long as I think, but again, telling time in Muspelheim is proving difficult. I miss the sun rising and setting or even the sky changing from darkness to light.

My worry and restlessness make me want to pace, but resisting the urge is essential in case it leads the lava monster to think something is amiss. I don't know who to expect. I hope Freya keeps her promise and doesn't come personally because that would expose her to the danger of being spotted by Surt. Not only do I not want that, but she's also my only hope for us being rescued.

My impatience nibbles at me, calling me to rub my thumb over the charm again. If I do it, finding out what's happening might ease my mind. Still, I resist the urge. Giving in could hinder the whole process and affect the outcome.

Instead, I take deep breaths to calm my nerves and mantra myself into thinking everything will be okay. The positivity is hard to retain as I stare out at the monster's dangling legs, partially blocking the way to the river.

As though picking up on my thoughts and restlessness, Elan angles her face toward me, her outline softened by affection. *Get some sleep, little one.*

I chortle. "What are you, my mother?"

She chuckles, turning her soft eyes on me. *In this instance, I think I should be. You're tired, Kara. You need to get some sleep.*

Worry creases my brow, and I fix my eyes on the glowing lava.

Elan insists, *Go on. Worrying won't help. It'll only make you more exhausted and unable to function properly.* She follows my line of sight then studies me again. *I'll keep an eye out.*

She's right. I couldn't do anything even if something came to attack us. Although I could try to defend us with my magic and my tiny weapons. I curl into a fetal position between Elan's front legs. I doubt anything I could do would help, and I am exhausted to the bone from having healed myself and Elan.

She nudges me softly with her nose. *That's it. I'll wake you if anything happens.*

Just knowing Elan is beside me and keeping an eye on things brings me some peace. Uncurling slightly, I lay my head on her front leg then cup my hands, resting my face on them and wriggling slightly to get comfortable. "Okay. But wake me at the first sign of danger. Or if anything happens."

I will. She brushes her lips against my face, which feels like the comforting kiss of a mother. *Relax. Get some rest. If someone does come, you're going to need your energy.*

In a matter of seconds, my eyes close, and I pull my knees closer to my chest, allowing my breath to slow. The needed sleep is overcome by strange dreams and haunted by an enormous lava monster and fire giant. Strong smells of sulfur are eventually overcome by the smell of rotting flesh, pushing my thoughts back to the times on Midgard when we were fighting the angels of death. Even in my dreams, I realize that hoping the angels of death would come is wishful thinking. More likely is the possibility that I've been dragged into the depths of Helheim. I imagine it's filled with the smell of rotting corpses even though I haven't been there. After all, that's where the dead without an honorable death go. Then again, maybe just the souls occupy it, not the bodies.

The smell grows stronger, overwhelming my senses until I can no longer smell anything else. A warm breeze brushes over my face, chilling the accumulated sweat. The coolness lures me from my light sleep, and I crack my eyelids. Wing shapes framed against the lava river background flutter before me, and I blink, attempting to clear my vision. The shapes remain, and I pry my eyes open farther.

Between the wings hang human male forms. After prying a hand from under my face, I rub my eyes to remove my hallucination. When it doesn't budge, I push myself upright and stare.

At first, fear rises within me. Every muscle tenses as I brace myself, ready to defend us with Elan's help. Then I realize it's a swarming flock of angels of death. Two of them fly in together. Between them hangs a strong male form with bulging muscles and no wings. The two angels of death sway as though unbalanced by his bulk.

Something is familiar about this man, and I watch their descent until they land with an ungraceful thud.

Excitement overcomes me as I rise to my feet. This must be Freya's rescue party. She must've sent them. Even though I know she instructs the dark warrior angels, I'm surprised they've come. They're the Valkyries' long-time enemies.

The human that had hung between them charges toward me.

Conscious that the lava monster is still above us, I say in a voice not much louder than a whisper, "Beowulf?"

He stands straight, crosses his forearms, and thumps his fists twice on his chest. "In the flesh."

I cringe at the level of his voice but smirk. This was how he greeted my friends and me when we first encountered him, and it made us laugh. We thought he was rather weird. However, he also saw us as the enemy then because we were riding our monstrous beasts, the dragons.

More angels of death fly into the cave, their faces serene and their landings soft.

Gazing upward, I watch to see if the monster shows any signs of knowing they're here. When his backside doesn't move, I return my attention to Beowulf and whisper, "What are you doing here? How did you know about this rescue party?"

"I'm Beowulf. Slayer of all monst—" His voice is still too loud, and instantly, the two angels of death that escorted him each slap a hand over his mouth, stopping his words while shushing him.

A frustrated expression crosses Beowulf's face

before it flattens in resignation. When they pull their hands away from his mouth, this time, he keeps his voice in a whisper. "I'm here to guide them in slaying the monsters. It's not their usual job. Because of this, and seeing they don't have magic, Freya asked me to come along." His eyes turn dreamy. "I would do anything for that goddess."

I roll my eyes and slap him on the back. "Thanks for coming, Beowulf. And thank you all for coming." I turn to the rest of the angels of death, their number close to thirty. "I didn't think that you would come. I'm very grateful."

One of the black-clothed angels moves to the middle of the group, his shoulders slightly broader than the rest. He seems to be the leader. "We understand that you've been taken hostage because of your connections with Freya." When I incline my head, he continues, "For this reason, we will come even though Valkyries are normally enemies."

My voice is husky when I answer, "Thank you."

Freya has risked a lot more of her soul reapers than I expected. I've seen how she mourns over them if they're lost.

I ask, "How did you know where to find me?"

An amused expression crosses the face of the leader. He spreads his legs, dressed in long black pants, and crosses his arms over his black top.

"Freya can track you by that charm she gave you. Did you think it was only so you could call her?"

I drop my gaze to the ground, feeling slightly stupid. "That would make sense, that she could track it as well as hear me. She's probably been keeping an eye on me these last couple of years."

My hinting is ignored with a one-sided smirk. "The goddess says if she taps into it properly, she can not only hear the charm, she can also find out where you are. It helps more when she knows what realm you're in."

Gazing at my quiver, I examine the charm. It looks innocent and inconspicuous, yet it can do so much. I'm tempted to rub the wings as I marvel at the brilliance, but I resist. "That's a lot of things this pretty little charm can achieve. How does that work?"

He shrugs. "I have no idea. But she's a goddess after all, and her magic abounds."

Pulling my attention away from the charm, I search their faces. Sadness crashes in my stomach at the memory of their past leader, Cael. I finally managed to win him over slightly, only to have him ripped away as he defended us in a battle against the dark elves. Also, Loki used the guise of an angel of death to befriend me. That was one of many times I trusted someone who turned out to be Loki in another form.

Quickly, I push these thoughts aside. From my trip to Freya's camp, I recognize some familiar faces in this small group, who fought by our side to protect Asgard. As I study their faces, I notice they all, including Beowulf, have large spears strapped to their backs and swords hanging at their sides. I don't know how well these weapons will work at getting us out of here, but I can only hope it will be enough with this many.

"Thank you again for coming..." I give the leader a questioning look.

He straightens his shoulders. "Ander. My name is Ander."

I smile at the start of this relationship. "What's the plan?" I ask, keeping my voice extra low.

His black eyes study Elan. "Can your dragon carry two riders?"

"Yes."

Ander narrows his eyes. "I've heard that she can also turn invisible. Is this correct?"

"Yes. But I don't have my cloak that can turn me invisible." I expel a disappointed sigh. "The monster is probably keeping an extra-diligent eye out for me trying to get out, more than anything else."

Rocks clatter around us, and I freeze, urgently whispering, "Take cover!"

Suddenly, all the angels of death squat and spread their black wings over their bodies. The two closest to Beowulf slam him to the ground and cover him and themselves with their black wings.

As the rocks continue to fall, I place a magical barrier above the strange-smelling angels to protect them from the tumbling stones. The legs at the river opening move away as the hole above opens and more rocks clatter around us.

Glaring at the hole above, I make sure Elan and I remain within view as a burning ember eye stares down at us.

My breath hitches in my throat, and Elan's does the same as we wait to see what the lava monster does. It continues to peer down as though it heard something. I don't know if the beast did hear something or if it's just conducting a checkup, but the pupil-less eye seems too curious for comfort.

With careful concentration, I maintain a blank expression so that the monster can't read my emotions. I'm still not sure just how smart these things are.

The cave around me lies motionless except for the disgruntled snorting of Elan. The efforts of the angels of death are laudable. Their ability to lie entirely still for so long while keeping the robust Beowulf stationary, protected, and quiet is a feat. The brazen Beowulf seems to have a short attention span, and he'll be itching to attack this monster. He doesn't seem deterred that it's much larger than a dragon.

Although the black-clothed angels are deathly still, I can't abolish that stench of rotting corpses, and I hope the sulfur masks it from the monster's sense of smell. Perhaps the molten material inside the beast destroys all scent. That would make sense.

The lava monster keeps peering down at us, and I make a show of sitting by Elan's side and resting my head against her. My tension rises as time ticks by slowly, seconds seeming like hours as I return the gaze of the fiery monster. I hope the angels of death can keep still for a while longer. Stretching my legs out, I cross them at the ankles, hooking one boot over the other as I feign casual boredom.

The beast's attention lingers too long, and I fear that the monster has heard my visitors. Beowulf wasn't exactly quiet a couple of times.

Picking up a rock from beside my leg, I throw it across the cave, allowing a deep grunt to escape with the effort. I do this a few times under the monster's curious glare, making sure my grunts are deep enough to be a man's.

Still sensing the glowing eyes on me, I stare into those pits and call out, "Did I disturb you?" I shrug and huff a laugh. "Sorry. I'm still here, and so's my dragon." I toss a few more stones, repeating the deep grunts.

Eventually, the lava monster pulls back, and the whole body shifts, causing rocks to fall on us as it covers the top hole and hangs its legs over the side entrance. Again, I block the stones from falling on the dark angels, who remain as still as death on the ground, and send the fallen rocks back to their original places, just as Gilroma taught me a couple of years ago.

When I'm sure we're no longer being watched, I whisper to the nearest angel, "I think it's all good now."

His handsome face, framed with long black hair, gazes up at me with uncertainty in his eyes.

"You can move," I whisper.

Slowly, the angels of death stand, their black eyes assessing the visible parts of the lava monster, ready to react again if need be.

Released from the embrace of the angels, Beowulf climbs to his feet. "These beasts are hideous." A mischievous smirk fills his face, but he's finally keeping his voice soft. "Now, there's a challenge to defeat, even a little scary, but I'm willing."

Shaking my head, I touch Beowulf on the back. "Let's hope it doesn't come to that. I'd rather sneak out than take on a monster from this realm."

Ander approaches with the bearing of a leader. "As you can see, when we cover ourselves with our black wings, that hides us in this dark realm. It will be best if you and Beowulf ride your dragon in her invisible form. Many of us will hover around you both, with our wings spread. Hopefully, this will block the view of you sitting on your dragon."

I raise my eyebrows. "Sounds risky."

One half of Ander's mouth lifts into a wry smile. "And staying here is not?"

Thinking that I've accidentally insulted my rescuers, I quickly say, "Oh no, I didn't mean anything by it." I rub an upper arm, pushing my eyebrows together. "Yes, you're right. Everything sounds risky." My words come out in a rush.

There's something about these angels of death with their high, smooth cheeks, firm jaws, and tanned skin that makes me nervous when talking to them. Although they are the Valkyries' enemies, they are somewhat handsome, almost like each is the other half of a Valkyrie, her matching male rival. All the Valkyries are females, while the angels of death are all males. It's a shame the smell of corpses shrouds them.

Attempting to change my line of thought before I embarrass myself, I turn to Beowulf. "Are you ready?"

He smirks. "I was born ready."

Pulling on Elan's scales, I slowly climb onto her back. At times like this, I miss the saddle I made for her. I have ridden her bareback, but I wonder how Beowulf will do. Once I'm up, I reach over the side and assist Beowulf, yanking him up by the collar of his tunic. He slips and slides while attempting to grab Elan's scales, which brings a smile to my face.

After a final pull, he manages to hook one leg over her back and lever himself up into a sitting position, then he shimmies forward to wrap his arms around my waist.

Several angels of death surround us. I'm not sure how they will pull this plan off, but we don't have any other choice, as Ander said. Their faces are focused, their expressions set in determination as though ready to tackle their next mission.

When my eyes connect with the leader's, Ander whispers, "Are you ready?"

Keeping my mouth shut, I nod.

He moves closer to make sure I can hear him. "Get your dragon to fly out in her invisible form, and a couple of us will hover over you. Hopefully, this will block the lava monster from seeing you and Beowulf."

"Let's do this," I say.

Changing into her invisible form, Elan pushes

into the air and slowly flies toward the river entrance. Her pace is slow enough to give the angels time to keep up and hover above us with their black wings, which I can't help but be mesmerized by. From birth, I've always had a fascination with wings. They're so beautiful, and I feel a slight pang of jealousy churn within me—just like when I watch the winged Valkyries. The black wings of these angels of death are as beautiful as the Valkyries' white ones. Even though I now have Elan, who acts as my wings, my life would have been much easier if I was born with my own.

We exit the cave under the cover of the angels' wings and quickly cross the river, away from the glowing red lava. The dark wings wouldn't be incognito with a glowing background. We're better off flying over the dark land, where their wings have a better chance of blending in.

After reaching the far side, we follow the edges of the river. Many more angels of death surround us, their wings beating in an alternating synchronization, providing us with more shelter. I manage to catch a small glimpse of the cave, and the tension in my shoulders releases slightly when I see the monster still sitting on top, seemingly oblivious to our escape. Full of gratitude, I gaze at my rescuers' faces and long, flowing black hair. Viewing them as my rescuers doesn't detract from how handsome each one is, dressed in all black, with powerful black wings.

I marvel at our escape, realizing that Freya was quite smart to send these dark heroes to come and get us. I hadn't realized how their black wings and uniforms and hair would benefit us in this land. Freya must've known of the nature of this place. I hope to the gods that she hasn't been here or let her knowledge of the realm become known to Surt. That would just encourage him.

Under the dark warriors' protection, we manage to travel quite a distance in a short period. I don't know where we're going, but I assume they do. They only recently arrived and weren't blindfolded or kidnapped when they did.

The angels seem to be heading in a specific direction, with Ander leading the way. We accelerate to a speed that indicates they must know where they are going. They seem to have a homing mechanism leading them back to the entrance. I gaze over my shoulder and catch another glimpse of the cave in the distance. We have traveled quite far, and the monster hasn't pursued us. With each beat of Elan's wings, my hope rises. Perhaps we will get out of here without being missed.

The lava river swerves to the right, and we dive

toward the ground as Elan follows Ander and a few other angels of death. As we maintain a height several feet from the ground, I wonder why, for we don't seem to have a reason for the descent. I'm about to ask, thinking of a diplomatic way to question the leader, when Elan swerves to the right and lowers farther. Suddenly, a loud spine-tingling roar reverberates across the desolate and burning black-stone countryside.

- Chapter Eighteen -

A chill settles into my bones. The sensation is strange as my skin is slick with sweat from the heat of the fire realm. That roar sounds familiar. The cover from the angels of death parts slightly as each one twists to find the source of the cry.

At first, the blackened fields behind us seem vacant—not a pair of lava-filled eyes to be seen anywhere. But suddenly, about ten feet behind us, the river springs to life and sucks the lava from the riverbed as a sizeable gaping jaw rises from it.

Dragon scales! Elan pulls up, bringing us out of the protective barrier of the angels of death, who remain behind, too stunned by the sight of the creature forming before them to move quickly. *It's the lava dragon.*

Beowulf's voice croaks behind me. "It's the what?"

Peering over my shoulder, I meet his wide eyes.

Even the slayer of monsters is stunned by this creature. "It's a dragon that forms out of the lava river. We encountered it when we tried to escape." I gaze back at the angels, who still haven't moved yet. "Go! Fly!" I scream.

My demand seems to knock away their shock, and they jolt into action, flapping their wings and darting upward, away from the creature-forming river.

We're too late. The dragon forms quickly, its figure shooting toward them with its mouth open wide. It devours one of the angels of death, snapping its jaws shut.

"Mother of Midgard!" Beowulf curses behind me.

I'm jerked from behind as my Valkyrie fighting leathers are grasped at the back of my neck.

Turning, I see Beowulf has risen to his feet, his spear set ready in his spare hand. He hurls it at the dragon, the action yanking at my uniform. Thankfully, the front of my uniform doesn't rise to my neck, or it would have choked me.

The maneuver causes him to slide.

I slip on Elan's back and clench my legs harder around her neck as I grasp her scales, feeling their sharp edges bite into my flesh. "Beowulf. Sit down!"

The spear aims straight for the dragon's enormous chest, disappearing into the crawling molten skin with a slight burst of flame as the wooden shaft catches aflame.

"Argh!" Beowulf's disappointed grunt attracts the attention of the lava dragon.

Beowulf, sit! Elan commands.

With a huff, Beowulf does as he's told just before Elan rapidly changes direction, aiming higher, away from the gaping maw of the enormous dragon.

Looking over my shoulder, I watch as the angels of death throw their spears at the dragon's heart, or where the heart should be, as though following Beowulf's guidance. Each one of the spears combusts into flames.

The dragon rises up and up, the dark pits of its eyes following our progress. Suddenly, Beowulf yanks my sword from its sheath on my back and throws it at the dragon. I use my magic to aim it at the beast's temple, hoping that the metal doesn't disintegrate as his spear did. I've grown rather attached to my flying sword.

For a human, Beowulf's throw is strong, and my sword shoots straight through the lava dragon's head and exits the other side. The dragon roars in frustration as the strike aggravates the dragon rather than killing it.

"Can this thing die?" Bewilderment laces Beowulf's voice.

Shaking my head, I hold out my hand, calling to my sword and happy that it hasn't melted. "I don't know. Why did we fly so low in the first place?"

Beowulf points at a location on the ground. "Because this is where we entered Muspelheim."

Following his finger, I spot Ander disappearing into a hole below, followed by a few angels of death.

"Then we need to follow if we can avoid the dragon." Worried that my sword is still hot, I magically instruct it to follow, and its tiny wings flap, hovering nearby. "Do you think we can make it through that hole, Elan, before the dragon blocks our way?"

I shall try.

Several more angels of death give us one final glance before disappearing into the hole. Their eyes are wide, and they look ready to leave this horrid realm as soon as possible. They cast a last glimpse into the realm, seemingly to make sure I've seen where they're disappearing. A few dark warriors remain floating around the lava dragon, trying to keep the dragon occupied for a little longer.

Another roar sounds in the distance, and I pull my attention away from the lava dragon. Over the mountains with cascading lava waterfalls, Surt stomps toward us. His massive lava-filled mouth opens as he roars again. Even in the distance, the large horns circling out of his head are intimidating, framed by smaller circular horns. His burning red eyes glare in our direction as he realizes his pawn to lure Freya here is escaping. I'm amazed that those eyes without pupils can see so far.

My attention falls toward the hole, growing smaller beneath us as Elan rises to avoid another attack from the lava dragon. "We need to get out of here, Elan. As soon as you get a chance, dash for the hole even if it makes our ride difficult. We'll just have to hang on."

Without needing instruction, Beowulf wraps his hands tightly around my waist, and I feel his legs tighten around Elan's frame. My knuckles are already white from hanging onto her scales, but I tighten my grasp anyway.

Elan's speed increases, and I feel a rush of hot air as the dragon's jaws clamp shut, narrowly missing us. Suddenly, Elan flips to the side and dives. The lava dragon is too slow to catch us in its mouth. Hot air blows over my face, and my cheeks push back from the pressure as she flips, plummeting toward the hole as another angel disappears into it. Taking in the size of the hole, I grow concerned. It's not very big.

"Are you going to fit, Elan?"

Not sure. I'll have to make it work.

The rumbling of giant footsteps grows louder.

Surt is progressing rapidly, his glowing eyes remaining fixed on us. We dodge the swipes of the lava dragon, now twisting to pursue us again.

"Hurry!" I yell. My heart is thumping profusely in my chest, desperate to break free before he closes the gap between us. "Hurry!" I repeat.

Elan flips a couple more times then lands when we reach the hole.

Surt moves closer, his large frame swerving between the last two mountains.

Elan pauses before the hole.

"Go! Go! Go! Go! Go!" I yell in frustration at Elan's immobility.

Surt's footsteps pound the ground harder, the vibrations traveling through my spine as he is nearly upon us. My heart stops beating, and my breath catches in my throat. This must be the end. If we don't leave now, we're done. I wish again that I had wings so I could be the one responsible for my own flight.

The large fire giant stoops from the waist, sweeping his large hand in our direction. My face turns clammy.

When the hand is only a few feet away, Elan cries, *Duck!*

Both Beowulf and I lower toward her back, and she squeezes through the hole, barely making it with us on her back. The space inside is dark, dimly lit by the lava light from Muspelheim. Fortunately, the hole widens inside, allowing Elan to fly through the strange tunnel. It reminds me of the tunnel through Yggdrasil's trunk to Jotunheim.

As Elan steers upward, I suck in an overdue breath as Surt's figure disappears. All my joy at making it through the hole is squashed as the entrance is blocked by a large hand charging through the opening, shaped like a claw and swerving upward.

I yelp then scream, "Go! Go! Go!"

I'm giving it my best, Elan snaps.

I clamp my mouth shut and look ahead to see several sets of black wings blocking out any light shining from a potential escape hole ahead.

"Mother of Midgard!" Beowulf curses, grabbing my attention. He gazes over his shoulder.

A strong breeze blows over my face as the hand swipes, trying to reach farther inside the hole. It jerks to a halt as the length of the arm has reached its limit.

My heart cheers, and facing forward, I concentrate on where we're going. The angels of death pass a portal filled with light. Elan flies past so quickly that I can't get a good look to see what realm the hole may lead to. Eventually, the inside of the tunnel resembles the inside of a trunk of a tree, the walls more wooden rather than stony in appearance, making Muspelheim's part of the Yggdrasil appear burnt out and dead. The beautiful trunk turns into petrified wood.

With each flap of Elan's wings, the heat abates. The pressure slowly seeps away from the back of my shoulders. The headache that had been growing in my temples eases as my stress melts away. I gaze over my shoulder to take in the difference in the World Tree's insides, barely able to make out the stony edges of the hole deep below, where we entered.

Suddenly, we burst through a new hole into a land lush and green, with long flowing rivers full of actual water and sky a color slightly lighter than Naga.

I throw my arms around Elan's neck, hugging her with joy. "This has to be Midgard." I look over my shoulder at Beowulf.

His rugged face is beaming with a smile. "Yes. This is Midgard. I would recognize it anywhere. There's nothing like it."

We rise higher, giving me a perfect view of the sun, which is lowering over the horizon, displaying an impressive array of yellow, orange, red, and blue as the east darkens. The day must be almost over for Midgard, causing me to wonder just how long I was in Muspelheim. As we continue to follow the angels of death, I take in a deep breath, filling my lungs with fresh air, thankful that our flying distance eliminates the angels' odor. The songs of different birds surround us as they settle in for the night. I never grow tired of their beautiful sounds, each bird having an individual tone and song to sing.

Midgard is so beautiful that I could almost live here. Although that's a pleasant thought, it brings me sadness. I must rectify my banishment. Asgard is my home. All my friends are in Asgard, and something tells me I wouldn't fit into Midgard for the rest of my life.

Eventually, we land on soft grass near a large lake. Elan lowers herself, and we climb off. I charge straight for the lake to lap water from my hand like a thirsty animal. I missed food and water in Muspelheim.

When I stand and approach Ander, his face is twisted with grief.

"How many did you lose?" I ask.

The pain in his eyes deepens. "Five."

Sadness rocks my soul. "I'm so sorry." I mutter the useless apology, not knowing what else to say. My gratitude seems dismal in comparison. "Thank you. Thanks so much for saving us. I couldn't have done it without you."

He inclines his head, his face unreadable. His expression is a mask to hide either the pain of loss or his hate of Valkyries. I'm not sure which.

Hoping to get the message through, I reinforce my sympathy. "For what it is worth, I'm so sorry for your loss. I know Freya will be devastated."

His face sharpens.

"I can tell you don't like my kind much. Please know that I and my few wingless friends are not like the other Valkyries. We don't have much to do with the reaping of souls. Although we have taken part in it at times."

His expression stays the same.

"I believe the reaping of souls could be done less aggressively and more fairly. I hope we can be friends to a point. I have much respect for Freya and all the angels of death."

"Noted." The word lacks empathy, a silent reminder that he isn't going to be my friend. He has done his duty, and that is as far as he is going.

My shoulders arch slightly as I release a sigh of defeat. "So what next? Are you taking me to see Freya?"

He shakes his head. "When she's ready, Freya is coming here."

"Oh? Why? Wouldn't it be best if you take me to

her?" I try to sound like I'm not being bossy. "I know she's busy."

"It's easy to blindfold you and Beowulf but not so easy to blindfold your dragon. I know she's an intelligent creature. On top of that, we can't carry her. She's massive. So Freya will be coming here." He nods, clicks his heels, and marches off, leaving me staring at his back.

- Chapter Nineteen -

Hearing the birds chirping in the trees of Midgard shrouds my soul in peace. The sound is comforting and refreshing after having been kidnapped and taken to a place filled with arid ground and lava with a sulfur stench. Muspelheim is a place where everything seems to be burned and dead. Even the fire giants and their creatures are either filled with lava or made from lava.

Heading down to the water's edge again, I splash some water over my face, washing off the grime and sweat I've accumulated during my time in the hot realm. Splashing sounds beside me, and I turn to find Beowulf squatting by my side, washing his arms.

Giving my face one final wipe, I sit down. "Thank you for your help, Beowulf. I'll make sure to tell Thor that you aided me, along with the angels of death."

Beowulf smirks, his eyes turning soft. "I would

do anything for the goddess Freya. Her beauty is something to behold."

I look to the sky, silently pleading for help.

"Don't you roll your eyes at me, young Kara. It is true. It's the first time I've laid my eyes on such beauty." He twists his mouth to one side. "Although I would also rescue you if Thor asked me."

I chortle. "So you wouldn't do it just for me?"

He raises a bushy eyebrow. "Your last visit to Midgard was interesting, to say the least. You and your young Valkyrie friends are good warriors that I would gladly fight beside. It was especially educational for me when you brought your beasts." He glances over his shoulder and nods at Elan. "I've never been so close to a dragon that I wasn't fighting."

Elan's eyes narrow.

Beowulf grins at the golden dragon. "Don't be alarmed. You're my friend. We won't be enemies." He rises to his feet and approaches her. "You're the first creature that I've said that to."

A fire burns in Elan's golden eyes, and she lifts her head and snorts. *You're somewhat self-confident, aren't you, Beowulf? As if you'd have a chance against me as a dragon. I'm appalled that you have attacked any dragon without getting to know them first.*

Beowulf chuckles and elbows me. "She's a feisty one, that one. I think I'm going to like her more than I expected."

Judging by the look in Elan's eye, I have to admire his courage—or perhaps stupidity—when he moves closer to her.

"Don't worry your strange scaly head. After meeting you and your friends, I'll make sure I give dragons the benefit of the doubt before I attack." He leans against her side and crosses his legs. "Although if they attack me first, they're fair game."

Something trickles in the water, and I spring to my feet, backing away from its edge. A scaly brown shape slithers not far from the border of the river.

Beowulf catches sight of the monster and yanks me farther away from the water while backing away. "The Midgard Serpent. He's still restless."

I frown. "I thought Loki's children weren't supposed to be restless anymore."

Beowulf's grip tightens around my upper arm. "Never underestimate Jormungandr," he says. "He's never happy with being peaceful. For as long as I've known, he has always had an evil gleam in his eyes."

The water stirs more, and I'm again surprised at the scaly creature's width when it shows some skin above the surface. The water ripples and swirls with each slithering movement. A chill runs down my spine as it glides past, and I back farther away. We have no guarantee that it won't leave the water and come after us.

"Isn't this a freshwater river?" I ask.

"The ocean must be fairly close to here. It's quite normal for the Serpent to visit some of the rivers that join the ocean," Beowulf says.

A low rumble sounds in Elan's throat as the scales slither closer. Still, the Serpent doesn't move away, unthreatened by a dragon only a fraction of its size. Elan growls again.

With an unexpected flick, the serpent's body kinks, twisting and turning, until beady black eyes rise above the water, followed by the Serpent's nose. The beady eyes move closer, staring us down.

Slowly, as though not to startle the monster, Beowulf moves farther away from the water's edge, pulling me along with him. Jormungandr watches as we make our retreat. The serpent slowly opens its mouth, larger than Elan's body, exposing its long fangs. Black venom drips from the points into the water, and few small fish nearby float to the surface, belly up.

Elan roars, and the beady eyes turn toward her. I want to stand in front of her to protect her, but I know that would do nothing. The distraction gives Beowulf time to dash backward and grab a spear, which he throws at the serpent after a few running steps.

The serpent spots it coming and swirls slightly, and the spear plummets deep into the water as the serpent heads closer to the shore of the river and rises onto the bank. Water drips away from the scales as it slithers farther onto dry land.

We back away while I glance over my shoulder, looking for the angels of death, making sure they're a safe distance away and the path is clear for us to escape. The angels are nowhere to be found.

Sensing Elan edging closer to me, I do the same. Catching Beowulf's attention, I discreetly indicate Elan with my head. He nods once and moves closer, ready to jump onto her back and take flight.

The Serpent continues to edge its way onto the shore, closing on us more quickly than we can move toward each other. I'm bracing myself, ready to run, when a bolt of lightning rises to the sky, forks, and is followed by a loud clap of thunder.

I huff in fascination. Not a single storm cloud was above us earlier. Now in the darkening sky, a large black cloud hovers directly overhead. I jump as another clap of thunder seems to shake the sky, and lightning pierces the ground just in front of the Midgard Serpent's nose.

The Serpent halts, retreats, and flicks itself back into the water in a few seconds. Joy surges within me as those murky brown scales disappear underneath the water.

More forks of lightning hit the ground just behind the Serpent in an additional threat. Judging by how the lightning hit the ground, only one explanation makes sense.

I scan the area and the darkening horizon until I see a figure on top of the mountain. Standing on the pinnacle, Thor clasps Mjolnir and holds it high. Lightning shoots from the hammer into the sky and bounces back to the ground. Another set of lightning forks across the sky in a magnificent display.

My breath catches as relief floods every pore in my body. Thor looks well. Not only that, he has arrived just in time to protect us from the Midgard Serpent.

I call, "Come, Beowulf. Thor's on the mountain. Let's go see him."

We climb onto Elan's back, and she leaps into the sky. She circles the pinnacle, and I spot Thor's two goats and his carriage, parked a small drop from the top. A fresh breeze blows against my face, a welcome change from Muspelheim, and the air grows colder as we climb. Elan lands on the mountainside, not far from Thor, her talons clacking on the rocks.

I jump from her back, Beowulf's thud sounds right behind me, and I scurry to Thor's side.

- Chapter Twenty -

With excitement coursing through me, I race toward Thor, my spirits rising. Seeing him back to his normal self is fantastic.

I'm baffled to see a vast smirk plastered over his face. My excited footsteps falter, and Thor closes the gap, his grin growing wider. He slaps me on an arm, lurching my thin frame sideways for a couple of steps and ramming me into Beowulf.

"Ha. Ha. Battle maiden. I knew you'd be an interesting companion when I asked for you to be by my side. Especially when things didn't go the way you wanted them to." Still smirking, he places his hands on his hips. "But I didn't think it'd be this entertaining. You've gotten yourself into so much trouble in the last few days. It's quite hilarious."

Regaining my balance, I cross my arms and narrow my eyes. "I'm glad I could entertain you," I say curtly, wobbling my head from side to side. "Nice to see you too."

His smile grows broader as he reads my expression. "There, there." He lightly taps me twice with an open hand on my cheek. "Don't get so upset. You know I love having you around." Then he nudges me with an elbow, and I topple off balance slightly.

I reset my legs in a firmer stance and form my mouth into a thin line.

With amusement twinkling in his eyes, he continues, "It's amazing how much you've been through lately." He feigns thoughtfulness. "Recently, you freed Loki, and then you traveled to Jotunheim to meet Angrboda on Loki's back. You've been kidnapped by a lava monster and taken to Muspelheim then almost eaten by the Midgard Serpent. Have I left anything out?"

"Yeah. Like you failed to save me."

"I saved you this time." His shoulders shake as he chuckles, then he rubs the top of my head as if I were a child.

Shoving his hands away, I move back and scrutinize him. "Yes. At least this time, you succeeded, but last time, you decided to take a little nap instead of rescuing me from the lava monster." Then I smile and fill my voice with warmth. "I'm glad to see you're all better. You had me concerned."

Thor scratches his auburn hair near his temples and looks sheepish. "Hey, I was just unconscious. You were the one kidnapped. Who had who concerned?"

I tilt my head. "Yeah, you were unconscious. Seeing you're the only person who knew I was missing, of course I was concerned."

"Ha. I know you miss me." He peers over my shoulder. "Beowulf. It's nice to see you, my Midgardian brother."

Thor thrusts his hands forward, and the Midgardian follows suit as they clasp each other's forearms and give them a shake.

Thor inclines his head toward me. "Can you see why I keep her around? With all the trouble she gets into, she's extremely entertaining."

Beowulf nods and grins. "Yes, I'm starting to realize. Maybe the Midgard Serpent is attracted to her, and that's the reason it attacked us on the shore before."

A hearty laugh bursts out of Thor, and he throws his head back. "Perhaps you are right. She is an attraction for danger and mischief. Or else I wouldn't have shown such interest in her."

I scowl. "Gee. Thanks a lot." Crossing my arms, I lean on one leg. "Thanks for *trying* to protect Elan and me from the lava monster that kidnapped us. If

I'm only interesting because I attract danger, why were you there in the first place?"

Thor lowers his eyes, a severe expression crossing his face as he adjusts his tunic and shifts his belt around his waist. "I was coming to tell you that my father knew that you let Loki out and that you traveled to Jotunheim with him."

My arms drop to my side. "Oh. Ratatoskr said I was banished. Is this correct?"

Thor's face remains somber as he nods, his blue eyes connecting with mine. "You know Father." He shrugs. "He is very unforgiving if he feels he's been betrayed."

"But I didn't betray him." I wipe my brow on my arm. "I let Loki out, only intending it to be for a few minutes. He was meant to heal Elan and then return. Once again, he backstabbed me."

Thor places a hand on my shoulder. "You know Father isn't going to forgive that."

"Even after everything I've done for Asgard?"

The god of thunder nods. "That seems to be the way it is. We'll have to rectify that somehow."

"How?" I groan. "I can't go into Asgard, and I've no idea where Loki is and what form he's taken. I don't even know it's him if I'm riding him. He can change into too many shapes."

Thor surveys the darkened valleys and the

minimal light remaining over Midgard. The creases on his forehead form dark lines in the dusk. "I will keep an eye on Asgard. But for now, you need protection, and you also need more training with your magic. I've given you much practical training on top of what you've already learned with the Valkyries. Loki has given you a gift, for whatever reason, and you haven't been able to practice or enhance that gift since he's been locked up... except for maybe a few things Anita has taught you about healing."

His eyes look almost sad as they scan the darkening land. "You need to be taught more and have time to practice it."

"And how am I supposed to do that? Where am I supposed to learn more about my magic ability?" I swing my hands out to the sides in exasperation.

His gaze eventually lands on me, his ally even though he's going against his father's approval. "There's a race that deals with magic all the time."

"A race?" I ask. "What do you mean?"

"The whole realm consists of light elves. You should know of it. It's Alfheim."

Annoyance fills me, and I frown. "Yes, of course I know of the realm. But I don't know anyone there who is going to teach me magic."

A soft smile spreads over his face. "You don't

have to find anyone. I have someone that will take you there and will lead you to the right company, someone who can take care of you and nurture you in your time in that realm."

"So I'm going all by myself to a strange realm to learn magic?" I look at him in disbelief. "Somewhere where I know no one, and I'm going with a total stranger."

He slaps a hand onto my shoulder, refraining from his usual force this time. "Oh, Kara. When you say it like that, it sounds dreadful. You won't be alone. You'll be under the good guidance of—"

Beowulf's awestruck voice interrupts us. "Ooh. There she is."

I'd forgotten Beowulf was with us. He gazes dreamily toward the valley, where the angels of death are hovering around a fire.

"There who is?" I follow Beowulf's line of sight down to the fire surrounded by angels of death.

Before I can focus, his irritated voice interrupts my thoughts, calling my attention back to him momentarily. His face is barely visible in the twilight. "And who's that male with her?" Beowulf's eyes, filled with admiration only moments before, constrict with annoyance.

My eyes meet Thor's, and amusement dances over his face before he focuses on Beowulf. "My friend, relax. That's Freya's brother, Freyr, not a lover." His smirk grows as he lifts an eyebrow, fixing his blue eyes on Beowulf. "Although I don't think you'll have a chance with Freya."

Beowulf huffs in disgust. "What makes you say that? I'm quite a catch."

Thor arches a bushy auburn eyebrow.

The beast warrior's chin rises, and he puffs out his chest and straightens his back. "I'm quite a catch for a Midgardian. I have big, strong muscles." He flexes, showing off his bulging biceps.

I shake my head. As much as Beowulf has grown on me, he can be a preposterous brute at times.

Thor chuckles and slaps Beowulf on the back. "Yes, my friend, and I do too. But she has her preferences, and it's not you or me."

Trying to distract the drooling males, I attempt a change in conversation. "Why is her brother here?"

Like his sister, Freyr has light blond hair that falls to his shoulders in soft waves.

Thor levels his gaze at me. "He's the friend I was talking about. He's the one that will accompany you to Alfheim and assist you in finding the right trainer for your magic."

"Him?" I squint down at the tall blond male and his white tunic, open at the front and exposing his chest.

He lurks close to Freya, his movements fluid yet bold and confident, oozing a smooth sexuality.

I swallow. "Why him?"

Thor shrugs as though it should be obvious. "He's a friend of mine. On top of that, he's a peaceful being who'll make sure that you're looked after, especially seeing you're friends with Freya. He cares a lot for his sister."

Pointing at the god, who looks as though he's cut out to please all females, I wave a finger, circling the spot he stands in the distance. "But... but he looks like he's interested in one thing only. It's not that I'm not interested in males—I just don't want to have some god trying to win my attention in that way. Besides, what would he know about anything?"

Thor places a hand on my shoulder, and my friend's reassurance works away some of the knots of apprehension. "Don't worry. He won't put a hand on you unless you want him to."

I cross my arms. "Well, that won't happen."

"Despite the obvious, he does know a lot about peace. You should fly down and meet him."

Shrugging, I realize I have nothing to lose. "I guess so." Clasping Elan's scales, I am readying myself to climb onto her bare back when Thor's voice stops me.

"Wait."

I gaze back over my shoulder.

Thor slaps his palm on his forehead. "I almost forgot." He slips his hammer into his belt and points down at his two goats, strapped to the carriage they pull, resting not far below the tip of the mountain's crest.

I let go of Elan's scales. Something large is sitting on the carriage, but I have trouble working out what it is in the dim light of the rising quarter moon.

"You're welcome!" Thor calls out. "That thing isn't light. I don't know how you've managed to haul it around. I almost had to put on my belt of strength to put it in the carriage."

Blinking, I frown before my heart thumps wildly in excitement. "It's Elan's saddle," I croon as gratitude warms my body. "I've missed that saddle. Thank you for thinking of me." Yanking on Elan's scales, I prepare to fly the short distance, and Beowulf climbs onto her back without invitation. As I look down at Thor, he seems small and lonely.

"Would you like a lift down?" I ask.

"What? You mean I get to ride a dragon?" His excitement is evident.

Elan turns on him with her teeth bared in a funny grin. *Take it easy, Thor. If you misbehave, god or no god, it may be the only time you get to ride a dragon.*

Thor grins. "I know you love me."

The Midgardian warrior offers a helping hand to Thor. "It's a fantastic experience."

Thor takes the hand offered, the muscles in his arms flexing as he pulls himself up. "And so is causing the sky to fork lightning and grumble with thunder."

"Oh, listen to him, would you?" Beowulf grunts. "You'd think he's someone special."

Elan groans under Thor's added weight. "Wow, Thor. You're heavy. It must be all those cows you eat."

"You're just jealous because I can eat more than you."

I can almost picture Elan's disagreeable face as she pushes off, carrying us to the goat carriage.

Without waiting, I jump off Elan's back and circle the carriage, studying the saddle in the dim light. Thuds sound behind me as Thor and Beowulf climb down to join me.

Taking in my excitement, Thor grins. "I had to smuggle it past my father. Fortunately in this case, he's still not up to full strength and still spends a lot of time in his room."

"Is he still getting over his prophecy from Mimir's Well?" Concern washes over me, temporarily displacing my disappointment over being banished.

"Oh, don't worry. The old man will get over that shortly. He's tough and will come back with a vengeance." Thor huffs. "It still doesn't keep him from getting annoyed and dealing out punishments."

My mouth stretches into a thin line. "I'm too aware."

Elan squats, and Thor helps me throw the large saddle over her back and secure the straps. The exhaustion from our ordeal in Muspelheim catches up with me, and lethargy creeps into my muscles, making me grateful for Thor's help. Hooking my foot in a stirrup, I grasp the edge of the saddle and heave myself up. I'm amused by how small the god of thunder looks from up here.

A thought crosses my mind. "So how did you know where I was, Thor?"

"Freya let me know. She sent me a message through Ratatoskr."

"Oh?" An image of the loving goddess flashes through my memory, unafraid to show her emotions, and her calm and collected, wanting peace and searching for the best in people. "I can't imagine her sending a message through Ratatoskr. Does she know how to send insults?"

Thor gives me an amused look. "Battle maiden, she comes up with the most interesting and disgusting messages that you wouldn't even comprehend."

My jaw drops, and my cheeks turn red when I think about whatever might be said by a love goddess to someone like Thor.

There must've been enough moonlight shining on

my face because Thor smirks. "Would you like me to tell you some?"

"No," I blurt too quickly. "Thank you. I don't need that image sparking the wrong kind of imagination. Let's go, Elan."

I breathe a sigh of relief as she pushes off and glides slowly down to the commune of angels of death, leaving Thor and Beowulf to catch up with us in the goat-drawn carriage. Having the saddle underneath me again feels good, giving me more grip and less chance of falling off her scaled back. Her scales glow in the dim light of the fire as we circle, listening to the rumbling of the carriage. When it nears the fire, Elan lands, and I climb off, waiting for Thor.

Arms wrap around me, and I gaze up in shock to find Freya embracing me.

"Thank goodness you're okay, Kara. I was so worried."

Hugging isn't my forte, but I return her embrace. A strange sense of peace fills me as I soak up the genuine concern that Freya feels for people.

"Thanks for sending your angels. I'm sorry I had to drag you into this. I didn't want Surt to get anywhere near you."

She shifts backward to study my face, clasping both of my upper arms gently. Her features are lovely, and I'm almost envious of her physique and mannerisms until I remind myself that she's a goddess. Nothing can be compared to her beauty, not even the beautiful Valkyries.

"Oh, Kara. It's because of me that you were in that mess in the first place. Besides, Surt is stupid to think he can take me as a wife."

Giving her a cheeky grin, I ask, "So does that mean that you're not going to say yes?"

One side of her face screws up with amusement. "Like I would ever say yes to that baboon. Could you imagine?" She waves a dismissive hand at me. "And that realm would be a horrible place to live. So much hatred and destruction. I couldn't do it."

"Are you going to introduce us, sis?"

Behind her shoulder stands Freyr, tall and thin with blond hair, his features similar to hers. "Is this the Valkyrie?" His eyes pass over my wingless shoulders.

Freya turns, opening a gap to let her brother into our small circle. "Of course. Why wouldn't I introduce you to her? This is Kara. Kara, this is Freyr, my brother."

Freyr moves quickly, clasping my hand and raising the back to his mouth, dusting a kiss on my skin. "And to what do I owe the pleasure of meeting such a beautiful woman?" Sensual tones filled with invitation lace his voice. The question is a greeting that doesn't expect an answer.

Heat rushes to my cheeks, which burn under his intense gaze, and I face away to hide my response. Sexuality and peace simply seep from him, just like his sister.

"I can't wait to take you with me to Alfheim." Sensual fingers coax my chin softly, directing my gaze back to his sweet smile. "You'll be under my protection and guidance, and I'll do everything in my power to make sure you're looked after."

Not knowing how to react or what to say, I gently pry my hand from his touch and look at Beowulf, almost begging for help.

The Midgardian warrior's eyes cut through my insecurity, and other than when I first saw him in Muspelheim, I've never been so glad to hear the warrior's boisterous voice. "Oh, Freya. It's so good to see you again. I'm at your service to use as you please as long as you grace me with your presence."

The words sound so foreign from the coarse warrior's mouth, and I have to stifle a laugh, especially when he bends at the waist in a bow, Freya's hand clasped in his.

"May I wash your feet or something else of more importance?" Beowulf's voice is laced with seduction, and I cringe, not so sure he's bringing me the distraction I want.

Freya's chuckle sounds like finely tuned bells chiming. Touching her loose hand to her heart, she gracefully pulls her hand out of Beowulf's grasp.

"Why, I'm flattered, Beowulf, but you aren't one of my warriors."

Disappointment flashes across his face. With eyes downcast, he straightens.

Freya clasps his chin and lifts it, looking into his

blue eyes. "But if you play your cards right while you're alive, perhaps you will eventually be one of my warriors."

Beowulf almost melts in front of Freya, his expression only changing when he's interrupted by Thor.

"Beowulf, you're a powerful, strong warrior, and I would hate to see your talents wasted. Perhaps when you die, you can come to Valhalla to serve by my side." Thor studies Beowulf's besotted face ogling Freya, and I think I see hurt showing in his eyes. "I thought that was your plan."

Beowulf makes an obvious effort to pry his eyes off the beautiful goddess to speak directly to Thor. "I don't see why I can't have both." Within seconds, his eyes return to Freya as he retakes her hand like a knight addressing his princess.

Freya chuckles, softly removing her hand again. "Then you would be an original first. Anyway, my darling Beowulf, we're here for Kara and her protection since Odin has banished her from Asgard." Smoothly, she turns to her brother. "Now, Freyr"— her stern eyes focus on him—"you must look after Kara and help her find a good teacher of magic without making unwanted passes at her."

Freyr affectionately hugs his sister around the shoulders, fixing her with innocent eyes. "I would never."

She raises an eyebrow at him. "You and I both know that you would. This isn't why I've put Kara into your care."

My attention flicks from one to the other, finishing on Elan, my eyes pleading. "Help me," I whisper.

Elan tilts her head to one side, pretending to look thoughtful. *Now, what would Naga say about it?* She lifts her talons and taps her temple several times. *Oh yes, he would say that you're of breeding age and in genuine need of finding a mate before you get too old.*

I glower at her. "Elan!" I cry in shock, causing everyone's eyes to fix on me, including the angels of death. Once again, my cheeks redden even though I know Elan didn't send that message to the rest of the group.

She grins, showing off her vicious smile.

Thor clears his throat, and I'm glad for the interruption. "I was afraid this might happen." He studies Freyr, his expression serious, almost like a protective father's. "As Freya said, you aren't to touch her unless she allows it."

The sensual god looks slightly offended, although unconvincingly.

Thor ignores him and continues, "Just as I thought. For this reason, I've called for one of her friends to go with her to Alfheim also."

My heart skips a beat, surging with excitement, and I want to hug my leader.

"This friend is probably a better suit for you and your realm in their attitude." Thor adjusts his hammer into a more comfortable position. "A Valkyrie whose heart is full of peace, love, and understanding, always wanting to see the good in people. And with her is her dragon, who carries the same beliefs."

The knowledge Thor holds of my friends surprises me. I know he can only be talking about one Valkyrie and her bonded dragon.

A soft voice sounds just behind me, almost a whisper. "Listen to that. He's saying such nice things about Naga."

Turning, I find Eir hugging Naga around the neck. I start briefly, not having realized they were there. They were so silent, sneaking up on me.

"Eir. I'm so glad to see you." Relieved, I wrap my arms around her neck and stroke Naga's blue cheek, smiling when the dragon leans into my hand. "You're so quiet. I didn't hear you two sneak up."

Eir shrugs. "We've perfected the art of walking without being heard—well, most of the time. It was easy while you were distracted. You probably heard us but ignored the sound."

I squeeze her hand, whispering, "Thank you. I'm

ecstatic to have a friend accompanying me this time." Naga catches my eyes with his big blue ones. "Two friends," I correct myself.

Eir leans to one side. "I wouldn't be surprised if Odin banishes me also for going with you." Catching my worried gaze, she shrugs. "It's something we'll tackle together. Besides, I want to come. When would I ever say no to learning more about peaceful magic?"

I chuckle. "Never."

Naga nudges me from the side with his nose. *Naga's excited to be coming. Naga has heard much about this land.*

I frown. "Oh. What's that?"

Naga has heard that there are peaceful dragons somewhere in one of these realms. Perhaps this is the place. Naga would like to meet friendly dragons, not like these dragons that want to breathe fire and fight all the time. His gaze turns to Elan. *Like the emperor dragons.*

The scales between Elan's eyes push together in a frown. *Naga, my breed is nothing compared to the dragon we ran into in Muspelheim. That dragon was na-a-asty!*

Naga's eyes widen.

"That's true," I say. "But that dragon remains in Muspelheim. It wouldn't be able to survive anywhere else. It would destroy everything it touched."

I catch Eir's shocked expression.

"It's a story I'll tell you on our travels," I say. "I'm glad to have you come with us, Naga. I couldn't think of any better companions than you two."

Catching Thor's attention, I say, "If you manage to speak to your father, please explain that I'm sorry. I didn't mean to set Loki free, and I'll do my best to bring him back. Asgard is my home. It holds all my friends and favorite gods. I'll always stand by and protect them."

Thor places a hand on my upper arm. "I'll do my best. You know I will, Kara. I want you back in Asgard. I have a lot more planned for you, and I'm not going to give up on you yet. I can see your loyalty even if my stubborn father can't."

I pull away from Thor's intense gaze and connect with the smiling blond god. Freyr stares at both Eir and me alternately for several moments, wearing a broad smirk.

I'm not sure if I want to cringe or be happy.

"Shall we get started?" the blond god asks.

My expression doesn't change.

He seems to realize my apprehension and inclines his head. "Do not worry, battle maidens. I'll do as instructed. I'll protect you and lead you through my realm. I think you'll find my followers very accommodating." He holds out one hand as an invitation.

Without grasping his hand, I step forward hesitantly. "Okay. Let's do this. I'm keen to expand my magic."

THE END

Hoodwinked: Book 4 Released January, 2021

If you enjoyed Entrapment, please take a few minutes and leave a review on Amazon. Thank you. Reviews help authors.

ACKNOWLEDGMENTS

Thank you to all of the creators of literature and websites who have spent time writing about Norse Mythology. Even though at times there has been contradicting information, it has been an interesting study. After all, of course a goat produces mead, and a dragon gnaws at the roots of the Yggdrasil, unhindered, threatening the existence of the nine realms attached to the world tree. Plus, there are many other "believable" tales told.

Norse mythology is such an impressive set of tales that I have incorporated some and invented others to create Kara and Elan's story.

I am touched by the enormous amount of support I have received from my immediate family. My husband has been a helpful first reader and, at times, been an excellent motivator, with hints of ideas to help me through the blanks. The support from my three sons has also been overwhelming. They have spent years putting up with my head in the clouds, thinking about the next plot twist or story, along with many hours spent working on my books and keeping in touch with my readers.

A big thank you to my extended family, who support me being a book enthusiast.

Safeguard: A huge thank you to my editor, Amanda K., her editing and writing tips, and my Proofreader, Kristina B, for picking up the things we missed.

Pursuit: A huge thank you to my editor, Kelly Reed, her editing and writing tips, and my Proofreader, Irene S, for picking up the things we missed.

Entrapment: A huge thank you to my editor, Kelly Reed, her editing and writing tips, and my Proofreader, Kristina B, for picking up the things we missed.

Thank you to all of my readers who have loved my work, and continue to read my stories.

BOOKS BY KATRINA COPE

Pre-Teen Books

The Sanctum Series

JAYDEN'S CYBERMOUNTAIN

SCARLET'S ESCAPE

TAYLOR'S PLIGHT

ERIC & THE BLACK AXES

ADRIANNA'S SURGE

~~~~~

Young Adult Urban Fantasy

Afterlife Series

FLEDGLING

THE TAKING

ANGELIC RETRIBUTION

DIVIDED PATHS

TRUTH HUNTER

Afterlife Novelette

THE GATEKEEPER

~~~~~

Young Adult Urban Paranormal Fantasy

Supernatural Evolvement Series

(Associated with the Afterlife Series)

WITCH'S LEGACY (Prequel)

AALIYAH

~~~~~

Young Adult Norse Mythology Fantasy

Valkyrie Academy Dragon Alliance

MARKED

CHOSEN

VANISHED

SCORNED

INFLICTED

EMPOWERED

AMBUSHED

WARNED

ABDUCTED

BESIEGED

DECEIVED

Thor's Dragon Rider

SAFEGUARD

PURSUIT

ENTRAPMENT

HOODWINKED

More to come

Get updates & notifications of giveaways

Would you like a FREE ebook?

Click here to get started: FREE copy of Marked or go to
https://dl.bookfunnel.com/f4cm1zh2qb

Through this link you can sign up for my newsletter and
receive a FREE copy of Marked plus updates about my
fantasy books, sales and notification of giveaways.

ABOUT THE AUTHOR

Katrina is a best-selling author of young adult fantasy and middle grade/tween novels. Her novels incorporate action, heart and an intriguing plot.

She resides in Queensland, Australia. Her three teenage boys and husband for over twenty years treat her like a princess. Unfortunately though, this princess still has to do domestic chores.

From a very young age, she has been a very creative person and has spent many years travelling the world and observing many different personalities and cultures. Her favourite personalities have been the strange ones, yet the ones under the radar also hold a place in her heart.

Katrina's online home is at www.katrinacopebooks.com

You can connect with Katrina on:

Facebook Group